MAGGIE SHAYNE

DAUGHTER OF THE SPELLCASTER

HARLEQUIN®
entertain, enrich, inspire™

Recycling programs
for this product may
not exist in your area.

ISBN-13: 978-0-7783-1380-9

DAUGHTER OF THE SPELLCASTER

Praise for the novels of Maggie Shayne

For Michele, Gayle, Chris, Laurie, Ginny and Theresa. Whoever said that writing is a solitary profession never attended one of our loud, laughter-filled, munchy-fest plotting sessions! What fun would this stuff be if we had to do it alone?

Love you all!

Prologue

In her tiny hand she held the vial of mugwort over her steaming cauldron and carefully let three drops escape. No more, no less. Then she looked up at her mom and smiled.

Mamma nodded her approval but didn't let little Magdalena bask in it for very long. "Now the eyebright. Just a pinch."

Lena set the vial aside and picked up the old brown crockery jar with the dried herb inside. She plucked out a pinch and dropped it into the squat iron pot.

A little more, said Lilia. *You have tiny fingers, after all.*

She didn't say it out loud, of course. She spoke from inside Lena's head. Though her mom called Lilia an imaginary friend, to Lena she was a big sister and very real, even though no one—except Lena herself—could see her. No one else ever had. But that didn't mean she wasn't real.

Lena grabbed another pinch and popped it into the bubbling brew, eliciting a satisfying hiss from the pot.

Mamma frowned at her. "How did you know to add a little more?"

"Lilia told me to," Lena explained.

"Ahh. All right, then."

Mamma didn't mean it, though. She didn't believe in Lilia. Magic, yes. Witchcraft, most certainly. But not Lilia. Grown-ups could be so odd sometimes.

Aside from that, her mom was the best grown-up Lena knew. She was beautiful, first off. The prettiest mom in the whole town. And she didn't wear jeans like the other moms. She wore flowing dresses—she called them captains. No, wait. Kaftans—in bright oranges and yellows and reds, and sometimes deep blues and greens. And big glittery jewelry that she made herself. And she knew all about magic. So much that other witches were always asking her about stuff.

And she loved Lena more than the whole wide world. And Lena loved her back. So with all of that, it wasn't so bad that she didn't believe in Lilia. And anyway, she never came right out and said it. Just said she was "keeping an open mind," whatever *that* meant.

Lena took the wooden spoon and gave her mixture a stir, leaning over to sniff the steam. She had insisted on a drop of dragon's blood—not from a *real* dragon, of course—as she did in almost all her potions. She loved the smell, and it always felt like a kick of extra power to her.

Her mom, who'd been a witch since she'd been in college, which was a *long* time ago, had taught Lena to trust her instincts.

They let the cauldron simmer for exactly thirteen minutes, then Lena blew out the candle that was heating it from underneath its three long legs and let things cool for thirteen more. Then she dipped a soft cotton ball into the concoction and used it to wash Mamma's magic mirror.

It was Samhain, the perfect time for divination, and her mom wanted to teach her how to scry. Lilia had said it would be easy and promised to help.

Once the black mirror was all gleaming and wet with the potion, Mamma placed it in a stand, the kind you would use to display a special plate, and turned Lena's chair so that she could look directly into it.

"Now you probably *think* you're supposed to look at the mirror. But you're not, really," Mamma said. "Just let your eyes go sort of sleepy. Let them be aimed at the mirror but not really looking at it. It takes time and practice, Lena, but eventually you'll—"

"Something's happening!"

Mamma blinked at her in that way she had. Lena didn't see her do it, but she knew. "What's happening, Lena?"

"It's all…foggy."

"Good. Just relax and see if the fog starts to clear."

"Oh, look!" Lena pointed at the images that were playing out in the mirror as clearly as a movie on TV.

"I can't see what you're seeing, Lena. Tell me about it as it unfolds."

She thought she heard a little bit of doubt in her mom's voice. Sometimes, Lena knew, her mom thought she was making things up, or at least stretching them out with what she called her turbo-charged imagination. But she *was* seeing that stuff in that mirror. Not in her imagination. But for real.

Go on, tell her what you see, Lilia whispered.

"There are three girls, all dressed up like Jasmine

from *Aladdin*. Hey, I think one of them is Lilia. It is! It's Lilia!"

"Your imaginary friend?" Mamma asked.

"Yes! Oh, my goodness, that one is me. Only…way different. I'm all grown up in there. And my hair isn't red like now. It's black." Lena giggled. "I've got *boobies*."

"What am I ever going to do with you, witchling?" Lena could hear the smile in her mom's voice, but she couldn't look to see it for herself. She just couldn't take her eyes off of the images in the mirror.

"It's getting dark, and I'm sneaking out. Gosh, look where I live. It's like on that show, *I Dreamed about Jennie?*"

"I Dream of Jeannie."

"Yeah. You know, how it looks inside Jeannie's bottle? It's like that."

"Makes sense. You said you looked like Jasmine."

"Oh, and there's a boy. A man, I mean. A prince! A *handsome* prince. Just like in one of my books." She frowned, then blinked hard. "Oh, no."

"What, baby?"

"I'm crying. He's going away. But he says he's coming back for me soon, and that we'll live happily ever after. Oh, and he's kissing me like in a grown-up movie!"

"I think that might be enough for now, Lena."

One more thing, Lilia whispered.

"Wait, Mom. There's one more thing." Lena blinked and relaxed back in her chair, because the fog had returned. It cleared again, though, and she leaned forward and stared eagerly, but then she sighed. "It's just a cup. It's just a stupid cup. Not a story. Just a cup."

"What does it look like?" Mamma asked.

"Fancy. Silver, with jewels all over it."

"Sounds like a chalice."

"As the chalice is to Alice," Lena chirped. It was a secret joke just between the two of them. See, there was this thing in witchcraft called the Great Rite. In it, a witch lowered her athame—that was a fancy knife— into a chalice. She was supposed to say "As the rod is *to* the God, so the chalice is to the Goddess." It never made much sense to Lena, though her mom said it would when she got older. It was supposed to be a powerful rite, one of the most powerful in the Craft, and it was done right at the beginning of every ritual.

Lena had once commented that "As the rod is to the God" rhymed, so the second line should, too. And then she changed it to "So the chalice is to Alice."

Some witches got really mad over that, so she wasn't allowed to say it in front of them anymore. Mom said some witches just had no sense of humor at all, but that she thought the Goddess would find it funny as hell.

That was just the way she said it, too. "Funny as hell."

"Lena," Mamma prompted.

Lena was still staring at the cup in the mirror. "It kinda feels like I've seen it before, Mom, but I don't know where."

Then the fog returned, and in a second the mirror was just a black mirror again. She sighed and lifted her gaze to her mom. "Did I do all right?"

Mamma looked a little worried. "You did great, honey. I'm very surprised. Most people try for weeks and weeks before they can see anything in the mirror. And then it's usually shapes in the mist, maybe an image or two, but not a major motion picture."

"It's 'cause I'm so young," Lena explained to her. "Grown-ups have spent too much time forgetting how to believe in magic. I haven't forgotten yet. That's what Lilia told me." She frowned and lowered her eyes, a sad feeling kind of squeezing her heart. "My prince never came back, though. At least, I don't think so."

He will, darling. He'll come back to you, just at the right time. And so will the chalice. You'll see. And the curse will be broken, and everything will be right again.

"What curse?" Lena asked Lilia very softly.

But Lilia only smiled softly before disappearing.

1

Twenty years later

Magdalena Dunkirk waddled to the front door of her blissful, peaceful home outside Ithaca, New York, with one hand atop her watermelon-sized belly. "I'm coming!" she called. It took her longer to get around these days, and her mother was out running a few errands.

They didn't get a lot of company. They'd only been living at the abandoned vineyard known as Havenwood, on the southern tip of Cayuga Lake, for a little over six months, and aside from their nearest neighbor, Patrick Cartwright, a kind curmudgeon who was also a retired doctor, and the two middle-aged, strictly in-the-broomcloset witches her mom hung out with, they barely knew anyone. Then again, she and her mother tended to keep to themselves. Lena liked it that way.

She got to the big oak door and opened it to see the last person she would have expected. Okay, the second-to-last person. Waist-length dreadlocks—both hair and beard—a red-and-white sari, and sad brown eyes staring into hers. She met them for only a moment, then looked past the guru for his ever-present companion. But Bahru was alone. Only a black car stood beyond him in the curving, snow-covered drive. "Where's Ernst?" she asked.

"Your baby's grandfather has gone beyond the veil, Magdalena."

Ernst? Dead? It didn't seem possible. Lena closed her eyes, lowered her head. "How?"

"He died in his sleep last night. I wanted to tell you before you heard it on the news."

Blinking back tears, she opened the door wider. A wintry breeze blew in, causing the conch shell chimes to clatter and clack. "Come in, Bahru."

He shook his head slowly. "No time. It's a long drive back."

She blinked at him. He was eccentric, yes. Obviously. But… "You drove all the way out here just to tell me Ryan's father is dead, and now you're going to turn around and drive all the way back? You could have told me with a phone call, Bahru."

"Yes. But…" He shrugged a bag from his shoulder. It was olive drab, made of canvas, with a buckle and a flap, which he unfastened and opened. "He wanted you to have this," he said.

Lena watched, wishing he would come inside and let her shut the door but not wanting to be rude and tell him so. So she stood there, holding it open and letting the heat out into the late January cold, and watching as he pulled an elaborately carved wooden box from the bag.

It caught her eye, because it looked old. And sort of…mystical. It was smaller than a shoe box, heavy and hinged, with a small latch on the front. As she took it from him, he went on. "Of course there will be more. I came to tell you that, too. You must come back to New York City, Lena. You and the child are named in his will."

She looked up from the box sharply and shook her head. "That's sweet of him, but I don't want his money. I never did. I won't—I can't take it, you know that, Bahru. It would just convince Ryan that everything he ever thought about me was true." She clutched the box in her hands, her heart tripping over itself. Maybe because she'd said Ryan's name twice in the past two minutes after not uttering it once in more than six months. "How is he taking his dad's death?"

"As if he doesn't care."

"He cares. I know he does. He's angry with his father, has been since his mother died, but he loves him." God, it was a crying shame he'd never gotten around to telling his father so. She wondered what would happen to the businesses, the empire Ernst had built, since his only son wanted no part of any of it.

Bahru said nothing for a long moment. He just stood there, fingering a crystal prism that hung from a chain around his neck. Lena noticed it because she was into crystals—so was her mom—and because Bahru always wore exactly the same things. Same robes, just with an extra white wrap over top in colder months. Same shoes, the faux leather moccasin-style slippers in winter and the sandals Mom called "Jesus shoes" in the summer. Same green canvas bag over his shoulder everywhere he went. The crystal pendant was new. Different. She'd never seen him wear jewelry before.

"Will you come?" he asked at length.

Lena pushed a long auburn spiral behind her ear. "Ryan still doesn't know about…about the baby, does he?" she asked, looking down at her belly, which made the tie-dyed hemp maternity dress Mom had made for her look like a dome tent lying on its side. She wore a fringed shawl over it, because the dress was sleeveless and the old house was drafty. And haunted, but you know, being witches, they considered that a plus.

Bahru smiled very slightly. "He does not know. He still has no idea why you left. But he will guess when he sees you. You knew you would have to face that eventually, though."

She nodded. She didn't believe in lying and had no intention of keeping Ryan out of their child's life. She just kept putting off telling him, feeling unready to face him with the truth when she knew what he would think. And now… Well, now it looked as if she had no choice.

"I really wish I'd told him sooner. He doesn't need this to deal with on top of everything else."

"Perhaps the distraction will be welcome."

She lifted her brows. "Well, it'll distract him, all right. But it'll be welcome news about the same time pigs fly."

Bahru frowned.

She didn't bother explaining. In all the years he'd spent in the States since leaving his native Pakistan, there were still a lot of American expressions that perplexed him.

"Will you come?" he asked again.

Lena knew she had to go. Ernst McNally was her child's grandfather, after all. "Of course I'll come. When is the funeral?"

"Tomorrow at one. St. Patrick's Cathedral, of course."

"Of course." Nothing but the best for one of the richest men in the world.

"Good." He patted the box she was still holding. "Take good care of this. We found it in a Tibetan street vendor's stand amid piles of worthless trinkets. Ernst believed it was special. He said it had your name written all over it, but I never knew what he meant by that." He blinked slowly. "He would never let me touch it, never let anyone touch it. Said it was for your hands alone. Very strange. But I've respected his wishes and never touched it until it was time to bring it to you."

"Thank you, Bahru." She was curious, but too distracted by the thought of seeing Ryan again to open the box just then. "Are you sure you won't come in? Mom's out, but I could make some tea—"

"No. But I will see you soon, and perhaps…perhaps more. After."

It was her turn to frown. What did he mean by that?

Turning, he walked in his fake leather moccasins through the half inch of fresh snow—there had been so little that year that winter had felt more like late fall—to the waiting car. It was a black Lincoln with a driver behind the wheel, cap and all. Probably one of Ernst's. The billionaire-turned-spiritual-seeker had dozens of them, and whatever he had was at his personal guru's disposal.

Ryan wasn't likely to let *that* continue. He'd always thought the former guru-to-the-stars was a con artist, out to scam his father at his weakest moment, right after the untimely death of Ryan's mother twenty years ago. But Bahru had been at Ernst's side ever since, guiding him in a quest for understanding that had taken him to the far corners of the world. His businesses had been left in the hands of their boards of directors. And his son in the hands of boarding schools and nannies.

She wondered if Ernst had ever found what he'd been looking for, then decided he probably had *now*. Bahru eased his long limbs into the backseat, pulling the tail of the sari in behind him and closing the door. The car rolled away through the snow, and Lena stepped back and closed out the cold at last.

She was going back to Manhattan. She was going to see him again. Ryan McNally. The father of her unborn baby. The man she had once believed to be the handsome prince of her childhood fantasies come to life. Carrying the wooden box with her, she all but sleep-walked to the rattan rocking chair in front of the stacked stone fireplace that was one of her favorite parts of the house, even though it was old and had gaps where the mortar had fallen away. It was comforting, and she loved it. She sank into the chair and started rocking, memories flooding her mind.

She remembered the day she had first set eyes on her long-lost prince—other than in the face of her mother's magic mirror, and her childhood dreams, and the stories she had created out of them in construction paper and crayons. She'd taken one look at him and the impossible visions of her childhood had all come rushing back.

She had been completely at peace, loved her life, her job at a PR firm in New York City, where she made scads of money, and her pricey Manhattan apartment. Her practice of the Craft had matured. As she'd grown up, she had come to understand that magic was more about creative visualization and positive belief than flashes of light and sparkles. Her imaginary sister-friend Lilia had stopped showing up somewhere around the middle of fourth grade, as near as she could pin it.

It was all good. Or she thought it was. And yeah, she'd probably been skating, pretending there was nothing underneath the ice but more ice, ignoring the stuff she'd pushed down there, the stuff she'd frozen out. The undeniable experience of real magic. Those visions of past lives that had been so vivid and convincing at the time. Lilia, the chalice…the curse. A little girl with a witch for a mom and a huge imagination, that was all it was.

Only it wasn't.

She'd managed to deny every last bit of it until the night she met Ryan McNally. Her handsome prince, right down to the roots of his hair.

She'd been handed his father's account—temporarily, of course, while Bennet, Clarkson & Tate's senior partner, Bill Bennet, was recovering from a triple bypass. Timing was everything. Ernst McNally, billionaire, philanthropist, world traveler and spiritual seeker, had been named *Now Magazine*'s Man of the Year and would receive the honor officially at a posh reception at the Waldorf Astoria. The other partners were booked, and Ernst was an important client. Lena was tapped to be the firm's stand-in, and she didn't kid herself by pretending it wasn't because, of all the younger associates, she would look best in a halter dress. It went against her grain, but she wasn't confrontational and she wasn't an activist. She figured she would use the opportunity to show them she was worthy by doing a bang-up job. Instead, she had pretty much proved the opposite by getting pregnant by the client's son, but that was getting ahead of the story a little.

That night changed her life forever. It was not only the night she had met the father of her baby, it was the night her imaginary childhood friend had returned as big as life and nearly given her heart failure. The night… she had learned that there might be a little bit more to magic than she had come to believe.

Either that, or that a high-pressure job in the big city was a little more stressful than she was equipped to handle.

"Lena?"

She had no idea how long she'd been sitting in front of the crackling fireplace, staring into the flames. But when she heard her mom's voice, she brought her head up fast. Selma was standing there looking down at her, frowning. Her glorious red hair was shorter these days, and a few strands of gray dulled its old vibrancy a little. She still wore the big gaudy jewelry and jewel-toned, free-flowing kaftans, though.

Captains, Lena thought, smiling at her inner witchling.

"Are you okay?" her mother asked.

"I… Ernst McNally is dead."

Her mother's hand flew to her chest. "Oh, honey— I'm so sorry, I know you cared for him. How did you hear? Did someone call?"

"Bahru came by."

"Bahru?" Selma blinked her surprise, turning back

toward the big oak door she'd just come through. "He was here?"

"Yeah. Showed up in a big Lincoln with one of Ernst's drivers at the wheel. I tried to get him to stay, but he was in a rush to leave."

"I wish I'd seen him," her mother said.

Lena sighed, recalling how much her mother and Bahru had seemed to enjoy bickering over tea recipes. Mom was a top-notch herbal-tea maker. Bahru was no slouch. But that was before…

"He says I'm named in the will, or the baby is, or something. Anyway. The funeral's tomorrow. He made me promise that I'd be there."

Selma's still-auburn eyebrows pressed against each other. "Do you think that's wise, honey? To travel that far, this late in the pregnancy?"

"It's only a few hours' drive. I can handle that."

"It's not just the drive I'm worried about. *He'll* be there. Can you handle *that?*"

She meant Ryan. Of course. "I'm sure I can. I knew this day would come, Mom. I have to face him sooner or later. He has a right to know."

"You could tell him later. After the baby's here."

"Keeping it from him this long was wrong. And you know it. And I know you know it, because you're the one who raised me never to lie."

"You didn't lie to him."

"And you're also the one who taught me that omissions of this magnitude are the same things as lies."

Selma pressed her lips together. "Damn thorough, wasn't I?" She ran a hand over Lena's hair. "You sure you can handle him?"

"I'm sure." So why did she feel compelled to avert her eyes when she said it? Lena wondered.

"Okay, if that's what you want to do. You want me to go with?"

"Mom, I'm not six."

Selma smiled and nodded, her spiral curls—even tighter than Lena's longer, looser waves—bouncing with the motion. "What's that you have there?" she asked, nodding at the box in Lena's lap.

"I don't know. Bahru said Ernst wanted me to have it." Lena stroked the box. "I got lost in thought and forgot about it."

"Memories?"

Lena nodded and tried to ignore the hot moisture in her eyes.

"You really loved him a lot. It hurts. I know, honey."

She wasn't talking about Ernst, but that didn't need to be said. They both knew what she meant. Flipping open the tiny latch, Lena lifted the lid as her mother leaned over her from behind.

An old, very tarnished chalice lay inside the box, nestled in a red-velvet-lined mold that fit its shape perfectly. Frowning, she lifted it out, held it up, turning it slowly so she could see the dull stones embedded around the outer rim.

"I think that's silver," her mother said. She hustled to the kitchen, and returned with a bottle of tarnish remover and a soft cloth. Then she took the chalice and went to work. Leaning forward in her chair, Lena watched the tarnish being rubbed away, the heavy silver gleaming through. Her mother sat down in the matching rocker on the other side of the fireplace, rubbing and scrubbing and polishing. "It's real silver, all right. Heavy. It must be worth a small fortune. Where on earth did he get this?"

"A street vendor in Tibet. Bahru said the stand was mostly junk, with this just mixed in with all the rest. He said Ernst took one look at it and knew it was meant for me."

Her mother sighed. "Never knew a rich guy as decent as that one." And then she paused and held the chalice up. The firelight made it gleam and wink in what Lena now saw were semiprecious gemstones: amethyst, topaz, citrine, quartz, peridot, three others that she thought might be a ruby, an emerald and a blue sapphire.

"It's old," her mother said. "And if these stones are as real as this silver is, and I think they are—I know my rocks—"

"I know you do." Most of the jewelry her mother wore, she had made herself.

"Lena, this cup could be worth thousands. Maybe tens of thousands."

"It's worth a lot more than that," Lena said very softly.

Her mother frowned at her. "What do you mean?"

"Remember when I was little, Mom? My first attempt at scrying? The vision I had?"

"The one where you saw your handsome prince. The one you later thought looked just like Ryan."

"Didn't look like him. *Was* him." She reached for the cup, and her mother handed it to her. "And do you remember the cup I saw in that vision? The one I described to you?"

Selma seemed to search her daughter's eyes. "Lena,

you don't think—wait. Just wait here, I'll be right back."
She was out of her chair and up the stairs, heading, Lena
had no doubt, to their temple room on the second floor,
where they kept their altar and all their witch things.
Herbs, oils, books. It was their own sacred space. The
house's chapel, so to speak. Lena studied the cup while
she was gone, wondering what on earth all this could
mean.

Her mother returned, a Book of Shadows in her hand.
An old one. Goddess knew they had filled many over
the years, Selma more than Lena, of course. She was
flipping pages as she walked. "I remember, I had you
draw what you'd seen. You were only eight, but—here.
Here it is." She came to a standstill in front of Lena's
rocker, blinking down at the page, and when she looked
up again there was no more doubt in her eyes. Just astonishment.

Turning the book toward Lena, Selma showed her
what her eight-year-old hands had drawn in crayon.
The shape was the same, the color—well, she'd used
the crayon marked "silver," though what resulted was a
pale shade of gray. But most interesting were the gemstones, because they were each a different color and a
different shape.

And they matched the ones on the cup.

"They're even in the same order, at least the ones that
show," her mother whispered, staring at her as if she'd
never seen her before. "My Goddess, Lena, it wasn't
your imagination. It was a *true vision* you received that
day."

"Looks like," Lena said. "The question now is—what
the heck does it all mean?"

"I don't know." Selma moved closer, hugging her. "I don't know, baby. But we'll figure it out."

That's what I'm afraid of, Lena thought.

Ryan McNally sat in the front pew, and felt small and insignificant inside the magnificent cathedral. But it was fitting that his father be memorialized here. He'd been bigger than life, too. Until his wife's death had brought him to his knees.

When his mother died, Ryan thought, the best part of his father had died with her. He'd loved her so much that losing her had all but demolished him. Ryan had been eleven, and even then he'd known he would never let that happen to him.

He was seated near several of his father's closest friends—old men, all of them—and Bahru, who had added a black sash to his red robes today, and who looked as if he'd been crying. His eyes were red-rimmed and puffy, his cheeks even more hollow than usual.

Seeing the old guru like that almost made Ryan rethink his twenty-year belief that the man was nothing but a con. But only until he reminded himself that Bahru had spent a lot of time around actors, prior to latching on to a broken and grieving widower. He'd probably learned a few tricks of the trade, like tears on demand.

Ryan had to give the eulogy. He'd spent a lot of time on it, yet when the priest nodded at him to come up, he found his knees were locked and he couldn't quite force himself to move.

Bahru put a hand on his shoulder. "It's all right," he said. "I promise you, it's all right."

He didn't like or trust the man, even resented him—

and yeah, that was mostly because Bahru had been closer to his father than Ryan had been himself. Not Bahru's fault, though. "Of course it is."

"Would it help to focus your mind elsewhere?"

"Not much could accomplish that today, Bahru."

Bahru met his eyes. "Magdalena is here."

He could have sucker punched him in the gut, Ryan thought, and it wouldn't have distracted him more. Lena had come. He hadn't thought she would. He'd figured she would send flowers, maybe call, but he hadn't expected her to come.

He rose easily, moving up to the front, taking his place at the podium and scanning the magnificent cathedral from a brand new angle. The stained glass, the architecture, the statues—the place was more beautiful than a museum, and it touched him. Beautiful things always did, especially art and architecture.

The sacred place was filled to capacity. No press—they'd been asked to remain outside, where the hearse was waiting and the black stretch limos were lined up around the block.

That thought drew his gaze to the fabric-draped coffin that held his father's remains. And suddenly his throat closed up so tightly that he didn't think he would be able to force a word through. His father was inside that box. His *father*. Lifeless. So hard to believe. He was suddenly awash in regret that his old man's time had run out. He supposed he had always expected they would make things right between the two of them again before it came to this. And now...now he was just gone. Hell.

Someone cleared their throat, and he lifted his head and looked out over the somber crowd, taking in the men in their black suits, the black dresses and even hats on the older women. White tissues flashed like flags here and there. Sniffles and clearing throats echoed from one direction and then another. People he knew, people he didn't want to know. A few genuine tears, more phony ones. But even with all of that, his eyes found hers without trying. He looked up and right into them. They were wet, and her tears were genuine. *She* was genuine. Had been all along, but he'd ruined it. Somehow. She was in a pew toward the back, probably hoping to make a quick exit without running into him. But she was staring right at him, and he got lost in her eyes for a second as their gazes locked. He felt her sympathy, her caring, and wondered yet again why the hell she'd left him. Certainly not because he hadn't been ready to offer her forever after only six weeks. She wasn't that unreasonable. She wasn't unreasonable at all.

Or hadn't been—until that day.

She gave him a sad half smile and a "go ahead, you can do this" nod. He realized that he could, and began. He read his speech with very little emotion, talked about his father's generous contributions to various causes over the years, the people he'd helped, the jobs he'd created. And then he stopped and shook his head, looked up from his notes and blinked back the first tears he'd shed since he'd heard the news.

"You know, I've always believed that most of my father died twenty years ago when his beloved wife, my beautiful mother, was taken from us by a drunk driver. He gave up everything after that. His businesses, his friends…his son. I don't blame him. Her death destroyed him. And ever since she left us, my father has been on a spiritual quest, traveling the world with Bahru by his side, trying to find the answer to one question. *Why?*"

He closed his eyes momentarily to compose himself, then nodded and went on. "I'm not a religious man. But I don't think it ends like this. I would like to think my father is finally getting the answer to that question. And I don't think we should be sad about that. Because I want to believe he's getting it straight from my mother."

He looked at the coffin, pressing his lips together hard to try to stop their trembling. "Yeah. That's what I want to believe."

He stepped down as numerous heads nodded in agreement. And then he sat again, and just tried to block it all out and hold himself together. He felt an emotional storm brewing, and he damn well didn't intend to let it break out in public.

So he thought about Lena instead. She wouldn't really leave without seeing him. Would she? What was he going to say to her when he saw her again? After all this time, would she finally tell him why she'd left? It had been—almost seven months now.

Seven months without a word. She owed him an explanation.

He couldn't imagine what it would be, though he'd tried a thousand times. He'd seen it all play out in his mind, had invented lines for her, none of which had ever made any sense. He couldn't think of a thing that would explain her walking away when they'd been so damn good together. But right now there were a lot of speakers waiting to say a few words about Ernst McNally, most of them hoping to find the ones that would ingratiate themselves with his heir. He had time to kill, and listening to all that insincerity would only make him angry, and he didn't want to be angry when he saw her again. So instead he forced himself to relax in the pew and thought back to the night he'd first set eyes on her.

"Who is *that?*" Ryan asked softly, staring past the beautifully dressed elite filling the Waldorf Astoria ballroom, all of them there to honor his father as *Now Magazine*'s Man of the Year, to the woman who stood chatting with his dad and Bahru. Even among the wealthy, his father stood out. He had a charisma that lifted him head and shoulders above the others. His steel-gray hair was still thick and wavy, his beard just long enough to qualify as "dignified-eccentric" without crossing the border into "aging hippie." And Bahru was always easy to spot, with his endless graying dreads, leathery skin and his red-and-white robes.

But she was different. She stood out for an entirely different set of reasons, some of which, he sensed, went beyond her appearance. She was beautiful, yes. Piles of dark red hair spiraling and twisting like satin ribbons. A perfect porcelain face. But there were plenty of beautiful women in the room that night. Actresses, models, women who made their living by their beauty. He'd banged many of them.

But this one…this one called to him somehow. Once he spotted her, he couldn't look anywhere else. "God, what is she doing with the old man?"

Paul, his best and pretty much only real friend, lifted his brows. "You're asking me as if I'd know. I'm the outsider here, remember? I'm still not sure why you dragged me to this shindig, pal."

"No, *I'm* the outsider. And I dragged you here because I *had* to come, and I didn't want to do it alone. Remember, though, not a word about our potential venture to anyone."

"Don't worry. I don't have a thing to say to any of these silver spoons types." Paul blinked. "No offense."

"None taken." Paul was a family court lawyer, an entrepreneur, a freaking genius, and had taken to the streets with the 99% protestors a while back. He didn't care much for the filthy rich. He probably would have lumped Ryan in with the rest if they hadn't become best friends in college, before Paul had known who Ryan's father was.

Not that it had mattered. His dad had been long gone at that point. Physically and in every other way.

Ryan nodded in the direction of the woman, just as she laughed, revealing a wide, sexy mouth, perfect teeth. He wondered if it was a real laugh, or if she was faking it for his dad's benefit. She wore her mounds of fox-red hair in a way that looked careless and pretended to be coming loose but wasn't really. Her dress was a long black number that hugged her curves like a lover, with a plunging neckline that revealed cleavage to make his mouth water. He couldn't take his eyes off the swell of her breasts until she turned just so and the slit in the dress parted to reveal a long, long leg and a thigh he wanted to trace with his tongue.

Damn.

"You're like something out of a monster flick," Paul muttered. "Perfectly nice guy transforms into a wolf right before my eyes."

Ryan shrugged. "Call it a hobby."

"I call it a lie, but you do what you want. I'm out of here. We still on for that meeting tomorrow?"

"Yeah." Ryan jerked his eyes away from the woman and returned them to his friend. He hadn't been looking for a friend back when they'd met, but Paul was one of those guys you couldn't help but like. Salt of the earth, as honest as the day was long, just a purely decent human being. So few of those around these days. And he decided not to make him suffer another minute. "Paul, the meeting's a formality. I've already decided. I'm going to fund the project. I think it's amazing technology, and there's no one I'd rather partner with."

Paul just stood there blinking at him. He ran a hand over his bristly chin and blinked. Ryan thought there were tears forming in his eyes behind those Steve Jobs glasses he insisted on wearing.

"Just remember, not a word to anyone, okay? I'm a *silent* partner. Though I hope you won't mind if I come around to watch your team in action. I'm as excited about affordable solar energy for everyday Joes as you are."

"I don't understand you," Paul said softly. "I mean, yes, of course I agree to all of that, and thank you. Thank you a million times over." He cleared his throat, looked down into the glass he held in one hand and had yet to sip from. "But why do you want to be so secretive about it? I mean, come on, Ryan. Wouldn't it help your image to be known for funding a project to put solar energy within the reach of every American household?"

Ryan smiled. "*Help* it? It would *destroy* it."

Paul blinked. "But—your image is that you're a spoiled, self-centered, overly indulged, lazy playboy."

"Exactly. And now, if you don't mind, I'm about to go play that role to the hilt. See you tomorrow."

Frowning and shaking his head in bewilderment, Paul muttered good-night, then turned and headed for the hallway and the curving red-carpeted staircase beyond.

Ryan watched him until he was out of sight, just to be sure he didn't get waylaid by anyone demanding to know who he was and what he did. If his father found out, he would want in. Because though he'd ostensibly walked away from everything, he still had that profit-seeking missile inside him, and he could smell money to be made even from a mountainside in Tibet. He would just order his "people" to handle it—buy Paul out, make him an offer even he couldn't refuse, and then Paul would see his beautiful, world-saving, idealistic notions slowly taken over by profit-seeking bottom-liners who would turn them into something ugly but lucrative.

Besides, Ryan needed to be part of a few projects where he could be his own man, completely free of his father's shadow.

Once Paul was in the clear, Ryan made his way through the throng, pausing to return the greetings of all those in attendance, most of whom disapproved of him and made no secret about it, not that he cared, to his father, who stood out even in this crowd of stand-out individuals.

Ryan had inherited his height from Ernst, who was broad-shouldered and narrow in the hip. In a tux, the man could stop traffic and impose palpitations on female hearts of any age, race or, Ryan suspected, sexual orientation.

But he didn't care. As far as he knew, Ernst hadn't been with a woman since his wife, Sarah. Since her death twenty-two years ago, when Ryan had been eleven, Ernst had never been seen, photographed or even rumored to be dallying with any other woman. He must either have gone celibate or been impeccably discreet. Ryan didn't see him enough to know which, because, as far as he was concerned, Ernst had also lost his mind at that time. His love for Ryan's mother had been— all-consuming. Too strong. In the end it had destroyed him.

You wouldn't know it to look at him. He was still a billionaire, still one of the most striking, fascinating men in the world, but a part of him had died that day. The good part.

Beside Ernst, as always, was Bahru, his "spiritual advisor." He always wore red-and-white robes, was bone-thin, and both his hair and his endless beard of thick, dark dreadlocks had puffs of white showing through here and there. His age was impossible to determine, but for the first time Ryan thought he was showing signs of aging.

Ryan nodded at Bahru, who gave him a pressed-palm "namaste" bow in return. Then he extended a hand toward his father. "Congratulations, Dad."

"Thank you, Ryan." His father took his hand in a firm shake and lifted his free arm as if to embrace him, but then sort of eased off and settled for a shoulder pat right at the end.

Awkward. But that was just how things were between

them. His father had abandoned him, motherless and eleven, to go off with his guru. He'd put a gulf between them, and it had only widened since.

Then Ryan turned his attention to the actual reason he'd crossed the room to begin with. The gorgeous female. He didn't look her in the eye but let his gaze stay lowered while he clasped her hand and brought it to his lips. "Ryan McNally," he said, before he kissed the back of that hand.

Then he straightened and met her eyes.

She stared at him, her big green eyes getting even bigger. She looked at him almost as if she recognized him, but he was damn sure he'd never seen her before. *That* he would have remembered. "It's *you*," she whispered, and then she jerked her head to the left, as if someone standing next to her had said something.

But no one was standing there.

She tugged her suddenly cold, suddenly trembling hand free of his and said, "Um, I— Lena. Magdalena Dunkirk. I have to go."

Turning, she hurried away, then stopped and looked over her shoulder. "I'm so sorry. It was lovely to meet you."

Then she was gone, hurrying through the ballroom in heels that should have made speed impossible, while Ryan kept his eyes on her ass the entire way. The dress hugged it tight enough to show what a really nice ass it was.

"Was it something I said?" he asked, turning back to his father only after she was out the door.

"Maybe your reputation preceded you," Ernst said.

"But that's just as well. She's a nice girl. I wouldn't want you breaking her heart."

"I don't really want anything to do with her *heart*," Ryan said.

I should have known right then that she was trouble, he thought. *Should have steered clear of her at all costs.*

But how could he have known that *she* would be the one to break *his* heart? For the first and only time in his life.

She had run away after a nearly-two-month-long relationship that had been sheer fire because he hadn't become serious about her fast enough for her liking. At least that was the explanation he'd constructed in his mind as he'd tried to figure out what had happened. He'd always gone out of his way to be very clear with every woman, right from the start, that he was not the getting serious type. He'd tried even harder to play the playboy for Lena's benefit. The more she got under his skin, the harder he played the role. Apparently she'd realized she was making no progress and walked.

The ironic part was, she was the one woman he'd ever been with who might have had a shot at making him want to get serious. If she'd waited around, maybe…

But in the end, he knew it was for the best. He never wanted to find himself mired in grief the way his father was. To love someone so much that he fell apart when she left. Hell, he'd had a taste of it, the sleepless nights, the recriminations, the missing her, the getting sappy every time any TV show or radio song or meal reminded him of her. If it had been that bad after two months, he'd definitely been heading for trouble. Doing exactly what he'd sworn he would never do.

It was good that she'd left. Now he was back on track again, cool and free, and not caring. Playing the play-boy. It was easier to maintain that image without her.

The crowd of people filling the pews of St. Pat's were muttering, which was his signal to stop reliving the past and start paying attention again to his father's funeral service. It didn't matter anyway. She'd dumped him and run away. It was over. She had come here to pay her respects to his dad. It was the decent thing to do, and she'd always been decent.

The priest had finished, and the pallbearers were moving up to take their places beside the coffin. Bahru and Ryan were the lead pair, so he had to get in gear. Reaching the front, where the casket rested on a stand, he took hold of the brass handle. It was cold to the touch, and the coffin wasn't as heavy as he would have expected it to be. Then again, there were six of them. The other four were all on his father's board of directors.

Fine showing at the end of a life. An estranged son, a Hindi con man and a handful of business partners as pallbearers. That said a lot. Said it all, really.

He didn't want to go out that way, he thought. Friendless and alone.

And then he wondered, as that thought flitted into his mind and he carried his father's casket down the aisle toward the big doors, if he died right now, today, who would be carrying *him* to his waiting hearse? Paul, he guessed. And a handful of other men he'd helped in their businesses and who he supposed were friends. Sort of.

He really didn't *have* any friends other than Paul.

Maybe he wasn't as different from his old man as he liked to think he was.

As he passed by the pew in the back where Lena had been sitting, he looked for her, but she was gone, and a sigh of disappointment rushed out of him. Involuntary but unavoidable. Maybe she would be at the graveside service.

He hoped so.

2

Lena ran into Bill Bennet, her former boss, outside the cathedral under bright sunny skies. Manhattan winters were so different from winters anywhere else in New York State. No snow on the ground here, though sometimes there was, and it rarely lasted long. The temps ran ten degrees higher than they did outside the city, because heat radiated from the pavement and was held in by the buildings and the smog, and Lena had always thought still more was generated by all the bodies, all the machines, all the frenetic human energy. Today it was warm even for January in New York City, maybe forty degrees on the sidewalk outside the cathedral.

Bill was standing in one of those little huddles of humanity that always form outside funerals. People leaning close, all dressed in dark colors, speaking in low tones about what a shame it was and how the family was doing, and who else had died in recent memory. There was never a positive conversation at a funeral. It was all about death and dying and mourning and loss, insurance and health and diseases and accidents. It put her head right into the frame of mind to attract something she did not want.

Lena hated funerals.

But not as much as she hated seeing the stunned looks on people's faces when they got their first glimpse of her midsection, which looked roughly like an over-inflated beach ball, minus the stripes.

Bill saw her face, started to smile underneath his gray-with-a-lingering-ginger mustache but then froze when his gaze found her belly. It was comical, in a way, or would have been if the belly had been attached to anyone besides her. His blue eyes went wide, and he walked right up to her, hugged her and said, "So *that's* why you left."

"Pretty much, yeah."

"Are you—I mean, is the father—"

"I'm doing this alone. That's the way I want it, Bill." She patted his back twice, the international signal for "this hug is about to cross the boundary from friendly to awkward," and he let go and backed a step away.

"You look wonderful," she said before he could continue on the topic of her pregnancy. "Better than before the heart attack, honestly. You've lost weight."

"Thirty pounds." There was pride in his voice. And then he was going on about his new diet, and having given up alcohol, cigarettes and mayonnaise.

She listened, because she was not only polite but truly interested in how her former boss was doing. But she still glanced back toward the ornate doors of St. Pat's whenever she could manage it without being rude, and on the third such peek she spotted Ryan. He hadn't seen her yet, and she scooted around to Bill's other side so he wouldn't. She just wasn't ready to see his reaction to her baby bump. Not yet. Not there.

She guessed there would be no hiding it at the graveside, but she felt she had to go. And really, she couldn't keep it from him forever. Had never intended to. Just… well, the more time she had let slide past, the easier it had become not to call. And now there she was, and there he was, and it was time. Past time.

"Do you mind if I ride with you to the cemetery?" she asked Bill, cutting him off in mid-cholesterol count.

"Well, of course not. We're parked back here." He put a hand at the small of her back and steered her further away from the cathedral, thank goodness, and around a corner. It was going to be a long ride to the cemetery, she thought, as he began listing off the others from the firm, and the spouses of same, who were riding in the stretch limo they'd hired for the occasion. The thing was huge, and there was definitely room for one more.

She eased herself into the vehicle, and spent the next forty-five minutes catching up with former co-workers and trying to describe her new life in a way that didn't sound painfully boring to them. And it *was* boring, really. Utterly tranquil, filled with peaceful bliss. Lonely, of course, but she had her mom. And aside from that loneliness and the odd presence they referred to as their house ghost and who was, they'd decided, harmless, their lives were perfect. Besides, Lena figured the loneliness would be gone the minute the baby arrived, so…

Yes, she thought, it was a long ride to the cemetery.

But not long enough.

She stood behind a crowd of people, wearing a cape-style coat, and holding her purse, brown knit beret-style hat, matching scarf and leather gloves in front of her belly.

It was roughly like a bear trying to hide behind a dandelion, but trying was automatic. Ryan was up front, near the graveside, which was clearly a hole in the ground even though it was decorated in an effort to keep it from looking like one. The shiny brass frame that held the casket was draped in fabric. But nothing could hide the fact that it covered a rectangular pit in the dirt.

As the priest spoke, Lena caught Ryan looking for her, his probing eyes scanning the crowd as she tried to shrink into herself. Eventually he spotted her, as she had known he would. Their eyes met, and just like that her heart flipped in her chest. Was he *really* more beautiful than he'd been before? Was she really that hungry just for the sight of him? Emotions started hurling themselves, like rampaging waters demanding release, against the floodgates that had been keeping them where they belonged for the seven months since she'd left him. Her eyes filled with tears and some of them leaked through. Pregnancy hormones, she told herself. Damn them.

She shifted sideways, breaking the eye contact and silencing those raging waters inside her—for the moment. There was a chest-high tombstone right beside her, and she moved to stand behind it. But all too soon the mourners were filing forward one by one, shaking Ryan's hand, wishing him well. Some threw dirt. Some laid flowers on top of the shining wood of the casket.

Lena didn't get into the line. She stayed where she was, feeling trapped. The shielding crowd of bodies around her had dissipated. If she stepped into the open, she would be fully exposed to Ryan's eyes. So, like a coward, she stayed where she was and just waited.

And soon they were all gone. Even the priest. Bahru met her eyes and gave her a silent nod, and then he, too, went to a waiting car.

The only car left was clearly Ryan's. A sporty little black thing that she had no idea how to identify. He ignored it, brushed the dirt from his hands and came closer. Lena leaned her folded hands on the tombstone, as if that would explain why she was still standing behind it, when she knew it wouldn't. She just looked dumb. But soon enough he would understand why.

"I'm really glad you came." Blinding sunlight streamed from the January sky. There was only a little snow in the cemetery, tufts and puffs clinging to the shadowy places. The rest of the ground was sticky with mud, more like spring than late winter.

"Of course I came. I loved him."

A corner of his mouth pulled upward. "He loved you, too."

He'd lost weight, she thought. There were harsher angles to his face now. As if he'd been sick, maybe, or just getting over the flu. And she noticed, too, that his whiskers were coming in. Ryan had a beard that just wanted to grow. Every morning he shaved, and every night he looked like he hadn't bothered.

She'd loved that about him. By midnight those bristles were just the right length to give her chills when they rasped over her skin in bed.

Her heart skipped; her belly tightened.

"Are you coming to the mansion?"

He was getting closer, taking a few steps, then stopping as if he expected her to move toward him, looking more and more puzzled that she didn't.

"For the reception?" she asked, knowing that wasn't the right term but thinking there wasn't one. Food, alcohol, stories about the deceased, traditional post-funeral activities...what did you call that? "I don't think so."

She didn't want to put herself through the pretense, much less parade her belly around for the world to see and wonder about, maybe even ask about—at least the rude among them.

What she wanted to do was to rush into Ryan's arms. At the same time she wanted to run away without giving him a glimpse of her belly or an answer to what had to be his countless unasked questions.

She didn't do either. She just stood there.

"I don't blame you. I don't want to go, either."

"Then don't go. You need to take care of yourself first." It was automatic, that answer.

Ryan smiled softly. "I've missed those affirmations of yours. Your positive-thinking tips of the day, I used to call them. You always seemed to have one for every occasion."

"And you always thought they were cute but useless."

"Or so I said at the time. Truth is, they stuck with me. I've even put a few of them into practice."

"Oh yeah? And how's it going so far?"

He shrugged. "I guess I ran out. I've been wondering what you'd say about today, about how I'm supposed to deal with things. I couldn't come up with anything for this."

She drew a deep breath. "Try to find something to focus on that feels just a little bit better. Try to do whatever will help you feel a little bit of relief. If you don't want to go to the gathering at your father's mansion, then don't go."

"That wouldn't look very good."

"Ryan, since when do you care how things look to other people? You drove your own car today instead of riding in a limo, for heaven's sake."

He lifted his gaze to hers. "That's a good point. But what about my father?" He turned to look at the casket as he asked the question. "Wouldn't he expect me to be there?"

"Right now, Ryan, your father understands everything. He's at complete peace, at complete oneness. He's achieved enlightenment and would no more put any expectations on you than he would...jump out of that box and dance a jig. He's not there, Ryan. He's in bliss. He's with your mom. And they both understand everything you ever did, felt or thought, and it's okay. It's all okay."

"That's good. That actually helps a little."

"I'm glad."

"Anything else? Other bits of witchy wisdom for the infidel to try?"

"Yeah. When the things that have your attention are very bad, the be-all and end-all solution is to get distracted."

He stared at her, even tried for a lecherous leer. "Are you...offering to distract me?"

"Yeah, just not in the way you think." She drew a deep breath and stepped out from behind the headstone. She had unbuttoned her coat, so her belly was in plain sight.

"Son of a—"

"Or daughter. I didn't let them tell me. But I'm pretty sure she's a girl."

He was dead silent, just staring at her belly. Then, all at once, his expression changed, and she knew he was asking himself the obvious question and doing the math in his head, counting how many months since she had left.

And then his head came up and he stared into her eyes. "Is it mine?"

"Yeah."

He gaped, then clamped his mouth shut, looked up at the sky, clapped a hand to his forehead, turned in a complete circle and faced her again. "My God, Lena. My God, why the hell didn't you tell me?"

"Do you really need to ask me that?"

He frowned at her. "Uh, yeah. I really need to ask you that."

She said, "Think about it, Ryan. Think about our last night together and then ask me why I didn't tell you." Suddenly she realized how pointless this discussion was, that they were never going to see their way across the chasm between them. She yanked out her cell phone and flipped it open.

"Who are you calling?"

"A taxi. It's not like I can flag one down out here in the middle of nowhere, is it?"

"I'll drive you back." He lowered his eyes to her belly again, shaking his head in bewilderment. "It'll give us time to talk about this."

"There's nothing to talk about, Ryan. It is what it is, and trust me when I tell you, I don't want, need or expect anything from you. I can do this alone."

"Well, that's fine, but I get some say in this, don't I?"

"You had your say already."

"Bullshit."

Angry, and knowing she shouldn't be—he had every right to be upset—she accepted defeat and walked toward the car, pulling her coat closed and doing up the buttons on the way. She was wearing flats, but the ground was wet. She was almost there when her foot slid on a patch of slick mud and she started going down, her arms flailing like some cartoon character.

He was behind her instantly and caught her before she fell, so she landed against his chest, with his arms around her above her beach ball and below her boobs. He stayed that way for a second, his palms turning to rest on top of her belly, and her helpful progeny chose that moment to kick *hard,* three rapid-fire, Jackie Chan-worthy thrusts directly where his hands were.

Automatically she looked up at his face for his reaction to what he'd just felt and then wished she hadn't. Because his expression went from stunned to rapturous in the space of a heartbeat, and when he met her eyes again his were wide and delighted, like a little kid on Christmas morning.

She understood it. When she had first felt the baby kick, that was the moment when the whole thing took on a new level of...of *realness.* Up until then she'd thought of the baby more as a concept than a reality. But once it had kicked, it was real. That's when it became a she—or he, she admitted, but probably she—wiggling around inside her body, just waiting to come out.

Ryan's smile was the biggest, most genuine smile Lena had ever seen.

Okay, kid, she thought, *good call. You made him smile on the day he buried his dad, so I guess it was worth it.*

His smile died as he stared into her eyes, and his expression softened. "Are you okay?" he asked, straightening her up again but keeping one arm around her shoulders as they turned toward the car.

"Yeah, fine. I didn't fall."

"I mean—I mean, you know…overall? You've been pregnant for…"

"Almost eight months now. And yes, I'm fine, and the baby is, too. Healthy. Growing like a weed."

"I'm glad." He opened the passenger door and stood holding it while she got in, then went around to get behind the wheel while she fastened the seat belt in what had become her customary fashion, with the lap belt behind her, and the shoulder harness across her chest.

He started the engine and pulled the vehicle into motion, glancing at her as she buckled up with a puzzled frown. "When is the baby due?"

"Thirteen days past Imbolc."

He frowned in confusion.

"Sorry. Mid-February. I'm calling her my little groundhog."

He shot her a look. "'Her' again. What makes you so sure it's a girl?"

She was surprised at the line of questioning. He actually sounded interested. "Well, like I said, I haven't let the doctor tell me that for sure. But I have my own feelings about her, and I think she's a girl."

"Where have you been living?"

It was her turn to frown. "What do you mean?"

"I mean, you vanished. The firm said you resigned. Your building manager said you'd opted not to renew the lease on your apartment. Your mother sold her place in Brooklyn—"

"You looked for me?"

"*Of course* I looked for you."

"Huh." *That* she hadn't expected. She had kept the same cell number and he had called numerous times, but she'd chosen not to answer. And after a while he'd just stopped.

"You didn't need to hide from me, you know."

She sent him a quick, sharp look. "I wasn't."

The look he returned was an "Oh, come on now" sort of expression, as if she'd said something ridiculous.

"No, really. Bahru knew where I was the entire time. In fact, he's the one who tipped me off about the place."

Ryan sent her a searching look. "Bahru?"

"Yeah. I went to say goodbye to him and…and to Ernst. And as he hugged me, Bahru slipped me a note with a URL on it. Turned out to be a real estate listing. He said he had a feeling it was meant for me from the moment he'd seen the place. And when I saw it, I knew he was right."

"Yeah?"

"Yeah. It's an old vineyard near Ithaca, right on the shore of Cayuga Lake. Kind of decrepit, but we're restoring it as we go along, and it's just full of character. It was called Havenwood. Someday I'd like to replant the grapevines and try my hand at making wine."

She almost added that she and her mother were convinced the place had a resident ghost, too, but decided against it. He'd never taken her beliefs seriously, and frankly, she was enjoying his interest too much to want to ruin it by eliciting his skeptical indulgence of things he didn't understand.

"I'd love to see it," he said.

She met his eyes but didn't answer. Because he might be asking permission to visit, which might mean after the baby came, which might mean he was actually asking to be involved in her life. Both their lives. And she wasn't sure she wanted that. Nor was she sure she *didn't* want it. And moreover, she wasn't sure she had the right to make that call. It was really up to her little groundhog.

In response to her silence he said, "You look tired. Are you sure you're okay?"

"Yeah, I'm good. But it's been a long day. How about you? This must have been a grueling day for you. I know how things were between you and your father. Did you ever…you know, make up?"

"We weren't really estranged, just…"

"Cold," she said. "Distant."

He shrugged. "That was his choice, not mine."

Okay, still touchy on that subject, she thought.

"I'll be all right," he said. "Why don't you lean your head back. Close your eyes. We've got another forty minutes back to the city. Here, I'll find something soothing." He found a new-age station that was right up her alley—the same station she always used to tune in to during those beautiful weeks of their passionate and life-altering fling.

He remembered….

He was acting more like the prince she had mistaken him for than he ever had…in this lifetime, anyway. She took his advice and leaned her head back, closed her

eyes and drifted back to the night she had first met him
at that fancy-assed ball honoring his father.

It was him, it was him, it was him!

She had tried to contain her childlike enthusiasm
as she stared wide-eyed at her reflection. All alone in
the restroom of the posh Waldorf Astoria, she tried to
come to grips with the fact that she had just met the
very prince from her childhood fantasies. That vision
in her mamma's black mirror. Her prince.

"Don't be ridiculous, Lena," she whispered to her
reflection. "That was a fairy tale from childhood. A
fantasy. Imagination. There's no handsome prince, no
exotic palace, no garden oasis in the desert."

Oh, yeah? Then where the heck did she *come from?*
she asked herself.

Because the instant she had set eyes on Ryan Mc-
Nally, she had heard, very distinctly, a woman's voice
from close beside her saying "He's the one you've been
waiting for." Except no one was there. Then, as she had
scanned the crowd, she could have sworn she'd seen her
old friend Lilia meandering through it.

She closed her eyes and concentrated. "Lilia was an
imaginary friend. She was not—I repeat, *was not*—out
there. Because she does not—I repeat, *does not*—exist."

Soft laughter came from behind her. Oh, *hell,* she
wasn't alone in the restroom after all. She opened her
eyes and stared into the mirror again—and saw Lilia
standing right behind her left shoulder, all decked out
in white robes like a desert angel, shoulders bare, skin
like copper, hair jet-black and blowing in a non-existent

breeze like a model on a magazine cover. And glowing. She was definitely…glowing.

Lena spun around, but of course there was no one there.

All right, this is ridiculous.

She pulled out her cell phone, flipped it open, hit the listing marked *Mom.*

"I was just going to call you," Selma said without even a hello first. "I had the oddest feeling—"

"My imaginary friend is back, Mom."

Selma was silent. Lena could see her as clearly as if they were on Skype, frowning and fingering her over-sized pentacle the way she always did. Her mom wasn't a broom-closet sort of woman. She was more an in-your-face witch. Or had been until they'd moved to the country. She'd been a lot more discreet since then.

"Well? Say something, will you? I'm freaking out here."

"Where are you?" Her mother was calm, composed, like always.

"At the Waldorf Astoria. The reception for my new assignment, Ernst McNally, eccentric, world-traveling billionaire. Any of this ringing a bell, Mom?"

"Yes, of course, just calm down. Take deep, cleansing breaths. Come on, now."

Lena nodded, closed her eyes and set the phone down. Then she inhaled nasally, raising her arms over her head, and exhaled thoroughly, lowering them in front of her body. Three times was the charm. She was calm, centered. She picked up the phone again.

"Better?" her mom asked, uncannily knowing she had returned.

"Yes."

"Now tell me what happened."

"I was at the reception. Chatting with Mr. McNally and his spiritual guide, a really eccentric-looking man called Bahru. Wait, I snapped a pic when he wasn't looking." She took the phone from her ear, located the picture and emailed it. "I like him. He's very wise."

"Ernst or Bahru?"

"Bahru. Ernst seems more sad and searching than wise."

"Oh, got the pic," her mother said. "Wow, he *is* eccentric-looking. He wore *that* to the Waldorf Astoria?"

"Mmm-hmm," Lena said, seeing again the red-and-white sari-style getup. "Ernst says he wears it everywhere. And the dreadlocks are all the way to his butt."

"Go on, what happened next?"

"Okay. Okay, this is…this is…"

"Just tell me, Lena."

Lena nodded again. "This man came over. Ernst introduced him as his son, Ryan. I looked up at him, and—and I swear, Mom, he was the prince from that silly fantasy-vision I had when I was a little girl. You remember the one, the first time you let me try mirror-scrying?"

"The Arabian prince who was going off to war but promised to return to carry you away. How could I forget? You wrote an entire collection of storybooks about him. I didn't let you scry again for two years. But, Lena, you *do* realize that was the same summer *Aladdin* came out, right?"

She sighed. "Yes. But there's more. Just as I thought

it couldn't possibly be him, a woman whispered right into my ear—not my head, Mom, my *ear*. Out loud. 'It's him. The one you've been waiting for.' And I turned fast, but there was no one standing there, and it was clear no one else had heard her but me."

"Huh," her mom said.

"So I scanned the room and I thought I saw Lilia."

"Your imaginary friend?" Selma asked. *Now* she sounded worried.

"And then I came into the restroom and she was right here. Standing right behind me in the mirror, laughing."

"Hell's bells," her mother whispered. "Honey, maybe you'd better come home."

"Soon as I can. But I have to go back out there. This is my biggest assignment so far, taking over the McNally account while Bill recovers."

"All right, then," her mother said. "Here's the thing. None of this sounds dire. I mean, it's odd, but…you always insisted Lilia wasn't imaginary. I was obviously wrong in not accepting that. She's clearly some kind of otherworldly guide. That's nothing to be afraid of, honey. It's a blessing, actually. Later, when you're alone, talk to her. See if she can tell you why she's come. And as for Ernst's son—"

"Ryan," Lena said, and the name whispering from her lips sent shivers down her spine.

"Ryan. He's in the tabloids a lot, you know. Player. Big-time player. Irresponsible, spoiled, self-centered—you know the type."

"I do."

"But if he's your prince, then, baby, gird your loins and go for it."

Lena stared into the mirror. Her wide eyes had returned to their normal size and shape. Her lips stopped quivering and pulled into a little smile. Her spine straightened. Her cleavage rocked. "You always know what to say, Mom."

"Well, of course I do, sweetheart. It's my job. Have a great time. Call me tomorrow."

"I will. Thanks, Mom."

"Blessed be, Lena."

Lena snapped the phone closed and slid it into her handbag, then pulled out her compact and touched herself up. Then she smoothed her hair, popped a breath mint, plumped her "girls" and turned decisively to head out of the restroom.

Ryan McNally was waiting on the other side of the door.

She smiled at him. "Men's room is over there," she said, pointing.

"I was waiting for you."

"I know you were."

His brows went up. "Confidence. I like that. Would you like to get out of here?"

She smiled. "If by that you mean, would I like to go somewhere for sex, then no. But I *would* like to dance."

"Dance?" He turned toward the ballroom, where the band was playing something fast, then back to her. "Can we wait for a slow one?"

"Oh, no. Slow dancing must be earned. You have to make an idiot out of yourself in public first. But don't worry about looking bad, Ryan. Sometimes my dancing causes people to dial 9-1-1 and report a woman having convulsions."

He laughed. He smiled, and not that suave "charm the lady's panties off" grin he'd been wearing before. This one was real, with tiny laugh lines at the outer corners of his eyes that made them seem even bluer and a flash of white teeth. He had a thick layer of beard coming in, shadowing his jawline in a way that made her stomach knot up.

"If that's the price of a slow dance, then it's worth paying." He held out a hand, and she took it, and then he led her out onto the dance floor just as the band jumped from one very old song to the next: "Twist and Shout."

"Ah, the dance gods love me tonight," Ryan said. "Twisting I can do."

"Shouting, too?"

"Ask me later."

He had a twinkle in his eye, and she had to laugh, because he was clearly kidding, not hitting on her. Though maybe a little of that, too. They twisted, and she felt ridiculous, but she kept hearing her mom's voice telling her that if he was her prince, she should go for it.

She had never *gone for it* with a guy in her life. But it felt like now was the time. And she thought it was working, because he seemed to be enjoying himself.

They twisted to the end of the song, and then, when he went to get them drinks and asked her to scope out a table, she chose to join his father and Bahru at theirs. Ryan didn't look too pleased when he returned, but he tried to cover it as he put down their drinks and asked, "Dad, can I you get something? Bahru, a carrot juice or anything?"

That was slightly nasty, Lena thought. But Bahru only held up a hand and shook his head.

Ernst said, "No, I'm fine."

Then Ryan returned his focus to her. "Lena. Is that short for anything?"

"Magdalena," she told him.

"Magdalena." He nodded slowly. "It's an old-fashioned name."

"Very. My mother said it just came to her the first time she held me, and she never questions things like that." She leaned forward. "She's a witch." Normally she wouldn't bring that up in front of a client, but she knew Ernst was a spiritual seeker. She wasn't worried about judgment from a guy who traveled the world with a guru at his side.

"The Wiccan kind?" Ernst asked.

She nodded.

"So you were raised…?"

"Casting and conjuring since I was four," she said.

"Delightful." The billionaire really seemed sincere.

"You just get cuter and cuter," Ryan said.

"One's belief system is sacred," Bahru said softly. "Not *cute*."

She sent Ryan a "so there" lift of her eyebrows. He rolled his eyes.

"What's your belief system, Bahru?" she asked.

"I was raised Hindi, but I have learned from countless holy men, shamans, priests, priestesses, swamis, monks, nuns and more, all around the world. I am an eclectic, I suppose."

"That's fascinating."

"I have never studied with a witch," he said. "I would love to talk with you about your path one day."

"I'd like that, too," she told him.

"Hey, don't you owe me a slow dance?" Ryan asked.

She studied him. He was bored with their discussion. Strike one, she thought. But maybe he would come around, given time. "All right," she said, getting to her feet, "but I can't ignore the man I'm supposed to be working for tonight." She nodded at his father.

"Consider yourself off duty, beautiful Magdalena," Ernst said. "Enjoy the party. I think I'm going to call it a night anyway." He rose as well. "I am very much looking forward to working with you, my dear. I'll phone you in the morning." He opened his arms for a hug.

The feminist part of her thought he wouldn't be hugging a *male* PR person. But the rest of her was touched. She hugged him briefly, and he took the opportunity to whisper into her ear, "Be careful, my dear. He's a heartbreaker, my son."

"He's the one who'd better be careful," she whispered back. "*I* am my mother's daughter." She kissed him on the cheek, knowing they were going to be close, whatever happened between her and Ryan.

Then she extended a hand to Bahru. "It was lovely meeting you. I look forward to those talks."

"As do I." He clasped her hand in both of his and bowed over it twice.

Then she was swept into Ryan's arms, and she forgot all about his calling witchcraft "cute," along with his rudeness toward Bahru and apparent boredom with spiritual discourse. None of it compared in the least with the feeling that swept over her when he wrapped one strong arm around her waist and held her close. She inhaled, breathing him into her, and then closed her eyes against an inexplicable rush of dizziness, as if his aura was a drug and she had no resistance to it. Lowering her head to his chest, she let him move her around the floor as visions raced into her mind.

There was a bubbling spring, very small, shaded by a trio of exotic palm-like trees that all seemed to grow from the same roots. The ground around the spring was nourished by the nearby water and sprouted plants in gratitude. They had thick, fibrous stalks and coarse, sharp-edged leaves, and yet they bloomed in tiny pink and purple flowers. She did not know what they were called.

And there in that beautiful miniature oasis, she was in the arms of a handsome prince. She felt his chest beneath her head, his arms around her waist. She breathed him in, and it was the same. The same essence. More than a scent, it was an energy. An aura. The same man.

Fantasies I spun when I was a little girl, under the influence of Aladdin *and* I Dream of Jeannie *reruns. I'd had the Jasmine and Aladdin dolls. I'd created an entire life for them in which Aladdin was the prince and Jasmine the slave girl. I'd drawn pictures, made little chapter books that told their love story, their adventures, with construction paper and Crayola crayons. It wasn't real.*

Then how can he be the same? she asked herself.

He can't, that's the answer. This is some kind of break with reality, and I'd better get a handle on it, because I cannot afford a mental breakdown at this point in my life. My career is about to take off, for Goddess' sake!

She closed her eyes and tried to keep her head in the moment. Which was, after all, a pretty amazing moment, because Ryan was gorgeous and…

And his hand was trailing down her spine, lightly, gently, slowly, lower, over the ultra-sensitive small of her back to just above her tailbone, and then, just as exquisitely, back up again. She shivered, and she knew he felt it. He dipped his head a little lower, and his bristly cheek brushed over hers as he whispered near her ear, "You seem so familiar to me. Are you sure we've never met before?"

It's just a line, said her brain.

Oh, God, that warm breath on my ear, said her body.

"I've been asking myself the same thing," said her voice, because she didn't like to lie. She never had. "But I've decided not to worry about it. I'm just going to enjoy the moment."

"I think that's a very good philosophy."

"It's the only one, really. All your power is in the now. The past no longer exists, and the future's not here yet. Now is really all there is, and since it is always now, it's endless. The eternal present."

"Deep."

She shrugged. "I take it you're not all that into deep, philosophical discussions?"

He angled his head downward. "I'm afraid I'm guilty."

"Why? Your father is such a spiritual man."

"Exactly."

She frowned, searching his eyes. "Meaning?"

He smiled, a charming, killer smile. "Let's not go there. Let's be in the moment. You're in my arms, you're beautiful, you smell good, and I'm not going to think about anything else right now. Okay?"

She smiled. "Okay."

He twirled her around, pulling her even closer.

And she let herself surrender to the moment, which became another moment, and then another, all unfolding one after the next until the moment when he was carrying her, with her arms linked behind his neck and her legs wrapped around his waist, her black velvet dress bunched up around her hips while he kissed her, into his apartment.

They'd danced again and again, and she'd had several more drinks, probably a few too many. Enough so that she'd stopped questioning the wisdom of sleeping with the son of her firm's most important client. Enough so that she stopped wondering how he could be so identical to the man in her childhood fantasies—Aladdin to her Jasmine. Enough so that she just fell into those stories and let herself believe in them. Like a little girl, she was making believe that her fantasy prince had finally come to take her away, because really, there was no better way to fully relish this particular moment.

She let everything go and allowed it to just flow over her. His mouth fed from hers as hungrily as if he adored her, even though she knew he didn't.

Shut up and enjoy it!

As he kicked the door closed behind him, his fingers found the zipper low on her back, and he slid it smoothly downward, his hands following its path, hot fingers trailing over her spine, rubbing delicious tiny circles right at the base, then slipping inside her silky panties. He squeezed and pulled her harder against him at the same time.

They moved through his place in the dark, their way lit only by moonlight, which she saw when he mouthed her neck, making her tip her head back in pleasure. He nipped, and her eyes opened wide, startled and delighted at once. She saw the gibbous moon high above, through skylights in the ceiling, and realized this was the penthouse. Of course it was.

They stumbled through another doorway, and then he swept aside the blankets on a king-size bed and lowered her onto satin sheets, his knees between her thighs, his hands sliding the unzipped gown from her shoulders just before he laid her down on the plush nest of pillows. Then he was leaning over her, caressing her breasts, teasing their peaks, making her gasp and pant and want him. Her hands slid over his chest, and she unbuttoned his shirt and pushed it off. She kissed his naked chest, his magnificent shoulders, his belly, where she couldn't help but touch him again and again, because he had the kind of abs you only saw on fitness-club commercials.

He groaned, then backed up enough to make her reach for him. When he returned he was naked. He helped her wriggle the rest of the way out of her dress and panties, and then he was touching her where she so, so wanted him to, teasing her from "ready" to writhing and whimpering before he finally lowered himself between her thighs and nudged just a little.

Impatient, she reached to guide him in, closing her hand around him and smiling with evil delight at his size. He tore open a wrapper with his teeth, sheathed himself in latex. And then he was sliding into her, stretching her, filling her.

There was a flash of light before her eyes, and she thought there had been heat lightning outside. And then a voice whispered, *As the rod is to the God, so the chalice is to the Goddess. And together they are one.*

She wondered if he'd heard it, too, but by then he was moving inside her and she forgot all of it, forgot everything but the pleasure he was creating inside her. She moved with him, clinging to his back and holding on for dear life as he drove her beyond sanity, beyond reality, into momentary, mind-blowing, blissful release. In her mind she saw swirling desert sands and heard her beloved prince saying to her, *"I will return for you, my love. Never doubt it. And when I do, you'll be my bride."*

She snuggled closer, embracing the fantasy, a fantasy that lasted for several more hours of pleasure. Until, a few hours before dawn, just as she was falling into blissful, sated sleep in his arms, he bent to kiss the top of her head and said, "Would you like a snack before you go?"

Before I go? Before I go where? she wondered.

"I can make us some microwave popcorn." Instead of holding her, basking in the afterglow of what had been the most powerful and meaningful lovemaking of her entire life, he jumped out of bed and walked naked toward what she assumed was the kitchen. "I'll call down and have the doorman start the car for us, so it'll be nice and warm by the time you're ready for me to drive you home."

"How...thoughtful." She frowned and thought, *So much for my fantasy.*

3

"Lena?"

His voice was soft and close, and as she let it swirl around inside her head it melded with the dream, so that she thought they were back there, in the past, still dating. And that nothing in between the day she'd left him and now had ever happened.

And then she realized she had fallen asleep and dreamed all that.

"We're here," he said.

She opened her eyes, blinking things into focus and looking out the window at the familiar shape of his father's Westchester mansion. And then she frowned. "I thought you were taking me back to my hotel?"

"I am. But, uh—even if you want to skip the socializing, there's the meeting first. I thought you knew."

"Meeting…?"

"Dad's attorneys. The will. You're named in it."

"Oh." She blinked softly. "I didn't know. That Ernst was going to do that, I mean. It's not something I was looking for. I don't need—"

"Did he know?" Ryan asked. "About the baby?" She

met his eyes, saw the hurt in them at the thought that his father would have kept something like this from him. A hurt he'd once worked very hard to convince her he was incapable of feeling. "I honestly don't know, Ryan. We haven't been in touch since I left. But…"

"But?" he prompted when she trailed off.

"Bahru knew," she admitted. She felt as if she was tattling. "He knew before I left."

"Bastard could've told me."

She shrugged. "He might have assumed, like I did, that it wouldn't have mattered."

He slapped his palms on the steering wheel, not violently, but in frustration. "Why the hell would you assume that?"

She frowned at him. "How can you ask me that? Do you *really* not remember the last conversation we had, Ryan?"

He looked as puzzled as if she'd lapsed into ancient Babylonian.

She rolled her eyes, sighed deeply. "It doesn't matter anyway," she said. "Bahru did mention that I would have to be present when the will was read, but he didn't say when. So you're saying it's now?"

"Yeah." He looked at his watch. "Right now. In Dad's den." He looked toward the house, the people wandering in and out. Then he popped the clutch and drove the car around to the back.

The wide stone deck was devoid of furniture. The umbrella tables had been put away for the winter, and the pool was sealed tight. Even so, the back of the house had a much more relaxed feel to it than the front.

"Come on, we'll miss the crowds this way."

Lena got out. She was feeling pretty pissed that he hadn't yet figured out why she had left him, much less apologized for it. Or, God forbid, taken it back. But what the hell? It was water under the bridge. They had tried. And they had failed. She would never regret it. And maybe the whole thing—the vision, the fantasy, his resemblance to her prince—maybe all that hadn't happened to fulfill their star-crossed love affair from the long-ago past lives she was convinced they'd had. Resolving that, might never have been the reason. Maybe it was all about the baby. She'd found him, been drawn to him, and he'd given her a baby. Perhaps that was the purpose all along.

He came to her side quickly, his hand on her elbow irritating her for no good reason. She jerked it away from him before she could stop herself.

"What?" he asked.

"I'm pregnant, Ryan. Not injured or weak or fragile. I've been waddling around just fine without you holding on to me for months now. I think I can make it to the back door without help."

"Oh."

He stood where he was while she headed up the three broad stone steps onto the deck and across it to the French doors. And then she paused, because she wasn't sure whether to knock or wait or what the hell to do.

He came up beside her and reached past her to open the doors, and they headed inside. The French doors led directly into the den, which had been Ernst's favorite room in the house. And no wonder. From it you could see the entire back lawn and the gardens, and you could walk straight out to the deck and then to the pool off the far end of it, any time you felt like a break. It was a perfect place to work.

Bahru was sitting cross-legged on the floor, eyes closed, holding on to that quartz pendant around his neck. Another man sat at Ernst McNally's big desk, shuffling papers. They were the only people in the room.

Must be a small will.

"Ahh, Ryan, good. And you must be Lena," said the man behind the desk, getting to his feet and coming around with a hand extended. "Ernst spoke very highly of you."

"Thank you, that means a lot to me, Mr. . . . ?"

"Aaron Samuels," he said. "Please, have a seat."

She nodded and headed for the two chairs that were situated in front of the desk. Bahru was sitting just past them. As she drew closer he opened his eyes, and they flashed red as they met hers. She sucked in a breath and stumbled backwards, crashing into Ryan's chest. His arms came around her fast.

"Hey, I thought you said you could walk without help, sunshine?"

Turning her head, she looked up into his eyes. Her heart was pounding, and she opened her mouth but didn't know what to say.

"What is it, Lena?" he asked.

"I—" She looked at Bahru again. No glowing red eyes. He was getting to his feet and smiling as warmly as ever. So she glanced back at the French doors to see the bright orange of the sunset beaming in through them and sighed. "Nothing, I'm fine." And jumpy, she thought. "Good to meet you, Mr. Samuels. Hello again, Bahru."

He pressed his hands together and bowed slightly over them.

She let Ryan keep hold of her and seat her in the first chair, and then he took the other chair—the one she'd been heading for, the one that was closer to Bahru—himself.

"I know this has been a miserable day for all of us," the lawyer said. "So I'm not going to spend a lot of time on the minutiae."

Lena glanced at Ryan as the man went on, and they shared an unspoken "Who the hell says *minutiae?*" moment. He even smiled a little.

The lawyer was still going on. "...right to the gist of it, which is really simple enough."

"Ryan, you of course inherit the bulk of the estate. The holdings, the money, the mansion, the fleet of cars, both jets, the businesses—"

"I was afraid of that." Ryan sighed and leaned forward a little, as if something very heavy had just landed on his shoulders.

Lena reached out and slid her hand over his, then tried to take back the intimacy of the move by patting it instead of holding it. "You can sell it all. You can let the board run it. It doesn't have to be a burden to you, Ryan," she whispered.

He nodded.

"As for you, Magdalena," the lawyer went on, "Ernst was very specific. First off, the deed to your home has been marked 'paid in full.'"

She blinked. "What? But I don't—"

"The vineyard belonged to Ernst, Magdalena," Bahru said softly. "He was afraid you wouldn't want it if you knew. He'd bought it long ago, hoping to retire there one day with his beautiful Sarah. They had such plans for the place—but then she died and…"

"*That's* the vineyard where you've been living?" Ryan burst out.

"I bought that vineyard from Ernst?" she shouted at the same moment.

Samuels held up both hands. "One of his holding companies, to be specific, but yes, that's what it comes down to."

"But I wanted to do this on my own."

"Dad didn't like to let anyone he cared about do anything on their own," Ryan said. "Trust me, Lena, I totally get your indignation." He tugged her arm until she looked at him. "But hey, it doesn't have to be a burden on you," he said, repeating her own words back to her. "You can always sell it."

"That's not the point."

"I know."

All right, all right, she knew what he was saying. Her homilies about him being able to sell his father's empire, about not letting it be a burden, were beside the point. The man had imposed his will on his unwilling son, and it didn't feel good. She shared the feeling firsthand now and acknowledged that with a slow nod. His expression said that he received the message.

"If you don't mind," the lawyer said, clearing his throat to get their attention, "there's more."

She sighed but didn't sit back down. "What else?"

"Ernst collected an impressive number of books and even some scrolls on his travels. Hundreds of writings, obscure religious texts and—"

"The sacred teachings of all times," Bahru explained. "He said you were one of the few people he had ever known who would appreciate his collection."

Lena blinked in absolute stunned shock, and thudded heavily into her chair again. Tears welled up in her eyes. "Oh, my God. I can't believe he did that."

"Wait, wait," Ryan said. "He gives you a vineyard, you're pissed. But he gives you a pile of musty old books and you're in tears?"

She spared him only a quick scowl before turning to Bahru. "But *you* should have them, Bahru."

He shook his head. "They were meant for you. Where would I put them, once I am free to return to my endless journeying?"

"The books will be delivered to you at your home by week's end, Magdalena," said the attorney. "I have people packing them up for shipping right now."

She opened her mouth, but he held up a hand. "I promise you, these are men who know how to handle precious and rare manuscripts. They'll be safe. Ernst also set up a trust for your child, the current balance of which is…" He shuffled papers. "Ten million dollars. With interest, it will be worth significantly more as time passes. But you are in complete control, and may use the interest at any time and in any way you see fit. The principal is to remain untouched until you deem the child mature enough to take control of it. He said he trusted you completely."

She felt as if the air had all rushed out of her body and her muscles had turned to gelatin. "But the interest on ten million dollars would be…"

"At the current rate, it's earning about five hundred thousand per year."

Her jaw dropped.

"As for you, Bahru, Ernst left you exactly what you asked for. The guesthouse on the vineyard, with the caveat that it's all right with Magdalena—"

"What's this?" Ryan asked, sounding angry again.

She put her hand on his shoulder. "Easy, Ryan." And then she turned to the bearded holy man. "Bahru?"

He smiled softly. "He wanted me to stay close to the child, Magdalena. To advise you and your baby just as I have advised him, and to watch over things."

"And is that what you want?"

"I want nothing more."

"Well, you got more," the lawyer said. "He's leaving you enough stock to provide a small income for the rest of your life, Bahru. And he told me not to take no for an answer."

Bahru's face darkened. "I told him no money!"

"He insisted."

Lena smiled, recognizing the irony of what she was about to say. "It's what Ernst wanted, Bahru. It would be an insult not to take it."

He frowned but looked down. After a moment, though, he met her eyes again and nodded once. "I accept—if you will accept my presence in the guesthouse, Magdalena."

"Of course I will."

"Lena, I don't know about all this," Ryan began, but he stopped when she sent him her patented glare. She had learned it from her mother, who could wilt roses with it.

"Fine. Fine. It's not like I have any say in it anyway."

"That's right, Ryan."

He was really fuming. She knew he'd never trusted Bahru, but surely he could see now that the guru had never been after his father's fortune. He'd been clearly angry when Ernst had left him money.

"Are we finished here, then?" Ryan asked.

"Actually," Samuels said, "Lena and Bahru can go now, but I need one more moment with you, Ryan."

Ryan sent Lena a look, as if to ask if she would be okay without him for a few minutes. She had been okay without him for her entire life, minus eight blissful weeks, she thought, but she didn't say it out loud.

"I'll venture into the reception," she said with a nod toward the door. "Come on, Bahru. It would be rude of us not to at least put in an appearance."

Nodding, Bahru got to his feet. Lena turned back to Ryan. "I'll wait for you, okay?"

"Yeah. I'll find you when I'm done here."

She didn't know whether to look forward to that—or dread it.

Ryan rose when they left, then stood there staring blankly at the door for a long moment. It was like a twister had just swept through his life. He'd buried his father and found out he was going to be one himself, inherited billions he'd never wanted, and learned that the man he disliked more than anyone he knew was being installed as a fixture in his child's life, when he himself had not yet been granted access. All in one day.

"Are you all right, Ryan?"

"Yeah. I—" He shook his head hard, as though he

was shaking away the fog. "Yeah. Good. Let's get on with this. I've got…a lot to deal with."

"That's got to be the understatement of the year." The lawyer bent to pick up an oversized briefcase, then laid it on the giant antique desk and snapped open the clasps. He opened it and picked up a wooden box that looked centuries old, at least. Its lid was completely engraved, so that there wasn't a smooth spot anywhere. Vines with leaves and buds, stars and spirals in between.

As the attorney held it out to him, Ryan took it and looked more closely, realizing that the more you looked at the thing, the more you saw. Swirls in the vine's bark-like texture revealed an eye here, a hand there, a crescent moon in another spot. He wanted to roll his eyes. "I don't know how many times I told the old man I just wasn't into all his spiritual hocus pocus bull. I guess he just had to try one last time to capture my interest."

And he had. The box was spectacular—there was no denying it as a work of art. And that spoke to Ryan's soul, though he would never admit it. But there was more. Something that seemed to grab his attention and pull him in.

He lifted the lid to see what was inside.

There was no earthly reason for him to feel as if he'd been hit between the eyes with an invisible blast, and yet that was what he felt at his first glimpse of the blade. It was a simple piece. A double-edged dagger with a gleaming gold hilt. It looked real. Weighed enough, too.

"That's it?"

"That's it. He said I was to give it to you in private, and to tell you to keep it to yourself."

"And why's that?"

Samuels shrugged, snapping the briefcase closed. "I don't know any more than that, Ryan." Then he rose and extended his hand.

Ryan closed the lid of the wooden box and accepted the gesture. "Thank you."

"You're welcome. I'm sure we'll be in touch. Let me know if there's anything you need. And again, Ryan, I'm very sorry for your loss."

"Thanks."

The lawyer nodded and left. Ryan watched him go. Then he opened the box again, wondering what the hell this was all about.

He went to pick the knife up, but his hand stalled just before making contact, as if he was afraid to touch it. Which was completely illogical. And then his palm started tingling like nothing he'd ever felt before. For just the barest instant the golden blade seemed to glow.

There was a knock at the door, and he slammed the lid as fast as if he'd spotted a cobra inside. Damn, he was jumpy. Emotional overload. A trick of the light. Some weird combination of the two.

"Ryan?"

It was Lena's voice. He shoved the box onto a nearby shelf and went to open the door. She searched his face, hers full of concern. "You okay?"

"Yeah. Fine. It's just been…it's been a crazy day, that's all."

"I know it has. For me, too. And the energy out there is just…" She raised her hands to her head and made the universal gesture for crazy.

"Nuts?" he asked.

"Frenetic. And fake, too. A lot of those people are

only here for their own ends. To see or be seen, or…I don't know. Definitely not out of any love for Ernst, that's for sure."

"They told you that?"

She frowned, cocking her head and wiggling her fingers in a woo-woo gesture. "Of course not. *Witch*, remember?"

He almost smiled, because he'd forgotten how expressive she was with her hands. And her face. She could never hide her feelings, and he didn't think she saw much reason to try. "Right."

"I've got to get back home, Ryan. I don't like it here anymore, and it's upsetting the baby."

He nodded, stepped aside and took her arm, drawing her back into the den. Then he closed the door behind her. "We can slip out the back, and I'll drive you to the hotel and your car."

"I took the bus."

"The *bus?*"

"Don't act like I just said I rode a donkey. For crying out loud, Ryan, not everyone can afford a three-hundred-dollar flight for a day trip."

"No, not everyone. But *you* can. Now."

She met his eyes, and hers flashed with what looked like anger. "I will never touch a penny of that money. It's all going to fold right back into itself for the baby. I don't want it, didn't ask for it and don't need it."

"All right, all right, I wasn't insulting you." Damn, she was sensitive.

She shrugged and turned away.

"Listen, I want to talk to you."

"About what?"

"Bahru. I don't trust him, Lena."

"You never have. But I thought his insistence that he didn't want any money from your father's estate might have convinced you that he was sincere."

"His insistence wound up getting him an income for life and a free place to live. Not to mention a VIP pass into the life of my child, who, in case you forgot, just inherited a fortune."

"*Your* child?"

"*Our*. I meant *our*." He turned away, pushing one hand through his hair, knowing he was blowing this utterly.

"You're jealous, aren't you?" she asked.

He gave her a don't-be-ridiculous look, but she went on anyway. "You've always been jealous of Bahru. And no wonder, Ryan. Your father abandoned you but took Bahru with him, and that was wrong of him. As much as I loved the man, I know that was wrong. But it wasn't *Bahru's* fault."

"I am *not* jealous."

"How could you not be? You were eleven. Your mother had just died, and your father left you behind and walked away with his guru. No one in their right mind could blame you for how you felt. And now it looks as if Bahru has once again usurped your place, this time in the life of *our* child. But you're forgetting one very important element in all this, Ryan."

"What element is that?" he asked. He knew he sounded angry, sarcastic, and while he regretted it, he couldn't seem to help himself.

She walked up to him, slid a hand over his shoulder. "Me."

Frowning, he lifted his head and turned to face her even though there were hot tears burning in his eyes, tears he hadn't thought he had in him—not for his father.

"I am not a stupid woman. Nor am I a gullible one. I am, in fact, probably the most powerful woman you've ever met in your life—besides my mom, anyway—even though I'm powerful in ways you don't respect or even understand. But you can trust me on this, Ryan. I would *never* keep you from being in our baby's life."

"I don't know if I believe that." How *could he* believe it? he wondered. "I mean, look at you. You've been pregnant for how long? And you never said a word."

She sighed as if emptying her lungs to the bottom, nodding, not arguing. "I know it looks bad. But, Ryan, I truly had no intention of keeping this from you. I just kept putting it off, and the next thing I knew months had gone by. And the longer I waited, the harder it was. But I always meant to tell you—and I swore I'd do it before she was born. That's the truth." She lowered her eyes, then they shot back up to his. Laser beams. "You know I don't lie."

He nodded. "I remember that about you."

"So you believe me, then?"

Long pause, then he nodded. "I believe you."

"And you can believe me about this, too. There is no way Bahru will ever be more involved in our child's life than her father. Not unless that's the way you want it to be."

His doubts thinned. Her honesty had never been a question to him. She didn't lie. His tension eased a little. "Thank you for that," he said.

"I'm not finished yet."

He gave her a half-genuine smile. "I didn't think you were."

"Am I talking too much? I am, aren't I?"

"You always talked too much. I've missed the hell out of it."

She averted her eyes all of a sudden. Had she felt what he had just then? That old familiar *unnh,* right between the belly button and points south? "Besides," he went on, "you're one of the smartest people I know. So please, keep on talking."

She got a little pink-faced at the compliment, but then something else replaced embarrassment in her eyes. Sympathy. Like she could feel the unexpected heartbroken sensation in his chest. Like she knew how he was hurting right then. Like she could see it in his eyes, but even more, like she could *feel* it.

"All right, I will." Her voice came out more softly than he'd heard it since she'd come back into his life this morning. Maybe softer than he'd *ever* heard it. "I just have one piece of advice for you today. Don't let things outside yourself control the way you live your life. Not your father, not all he put on you—the businesses, the money—"

What a notion that was. Not to let the 3000-ton weight on his back knock him flat. If only that were possible.

"And not me," she added, compelling his attention. "Not even this baby. You need to make up your mind what you honestly, truly *want* and then do it, no matter what it is. You want to keep being the spoiled, rich playboy? Then go ahead. Let the boards of directors run the companies, cash your checks and bag a different supermodel every night of the year. You want to be involved in your daughter's life? Then figure out a way to do that. That's all you can do. It's all you're *supposed* to do. Life should be lived, Ryan. Relished. Not spent enslaved to 'I shoulds.'"

He looked at her face, her beautiful face, the one he'd missed way too much, and wondered how she ever got to be so smart.

"As for me, I'm gonna catch a cab to Port Authority and a bus back home, because I had no idea how much I'd miss Havenwood. This has all been…too much."

He drank in the sight of her for a long moment. "I have a better idea."

"Really? And that is?"

"I'll drive you home. How 'bout that?"

She gave him a quizzical look, like a puppy who'd just heard an odd noise.

"Maybe I'll stay awhile," he said, leaning in to kiss her.

She dodged his mouth with an elegant dip and a bob, and wound up standing a foot away. She looked scared. "I said you could be in our child's life, Ryan. Not in mine." Turning, she headed for the exit. "She's due in February. You can come and visit then, if you want."

4

Lena didn't know what she was expecting when she made her exit. Maybe for him to come chasing after her, begging her not to go. Maybe at least an apology. But he did nothing, said nothing, just let her leave. So she sat amid the masses of humanity on the bus ride home, hiding behind a pair of very large, very dark sunglasses. She'd picked them up for three times their worth at Port Authority when she'd realized she was teetering on the brink of tears for the twelfth time since she'd jumped into the taxi.

Stupid to cry over him. So freaking stupid. Stupid to keep remembering that last night, the awful things he'd said. Stupid.

She leaned back in the seat, closed her eyes and thought about it anyway.

She'd decided she was going to tell him she was pregnant that night. It was time, she'd thought. She'd cooked dinner at his place, and she hadn't thought of it as trying to show him how domestic she could be or anything, although she could see where someone else might have thought so. She roasted a small chicken with lots of veggies and dollops of sour cream. It was nice.

He wasn't.

Oh, they were getting along great at first. And then, after they'd eaten, when they were all snuggled up on his sofa and surfing through the pay-per-view channels, she sort of took the cowardly way in. She told him a friend of hers was pregnant, and that she was wondering what the guy she'd been dating was going to say about it, and what did he think about that?

And it went *zoom,* right over his head. "If the guy has any brains, he'll run screaming in the other direction," he said, and he was dead serious.

Lena felt like he'd slapped her. "Why's that?" she managed to ask through her rapidly closing windpipe.

He was manning the remote, pausing to read the info on anything that looked interesting to him, not looking at her. "Isn't it obvious? She's trying to get him to marry her."

"That's not true! She doesn't want to *marry* the guy. She just thinks he has a right to know he's going to be a father."

"Right. She doesn't *want to* marry him." There was more sarcasm in his tone than there had been sour cream on their roasted veggies. "Tell me this, does he have money?"

"Well, yes. Quite a lot of it, actually. But that doesn't mean—"

"Yeah, it does." He set the remote down and looked at her. "No one gets pregnant by accident in this day and age, Lena. And believe me, before I met you, every woman I dated was after *one* thing and one thing only—

my father's fortune. They'd have done anything. Some of them even tried, but I was too smart. I was careful. I protected myself."

"Did you, now?" She focused on her hands in her lap, thinking she needed a manicure, unable to meet his eyes. Mainly because there were hot, angry tears surfacing in her own.

"I did." He shook his head. "I pity the guy, but it was his own stupidity. Guys with money need to be more careful than anyone about shit like this. He should have known better. Now he's doomed."

"Doomed?" That brought her head up, and the anger burning a path up the middle of her chest rose with it. "Marrying her would be his *doom?*"

"Marrying a woman who tricked him into it, yeah. Doom." He smiled at her, still completely oblivious. "You know, this is something I wanted to talk to you about right at the beginning, and I kept getting distracted. Totally your fault, by the way." His eyes softened, and he pushed her hair behind her ear and kissed the lobe, sending a warm shiver down her spine, despite how pissed off she was at him. She wished she could grab that warm shiver by its neck and choke it to death.

"Talk to me about it now, then," she said. She didn't think she was going to like this discussion, but she figured she needed to hear it.

"Well, I just…you know…have no intention of…you know…"

"No, I don't know. I'm a witch, not a psychic. You have no intention of *what?*"

He sat back, and the lightbulb *finally* went on in his eyes. "Whoa. You're pissed."

She crossed her arms over her chest. "No, I'm not." She sighed, then shook her head hard. "Yes, dammit, I am. I thought we had something wonderful happening between us, Ryan."

"We do," he said quickly. "We really do. I mean, it's been great. I'm enjoying the hell out of being with you."

"But you don't want anything…more?"

"No." He looked away. "I mean, certainly not *now,* anyway. It's been eight weeks, Lena. Don't you think it's *way* too soon for this particular conversation?"

"Oh. You think I should wait until I've put in eight *months* and *then* find out I've been wasting my time?"

He was hurt. She saw it in his face. She was being completely irrational. Under any other circumstances it *would* be too soon to be having this conversation. But she was carrying his child. Not that he would ever believe she hadn't planned it. She realized that now, and it was crushing her heart slowly. Like a vise with some big guy gradually turning the screw.

"You think that unless we're heading for marriage, you're wasting your time?" he asked, handsome and dense and so out of touch with his feelings that it was beyond belief.

Or was he just out of touch with *her* feelings? With who she wanted him to be? Her dream prince. The one who would have died for her.

She lowered her eyes, knowing she'd hit on the truth. "No. Of course I don't think that. Our time together has been…" She tried to swallow and couldn't. "It's been the best time of my life, really." Her tears were audible that time, her voice tight and strained and an octave deeper than usual.

He tried to look at her eyes, but she turned her face away. "Are you crying?" he asked.

"I have to go." She got up, went to the door, needing to escape. *Now.*

"Hey. Wait a minute." He followed. "What the hell just happened here?"

She turned slowly and forced herself to look up at him. To let him see her tears. It was the honest thing to do, though it made her feel like a fool. She saw him through her swimming eyes and knew beyond doubt that if she told him she was carrying his child, he would believe she had planned it that way, intending to trick him into marrying her so she could get her hands on his dad's billions.

Which was a joke. Ernst adored her. If she'd wanted money, she probably could have just asked him for it. But she didn't want his money. She wanted his son. She had allowed herself to fall—had fallen willingly, knowingly—into her own childish fantasies, where he had been her exotic desert prince and she had been his beloved slave girl.

"Lena?" he asked. And he sounded genuinely puzzled.

"I think we want very different things, Ryan." It was hard to talk, hurt to force the words through her spasming larynx. "I think my feelings for you are getting close to the point of no return. If you're not heading in the same direction, then…" She let the sentence just hang there.

He stared at her as if she'd grown a second head. "It's *good* between us. Why fix what isn't broken?"

"Because if I stay, it'll be my heart that gets broken."

She blinked as fresh tears flooded, and then she stood on tiptoe and pressed her mouth against his, drinking in the taste of him one last time, promising herself to remember it forever. "I don't regret a day of it, though."

And then she turned and she left. She knew his head was spinning, and that he must think she'd lost her mind. But he'd made himself clear. Which meant she didn't have a choice.

Lena snapped herself out of the memory, realizing it was doing her no good. She was more eager than ever to return to the rural community she now called home, the low-key people there, the easy, laid-back pace. The peace and serenity of it. That old vineyard had healed her since she'd been living there with her mom. She'd just reopened an old wound, that was all. Maybe she had to let out a little of the poison that had been festering there. She would heal again. Just as soon as she returned to Havenwood, her little piece of heaven.

Ryan sat in the den, doing what he supposed could be described as brooding, until it hit him that his father's mansion was emanating a feeling of emptiness. The post-funeral gathering must have ended. No one had come in to bother him. No one had come in to say goodbye. He doubted anyone even knew he was in there, other than Bahru, and God knew there was no love lost between the two of them.

The funeral and the attendant gathering were over. It was *all* over. Lena was gone, and she'd taken his baby with her.

Sighing, he got up out of the chair where he'd been

sitting like a tranced-out zombie for the past two hours. He had to get home.

Why? What's the hurry?

Shut up.

He went to the bookshelf to get the ornate wooden box, and for some reason he opened it again. The gold-colored knife lay there nested in its red velvet. He reached for it, and that same tingling sensation started up in his palm, but he ignored it this time. Pushing past it, he closed his hand around the gleaming hilt and picked up the knife.

The tingling moved up his arm, and as he frowned at that golden blade, it seemed to glow again. Just like before. Only the sun had gone down now and the desk lamp was on the far side of the room, so there was no believable explanation for that glow.

"What the hell *is* this?"

He lifted the knife a little higher, turning it slowly to examine that gleaming double-edged blade and then the engravings he realized were inscribed into every millimeter of the hilt. There was even a symbol on the flat end of it, he noted, and he tipped the blade forward to get a better look.

There was a pop and a recoil, snapping his wrist back as if he'd just fired a gun—and the curtains were on fire!

Ryan swore a blue streak, lunging across the room to yank the drapes, poles and all, out of the windows and stomp on them before they set off every fire alarm in the place. Finally it seemed he'd put it out. And he just stood there in the smoke, staring down in disbelief at the blackened edge of a burn hole about the size of a

grapefruit and the way the thin gray ribbons still winding up from it encircled his calves.

Blinking, he looked from that smoke to the blade in
his hand, and then, after a few final stomps to be sure
the fire was out, he retrieved the box and pulled out the
red velvet in search of an explanation.

Underneath the velvet lining there was an envelope
with his name scrawled across the front in his father's
unmistakable handwriting. He opened it and started
to read.

Ryan,
I found this knife in an undiscovered burial
mound in the Congo. Could've been arrested if
I'd been caught smuggling it home, but something
told me I had to. That you needed it. I know you
don't believe in that kind of thing, but I do, son.
I do. And I'm sorry I haven't been a better father
to you since your mother died. I fell apart. I don't
know why, but something told me this was the
best way I could make up for it. To get this blade
for you. So I did. And I keep dreaming that you're
not supposed to tell anyone you have it. So, keep
it to yourself. It's something to do with you and
Lena. That's all I know. I love you. And I'm sorry.

Him and Lena? Ryan thought, almost bitterly. Why
did everything have to keep coming back to him and
Lena?

He returned the knife to its box and set it in an empty
drawer, kicked the ruined curtains behind the sofa and
sank into his father's chair, remembering that first night.

That very first time. When he and Lena had been snuggled in each other's arms in his bed right after round one and she'd said, "It felt powerful to me. Did it…did it feel that way to you, too?"

Here we go, he'd thought. He didn't think she was a gold digger. She was probably one of the romantics. Those who thought they were in love after their first—and subsequently only—encounter.

And yet, beyond his cynical side, some deeper part of him whispered that he'd felt it, too, and he knew it. "Powerful how?" he'd asked, stalling for time.

"Like the Great Rite."

Frowning, he'd rolled over and searched her face. God, she was beautiful. "The great what?"

"The Great Rite. It's the most sacred ritual of witchcraft."

"Witchcraft?" Rising up to rest his head on one elbow, he said, "Tell me more."

"Well…" She pulled on one of his T-shirts that he'd tossed onto a nearby chair and bounced out of the room, flipping on lights on the way. "Wow, this is nice," she called. He heard rattling, water running. Her footsteps headed back in his direction, lights going off in her wake.

Then she was beside the bed, a wineglass half-full of water in one hand and a carving knife in the other.

A little sizzle of alarm shot up his back. "What the—"

"The Symbolic Great Rite." She cleared her throat and held the knife up over her head in one hand, the cup in the other. "As the rod is to the God," she intoned. She flipped the knife, point side down, lifted the wineglass up a little and said, "So the chalice is to the Goddess." She lowered the blade slowly, until it was dipping into the wineglass. "And together they are one."

"Wow. These witches don't use obvious sexual symbolism much, do they?"

"That's the whole point." She put the glass down, wiped the knife blade on the T-shirt and set that down, too, then climbed onto the bed. "The force, or male energy—or god, or semen—is represented by the blade. The cup is the form, the goddess, the womb. Only the two combined can create life. Only the two combined can create magic."

"Ahh. I see." Then he shrugged. "I'm surprised they don't do it for real. You know, sex in the old magic circle?"

"Who said we don't?" she asked, with a slow smile.

"Damn, you're sexy as hell, you know that?" He pulled her close again, started kissing her, and then they were off and running for round two.

He came back to himself when Bahru opened the door and peered in at him. "I think we are both heading in the same direction, Ryan. Perhaps we should travel together."

Ryan didn't like Bahru. Didn't like him and didn't trust him. But the man was right—Ryan had no intention of letting Lena walk out of his life—and right then, he realized, he needed the graying guru. And Bahru needed something too. A ride.

There were about twenty big boxes of books—the ones his father had left to Lena—all packed, labeled and ready to be shipped out. Instead, Ryan called U-Haul, had a small truck delivered to his father's mansion and had the books loaded into it, all within hours of her departure. It was amazing what money and the family name could do.

Once he'd made his decision to follow her, he didn't feel like wasting any time. He'd been mulling over the pros and cons from the minute she'd walked out the door. But once he'd set the curtains on fire with what appeared to be a magic knife, well, that tipped the scales. He needed to figure out what the hell was going on, and who better to ask than a self-proclaimed witch? Add that to the fact that she was a few weeks away from making him a father, and that he'd apparently done much too good a job of convincing her that he was the most unsuitable father-to-be on the planet, and he figured he had more reasons to go than to stay.

In fact, his only reasons not to go were that she apparently didn't want him to, and that he didn't exactly relish the idea of Bahru's company.

But the damn guru was right, they were both heading in the same direction. And this would make it easier to keep an eye on the con artist.

Okay, there was more than traveling with Bahru bothering him about this trip. There was this odd thing that felt a lot like fear twisting around in the middle of his chest, but that didn't make any sense, so he ignored it.

After the truck was loaded, he went off in search of his bearded nemesis to offer him choice of radio stations in trade for letting him bunk with him in the cottage, just in case Lena refused to let him in. Ryan figured the guesthouse was Bahru's, lock, stock and doorknob. Lena couldn't throw him out of *that*.

Bahru took him up on the trade—only because he said he was going to offer anyway, and because Ryan swore he wouldn't be staying more than a day or two.

It wasn't entirely untrue. He currently had no idea how long he would be there.

So they made the long drive together, with what sounded like Bollywood soundtracks playing the entire time. Eventually he turned the volume down to save his own sanity, using the excuse of wanting to talk. He actually *did* want to talk, he realized as he spoke. He wanted to ask the holy man some pointed questions.

"So, Bahru, how did all this happen? This—vineyard my father owned, what's the story?"

"Havenwood? He never talked to you about it?" Bahru's expressionless features belied the curiosity in his question.

"I knew it existed. That was it." Like Bahru, he didn't let any emotion show through. But while Ryan knew his detachment was generally perceived by others as coldness, Bahru's looked more like...serenity. The man was always unflappable, calm. For a long time Ryan had thought it was an act, but he'd never seen so much as a crack in the fabric of it, so if it was fake, then Bahru deserved an Oscar.

"Your father told me he'd bought the place on a whim, before your mother made her transition."

"Made her transition?"

Bahru nodded. "Back into spirit."

"Oh. You mean before she died."

"There is no such thing as death, Ryan."

Ryan closed his eyes briefly, biting back the sarcastic comments that sprang to his lips. He hadn't brought the man along looking for spiritual platitudes, but with this guy, every conversation was sprinkled with them, so he supposed he had to put up with it. It wasn't as if he hadn't known what he was in for, so he just kept quiet and waited patiently.

And it paid off. Bahru began speaking again. "Your parents had spent a weekend together at an inn in the area once— an anniversary, I think—and while driving around the countryside they found the vineyard. He bought it, and they planned to move there when he retired." Bahru sighed, lowering his head. "But when your mother passed, he forgot about those plans. Forgot about the vineyard. Or pretended to. It fell into disrepair. He'd decided to finally let it go just before Lena left us, and then I—I received a strong message that he had held onto it for a reason. That she…belonged there."

"Received a message from whom?" Ryan asked.

Bahru fingered the quartz crystal around his neck. "I do not ask that question. Sometimes things just come. Your father and I had visited Havenwood only a week before, and he had made arrangements to put it on the market. The energy there was very strong. *Very* strong."

"Energy? I don't know what that means, Bahru."

The older man shrugged and ignored the implicit question. "When Lena told us she was leaving, I told your father about my feeling that she should live at Havenwood, and I told Lena about the listing. Your father asked the real estate agent not to reveal that he was the seller, and she bought the place, as I knew she would."

"He went along with all that?"

"He did." Bahru sighed. "I think he felt it, too—that the timing was too perfect to be coincidental."

Ryan lifted his brows. "And the baby? He knew about the baby?"

"He knew the doctor she saw and he…heard. Unethical, yes, but…your father's friends were very loyal."

"My father didn't have friends. If that doctor cooperated it was because he was afraid not to. Afraid of my old man's power."

"Perhaps."

"And what about him leaving you the guest cottage as part of the deal?"

Bahru lifted his chin and stared off through the windshield at some empty spot in the distance. "I was led to your father. But not for his sake. He knew that as surely as I did. He was only a guidepost on my way to my true mission."

"Your true mission?"

"Yes. At one time I thought that mission might be you—but now I believe it is your child. Ernst's grandchild. The baby is my mission."

I don't fucking think so. Ryan cleared his throat. "What is it you think this…mission will entail?"

Bahru shrugged. "That I cannot say. I haven't yet been told. But I've been guided this far, and I trust I will continue to be led to do what I am meant to do, to be where I am needed, to serve the Whole."

"I see." The hell he did.

"The closer we get, the stronger the pull," Bahru said, fingering the crystal again. "It's beyond anything I've felt before."

The guy was nuts, maybe even dangerous, Ryan

thought. And quite possibly obsessed with his child. He was more convinced than ever that he was doing the right thing by going up there and staying close to this situation. Maybe he could convince Lena to send Bahru packing. It wouldn't be easy, though. She adored the guy. They were birds of a feather, with all this mysticism and shit. What he did know was that he had to get close, and stay close. He did not trust this nutcase with his baby.

5

"You won't believe what I dug out while you were gone," Lena's mother said, after she'd hugged Lena breathless, nudged her into their big, comfy teddy bear of a rocking chair and pressed a cup of herbal tea into her hands.

The fireplace was snapping and dancing. Lena's overnight bag was still on the floor just inside the doorway where she'd dropped it when she had come in. Her mom had picked her up at the bus station, and she could barely believe the feeling that had come over her when she'd stepped off that Greyhound. Peace. That was what it was. As they drove back to the house, the tension just seeped out of her with every mile that passed. And by the time she walked through the front door, she was almost limp with it.

It was good to be home. It really was.

She sipped the tea, heeling off her shoes and relaxing into the chair's bear-hug cushions. "What did you dig out?"

Grinning and sappy-eyed, Selma went to a cardboard box on the coffee table and pulled out a stack of books.

Not real books. These books had construction-paper covers in full Crayola color. Their bindings varied from staples to masking tape, depending on what had been available at the time. Selma set the whole stack of them on her lap, and Lena smiled as she looked through the stories she'd created when she had been seven or eight years old. There were a dozen or so, all based on her little-girl fantasies.

Lena and the Prince Meet the Littlest Slave Girl
Lena and the Prince Find a Magic Cup and Knife
Lena and the Prince Meet the Evil Bad Guy
Lena and the Prince and Lena's Two Sisters
Lena and the Prince Get Lost in the Desert
Lena and the Prince and the Kiss in the Garden

She sighed, remembering every story. They'd seemed real to her.

"When you first met Ryan, you were so sure he was that prince you used to daydream about," Selma said softly.

"Well, it's obvious, Mom," she told her, holding one of the flimsy volumes toward her, face out. "Can't you see the resemblance?"

Selma laughed. "Identical. Clearly it has to be him." But her smile died slowly. "You've had some time and distance, Lena. Do you still believe he's the one?"

"Yeah. I do." Lena drew a breath, sighed and set the stack of books beside her chair. "I need to get out of these clothes, put on something cozy. Do you mind if we catch up later?"

"Of course not. I made you an overly indulgent dinner. Comfort food. I'll warm it up whenever you're ready. Okay?"

"Just what I need. Thanks, Mom."

Lena took a long, steamy shower and then put on her most comfy nightgown, a soft flannel "granny gown" with three-quarter-length sleeves and flowers embroidered down the front alongside the buttons. Her slippers were warm and cozy, and her robe felt like a blanket around her shoulders. But she didn't go downstairs when she finished getting dressed. Instead she sat down in their temple room—the place had five bedrooms, so there was still one left for the baby and one for guests—and took that magical chalice out of its beautiful box.

She went to the antique Shaker cabinet that stood in the corner, opened its doors and took out the big jug of witches' holy water she and her mother had made last full moon. She didn't worry about exposing it to sunlight, as it was already dark outside. After filling the chalice and leaving the jug where it was, she placed the chalice on the floor in the middle of the room. She sat down beside it and relaxed herself into a magical state. Entering that nearly hypnotic place was one of the most powerful skills a witch possessed. Newbies took their time about it, going through various mental exercises and breathing techniques, maybe mixing in some yoga, to get there. But for a born-and-raised witch like Lena, it was a process that took all of about three seconds.

She opened her eyes and gazed into the chalice, letting her vision go slightly out of focus so she wasn't looking *at* the water, but rather at some uncertain point beyond it. The surface of the holy water got all misty, like fog, and she relaxed her eyes. Then the mists started to clear, and images began rippling into and out of existence in the water.

She saw the shape of a man, and glimpsed dread-locked hair and a beard. *Bahru.* A red flash in his eyes, just like she'd glimpsed in Ernst McNally's den. *What the hell was that?* The image was there and gone just that fast, then the mists took the shape of another man. Ryan. She recognized him immediately. And then he changed shape and another form took his place in the cup—a dark shadow, shaped only vaguely like a man. Lena got chills up her spine when she saw that shape, and the baby inside her kicked frantically, almost jarring her out of her trancelike focus.

She rested her palms on her belly. "Hush, little one. It's all right."

No, it's not, her mind whispered.

Her attention returned to the shifting images in the chalice. She saw a woman there now. A beautiful woman whose face stayed the same even while her hair rippled from jet to corn silk, her eyes from ebony to robin's egg, her complexion from sun-bronzed to china-white. Her lips moved, and the vision became audible.

Your baby is in danger, Magdalena. And so are you.

Before she could even frown at that completely familiar face, the waters in the chalice began to swirl, forming a whirlpool that grew bigger, emerging from the cup and rising toward her, until it sucked her right inside. She was spinning, whirling, dizzy, and somehow breathing as the water swallowed her up and then spat her out again.

She was lying on the ground. It was hard, stone, and hot to the touch.

"Get up."

It was a man's voice, and he was speaking in another

language, but Lena understood it perfectly as she got to her feet. Then she looked down at her body and went cold in shock.

She was…someone else. She was bronze-skinned and slender. Her baby bump was gone. But *not,* she somehow knew, the baby. The sight of her flat belly stunned her when she glimpsed it between the scrap of silky sheer fabric knotted at her hip and the matching scrap that covered her breasts. An icy shiver of panic shot through her as the man grabbed her arms, which were bound behind her back.

"What is this?" she demanded, and the words emerged in that same, exotic tongue she did not, *could not,* know. "What are you doing?"

"Take hold of yourself, Magdalena," said a woman.

A woman dressed—and bound—just like her. The woman from the chalice. *Lilia.*

"There is no end to love," Lilia whispered, and her eyes were full of the emotion she spoke of. "Remember what we must do. We cannot cross the veil until it is done."

"We can do this," whispered another voice, and Lena turned to see another woman standing on the other side of her, dressed the same, bound the same, and just as beautiful. *Indira,* someone whispered in her mind.

"There's no such thing as death," Indira said. "We have nothing to fear."

Lena's field of view widened. She'd been seeing only what was close to her, as if she were caught in some sort of hazy vignette. But now she saw everything. The desert, far in the distance, a city glittering like a jewel beyond it, and closer, right at her feet, the very edge of the cliff on which she stood and the dizzying distance to the rocks below.

And she felt the hands of the soldiers at her back.

"I don't understand," she whispered. "What's happening?"

The other two women edged closer, so close that she felt the heat of their smooth skin pressing against hers, shoulder-to-shoulder. "We will triumph, my sister," said Lilia. "These murderers have not seen the last of Indira, Lilia and Magdalena."

The hands at her back pushed, and Lena screamed. The last thing she saw as she plummeted downward, the wind burning past her ears and pulling her hair, was a lone horseman galloping on a white stallion across the desert toward them.

My prince was coming to save me, she thought, *but he was too late.*

Ryan pulled the rented moving truck into the washboard-like dirt driveway, and brought it to a stop outside the farmhouse. It was a big old house, emphasis on *old,* and he figured it was probably supposed to be white. "Dad bought *this?*"

Bahru nodded. "Don't let its appearance mislead. It is solid, the roof, wiring, heating system and plumbing are all completely new. He was having it restored a little at a time."

"Why didn't he have it painted, or sided or landscaped or—"

"He intended to do the cosmetic things himself. He and your mother."

"But he dropped those plans when she died."

Bahru nodded, but he was staring at the house. Ryan followed his gaze to an upstairs window, but aside from a brief shadow beyond the glass, which he thought was just an optical illusion, he saw nothing worthy of interest.

He opened the door of the truck, stepped down and walked over the driveway, which had bits of snow here and there, up the front steps and across the front porch. He could see it was solid, just as Bahru had described. He was almost to the door when he started getting cold feet. After all, he had no reason to anticipate a warm welcome. He turned to see what was taking the guru so long and saw that Bahru was already trekking along the driveway where it forked off and led to the little guesthouse in the distance, a small drawstring bag over one shoulder, along with his green canvas satchel. That was all he'd brought. Ryan noticed that he'd traded his sandals for a pair of cloth moccasin-like shoes that could have been made this year or last century. No way to tell. At least he wasn't barefoot in the snow.

Straightening his spine, Ryan lifted his hand to knock on the door and heard a scream. Lena!

He opened the door and lunged into the house before he even thought about it and was just in time to catch a glimpse of Lena's mother running up the stairs to the second floor. He didn't hesitate. He raced up the stairs and down the hall behind Selma, his heart in his throat when the two of them burst through a bedroom door and stumbled to a stop inside what was not a bedroom.

It was some kind of witchcraft den, and Lena was lying on the floor with her eyes closed, her belly so huge it made him blink and look again. Her head was rolling back and forth, her arms and legs twitching. He dropped to his knees next to her as Selma did the same on the other side.

"Lena," Ryan said, sliding one hand under her neck, cradling her nape to try to keep her head from thrashing back and forth. "Lena, can you hear me? Are you all right?"

She moaned, and Ryan looked up and met Selma's eyes. "Call 9-1-1," he told her.

"I'll do better than that." She got up, turning to run out of the room, but as she passed, she reached down to squeeze his shoulder. "I'm *really* glad you're here, Ryan."

Lena opened her eyes to find herself lying in bed and staring up into the face of her prince, and for just an instant she was there again on the cliffs.

"You came," she whispered, lifting a hand to his cheek as if to assure herself that he was real. And he was. He *was!* "You made it in time. You saved me." And then she blinked as panic bubbled up in her chest. "What about my sisters? Lilia? Indira? Where…?"

The way he frowned, as if she were speaking gibberish, made Lena bite her lip. And then he lifted his gaze to meet someone else's, and she got hold of herself, turning her head, scanning her surroundings. She was in her own bedroom, and her mom and Doc Cartwright were standing nearby. Doc was closer, his hand on her wrist as he counted her pulse.

"Oh." *This* was real life. *That* had been a dream. Or something.

"What…happened?"

"I don't know," Selma said. "You were in the..." She glanced up at Doc very briefly. "The *meditation* room, and we heard you scream. Ran in there and found you unconscious on the floor."

Lena knew she meant the temple room. She and her mother hadn't advertised the fact that they were witches, and clearly her mother still didn't trust the doc enough to share that tidbit with him. They'd only been there half a year, after all.

Lena looked at Ryan again. "What are you doing here?" Then she gaped at her mother. "Did you call him? God, how long have I been out?"

"Overnight." Ryan said, his voice soft and a little unsteady. That really scared her. "I was just about to knock on the front door when you screamed."

"But...what...?" She swung her gaze toward Doc. Had he been here all night, as well? He looked as tired as if he had. "Is the baby okay?"

"Fine and healthy," he said. He had a deep, steady voice, as if a mountain could talk, and she found it reassuring. His smile was genuine, wrinkling his forehead right up to his receding hairline. "No problem at all. Can you remember what happened, Lena?"

She blinked slowly, thinking back, and then her eyes widened. She had been sucked into the chalice. She had been transported into another dimension or existence or...something. Lilia had been there. And another woman. They were her sisters, and the three of them had been shoved off a cliff to their deaths, and there'd been something about—

"Lena?" Doc prompted, interrupting her train of thought.

She blinked away the memories. "No. No, I don't remember a thing." He frowned at her, as if he knew she was lying. "I think I must have fallen asleep and had a bad dream."

"About what?"

She shook her head. "Darned if I know."

"Huh," he said.

"Should we take her to a hospital, Dr. Cartwright?" Ryan asked.

Doc smiled at him. "No, no, I don't see any need for that. Everything looks fine, just as it did last night. The baby's heart sounds perfect, as always. There's no bleeding. Do you have any pain, Lena?"

"No, nothing."

"Well, good, then." Doc nodded at the others. "If this should happen again, I'd like to know about it." He headed into the adjoining bathroom, leaving the door open, still talking while he washed his hands. "You call me if you notice the least little thing wrong," he instructed. "And I think we're nearing the time when you might want to take me up on my offer to find you a live-in nurse. You're getting close to your time, and since you intend to deliver at home—"

"Deliver at home?" Ryan gaped at her. "Are you out of your *mind?*"

Doc returned from the bathroom, chuckling down deep in his belly. "Trust me, son, back in my day, that was the norm out here. She'll be fine. You can take my word on that. And now I need to head home. It's poker night with Sheriff Dunbar and the wives. Mary's gonna think I've run off with a hot blonde."

"Thanks for everything, Doc," Selma said, laughing at the same joke he'd used for a dozen exits before. "I'll walk you out."

Ryan stayed after the other two left. He stood beside the bed, nervous and awkward. Lena met his eyes and sighed.

"What really happened?" he asked.

She blinked, debating whether to tell him the truth. About the chalice and the vision, about her imaginary friend Lilia and his role as the prince in her lifelong fantasy that maybe wasn't just a fantasy after all.

But no. He thought witchcraft was *cute.* It wasn't like he would take her seriously.

"What are you doing here?" she asked.

"Been here all night. Even though Doc said you were only exhausted and in need of sleep, I was...worried." He sighed and pulled a rocking chair up closer to her bedside, then sank into it.

"I mean, why are you *here?* At Havenwood?"

"I don't really know. Bahru was moving into the cottage, and those books were about to be shipped, and I just got the crazy notion to deliver both of them personally."

"Why?" And why was that stupid hope flooding into her heart again? He wasn't her prince. He never would be.

But Ryan held her eyes. "Look, it's my kid, too. I just...I don't know, I feel like I ought to be here for this. And like I should have been here for this from the beginning. But you didn't give me the chance."

"I did."

"Bull. You told me some bogus story about a friend of yours getting pregnant."

"You said no one gets pregnant by accident in this day and age."

"Well, clearly I was wrong about that."

She rolled her eyes. "Are you sure? I wound up controlling a big chunk of your father's money after all. If that was my plan, I sure pulled it off in spades."

Ryan was scowling at her. "Don't put words in my mouth, Lena. I know you're not one of those schemers. I never would have thought you *were*. And even if I had, you sure as hell proved me wrong by running off without a word."

"Maybe that was part of my plan." She looked away as she said it.

"You couldn't have known my father would die, much less that he'd leave so much to the baby."

"I didn't think he even knew I was pregnant."

"Bahru told him," Ryan said.

"But how did Bahru know?"

"You didn't tell him?" Ryan asked.

"No." She sighed. "So he came with you?"

"Yeah, headed straight for the guesthouse." Ryan got up and wandered to the window, parting the curtain to look out while she stared at his back and wished it was shirtless, and that she was running her hands over it. "That's odd," he said, breaking into her fantasy.

"What?"

"Doc's pickup is parked in front of the guesthouse. He and Bahru know each other?"

"Not that I'm aware of," Lena said, frowning.

Ryan dropped the curtain. "Must've met on one of my dad's trips out here, I suppose."

"So...what do you want, Ryan?" She was restless,

simultaneously itching to fling back the covers and get up, wanting him to leave so she could tell her mother what had happened in the temple room, and longing for him to crawl into bed with her and hold her close.

"I want to stay. I can bunk with Bahru. But I want to be here for the final weeks of this pregnancy, and for the birth of my child."

"*Our* child," she corrected. "And that's all?"

He frowned, meeting her eyes. "I don't know. Hell, Lena, I've only known about the baby for a day, and it's been a day when a lot of other things have happened. My whole freaking world just had a hurricane whip it to the ground, you know?"

"Like mine hasn't?" she snapped.

"Hey, you've had months to adjust. I'm on Day One here. Cut me some slack, okay?"

She huffed, turned to, stared at the wall. A rippling shadow caught her attention, as it so often had since they'd moved here. It was always in a dark corner, always in her peripheral vision, and always vanished when she looked at it straight on. Like a floater in the eye. Her mom had glimpsed it, too, and they'd decided it was some kind of ghost or trapped energy from times gone by. They'd saged the hell out of the place, cleansed it with holy water and sea salt, bells and rattles, but nothing had worked. Selma had been threatening to use "Devil's Dung," but Lena had vetoed the suggestion. Asafetida was a last resort, because its smell lived up to its folk name, and besides, the *presence* didn't seem at all menacing. Not to her, anyway.

"So can I? Stay?" Ryan asked.

Lena looked into his eyes, went soft inside, sighed

heavily and nodded. She really had no right to keep him out of their child's life. "But you can't stay with Bahru. That guesthouse is barely bigger than a closet, and it's his. Your father left it to him, it wouldn't be fair for me to stash my guest out there."

"Okay, you're right. I'll check into the nearest motel and—"

"Don't be ridiculous. You can stay in the guest room —for now. But if this doesn't work out, Ryan…"

"I'll make it work out."

She kept probing his eyes, looking for the playboy she'd fallen in love with, or the prince her stupid sub-conscious insisted on believing him to be, and she saw neither. She saw a wounded man, adrift at sea, looking for something to hold on to in the middle of a storm. And *that* she could not resist.

Ryan left Lena to spend the day in bed, as the doctor had instructed her to, and, after an amazing breakfast courtesy of Selma, headed out to the truck, backed it up as close to the front door as he could. Then he started carrying in the boxes of books. There were twenty-four of them, each one seeming to weigh more than the one before. Since he didn't know where the women wanted them, and didn't want to track dirt and snow through the house, he just piled them between the front door and the fireplace. One of the lids worked itself open, and he glanced down at the book right on top. *The Chalice and the Blade: Sexual Symbolism in Pagan Rites.*

"Huh." He tried to ignore the memory it elicited, struck by the coincidence that out of all the books his father had left to Lena, this one was on top, featuring *that* ritual. The one Lena had told him about the first night they'd had sex. Just out of curiosity, he flipped open the cover. The illustration on the very first page showed a double-edged dagger, not a whole lot different from the one he'd inherited from his father, which, he was pretty sure, had some kind of…powers. The one on the book cover had a silver blade and a wooden hilt, also engraved with symbols. It was standing point-down inside an ornate silver goblet. He frowned but didn't look further. Maybe later he would check out what the book had to say. Yes, he knew the basic symbolism of the Great Rite, as Lena had called it. But he would like to see if there was anything more—any mention of fire-starting daggers, for example.

He was still planning to ask Lena what she thought about the golden knife, despite his father's request that he keep it to himself, but frankly, the timing felt wrong. She had an awful lot on her mind at the moment. Or maybe he was just being a big chicken, because he was afraid she would think he was nuts. Yes, she called herself a witch, but he was pretty sure she wasn't insane. Just…whimsical. And she pretty much seemed to consider her "craft" more a spiritual thing than a magical one. For the most part, anyway. At least, as far as he knew.

Not that she'd told him all that much about it. She'd pretty much clammed up after he'd called it cute.

That memory made him wince. Man, he'd *really* blown it with her.

An hour later, with the books all neatly stacked, Selma still upstairs with Lena and the doc's truck still in front of Bahru's cottage, Ryan decided to wander out to the guesthouse and find out how those two knew each other. He bundled up in his lined denim coat, pulled on a blue knit hat, stepped into his all-weather hiking shoes and trudged out the door and down the long driveway. Everyone kept saying how mild this winter was. Well, it didn't feel mild to him. Thirty degrees, with a biting wind, was not what he'd call pleasant.

He pulled the cap lower over his ears and tried to enjoy the scenery. Havenwood's long dirt driveway rolled out between a pair of open fields that had once been vineyards. The one on the left turned into woods after about fifty yards. Directly across the way stood the guest cottage, a little white clapboard building with red shutters and a red door.

The former vineyard on the right side of the drive, behind the cottage, was narrower, with another patch of woods backing it and Cayuga Lake beyond that, far below. He could see it through the leafless trees but figured it would be almost invisible in summer. If it were him, he would clear away just enough of the woods to provide a nice year-round view of the lake. The vineyard was on high ground overlooking the water, and that was too perfect a vista not to embrace.

He'd made it to within ten yards of the cottage when the aging medic came limping down the three front steps, adjusting his fur-lined hat. He walked strongly, but slowly, deliberately. He didn't shuffle like so many guys his age, and Ryan got the feeling it was because he was determined not to. The doctor had dignity, a lot like his father. He didn't like to show weakness.

He climbed into his '80s model Ford F150 pickup, which looked as pristine as if it had just rolled off the showroom floor. Ryan was willing to bet the doctor had owned it since it was new and babied it ever since. He liked a man who took care of his things. Said a lot about his character.

The doc reached up to adjust his mirror, glimpsed Ryan in the rearview mirror and, turning, lifted a hand to wave through the rear window.

Ryan returned his friendly wave but froze at the flash of red from the old man's eyes. *What the hell?*

But Doc had already faced front again and his truck was rolling away. Ryan turned to glimpse the moon over his shoulder, gleaming from beyond the house. It was sinking fast and glowing a strange shade of orange behind the cloud cover. That must have been it, then. He must have seen a reflection in the glass. That was all.

He continued up the steps to the cottage door, shaking off the odd feeling that had crept through him, and knocked hard.

The cottage was small, maybe twenty-four by twenty-four, with a peaked roof and a smaller peaked dormer over the entry. Bahru opened the door and offered his typical bow in greeting, then stepped aside to let him in.

"What brings you by, Ryan? Would you like tea?"

"Just wanted to see how you were settling in." He shrugged off his coat and pulled off his hat as he stepped inside, pulling the door closed behind him.

"Nice and warm in here, that's for sure."

"There is a woodpile right behind the cottage. And while I'm proficient at starting a fire, I've no idea how to regulate the temperature of one. It's actually too warm."

"Huh." Ryan walked to the little woodstove, saw a knob on the bottom that slid a draft open and closed, and closed it tight. "This little doohickey controls how much air the fire can suck in. Fire gets too low, you slide it open to give it a boost. But when it's burning well, close it up tight." He rose, noting the damper in the chimney pipe, its handle straight up and down. He twisted it until it was just a bit short of horizontal. "This works the same way. Any time you're gonna open the stove door to put wood in, you want to turn it upright to let the smoke out. Then turn it this way again to slow down the burn and prevent chimney fires."

Bahru was watching intently, nodding. "I see. Thank you, Ryan, that's very helpful."

"You're welcome."

"I did not expect you to know the inner workings of a woodburning stove."

"A friend of mine has one." Paul, in his fishing cabin, where he liked to go and hang for a weekend every now and then, pretending he was a normal guy and not the heir to his father's kingdom.

Ryan accepted the mug Bahru offered, though he hadn't said yes to the offer of tea, and sat down in a corner chair. "How do you know the doc?" he asked, looking the place over. On the right-hand wall there were a kitchen sink, an apartment-sized range and a freestanding white metal cabinet, with about three feet of Formica countertop in between. The back wall of the cottage, facing the door, sported a bedroom and a bathroom, side by side. The place was tiny, but functional. Apparently Lena and her mother had cleaned it up and furnished it before knowing it was going to Bahru. They'd even hung frilly white curtains in the small windows. Ryan wondered who they'd expected to come for a visit.

Bahru sat on the mini-sofa—Ryan supposed it was technically a love seat—kitty corner to the chair. "I met Patrick and his wife, Mary, when your father and I journeyed out here to put the place on the market last year. Why do you ask?"

"So you don't know him well, then."

Bahru shrugged. "Does anyone truly ever know anyone? How can we claim to know another, when in truth—"

"Cut the philosophical discourse, Bahru. I just want to know how such a brief acquaintance warranted such a long reunion visit."

Bahru shrugged again. "We'd all had dinner together on our last visit. Your father, the Cartwrights, the real estate agent and I. We spent several lovely hours immersed in conversation. I suppose you would say we… hit it off." He face gave away no more, to one side, his brown eyes were opaque.

"You must have." Ryan frowned.

"Naturally he was saddened to hear of your father's passing. No one had told him."

"I see."

Bahru nodded. "Do you have…concerns about Dr. Cartwright, Ryan? He is planning to bring your child into the world, after all."

"I don't know." Ryan debated whether to say anything, then decided he had nothing to lose. He certainly wasn't going to sound weird to *this guy,* right? "Did you notice anything…odd about him?"

Bahru lifted his bushy brows. "I don't know what you mean. He seemed no different than before."

"Yeah. That's what I figured."

"You are concerned. Your father liked and trusted him, if that's any consolation to you, Ryan. And my own intuition tells me he's the best man to welcome the child."

Ryan nodded but thought Bahru's intuition wasn't a hell of a reliable recommendation, given that he didn't trust the guru any more than his gut was telling him to trust the old doctor.

"You did not bring your bags, Ryan? There is only one bedroom, but it has two small beds. I'm sure we can—"

"That's the other reason I came out here."

"Yes?"

"Lena says I can stay in the house."

Bahru's frown was instant and, Ryan thought, involuntary. Also honest. He looked pissed, something Ryan had never seen in him before, but hid it quickly. Could he be feeling as competitive over Lena and the baby as Ryan was? Or had he just been counting on having a roommate to help him figure out how to do things like operate the woodburning stove?

"For how long?" the older man asked, clearly trying hard to mask his irritation.

"I haven't decided yet. I just thought I'd let you know. My stuff's still in the truck, so..." Ryan sipped his tea uncomfortably, not sure what the hell to say or do next. Bahru was still looking at him. "I get the feeling," Ryan said at length, "that you have...some kind of problem with me being here?"

Bahru focused on a speck on the wall behind Ryan's head, and sounded almost bored when he answered.

"Lena has a support system around her. Dr. Cartwright and Mary, of course, and there's a very skilled nurse who will come and stay with her when the time is right."

"And there's her mother," Ryan put in.

"Of course. And now that I'm here, that system is complete. She doesn't need you here, but that's beside the point, of course. You have a right, as the child's father. I just fear…well, I fear your presence might upset her."

"You think my being here is upsetting her, yet you haven't even seen her yet."

"I am only repeating the doctor's concerns."

"I have a right to be here."

"I have acknowledged that. But you should consider that Lena's emotional state is key to the safety and health of the child."

"I knew it." Ryan got up slowly. "I knew you were going to come out here and try to insinuate yourself into my kid's life and push me out in the process. Just like you did with my old man."

"I did not—"

"It's not gonna happen, Bahru. I'm not gonna *let it* happen. Not this time."

Bahru shrugged and lowered his eyes. "Things have been set in motion. They will unfold as they will unfold."

"What the fuck does that mean?"

Shrugging, the guru turned toward the nearby window, gazing outside and fingering his pendant, as if he'd grown bored with the whole conversation.

Ryan pulled his jacket back on and stomped out the

door. He liked the bearded schemer even less than he had before, and he was more determined than ever to get the bastard out of his child's life.

6

"I hate to leave you on your own, your first full night in the house, Ryan," Selma said. And he believed her. Selma had liked him from the get-go. Of course, she'd also said she could see right through him, though he hadn't wanted to believe it. "But I have a feeling you'll be fine."

"You're going out?"

"Yeah. A little full moon ritual in a friend's backyard. But don't tell anyone. I don't want to stir up trouble among the locals."

He was surprised. "I'd expect Ithaca to be a pretty open-minded little place, with the colleges and all."

"Ithaca, yes. But we're not *in* Ithaca. We're in Milbury. Conservative, extreme-right Milbury. And despite there only being a few miles between the two, there's a world of difference in attitude."

"And yet you and Lena decided to live here."

"Well, the local narrow-mindedness was the only thing con on our list of pros and cons."

"Lots of pros, huh?"

"Lots. The asking price, the natural beauty, the lake

bumping right up against our property, the acreage, the outbuildings, this fabulous old house, access to just about everything, including culture. It was almost perfect." She shrugged. "And you know, the haters tend to die out. Evolution at work."

He nodded. Made perfect sense to him. "So you'll be late, then?" he asked.

"I'll be late. There are leftovers in the fridge, or you can whip up anything you want for dinner. Lena's still asleep. You should probably check on her every now and then. Okay?"

"All right, sounds good."

Selma smiled warmly and clasped his upper arm. "I know you don't believe in anything beyond what you consider reality, Ryan, but you will, once you realize what's going on here."

He frowned. "Something's going on here?"

"Mmm-hmm. I don't know details, but I do know that it's fate. Lena's been waiting for you since she was a little girl. Talking about you, writing about you, dreaming about you. You two go back a long, long way. You just don't know it yet."

He felt his eyebrows arch, but before he could decide which one of his ten thousand questions to ask first, she turned away. Her emerald-green-and-yellow tie-dyed dress flared out like a flower opening its petals. She pulled her coat off the row of hooks near the door and left him standing there, wondering about past lives and magic knives and what, exactly, witches did on full moon nights in their friends' backyards.

Lena was lying in her bed, and there were people all around her. Doc Cartwright was there, and so was his wife, Mary. Bahru was there, and so were Ryan and her mother. They were all looking down at her, and she was in labor. The pains were crippling, way beyond anything she had expected. She looked up at them, meeting their eyes one by one, wanting to ask them to help her. To do something. To make the pain stop.

But there was something horribly wrong with them. All of them. Their eyes were all red and glowing and evil. They all wore pendants just like Bahru's, which also glowed. And then Ryan was lifting a knife above her—aiming it right at her chest. It wasn't just any knife, but a golden athame, a ritual dagger. Its hilt was engraved with symbols that looked like some ancient form of writing.

She moved her lips to ask what he was doing, only no sound came out, and it felt as if her body was being torn in two as her baby emerged. They were all muttering, chanting something. She searched the room for someone, *anyone,* who would help her, but she saw only that dark shadowy form in the corner, and she knew suddenly that it wanted her baby.

She came awake fast, sitting up straight in the bed before her eyes even opened. When she did manage to look around and reassure herself that no one was there but her, and that she was still pregnant and not in labor, she went almost limp with relief.

It had been so real!

She sat there, breathless, her skin a little damp with perspiration. "Just a dream. It was just a dream. That's all, just a dream."

And yet, that was two clear warnings now. This one and the vision in the chalice: that ancient setting, three women being murdered, one of them herself and another her childhood imaginary friend, Lilia. A red-eyed Bahru had appeared briefly in that vision, and she'd heard the words *Your baby is in danger.*

She had to put this all together.

It wasn't just pregnancy hormones or nervousness over the impending birth.

Was it?

A beloved friend had just died. The man her subconscious believed to be her soul mate from some long-ago lifetime had come crashing back into her life. Bahru had become her neighbor.

A lot had happened. Everything had changed. Ryan's constant suspicions of Bahru, combined with that brief trick of the setting sun back at Ernst's mansion, could, she supposed, be playing games with her mind. Plus she was stressed, tense about the baby. And yes, her hormones were raging.

She flung back her covers and sat on the edge of the bed for a second or two before standing, her hands on her baby bump. The child twisted around inside her, and she imagined her daughter stretching her little arms and yawning. Apparently her mommy's nightmare hadn't disturbed her.

Stress? Or warning?

But why would her baby be in any danger? She was out here in the country, living a quiet existence and not bothering anyone. She had no enemies. Who would want to hurt her baby?

Bahru was a holy man, a guru, who'd traveled the world and studied the wisdom of the most learned sages. He was a pacifist. He refused to even swat a fly.

The house ghost had been harmless up to now and had done nothing to make her think that might be changing.

And Ryan would never harm her. He might not be the prince she'd been dreaming about since she was eight years old, but he wasn't going to hurt her, for heaven's sake. Much less with a golden athame. Where would he even get one? He wasn't into ritual magic.

Sighing, she got up and shuffled into the bathroom, cranked on the shower taps and spent the next half hour rinsing away the remnants of the dream. The entire time she reminded herself how good she had it here, how much she loved Havenwood, what a beautiful life her little girl would have here, and how lucky they were to have Bahru—and Ryan, too—looking out for them.

Feeling better and better, she put on a pretty smock top and a pair of whale-belly jeans, and sat down again on the edge of the bed, preparing herself for the challenge of her socks.

"You're awake," said the man who'd been about to drive a knife through her heart half an hour ago. The sound of his voice brought that nightmare image rushing back and made her heart take off like a racehorse. He was leaning in the bedroom doorway, looking too handsome to be real. Her nightmare was nudged aside by the sight of him, a sight that made her want to curl up in his arms and never come out.

He was so beautiful. She wanted him *so much*.

"Yeah, I…" She pressed her lips tight, deciding that telling him about the nightmare would be the wrong move. Really, how much drama did she want to dump on the man his first day here? "I finally woke up. Took a shower."

"Smells like. I mean…you smell…nice. Your soap or shower gel or whatever you—" He cleared his throat. "And your hair's wet."

How could she have dreamed of him murdering her? He was actually stammering. "Yes, it is." She had ponytailed her ringlets up high, so wet tendrils were spiraling every which way. "It behaves better if I tie it up and let it dry that way. I just can't seem to wield the hair dryer without my arms getting ridiculously tired."

"I could help." He lowered his eyelids to half mast. "That sounded so stupid. I've never dried a woman's hair in my life. I think I'm feeling kind of guilty that you're…you know, doing all the heavy lifting with our baby. Have been for all this time." He swallowed hard while her mind painted pictures of him running his hands through her hair, blow-drying it for her, touching her.

"Are you hungry?"

She met his eyes as guiltily as if he could see her thoughts. "At this stage, I'm pretty much always hungry."

His smile was quick and real. "That's good. I made dinner."

"You did?"

"Yes, I did. Your mom said she had to go out. Said she wouldn't be back until late, so—"

"Where did she go?" The thought of being alone in the house with him sent an unreasonable frisson of panic up Lena's spine. She wasn't sure if it was due to that stupid dream, or fear due to the fact she wanted to throw him down, rip off his clothes and molest him until he admitted that he loved her, always had and always would.

"She said she had some full moon thing in a friend's backyard. Said you knew about it."

"Right. I forgot."

He frowned at the socks, which were still balled up in her hand. "Are you going to put those on?"

"I was just gearing up for it." With a sigh, she took a sock, then pulled one leg up across her other knee and bent as much as possible, reaching for her foot. Her belly was in the way, of course, but she'd found that if she really pushed herself, it sort of smooshed down enough so she could just about…

"Hey, hey, hey, stop now. Here, let me." He took the sock from her hand, then sat on the bed right next to her. His hands were warm as they clasped her foot. "Jeeze, like ice," he said. But his fingers were on her skin, even if it was only her foot, and she sighed in pleasure. She'd been aching for him to touch her ever since she'd seen him again.

No. Ever since she'd left him. It had never gone away, that yearning for what felt like a part of her. A missing limb.

He stopped moving at the sound of that sigh, and then he set the sock aside and rubbed her foot between his big hands. Slowly, like he was just trying to get it warm again. But it was turning into a foot massage, the kind they used to give each other lying on his sofa, her head on one end, his on the other, some movie playing on the DVR.

She didn't dream of arguing. He moved her pillows

behind her, and she let herself collapse backward onto them as the tension eased out of her in a long, slow, steady whoosh. Every touch—the pressure of his thumb in her arch, the gentle kneading of every toe—was making her feel better and better.

"God, that's good," she whispered.

"You're such a little thing," he said. "Carrying that baby around must be straining every muscle you've got. You should be getting a massage every day of the week."

"I'm all for that." She closed her eyes, reveling in bliss. "I forgot it was the full moon tonight."

He kept working. "I have to admit, I have no idea what Selma and her friends are up to. But I'm curious."

Lena almost gasped in surprise. "Since when are you curious about the Craft?"

"Since I'm about to become father to a half-witch baby."

She opened her eyes long enough to meet his gaze. "She's all witch, Ryan. Make no mistake about that." But she said it playfully.

"Grounding her is going to be a bitch."

"Only if you have an aversion to lily pads and a diet of flies and mosquitos."

He laughed softly. It was nice, she thought, teasing, playing like this. Touching. Being together.

"Mom found a couple of witchy types in the area soon after we arrived. She always manages to sniff them out, don't ask me how. Anyway, they get together for new moons and full moons, lunar eclipses and all the usual holy days—ends up being weekly or so. It's nice for her to have some people to practice with. She had dozens of witch-friends in the city, and I know she misses them."

"'I guess the witches here keep a low profile, huh?" he said.

"Yes. Betty from the general store, and her sister-in-law, Jean, are mostly in the broom closet. I mean, people think they're eccentric, but no one knows they're witches." Her eyes widened. "Damn. I wasn't supposed to reveal it, either."

"Don't worry. I'm not going to go around outing anyone who's still in the, uh, *broom closet*." He grinned. "That's cute, by the way."

She frowned. So they were back to *cute* again.

"I meant the terminology. Not the belief system," he said as if he'd read her mind, then tucked her now-warm right foot under the covers and started massaging the left. "So how does one celebrate the full moon in the backyard with friends?"

"Bask in the moonlight, worship, give thanks, make wishes. We dance a little, we sing a little, we drum—a lot." She sighed softly. "It's a little like going to church."

"Do you usually go, too?"

"When I feel up it, which used to be often, but lately it's dwindling to almost never."

"So before I came, you would just stay home alone?"

"Uh-huh."

"You sure that's wise? I mean, given your condition and how far you are from help and—"

"My doctor lives next door, Ryan."

"'Next door' is a pretty relative term out here. He's gotta be at least a mile away."

She shook her head. "It's rural, Ry, but it's not a

desert island. I'm fine, really. We have 9-1-1, and ambulances with EMTs, and my mom's only a few minutes away. It's all good. Promise." Her stomach growled rudely, and her eyes widened in embarrassment.

Ryan laughed. "All good—except you're starving. Okay, we'll postpone the full-body massage until a later date." He took the socks from inside his shirt, where she hadn't realized he had tucked them, and put them on her feet. They were warm from his body heat. Damn, he was good. "There, now. Better?"

Lena nodded, sitting up again. "Much. Why are you being so nice to me?"

He looked her squarely in the eye. "I was *always* nice to you."

That was true. But he was also nice to every one of his conquests—until he got tired of them, or they started pushing for more than a sex-based relationship.

"Why so suspicious of me?" He took her hands to help her get up, and she let him.

"I don't know. Probably because I just dreamed that you killed me," she said. She hadn't meant to tell him, but the words just came out.

He froze, and they just stood there, toe-to-toe, only a belly's width apart, as his eyes went wide. *"What?"*

"I dreamed…you stabbed me. You had this athame—"

"Atha-what?"

"Athame—it's a ritual dagger." His gaze flicked to the side and then settled on the floor. "I was in labor, and you were going to stab me in the heart as soon as the baby was born."

His eyes shot back to hers. "What did this athame look like?" he asked.

She gaped. "Lovely. Not 'I would never hurt you' or 'that's the most ridiculous dream ever.' No, it's 'What did the murder weapon look like?'"

"I would never hurt you, Lena. And that dream is clearly either an aftereffect of whatever happened to you last night or some kind of pregnancy-induced nightmare. But I would *never ever* hurt you. Now what did it look like?"

"It was golden. Maybe real gold. Double-edged. Engraved with symbols I didn't recognize."

"I remember you telling me about the athame way back when."

She remembered exactly when. Wondering if he did, as well.

"I remember you telling me that it's the symbol of the witches' god. And of fertilization. A phallic symbol, and it's never supposed to be used to cut anything physical."

She blinked in absolute shock. "You *do* remember."

"So it kind of makes sense, doesn't it? In some kind of Freudian way," he said. "I mean, mating, pregnancy, the male and the female, the dagger as a phallic symbol, you know?"

"The chalice and the blade. The womb and phallus. You're right, Ryan. That's probably exactly what it was."

"See? I'm not so ignorant about your Craft after all."

"Guess not."

He nodded, taking her warm, fuzzy robe from her bedpost and holding it open so she could slide her arms into it. "Is the athame used for anything else?" he asked. "Besides the Great Rite, I mean."

She frowned. "Why so curious?"

He only shrugged. "I just am. Can't I be curious about the nightmares and religious practices of my baby's mother?"

She was still frowning at him when her stomach gurgled again.

"Never mind. Come on, let's go eat before my steaks get all dried out and my baby faints from starvation."

"Steaks?"

He walked right beside her, taking her arm as they started down the steep old staircase as if afraid she would fall. The oven timer sounded just as they hit the bottom step. "Perfect timing," he said. "There are also baked potatoes with sour cream, and what appears to be fresh broccoli, straight from your vegetable crisper drawer. *Fresh* being a relative term, given that it's January in New York State. Probably shipped in from Brazil or somewhere."

"That sounds like absolute heaven," she said, smelling all the yumminess in the air as they headed toward the dining room. "Is Bahru coming?"

"God, I hope not."

"Ryan..."

"Sorry. I know you like him."

She drew a deep breath to reply, then just gave up and slid into a chair at the dining room table, which he'd set. It really bothered her that Ryan distrusted Bahru so much, as little sense as that made, given that she'd dreamed the guru had turned into some red-eyed demon zombie or something.

But that was just a dream.

Ryan's dislike and distrust of the holy man were real.

She knew that part of the reason it bothered her so much was because it seemed like a judgment on her own beliefs, her own spirituality. Bahru was like her, a mystic, a man who walked far from the beaten path, a spiritual seeker on a constant quest for understanding and enlightenment. Every time Ryan dissed him, it felt like he was dissing *her*.

While she sat, he picked up their plates and took them into the kitchen with him. Minutes later he was setting Lena's in front of her, bearing a New York strip that was still sizzling, and she forgot to care what he thought about Bahru.

"Been a long time since you broiled me a steak," she said.

"Yeah, it has. Or since you made me blueberry waffles for breakfast."

"You were having those way too often anyway," she told him. "Heck, if I hadn't left, you'd probably have a belly to compete with mine by now."

His gaze strayed to her belly, which was so large that her chair had to remain a solid foot away from the table. "You carry it well, Lena."

"Pssh, *nobody* could carry this well."

"No, I mean it. You're…you're more beautiful pregnant than…than ever. I can't put my finger on it, but… it's there. It's real."

"If you tell me I'm *glowing,* I'm going to throw my food at you." She looked down at the steak, picking up her silverware, ready to dig in. "Well, maybe just the broccoli."

He laughed as they both started to eat. And it was nice. It was really nice.

Don't go getting all comfy with him, her inner voice warned. *He's no prince, he's a player. He showed you that. He was very, very clear and honest about it. Don't get your hopes up that this is going to turn into some domestic bliss scenario like a fifties sitcom. It's not. That's not who he is.*

They ate, and they talked, and they cleared up, then loaded the dishes into the dishwasher, and even that was nice. Would have been perfect, if she hadn't been so sure it couldn't be.

And then he said, "I put all those books up in the attic. The ones my father left you. Your mom thought that was the best place."

"Yeah, until we get the library done."

"Library?"

She smiled. "That's right. I take it you haven't had the grand tour yet, have you?"

"No. Not yet."

The house was huge, almost too sprawling. So she led him through the ground floor first, mostly because it was a way to distract herself from wanting to cuddle up on the sofa and watch a movie together, or spoon around him in bed like they used to.

Well, she supposed *he* would have to spoon around *her,* given her current shape, but still…

Lena thought the long, narrow room off the formal dining room had probably been meant to house a buffet table. But it was also tall, and lined now with the framework for floor-to-ceiling bookshelves. Lena and her mother had done the work themselves, and all that remained was to finish the shelves and slide them into place, and then it would be a perfect library.

Next she led Ryan up to the second floor to see the baby's room.

When she opened the door and flipped on the light switch, he just stood there in absolute silence for a moment. There were cans of paint and spackle, trays and ladders, and the floor was covered in drop cloths. It was nowhere near done, of course.

"Obviously we've still got a lot more to do," she said as he looked around. "There's a chandelier all made out of shoes from different fairy tales that we need an electrician to install, and we still need to paint and decorate, add furniture, curtains."

"Carpeting?" he asked.

"I'm thinking not. It would be nice—warm and soothing—but also a haven for dust mites and allergens. I'll keep the wood."

"Smart." He looked up at the bedroom doorway and spotted the old-fashioned glass baby bottle filled with swirls of colored ribbon, pretty stones, shells and a couple of tiny yellow feathers. It was hanging from the outside of the door frame. "Now that's interesting. Did you make that?"

"Mom and me, yes."

He peered closer, examining the items inside the bottle. "I'm guessing there's more to this than just a decoration."

"It's a witch's bottle. It's...sort of like a HEPA filter for energy. Traps anything bad, keeps it out of the room." He lifted his eyebrows. *Don't you dare ridicule this,* she thought. "In the old days it would have been filled with rusty nails and spiderwebs, but you know, it's the energy that counts. The intent, the focus you put into it while making it."

"The ingredients don't matter so much, then?"

He was asking a good question, with real interest in his eyes. Go freaking figure.

"The ingredients *do* matter. They carry an energy all their own. But tangled ribbon can represent spider-webs quite effectively, if you're thinking spiderwebs while you're tangling it."

"I see."

She was so pleased that she could barely keep from grinning. "We haven't even bought a crib yet. We're a little behind schedule in here." She pulled the door shut as the phone started ringing and opted to grab the extension in her bedroom instead of racing—or rather, waddling quickly—downstairs.

"Hey, Lena, it's Betty. Your mom left her favorite scarf here. Can you tell her so she doesn't drive herself crazy looking for it?"

"Sure, I'll tell her as soon as she gets home."

"What do you mean?" Betty asked. "She's not home yet? Lena, she left two hours ago."

An icy chill of foreboding raced up Lena's spine, and she turned, her eyes instinctively meeting Ryan's.

Selma was driving slowly and listening to James Taylor on the radio when she spotted the unmistakable light of a balefire in the woods. *Their* woods. Hers and Lena's. All right, she supposed it could have been an ordinary campfire. But she could tell from the shadows that there were people standing around it, moving in time, so it had to be some kind of ritual.

Which was really odd. She and Lena, along with the friends she'd just left, were the only locals she knew of who would be prone to dancing around balefires in the woods by dead of night, especially this time of year.

Well, this was Havenwood property, so she supposed she had the right to investigate. She pulled the car over and shut it off, then got out and hugged her coat a bit more tightly around her body. She hadn't worn gloves, and while the winter had been noticeably mild so far, it was still a January night in upstate New York, which meant it was cold. Her slipperlike shoes had never been intended for traipsing through the woods, much less when there was snow on the ground.

She moved carefully downhill, heading toward the light of the fire. The shapes of the people who stood around it were still just black outlines, but she could hear the murmur of voices now. No faces, not yet. And she couldn't tell what they were saying, but she clearly heard at least one member of each gender.

A shiver of unease whispered over her nape, and she paused, glancing nervously back at her car, suddenly thinking this little investigation might not be the best idea. Selma never ignored her intuition, and she decided this was no time to start. She should never have come out here.

She pushed aside the needle-covered limb of a pine and took one last look toward the fire, which was snapping and dancing unattended now. Where had all those shadow-people gone?

Suddenly a pair of powerful arms snapped around her body, jerking her backward and pinning her own arms to her sides while one hand covered her mouth.

She twisted and struggled, but it was no use. And then something sharp pierced her upper arm, and her entire world went dark.

7

Ryan stood in Lena's bedroom doorway, read her look and frowned. "What is it?"

She covered the phone with her hand. "Ryan, would you please look outside and see if Mom's car is out there anywhere? Maybe by the guesthouse? Betty says she should have been home by now."

Nodding, he headed across the hall into the guest room—his room, he mentally corrected. Going to the window, he pushed back the curtain. "No, I don't see it anywhere. How long ago did she leave?"

"Two hours, and it's only a twenty-minute drive." Lena spoke again to the woman on the phone. "We'll track her down, Betty. I'm sure she's fine. Thanks for calling, though…Yes, yes, of course we'll let you know. I'll have her give you a call as soon as we find her." She hung up the phone, and Ryan could see in her eyes that her confident answer had been completely false. She was worried.

He was glad he was there but couldn't help wondering what Lena would have done if he hadn't been. In fact, what would she have done all along if an emergency came up and there was no one around to help out? Clearly she had a caring neighbor in Dr. Cartwright, and she'd mentioned his wife more than once. Selma was obviously her chief ally, but damn, sometimes you needed more than that. A man, to be sexist about it. A young, strong man.

Meanwhile, the immediate problem was that her mother had taken the only car.

He was going to need a vehicle out here, that was for sure. He'd driven the rental truck, but that needed to be turned in tomorrow. He thought about that as he helped Lena climb up into the truck and started the engine. With a twist of a knob the headlights cut through the darkness, and then he headed down the driveway toward the guesthouse.

"You think Bahru might have seen her?" Lena asked.

"We might as well ask. Then we'll retrace her route. You know where her friend's house is, right?" She nodded. "Is there more than one way to go?"

"No, it's pretty much a straight shot, two turns, not really any alternative way to get there that I can think of, so if she's had engine trouble or a flat tire or something like that, we should find her."

"Good." Confident words, but he knew she was worried. He stopped the truck in front of Bahru's cottage and climbed down. "Wait here. I'll be right back." Then he slammed the door and headed up the front steps to knock.

No answer.

He knocked harder, then cupped his hands around his face and peeked through the glass. "Bahru! You in there?"

No reply.

Giving up, he headed back to the rental truck and got in. "I think he's out."

"Out where? Where would he go?"

Ryan shrugged. "He might have gone into town for supplies. I doubt he had any groceries or anything."

"Ryan, they roll up the sidewalks at six around here. Eight on weekends. It's after nine. Plus it's five miles into town and he's on foot."

Ryan met her eyes. "I suppose he might be hiking, or more likely sitting in the snow meditating, maybe communing with an owl."

"Yeah." Lena lowered her eyes, but she looked troubled, and he got the feeling she was keeping something to herself. "Yeah, that must be it."

"Hey, what is it? Don't tell me you're starting to mistrust the deep and spiritual Bahru? I thought that was my job."

"Of course not," she said. "I just…I don't like not knowing where Mom is."

"We'll find her." He covered her hand with his, and his throat got tight when he realized hers was shaking a little.

She lifted her chin, met his eyes. "I'm so glad you're here tonight, Ryan."

"I was just thinking the same thing," he admitted.

They drove in silence back down the long, curving driveway to the main road, and then turned left. In only a short time they were stopping again, because Selma's car was parked along the shoulder, right beside a big patch of woods.

He pulled the truck over, but he didn't like what he

was seeing. No flat. The hood wasn't up. And, worst of all, there was no one inside the car.

"Why would she have stopped here?" he asked.

"I don't know. Do you have a flashlight or—"

"My phone has one." He pulled the cell from his pocket, glad he'd grabbed it, even though reception was spotty out here. Activating the flashlight application, he climbed down, about to tell Lena to wait. Too late. She was already getting out. He rushed around the truck to help her, but she was already standing on the road by the time he got there. And then they both headed to the car.

He shone the light around inside. "Keys are in the ignition."

"I don't understand it. Bring that light here," Lena said, and pointed at the ground

Footprints in the dusting of snow led around the front of the car, and then off the road, through the ditch and into the woods.

"What the hell?" Ryan asked.

"Mom?" Lena started down the hill, following the tracks. "Mom? Where are you?"

Ryan caught up to her, touching her shoulder. "Lena, why don't you take your mom's car back to the house and call the police, maybe a few neighbors? In the meantime I'll search the woods."

"But—"

"It's dark, the ground is wet and uneven. You could get hurt out here. Come on." He took her by the arm and helped her back up the slope to her mother's waiting car. "Go on. I've got this. Go home, send help. Okay?"

"Okay, yeah, you're right. We need more people and

some real flashlights. But I'm coming right back as soon as I call."

She met his eyes, squeezed his hands in what he thought was gratitude, and then hurried to her mother's car and got in.

She had phoned Sheriff Dunbar and Doc Cartwright, located two flashlights—one of those long, heavy ones that could double as a billy club, and a tiny yellow one that was bright for its size—and written a note that she'd left on Bahru's door. Now she was driving her mother's car a little too fast on her way back to Ryan.

Suddenly her mother staggered out of the weeds along the roadside and into the beam of Lena's headlights. She hit the brakes hard. The car skidded sideways on the snowy road, coming to a stop so close to Selma that she was sure she was going to hit her.

But she didn't. She slammed the car into Park, her heart racing, then wrenched the door open and ran to her mother, who just stood there staring at her, a vacant expression in her eyes that Lena had never seen there before. Blinking, tipping her head from one side to the other, Selma said nothing. Her red curls, shorter than Lena's, were a mess, full of twigs and debris. She had mud on her hands and all over her coat, and her poor legs were streaked with it. Her light fabric shoes were soaked.

"Mom, what happened? What happened to you?"

Selma stared blankly and then shook her head. "I…I don't know."

And that scared Lena more than anything.

* * *

Selma sat in the rocker close to the fire, which Ryan had just stoked. She was wrapped in two blankets and still shivering, her expression making her look like a frightened little girl. Doc Cartwright was examining her eyes with a tiny penlight. He'd already listened all over with his stethoscope, taken her blood pressure and given her an aspirin, "just in case."

The word "stroke" whispered through Lena's mind like a monster through a child's nightmare.

Sheriff Dunbar was outside looking over the car with a flashlight, or had been. Just then he was opening the door and ushering Bahru in, one hand on the old man's shoulder like he was a suspect or something. "Lena, you know this fella?"

Lena left her mom's side to rush to the door. Big Larry Dunbar reminded her of a large bear. Huggable, but fierce when he needed to be. He had a thick shock of black hair that never really did anything, just sat on his head like a woodland creature that had taken up residence there. His brows were like its smaller siblings. And he always looked vaguely sad.

Sheriff Dunbar had an old-school approach to protecting women and kids, and considered her to be both of the above.

Bahru looked frightened, and no wonder. He had no idea the man was harmless. "I saw the sheriff's SUV and Patrick's truck, and thought the baby might be coming," he explained. "What's happened to your mother, Lena?"

"We don't know." She sidled between the sheriff and the guru, slid her arm around Bahru's and walked him further into the house, just a step or two, to get him away from the sheriff, who clearly frightened him. "Bahru, why don't you make her a cup of tea?"

"Way ahead of you, Lena." Ryan came in from the kitchen with a big dishpan full of steaming water in his hands, a towel over one arm. "But you can grab it off the counter and bring it to her, Bahru."

The guru nodded, wiping his feet before heading into the kitchen to fetch the tea. Meanwhile Ryan lowered the dishpan to the floor in front of Selma, who was having trouble keeping her eyes open.

"Here you go. Just settle your feet right in there." He helped her, and she sighed deeply as her cold feet sank into the warm water.

"Here is the tea," Bahru said. His deep brown eyes were full of concern and that innocence Lena had always seen in them. It was partly the thick black lashes that gave him that little-boy look. But not entirely.

"Thank you, Bahru." She took the mug, and held it to her mother's lips, and her mom sipped automatically, not even opening her eyes.

Lena set the mug aside and turned to Doc. "What do you think's going on?"

"Not a stroke, of that I'm certain. I suppose it could be a TIA, but–"

"No initials. Use words, Doc."

"Transient ischemic attack. Kind of a ministroke, can be a precursor to the big one. But I don't think it's that, either."

"Well, then, what the hell is it?"

He shrugged. "I feel like she either banged her head pretty danged hard– in which case I'm sure I'd see a lump somewhere—or ate or drank something she hadn't ought to have. Your mom's not a…well, she's not into the wacky-tobacky or anything, is she?"

"Not for twenty years, anyway," Lena told him honestly.

Doc looked to the sheriff. "You find anything in the car?"

The sheriff nodded and lifted up a bottle of wine Lena and Ryan had missed.

"Wine?"

"Label says Mead. Homemade, by the looks of it. It's not sealed—not that I suspect your mother of drinking and driving, Lena. The bottle's full. Just not sealed, like it would be if she bought it somewhere."

"Her friends make mead sometimes," Lena said. Doc and the sheriff both frowned. "It's a kind of an ancient beer, made with honey, and fermented to—"

Doc said "Ah, that must be it, then." His eyes shot to meet the sheriff's.

"What must be it?" Lena was still waiting for an answer.

"Any kind of fermentation can go wrong, turn toxic. Whoo-boy, it can do a number on a person."

"You think she drank some bad mead?" Lena asked.

"Can't think of a better explanation," Doc said. "Could've been a lot worse, hon. But I'll tell you, it's been long enough that it's pretty much worked its way through her system by now. Best thing for her is gonna be a long, hard sleep."

Lena shot a look at Ryan. He met her eyes, and she knew, just like that, that he was thinking that Doc was full of blue mud. She thought so, too.

"I think I'd like to get her to the hospital," she said. "At least have some blood work done."

"It comes back wrong, I'll have no choice but to issue a DUI, Lena," the sheriff said softly. "I mean, we're friends, neighbors, and Molly would slit my throat if she heard me say so. But technically, this is an open container. Now, I'm not gonna write anything up, and far as I'm concerned, this can stay right here between us. But we start getting the E.R. staff involved and I'm not gonna have a choice."

"I think we should err on the side of caution," Bahru said slowly.

Doc and the sheriff sent him surprised looks. He shrugged and went on. "Smell her breath, Lena. At least then you will know if she drank the mead."

Lena bent over her apparently sleeping mom, leaned close, sniffed as Selma exhaled, then backed away blinking. She smelled like she'd had more than a sip or two.

"I think your mother will be fine, Lena," Doc said, sighing in apparent relief. "The mead might not even be bad. She might just have…overindulged."

"And then driven herself home? No, no, my mother would never do that."

"Well, either way." He closed up his black bag with a snap. "You need help getting her up to bed?"

"No." She was pissed and didn't care if he knew it.

"Well, then, I'm glad everything's all right." Doc turned to leave. "You call if you need anything at all now, Lena," Doc called as he jammed his hat down over his ears. "Offer you a ride back to the cottage, Bahru?"

"If I am not needed here?" Bahru said, turning to Lena and making it a question.

"It's fine, Bahru. Go ahead, get some sleep. It's late."

Pressing his palms together, he bowed, then turned and followed Doc Cartwright to his pickup truck.

The sheriff grabbed his hat, as well. "Well, I guess I should be heading out, too."

"Actually, Sheriff Dunbar," Ryan said, "I was planning to head out to those woods, take a look around. Just…you know, to make sure nothing…weird is going on. Do you want to tag along?"

The sheriff frowned at him. "All right, son. All right."

The two of them left, and Lena returned her attention to her mother. Drunk? Tripping on badly fermented grains? She didn't freaking think so.

Kneeling, she found a soft cloth in the warm water—Ryan again. He'd thought of everything. She used it to wash the remaining dirt off her mother's legs, and then her hands. Finally she coaxed Selma to her feet, and she managed to walk her up the stairs to her room.

Lena pulled back her covers, peeled the orange-and-yellow kaftan over her mother's head, then unhooked her bra and noticed what good shape she was in. She didn't look old. Hell, she *wasn't* old. Fifty-four, and she looked ten years younger. What could have happened to her? Lena knew she wasn't foolish enough to get drunk on mead and try to drive herself home. Aside from a few scratches on her legs, there were no signs of injury. She slid a soft cotton nightgown over her mother's head, and then eased her into bed and tucked the covers around her.

Selma let her head sink into the pillows and closed her eyes. "Oh, this warm bed feels so good. And that soak, too. My poor feet were frozen."

Since she sounded coherent, Lena decided to see what she could find out. "Mom, do you remember anything that happened to you tonight?"

Selma frowned hard. "Well, there was the balefire. The ritual. It was very cold. And I think I was stung by a bee."

"It's January, Mom. There aren't any bees."

"Wasp, then. Good night, honey. This is a nice room, but in the morning I think we should go home."

Ryan didn't know what the hell to think about Selma Dunkirk's condition. He hadn't seen the woman in over half a year, and he'd barely had the chance to get to know her then. For all he knew, she might have been going on drinking binges for a long time now.

But he didn't think so. He didn't think so, because Lena would have noticed. Not much slipped by her. And because Selma just hadn't seemed drunk to him.

Call it a hunch, but he didn't like the odd feeling running through his head. The feeling that something was off. That something needed…looking into.

So he rode with Sheriff Larry Dunbar out to where they'd found Selma's car, equipped this time with a heavy-duty flashlight. He directed the local lawman to the right spot. "Right there, see the tire tracks?"

"Sure do." The sheriff pulled the big SUV over. He picked up his own flashlight, got out of the vehicle and slammed the door, which made Ryan wince. If there were anyone in the woods with something to hide, they'd just been forewarned.

Not that there was anyone in the woods with anything to hide. Probably.

Aiming their lights at the ground, the two men followed Selma's footprints in the soft, wet earth and occasional puffs of snow, into the woods.

As soon as they entered the thick pines, where every
breath was a sensory explosion, the tracks pretty much
vanished. There were probably still impressions in the
ground, but even with the flashlights they couldn't make
them out very well. Still, one of them would catch a hint
of one every now and then, and so they moved slowly
in the direction she had probably taken.

Ryan figured he could do a more thorough search tomorrow, by daylight. But if there was anything to hide,
it would be hidden by then. If there had been any...foul
play—God, listen to him. *Foul play*. He was starting to
sound like a TV detective.

And yet there he was, traipsing through the woods in
the dead of night with a lawman he'd just met, in search
of...what? he wondered, moving the powerful flashlight
beam over the ground.

Something flashed, a reflection, and he stopped,
backed up. "Sheriff Dunbar, over here."

"What have you got?"

"That," Ryan whispered. Kneeling in the dirt, he
picked up the dropped cell phone. Selma's cell phone.
He would bet money on it.

He held it out to the sheriff, who took it from him,
bare-handed, and turned it over. "It's a phone," he said.

"Shouldn't you...you know, bag it or something?"

The sheriff looked at him, tilted his head. "You're
from the city, aren't you, son?"

"I don't see what difference that makes."

"Let's see if I can explain it to you, then." Ryan bristled, but took a calming breath and told himself to just let the man talk. "See, if this were the big city, then yeah, odds would be pretty good that something criminal was going on. And if that was the case, then yeah, I'd bag this cell phone as evidence. But that *isn't* the case, 'cause this isn't the big city. Out here, people don't go around hurting each other that way. I mean, we get a teenager playing pranks now and then—but nothing like what you're thinking." He clapped Ryan on the shoulder. "It's different out here. Not your fault at all that you're confused, though. I'd be as apt to jump to the wrong conclusion in your neck of the woods as you are in mine."

"So you think…?"

"I think the lady drank what she thought was a reasonable amount of that mead stuff, and it was stronger than she realized and knocked her on her keister. Probably didn't even realize it till she was halfway home, then pulled over once she did, 'cause she's a smart lady, and decided to walk the rest of the way, just to be safe. Thanks to the booze, she made the poor decision to take a shortcut. Fell in the mud, got disoriented, wandered around, dropped her cell phone, found her way to the road, end of story."

Ryan nodded slowly. "I gotta tell you, it makes perfect sense the way you're telling it. And I do get what you're saying about that being a far more likely scenario, given the small-town lifestyle you all have going on here."

"Reasonable. I like that about you."

"There's maybe something you're not aware of, though. I hate to even think it, but…" They were still standing in the dark, in the pines. The night breeze was whistling through the highest boughs like a high-pitched whine, coming and going, then coming back again. It was icy on his neck and ears and face.

"What's that, son?"

Ryan hunched his shoulders a little, turning his back to the wind. "My father is—was—Ernst McNally." He didn't think he would have to elaborate, and he could tell from the sheriff's response that he was right.

"*The* Ernst McNally? The one who just— Aw, hell, I'm sorry for your loss, Ryan." One big hand clapped down onto his shoulder, while the other clasped his other arm in a gesture of comfort and familiarity.

Ryan found himself liking the guy. He had a kind of John Wayne vibe about him. "Thanks. The thing is, he left a pile of money to the baby, and Lena's the trustee."

"Keeper of the purse strings. I get it." The sheriff gave one last squeeze, then lowered his hands. "So then…you're the father?"

"I am."

"You gonna do the right thing? Marry her?"

Ryan's jaw dropped. "Um, you know, I just— That's not the point." He bit off the rest of the explanation he did not owe the man. "The point is, there's reason to be extra careful, maybe look at things extra close, because that money could be a motive for some nutcase to try to mess with them."

The sheriff pursed his lips thoughtfully, shrugged. "Can't see how that fits with this, though. How did he make Selma forget where she was, and how could that help him get access to the money?"

"The operative word was *nutcase,* Sheriff."

The big man nodded. "Well, I'll come back out and take a better look around tomorrow. You can join me then, if you want."

"All right, I'll do that."

They turned and headed back for the road. But halfway there, Ryan stopped as an odd tingle of awareness whispered up his spine. He turned slowly, getting the strongest sensation that he was being watched.

"Sheriff, hold up."

Dunbar stopped a few yards ahead and stood perfectly still, turning only his head. Ryan held a finger to his lips. And right then, he heard a distinct "crunch" in the forest, like a heavy foot coming down on a pile of dry twigs. He froze in place. The hairs on his nape prickled, and then, unable to resist, he turned around to look behind him.

Heavy pine boughs, swaying gently back and forth, filling the air with their scent. Leafless maple saplings springing up in between. Fallen, half-rotted trees with dinner-plate-size fungi and carpets of moss all over them. An owl soaring soundlessly in the distance. Nothing else. No one watching him.

Bullshit, he thought in silence. *I know when I'm alone and when I'm not, and I am* not *alone out here.*

Whoever was out there, though, was being careful not to be seen. But he was even more convinced than before that something just wasn't right. His spine stiffening, he lifted his chin and set his jaw, as the strangest sensation seemed to spread through his veins, pulsing in every part of him. A protective instinct. It was all he could do not to shout a challenge to whoever was lurking out there, telling them to get lost, to stay away from his territory.

The only thing that prevented him was the sheriff standing nearby, along with the notion it might be best to pretend he wasn't on to them. Whoever *they* were.

Turning, he walked up to join the sheriff, who waited for him to catch up. "Probably a deer," Larry Dunbar said softly. But Ryan didn't hear much conviction in his words.

8

Ryan headed upstairs. The house was quiet, and he was glad. It had been such a full day, he hadn't even had time to unpack. But he wasn't in any hurry to do that just yet. He peeked into Selma's room. Lena was sitting in a chair at the bedside, leaning over to one side. She'd fallen asleep holding her mother's hand. A single tear glittered on her cheek.

For just an instant he stopped right there and experienced the sensation of a hot knife sinking through his butter-sculpture heart. The pain was that of an eleven-year-old boy who'd lost his mother. He'd loved his mom just like Lena so clearly loved hers. Just that much. But he hadn't let himself grieve.

He had to look away fast. As much as he wanted to go to Lena and comfort her, he couldn't. Not just then. He needed to give it a few minutes. He started to back away from the door.

Then she whispered his name. "Ryan?"

Closing his eyes, out of sight, he said, "Yeah?"

"Did the sheriff go home?"

"Yeah, he's gone." The burning sensation was gone

from his eyes, so he stepped into her line of sight once more. "Are you okay?"

"I don't know." She sat up a little straighter in the chair, easing her hand away from her mother's. "Do you think we're doing the right thing? Not taking her to a hospital?"

He sighed. "I don't know. I really don't. I could make some calls, have the best doctors money can buy checking her out in no time."

She thinned her lips. "Money can't fix this. I was asking what you *feel*. In your gut."

His gut was churning. "I think it wouldn't hurt to get a second opinion. But I don't think we'll be able to do much about that until morning."

She nodded, sighing. "I was thinking the same thing."

"You should go to bed, Lena. Get some sleep yourself."

"I know. I will. Just a few more minutes." She sighed, then blinked and looked up at him. "Did you find anything out there?"

"Oh, right." He pulled the cell phone from his pocket and handed it to her. "It's a little dirty, but…is it hers?"

"Yes!" She brushed some of the dirt off it. "Needs a charge."

"Plug it in before you go to bed. We can check it out tomorrow."

"For…?"

He shrugged. "Damned if I know."

She sighed, set the phone down and turned her attention back to her mother. He watched her for a moment, feeling helpless. "I guess I'll get the rest of my things out of the truck, then. I never even unpacked."

"Okay. I'll just sit with her until you're done, and then I'll go to bed. Promise."

"Okay."

He left her there, pretending he didn't see her crying for her mother, and headed out to the truck to grab his duffel from the back. He looked off toward the guesthouse but saw no movement, just a small light glowing inside.

He opened his duffel and pawed around inside until he found the box, then he pulled it out and sat down on the edge of the truck bed, holding it in his lap. He'd brought the damn thing with him to try to figure out what it was. How it did what it did. What it meant. He'd thought he could ask Lena. She was a witch. She should know. But then she'd had that dream—a dream in which he'd been about to stab her through the heart with a blade just like this one. A golden blade, she'd said. The hilt etched with symbols even she didn't recognize. Yeah, that matched.

So he couldn't tell her. And he couldn't tell anyone else, either. That note his father had left lingered in his mind. *Keep it to yourself.* He'd never done a damned thing his old man had asked him to do. Barely anything, anyway. But this...this had apparently been important to him.

In fact, it was the one thing his father had ever shared with him and him alone. Not Bahru. He knew there were probably dozens of things—maybe hundreds—the old man had shared with Bahru and not him. But this one thing, this was *his.*

He kind of wanted to hold on to that for a while. This

secret between him and Ernst. Maybe he could figure it out on his own.

There were all those books, after all.

He slid off the truck, tucking the box under one arm, slinging the duffel over a shoulder, and then he walked around the big farmhouse into the backyard. It was dark there, or as dark as it could be with the big white moon shining down. Selma's bedroom was on this side of the house, but a little copse of trees blocked the view from her window. And Bahru's cottage was completely out of sight from here.

He set the duffel down on the two unadorned steps that led up to the back door—what a great spot for a deck, he thought. Nice wide, level patch of lawn, probably a gorgeous view, though he had yet to see it by daylight. Yeah, a deck would be perfect. And a swing set for the kid. Maybe a jungle gym.

He let himself smile. It was kind of fun, thinking about a child. His own child.

Sighing, he walked out across the back lawn until it sloped slightly downward into a cluster of leafless trees. They were gnarly, short and twisty. Something squished under his feet, and he looked down to see half-rotted apples all over the ground. The scents wafted up to his nostrils, varying from sweet and crisp to vinegar-sour, and hitting every note in between.

Okay, this was far enough. He took the box out from under his arm, opened the lid and, drawing a deep breath, closed his hand around the hilt of the knife. That tingling feeling shot through him immediately, rushing up his arm.

He held the knife, glancing around nervously. Then,

with great care, he pointed the blade at a broken branch that was lying on the ground, a good distance away from anything else.

Nothing happened.

Huh. He tipped the knife one way and then another, looking it over. There didn't seem to be any button or trigger that he might have hit by accident back in his father's office.

Or maybe that was some kind of hallucination on my part. The mind can play some pretty powerful tricks, after all. Look at poor Selma.

He aimed the blade again, even shook it menacingly at the dead limb once or twice. Still nothing.

"Hell, I don't know what I was thinking. It had to be some kind of…trick or…delusion or…" He looked up toward the house again. Time to get back. Get his stuff inside and check on Lena again. She needed to get to bed, get some rest. Talk about stress. If this incident with her mom hadn't stressed her out, he didn't know what would. He hoped it hadn't affected the baby.

The blade bucked in his hand, scaring the hell out of him as it blasted the ground at his feet and spread liquid fire all around his shoes.

He dropped the thing with a cry of alarm, and then he was turning in circles, stomping out the burning leaves and twigs as fast as he could, before the fire had a chance to spread.

When it was done, he just stood there looking at the knife and shaking his head. "Damn. It's real. Whatever the hell this is, it's real."

He picked the blade up again, this time with just two

fingers. "Don't go off, don't go off, don't go off...." He dropped it into the still-open box and slammed the lid.

He was going to have to get to the bottom of that blade, and soon. He couldn't talk to Lena about it—not after she'd dreamed of him killing her with it—and he didn't trust Bahru. Lena's mom might be of help, but she was basically out of commission.

There were all those books, though. Maybe he could find the answers on his own.

Tucking the box back under his arm, he carried it out to the truck, hiding it under the driver's seat. He couldn't risk keeping it inside and setting the place on fire while they slept, after all.

Lena had gone to bed, since her mother was sleeping soundly and seemed okay. Her lights were off, and her bedroom door was open, so she would hear Selma if she woke and needed help. Her own eyes were heavy, and she didn't think she could stay awake much longer, even if she wanted to. Ryan's bedroom was right across the hall. His door was open, too, lights off. She figured he was sleeping and had left his door wide open for the same reason she had.

But then she saw a glow, a light coming from out front and shining through Ryan's bedroom window, as if a car had pulled in. Except she didn't hear a car.

So she dragged herself out of bed and tiptoed across the hall, then leaned through his bedroom doorway. "Ryan?"

His bed was empty, and still made. Frowning, she crossed his room and pushed the sheer white curtain aside. Standing off to one side, keeping out of sight for some instinctive reason she didn't dare ignore, she looked down.

Ryan was outside, crouching beside the open driver's-side door of the rental truck, as if he were looking for something on the floor or under the seat. But when he straightened, he wasn't holding anything. Nothing she could see, anyway.

Huh.

He's hiding something from you, you know.

Lena spun around, the deep male voice sending icy chills right up her spine. Who the hell was in her house? She stepped out of Ryan's room to investigate, but there was no one in sight. She rubbed the goose bumps from her arms, straining her eyes to see in the darkness up and down the hall, now that the truck's light had gone out. Gauging the distance to the light switch, she decided to stop thinking and take action. Three lunges and *snap!* Light flooded the hall. Near the head of the stairs, one shadow seemed to fade a half beat slower than the rest, and she frowned, staring at the spot where it had been.

Their up-to-now silent and harmless house ghost? Or something else? Something darker?

She heard the front doorknob rattle and quickly flipped off the light before it opened, then closed again with deliberate softness. Ryan was back and trying not to be heard. No, that wasn't fair. Maybe he was just trying not to wake anyone. She padded quietly back into her room, sliding beneath the fluffy white duvet. Then she turned onto one side, curling her arms around her belly and closing her eyes.

Seconds later she heard his soft footsteps in the hall,

felt him pause and look in at her as she feigned sleep. She almost held her breath until she finally heard him sigh and move away into his own room.

Lena didn't know why he would be hiding anything from her, nor did she have a clue what it might be. But she was equally baffled as to why her house ghost would finally try to communicate after all this time without a damn good reason. Maybe the ghost was wrong. Maybe he'd made some kind of paranormal mistake. But if it was true, if Ryan *did* have something to hide, she was damn well going to find out what it was.

Her eyes blurred, drooped, opened again. Yeah, she was going to find out. Right after she got a little sleep.

Lena dreamed she had fallen into one of those storybooks she'd created as a little girl. She was a harem slave, though she hadn't called it that back then. She had seen herself as a slave girl, maybe a belly dancer, or perhaps a genie from a bottle. But from the eyes of an adult it was clear what her vivid imagination—second sight?—had conjured. "Harem slave" was a far more accurate description. She wore sheer fabrics in jewel tones that draped all around her while covering almost nothing. And oh, how she could dance! She could mesmerize the king and his entire audience with her moves, as could her sisters. They used their bodies like spells, wielding magic with every twist, shimmy and undulation.

But it wasn't the king's gaze that warmed her all the way to her toes and made her shiver with pure female power. It was the look in the eyes of the king's son, the prince.

Ryan.

Of course, that wasn't his name, not then and not in her books. She didn't know what it was, didn't care, because he *was* Ryan. No mistaking it. His hair, his eyes, his barely clothed body… His skin was a little darker than the Ryan in her waking life. His hair was raven-black instead of dark brown. But then, her own hair was jet in the dream, too, not a coppery curl in sight.

He was watching her. His smoldering eyes never left her body as she writhed and swirled to the increasingly frantic beat of the *lilis* drums. And it was more than just passion she saw in that gaze. When she dared allow the tiniest smile to tug at the corners of her lips, he returned it, just as subtly, and it was intimate. Familiar. Deep. And secret, a secret just between the two of them.

A deep moan brought her instantly wide awake, because it came in her mother's voice. She was on her feet almost before she was fully out of the dream, and then felt queasy and momentarily disoriented by the sight of her own pale porcelain limbs and white cotton nightgown protruding over her baby bump, instead of a belly dancing costume draped over skin of copper and impossibly firm abs. She shook off the confusion and darted to her mother's room. Selma was moving restlessly, turning her head back and forth. It was daylight, but gloomy, and rain was pattering gently against the windows. Lena bent over her mother and took her hand as she muttered in her sleep.

"What is it, Mom?"

"Ba… Ba—" Selma murmured, twisting from side to side on her pillows. "Ru."

"Bahru?"

"Bah…ru," Selma sighed.

"Okay, all right, hold on, Mom." Lena dashed down the hall into Ryan's room and then came to a halt in his bedroom doorway, arrested by the familiar sight of him. The sheet was low across his hips, his chest, magnificent shoulders and muscular arms all completely uncovered, so her greedy eyes could drink their fill of him. She knew the feel of him, the scent of his skin and how it set her on fire when they lay wrapped in each other's arms, naked and holding on.

But those days were over.

She shook off the images and went to him, bending over his bed and gently shaking him awake. The feel of his warm shoulders under her hands triggered a shower of fiery sparks in her mind and lower. But she pushed them aside as he opened his eyes wide and stared up into hers.

"The baby?"

"No, it's Mom." She warmed, though, at his very real concern for their child. "She's asking for Bahru. Will you go get him for me?"

He frowned, as if he wanted to argue, but then seemed to change his mind. He flung back the covers and got up, wearing nothing but his briefs. "I'll have him back here in five minutes. Less. Go take care of your mom."

"I'm sorry to send you out in the rain."

"I won't melt."

"Thanks." She started to leave, but he put a hand on her shoulder.

"What about you? Are you okay?"

Turning, she smiled at him. "Yeah, I'm good."

"Okay."

She headed back into her mother's room and sat down beside the bed again, stroking her hand. She seemed to have sunk back into sleep, though. No more muttering or tossing. Lena spoke softly to her, in case she could hear, and within a few minutes the scent of sandalwood told her that Bahru had arrived.

Barefoot, he walked into the room and over to the bed. "How is she doing?" he asked softly, his deep brown, thickly fringed eyes on Selma's still form.

"Better. She was really agitated, and then just...not."

"I could perform Reiki for her, if you wish it?" he asked.

"That would be wonderful, Bahru. Thank you."

He pressed his palms together and bowed a little bit, then rubbed them to get them warm and moved to the other side of the bed. Closing his eyes, he laid his hands on Selma's head, cupping the top of her skull, thumbs touching.

Lena backed away, then turned toward the door, where Ryan stood watching. "I think she'll rest now. We can leave her in Bahru's hands for a little while. I, for one, need a hot shower and a huge breakfast."

"What is it he's doing?" Ryan whispered with a nod toward the bed.

"Reiki. It's an eastern energy healing practice. Mom would want it."

"From *him?*"

Lena frowned. "He's only trying to help, Ryan."

He nodded. "Yeah. I guess so. But...then there's my gut." He was speaking quietly, but she kept thinking Bahru could hear them if he wanted to.

She closed her eyes slowly. It was nice that Ryan cared enough about her mother to even offer an opinion, especially one he knew was likely to piss her off. "So what do you suggest?"

"You stay in the room with him, I'll make us that huge breakfast. You can eat first, shower later. Good?"

She licked her lips. "I would argue with you, except…I've had your breakfasts before."

"Yeah. Heavenly, right?"

"Sinfully divine," she admitted. She wondered whether, if she just slid right into his arms right now, he would wrap his around her and kiss her good-morning like he used to do, all hot and steamy, especially if they'd just made love before getting out of bed. And if he did, would everything just magically go back to the way it had been before, only with him loving her this time?

"So it's a deal?" he asked.

She blinked out of the fantasy, had to work to recall what they'd been talking about. "Yeah. It's a deal."

"Good." He leaned in and kissed her on the mouth, a quick, familiar peck, as if they'd been doing it for years. Immediately he froze, and so did she. Their eyes locked, and she shivered right to her toes.

"I've got a storybook I want to show you later. Remind me, okay?"

"A storybook?"

Her stomach growled. "Go make my breakfast, already."

He smiled, then turned and hurried away. She watched him go, trying to still the ecstatic little girl inside who was jumping up and down, and conjuring visions of domestic bliss. *Shut up, kid,* she commanded. And then she turned to Bahru. "I'll help, okay?"

"Of course," he whispered.

Lena moved to the foot of the bed and pulled the covers from her mom's feet, then put her hands on them and mentally sent the sacred symbols of Reiki into her mother's body.

"There is something you should know about him, Lena," Bahru said softly.

"About who? Ryan?" she asked, her hands already growing warm as the power moved through them.

"Yes. I..." He looked at the floor. "I do not wish to cause him problems, but I feel you should know the truth."

"And what is the truth, Bahru?" She narrowed her eyes on the guru, watching him closely.

"Before we left, I...I overheard him on the telephone discussing...custody law."

The bottom fell out of her stomach. "Custody law?"

"A father's rights."

She pulled her hands away from her mother's feet, so the anger zapping through her wouldn't shoot into Selma and set her hair on fire. "A father's rights?"

"I suspect he came here to...to inspect the home you will provide for the little one. More specifically, to look for flaws he can use to his favor in any future custody battle."

"You think he's going to try to take my baby away from me?"

Bahru lowered his voice to just above a whisper. "I cannot claim to know what his intentions are. I only felt you should be forewarned, just in case."

"Son of a—"

"Take care, Magdalena. Anger isn't good for the baby."

She sent him a scowl. He closed his eyes as if to shut it out. "I am sorry. Believe me, I am."

"For what? You didn't do anything but tell me."

But he lowered his eyes as if he had. Just like Bahru to feel guilty for ratting out a McNally, right? Maybe his loyalty to Ernst was bleeding over onto Ryan. But Lena was grateful he had overcome it enough to give her the heads-up. If Ryan thought for one earthly instant that he could take her baby away from her…well, he'd better think again.

"I've done what I can," Bahru said softly, lifting his hands from her mother's head. "I can do more later, when things are less…tumultuous."

"Yes. Fine. Listen, Ryan's cooking. Would you like some breakfast?"

"Thank you, but no. I am fasting today."

"You're already barely more than a bag of bones, Bahru. If you were caught by starving cannibals, they'd throw you back out of mercy."

He grinned at her, looking like the old Bahru for just the briefest second. And only in that second did she realize how different he'd been before she'd left Manhattan. Before she had quit her job. Before Ernst had died. So much lighter. There was a new darkness around Bahru, a shadow behind his eyes and a heaviness to his being that she was only now seeing.

"I have already stocked my little cottage with supplies."

"And where did you manage to find wheat grass and goat's milk out here?"

His smile flashed again. "I bought enough to last an entire month from the Whole Earth Co-Op before we left the city."

"You're good to go, then."

"I am." His smile faded slowly. "You've never been anything but kind to me, Lena. I wish…" He hesitated, gathered himself, then went on. "I wish this wasn't necessary."

"What? Telling me Ryan's secrets? It's all right, Bahru. I won't shoot the messenger."

He couldn't seem to hold her eyes for more than a moment at a time. He couldn't have looked guiltier if he'd been caught stealing candy from her baby. "I will be nearby should you need me again."

"Thanks, Bahru."

Palm press. Head bow. Then he padded away into the hall and down the stairs.

She watched him go, then stared down at her mother's sleeping form. "You'd think we were having a funeral in here, wouldn't you? Hell, I guess he's still in mourning. You know how much he loved the old billionaire, right?" Her lips thinned. "It bothers him, ratting Ryan out to me like that."

Selma said nothing, just lay still, peaceful.

"I'm going down for some breakfast, Mom. If you wake up, I'll bring you something. And if you don't wake up pretty soon, I'm going to have to take you to a hospital so they can put an IV into you before you starve to death. But I'm willing to give you a little more time. Okay?"

Nothing. She bent to kiss her mother's forehead, then straightened again and headed down to the kitchen, where Ryan was looking as domestic, well-intentioned and innocent as he could possibly manage to look.

Her first instinct was to flay him to the bone—verbally, anyway—for daring to even think about taking custody of Eleanora—the name the baby had made it clear she'd chosen for herself. She paused halfway into the kitchen, gathering up her words and her wits, working up to a big explosion while he scooped a giant, perfect omelet from the pan and divided it onto two waiting plates. Before he even looked up, he said, "I need to return the truck to the nearest U-Haul place today. But I need a vehicle of some sort while I'm here. Is there a dealer anywhere close?"

"A dealer?" Her mind wasn't on what he was saying but on constructing the telling-off he was about to receive.

"A car dealer. Truck, really. I think out here we need a truck. Don't you?"

She blinked. He looked up at her, then seemed to wonder what was going on in her head and studied her curiously. "You all right? You look like you just swallowed a lemon."

It wasn't a lemon she was swallowing. It was her well-deserved rant. Because he had just reminded her of something. He was the kind of guy who could drive into town to return a rental truck and stop along the way to buy a brand-new vehicle, any kind he wanted. If it could be found, he could plunk down his credit card and drive it away.

He could afford the best lawyers in the world. And

he could afford to do whatever it took to win a custody battle.

Then again, so could she. But she wouldn't use the baby's trust fund that way, and he probably knew it.

She would fight him to the death, even if it cost everything else she had, but she hoped it wouldn't be necessary. However, it might be best not to show her hand too soon. And not to antagonize him until she had her own game plan laid out.

Drawing a deep breath, she focused on shifting her anger onto a back burner to keep it warm until the time was right. In the meantime, she would make nice.

"Lena?"

"No, I'm fine," she said, forcing a smile and moving toward the table. "Just tired, and of course worried about Mom."

"Yeah, I've been thinking about that."

"About Mom?"

He nodded, carrying the plates to the table, then spinning back to the oven and pulling out a tray of biscuits that wafted a heavenly aroma throughout the entire kitchen.

"You made biscuits?"

"The little pop-can of dough was just sitting in the fridge, so…" He quickly plunked a couple onto their plates.

Finally he sat.

She eyed the feast before her. A bottle of hot sauce stood in the center of the table. He'd remembered that she liked it on her eggs. Her tea was already poured. He had coffee, and it smelled heavenly. But no caffeine for their daughter.

Lena was reluctantly grateful, and seeing him like this, all helpful and concerned about her mother, she had trouble believing he was secretly plotting to steal her baby. On the other hand, both the house ghost and Bahru were warning her now. So there had to be something to it, right?

"Dig in, babe. You're eating for two."

She nodded, and since she was starved and it smelled delicious, she ate a few bites. Then she paused, and decided to go fishing. "Ryan?" she asked, after washing down the luscious omelet with a swig of tea.

"Yeah?"

"I...I ran away from you because I thought a baby was the last thing in the world you would want."

He nodded. "I know that."

"But I wasn't lying before, when I said I never intended to have this child in secret. I mean, I know I let an awful lot of time go by, but I really was going to call and let you know."

He stopped with his fork halfway to his mouth. "I know you were."

"You do?"

"Yeah." He searched her face. "Look, I was acting like an idiot back then. And the thing is..." He set his fork down and seemed to turn his attention inside for a moment. Then, with a firm nod, he faced her again and went on. "Here's the thing. I was doing it on purpose."

She blinked. "I don't...follow."

"I didn't want you or any woman to ever think of me as a guy who could be...you know, landed."

"Landed. Like a fish."

"Right." That wasn't the kind of fishing she'd meant,

though. "I was playing the role everybody expected me to. I think I might even have believed it myself, so I can't really blame you for buying the act."

"Act?"

He reached across the table and covered her hand with his. It was big and strong and warm, and it sent chills right up her arm. "I came out here to start trying to show you who I *really* am, Lena. I came out here to try to earn the right to be a part of our child's life."

"You did?"

"Yeah."

"Well, I…I mean I—"

"No, don't. I'm not asking you for anything right now. You've got enough on your mind. I'm here. Just let me hang, let me help, lean on me a little, and don't worry about anything else. Not right now. Okay?"

She wanted to believe him more than she wanted to finish the luscious omelet. And *that* was saying something. "Okay."

"Good. Now, eat, will you?"

Maybe Bahru was wrong. Or maybe Ryan *had* talked to a lawyer, but only because he was worried that *she* would try to keep the baby from *him,* not the opposite. Maybe…maybe a hundred things.

"Eat," he said again.

It made her smile just a little. "You don't have to tell me to eat. You're lucky I haven't eaten *you* by now."

His smile was instant and genuine. "I've really missed you, Lena."

Her heart did a little dance in her chest, and she whispered, "I've missed you, too."

9

He felt good—damn good—about the way things were going with Lena. Except, of course, for whatever the hell had happened to her mother. Not to mention that he was still antsy about the magic knife he had tucked under the seat of the rental truck, but he was trying not to let that bother him too much right now. Meanwhile, he had a project to get underway, and he needed a pickup.

He drove the rental through the pouring rain into nearby Ithaca and chose a big black F250 extended-cab truck, so he could fit a baby carrier in the backseat. The dealer handed him the keys and agreed to return the rental truck for him.

Before he left, he took that damned box out from under the rental truck's seat and tucked it underneath the front seat of the new one.

One task down.

Task two, the local hardware store back in Milbury for paintbrushes and rollers, trays and blue tape, sandpaper and more. He intended to make himself useful while he was taking up space in Lena's old farmhouse, and contrary to popular belief, he knew how to work with his hands. He'd helped more than one friend redo a room.

He was pondering paint colors for the trim—pink to go with Lena's premonition, or a gender-neutral yellow or green?—when he overheard a man's voice an aisle over.

"It happened last night. Ben Fromer's farm."

"No fucking way. A *calf?*"

"Just a few days old. Some bastard slit its throat, left it lying there. And get this—not a drop of blood anywhere."

"What the *hell,* man? Second time this month, isn't it?"

"That we know of."

"So what's the sheriff say?"

"Shit, he's as clueless as the rest of us. Thinks it might be kids playing around with occult shit or something, but what the hell are they doing with the blood?"

The two men stopped talking and looked at Ryan with undisguised curiosity, and only then did he realize he'd moved closer, inching around the corner and forgetting to be discreet. He was standing three feet away now, and looking right at the men, one of whom wore a red apron with the store logo on the front, so he shrugged sheepishly. "Sorry, I…was looking to get some paint mixed?" He held up the color cards in his hand.

They eyed him suspiciously, but the man in the apron, whose name tag identified him as Bob, took the cards from his hand and nodded, while the other guy wandered away.

"You're not a local, are you?" Bob asked as he yanked

a can of white base coat off the shelf and took it to the mixing stand.

"No, I'm visiting. Staying with Lena Dunkirk and her mother."

Bob's eyes shot to Ryan's. "Talk around town is those two are some kind of new-age crystal-wearing witches or something. You know anything about that?"

Definitely not good, Ryan thought. Lena seemed to believe they'd been "flying" under the radar. Clearly that was not the case. "Huh," he said. "I've known them for over a year, and I've never seen either one of them riding a broomstick. But I'll be sure to keep an eye out."

The guy grunted. "Been strange things happening since they came here."

"Since they came here? Really? 'Cause they've been here more than six months now, and didn't that other guy say the weird stuff started a month or so ago? Or is there other weird stuff, besides that thing with the calf blood?"

"No, no, that's the only thing. Unless you count the weather."

"The weather?"

The man nodded toward the front windows. "It's January, friend. And it's raining. It ought to be snowing. But it's raining. That's weird."

"That's global warming. I know people are still arguing about whether it's man-made or a natural cycle, but I don't think anyone's claiming it's witchcraft."

Bob shrugged. "Still and all, we never had calves with their throats cut *before* those two moved out here."

"Come on, now, you really think a woman who's

eight months pregnant and her mother are into sneaking out at night and butchering cattle?"

"Scuttlebutt is, one of 'em was out in the woods doin' *somethin'* last night, though."

Ryan's blood ran cold. "This town has some grapevine. But you ought to know better than to listen to gossip like that, friend. Someone could get hurt."

Bob focused on his work, running his finger along a color chart. "I'll have this ready for you in about ten minutes. You have other shopping to do?"

"Yeah, I do," Ryan said, knowing he'd just been told to take a hike. So he did. But damn, this kind of gossip, combined with what looked like ritual cattle murders, did not bode well for Lena and her mother.

Shit, maybe some local had taken it upon himself to do something about it. Maybe that was what had happened to Selma. He was suddenly eager to get back to the house, to warn the women about the sort of talk being generated about them. It was dangerous talk. And it needed to stop.

Lena had spent the entire gloomy, rainy morning working on her hand-stenciled sunflower border in the kitchen. When she heard the car in the driveway she smiled. It had to be Ryan, back from his errands, and the thought of him walking through the front door filled her entire body with a ridiculous warm, glowy feeling that was, she decided, very poorly thought out. Okay, not thought out at all. She had to be careful, because she could far too easily fall far too in love with him and get her heart broken all over again.

She'd decided to wait for him to get back from his errands to make up her mind whether to take her mother to the hospital or not. Doc had already phoned in to check on her, and he'd said she would probably sleep for a few more hours. It had been a late night, after all. He'd promised to come by later in the day.

When she heard a knock at the front door, though, she frowned. Didn't Ryan know he could just walk right in? She went to the door, wiping her hands on a rag, yanked it open and felt her welcoming smile freeze in place when she met the sky-blue eyes of the blond-haired, steely-faced woman in a white, faux-fur-trimmed raincoat standing at the door, a large tote bag over her shoulder.

"Ms. Dunkirk?" the woman asked.

"Uh...yes?"

"Eloise Sheldrake, R.N."

Lena frowned. "I'm sorry, do I know you?"

"Doc Cartwright sent me. He has a full day and asked me to check in on your mother for him."

"Oh." Lena stepped aside and waved the woman in. Just before she closed the door, she saw a little black cat streak across the driveway toward the small shed and duck inside through a broken board. She had no idea where it had come from, but at least it had found shelter.

She closed the door and returned her attention to her visitor. "I'm glad you're here, actually, because I just don't know what to do about feeding her. I mean, if she doesn't wake up soon, she's going to need an IV or something, right?"

"We'll see." Eloise smiled. It was a only a brief flicker, but it transformed her face. She was beauti-ful when she smiled. But the expressionless mask returned instantly. "Is she upstairs?" the nurse asked with a glance at the stairway.

"Yes. I'll take you up. Can I get your coat?"

Eloise took off her coat, revealing a uniform that could have come from the 1960s and went perfectly with her sensible shoes. Then she pulled an old-fashioned nurse's cap out of the bag and put it on, complete with two bobby pins to anchor it to her blond hair. She pulled a little black satchel from inside her bag, then gave a firm nod and met Lena's eyes again. "Take me to her now. Her name is Selma?"

"Yes. This way." Lena swallowed her misgivings as she led Eloise up the stairs. Doc had talked often about a nurse, had even tried to convince her to have one move in until the baby came. She was pretty sure this must be the nurse in question, though she'd expected someone a bit older. This woman was, she estimated, in her thirties.

She led the nurse into her mother's bedroom, then stopped, staring in shock.

Selma was sitting up in bed, thumbing through a magazine. She looked up when they came into the room and smiled. "Well, hi, honey. I don't know what's the matter with me this morning. I'm so *tired*. I think I might be coming down with something." Then her eyes shifted to the nurse. Her expression turned curious but remained friendly. "Hello."

"Hello, Selma."

"Mom, this is Nurse Sheldrake—"

"Eloise, if you don't mind," said the nurse.

"Doc Cartwright sent her over to have a look at you."

Selma frowned. "But...how did *he* know I wasn't feeling well?"

Lena bit her lower lip, then turned to the nurse. "Eloise, can you give us a minute? There's coffee in the kitchen. Why don't you make yourself a cup?"

Those striking blue eyes shifted from Selma to Lena, but her expression never changed. Stony. "Fine. I'll be back in five minutes." She turned on her heel and walked away.

"Hon, what's going on?" Selma asked.

Lena sat on the edge of the bed. "You never came home from last night's…" she looked toward the doorway and lowered her voice "…gathering." Her mother looked a little confused, so Lena clarified in a whisper. "You had a full moon esbat last night with Betty and Jean."

"Oh, right." Selma sent a look at the ceiling with a self-deprecating shake of her head. "Gosh, brain-dead this morning. I remember now. It was *great,* Lena. You should have been there. Betty got some flash paper and didn't tell us, so we damn near jumped right out of our skins when she—" She stopped there, her frown returning, deeper than before. "I didn't come home?"

"No. We got worried and went looking, and we found your car along the side of the road, near the woods. Apparently you went into the woodlot, then tried to cut across the field to the house."

Selma blinked rapidly. "I don't remember any of that. Are you sure?"

"Yeah. I was out looking for you when you came stumbling out of the field. You were muddy, confused…."

Her mother blinked, then said, "No. No, I don't remember that at all."

"What *do* you remember, Mom?"

Selma took a deep breath, pressed her hands to her forehead. "I remember the ritual at Betty's. I remember getting into the car to come home...."

"Was there mead?"

"Yes. Jean's homemade honey mead. She gave me a bottle to bring home. I promised to save it till after the baby comes and toast her with it."

"Did you drink any of the mead before you left Betty's?" Lena asked.

"Just the usual sip during the blessing of the cakes and ale. You know."

"Yes, I know." The customary Wiccan circle closing included the sharing of a bite of food, often fruit or a baked item, and a sip of some beverage, usually wine or juice, to acknowledge the blessings of the earth. "So you didn't drink any more than that? After you left or anything?"

Selma shook her head, her eyes vacant. "No, honey, I don't drink to excess, you know that." She frowned. "It's odd, though, I don't remember much after leaving Betty's house. There's a big empty hole in my memory, and my head feels like it's stuffed with wet cotton." Squeezing her eyes tight, she said, "And it's pounding pretty good, too."

"We'll get you something for that. And I'm gonna call Doc, too, let him know you're awake and everything." Lena studied her mom's face, looking hard for the telltale signs of a stroke or any other medical issue, but there were none. No lax facial features on one side, and she was speaking clearly and logically.

The phone, she thought. *I never looked at the phone.*

She had wiped it free of dirt and plugged it in to charge, then had gone to sleep before doing anything more.

Nurse Eloise was back, tapping on the door frame, even though the door was open. She had a tray in her hands, with a bowl of oatmeal, a tall glass of water and a cup of tea.

"Wow. You work fast," Lena said.

"Instant oatmeal, two minutes in the microwave. She needs something in her stomach." She moved closer, and her demeanor changed just a little bit. She seemed lighter, friendlier. "There now, Selma, how are you feeling?" Her voice was lighter, too.

This must be her bedside manner, Lena thought. Odd, how she turned it on like a light.

"My head is pounding, and I seem to have lost a chunk of time, but other than that..." Selma shrugged. "I'd rather have you fussing over Lena, though."

The nurse slid a sideways look at Lena as she lowered the tray across Selma's lap. As she bent over, a pendant fell from the neck of her white uniform, dangling over the bed. A quartz crystal point on the end of a long silver chain.

Selma grabbed it. "Oh, how pretty! It's just like the one Bahru has."

"Who or what is a Bahru?" Eloise asked, snatching the necklace and dropping it back inside her blouse.

Though her mother only laughed, Lena found herself shivering. Everyone in her dream had been wearing a crystal like that. What the hell?

"As for your daughter, I intend to offer my services, though Dr. Cartwright assures me she'll refuse."

"I'm gonna call Doc right now and let him know

you're awake," Lena said. "Be right back, Mom." She left her mother to enjoy her breakfast and the nurse to figure out what else she might need, and headed down the hall and into her own bedroom. She left her door open, listening for any sign of a problem, and located her mother's phone on the nightstand where she had left it to charge last night. Quickly she turned it on, and checked the call log. Nothing of interest. Recent text messages—nothing there, either. The last one had gone out to Helen soon after Selma had left the house. On my way. C U soon. Emails? Nothing near the time when she'd apparently blacked out.

She checked photos on a whim, not expecting to find a thing. But there were three of the same exact blurry, dark shot.

Squinting, Lena tried to decipher them. They'd been taken in the woods at night. There were people standing around a fire, but it was impossible to see who they were.

She supposed the shots could have been taken at some ritual her mother had attended, though unless last night had turned into something completely unexpected, they had to be from sometime earlier. Easy enough to check the time stamp.

A vehicle pulled in, loud, powerful. She couldn't see out front from her bedroom, but she could tell by the feeling in her belly that it was Ryan, so she pocketed the phone and quickly trotted downstairs to the front door, arriving just as he opened it.

Beyond him she could see a huge, shiny new truck, glittering with raindrops as more pinged off its surface.

There were several items in the back, tall boxes covered in clear plastic to keep the rain off them.

She looked from the truck to his face and tried to ignore the warm, gooey feelings coursing through her veins. "What, they didn't have a bigger one?"

"Aw, come on, you don't like it? It's my trusty charger. My noble steed."

"I don't even care what you drove, I'm just *so* glad you're back." She was almost embarrassed by how emphatic she sounded, but it didn't even faze him.

"Yeah, me too. We need to talk." He looked worried.

"What's up?" She closed the door behind him.

"You first," he said, taking off his boots. "Whose car is that out there?"

"Nurse Ironbottom. Though she prefers Eloise. Doc Cartwright got busy and sent her to check on Mom, though I think he had ulterior motives."

"As in?" he asked, dropping his new keys into his coat pocket and then hanging his wet coat on a hook.

"He's been trying to get me to hire her as a live-in until the baby comes." She thought of the pendant. Coincidence? Would she sound insane if she told him about it? She hadn't yet decided. "But that isn't the big news. Mom's awake."

His head came up fast, eyes wide. "She is? She okay?"

"As far as I can see, she's fine. Certainly doesn't look like she's had a stroke or anything like what I was thinking last night."

"Did you ask her about the mead? The woods?" He moved to the fireplace and started adding a log as he spoke.

"I did. She doesn't remember a thing after getting in her car to come home. But I finally remembered to check the phone." She pulled it out of her pocket. "Take a look at these." She handed him the phone as they walked to the stairs together and started up.

He looked at the photos, frowning as deeply as she had. "Have you asked her about them yet?"

"Not yet. I want to wait until we're alone for that, and the nurse has been here ever since I saw them. It's hard to see, but it looks like some sort of a ritual circle. And that's where she was last night, before all this happened—but the thing is, they use Betty's back-yard for circles. These look like they were taken in the woods."

"We can upload them, see if we can enhance them at all, maybe get a better look at a face or two."

"Yeah, and I'll ask Mom if she took any pics last night. As soon as the nurse leaves," she whispered as they stopped at the top of the stairs. "If you click on the info tab, there should be a time stamp."

"Good thinking." He frowned, thumbing the phone. "Just after midnight."

"I was afraid of that."

He put a hand on her shoulder, and she felt heat rush straight to her toes. "Lena, there's something else you should know."

She gazed up at him, and if the circumstances had been less troubling, she would have been tempted to lean a little closer and see if he would turn it into a kiss. But the nurse came out of Selma's room into the hall just then.

"She looks very good to me. I don't see any reason to

be concerned. I gave her some ibuprofen for the head-ache. She ate her meal just fine. She's gone into the bathroom for a shower—told me to take a flying leap when I tried to go with her."

"Nurse Sheldrake, do you—"

"Eloise," she corrected.

"Right. Do you think it's possible she had a stroke or a TIA, as Doc Cartwright mentioned?"

"I don't see a single thing to indicate that."

"Well, then, what *did* happen?"

"I don't know. Frankly, we might never know. Did you phone Dr. Cartwright?"

"No, I…got distracted." She glanced up at Ryan, then looked away when he met her eyes. What was wrong with her?

"Well, I'll stop by on my way home and fill him in. Now, as long as I'm here, why don't I take a look at you?"

"No."

The nurse blinked at Lena's quick response and even looked slightly offended. "Are you sure? Dr. Cartwright says you've been under intense stress for the past cou-ple of days."

"I'm fine. My baby's fine. I don't need a nurse." Lena turned and headed right back down the stairs. "Thank you so much for coming by. I appreciate it. We've got an awful lot to do, though, so—"

She was at the bottom of the stairs by then, and since she'd kept on talking, the nurse had no choice but to fol-low. Ryan stood at the top, watching, looking surprised by her rudeness, but…whatever. She couldn't explain it. She just didn't like the woman. Nurse Ironbottom followed Lena to the door, and Lena took her raincoat off the hook and handed it to her.

Hint delivered. "Thanks for coming. Bye, now."

The nurse held her gaze for an extended moment, no expression visible. She was completely impassive. Not angry, not amused, not hurt, not impatient. Just sort of *there.* She put on her coat, and then, hat still bobby-pinned in place, headed out the door into the rain.

"I do *not* like her," Lena said, watching through the small oval glass inset until the nurse was in her car and bouncing back down the rutted driveway.

Ryan was halfway downstairs, but Lena headed right back up. "I'd better get into the bathroom, make sure Mom doesn't fall and bash her head in."

"Good idea."

"I know you wanted to talk about…something."

"And you wanted to show me something. Something about a storybook, you said?"

She looked at him. "Yeah. That's right." Then she gnawed her lip. "Later tonight, after Mom's in bed and we can be alone. Okay?"

"It's a date. I've got plenty to keep me busy until then."

She looked at him curiously, but he didn't fill her in. "You're heading back to those woods, aren't you?"

"Actually, no. I called Sheriff Dunbar on the way home. He asked me to hold off until tomorrow, so he could come along. Didn't want to risk my disturbing anything out there."

"You agreed?"

He nodded. "I think the rain's probably already erased anything we might have found, anyway. Another day won't make a difference. And I kind of like the guy. He seems…real."

"I've always liked Larry, too," she said. "He and Molly are a real pair of characters. Punch and Judy, only playful, you know?"

He nodded.

"So what's going to keep you so busy today?" she asked.

"I'm going to finish the baby's room for you. I know, I know. You had your own notions, and I'm gonna stick to them, just maybe add one or two of my own. And you're not allowed to see it until I'm finished."

She blinked. "You…know how to do that sort of thing?"

"I knew you'd doubt my construction skills. But yes, as a matter of fact I do. I actually do a lot of this sort of thing."

"How did I not know this?"

He drew a deep breath, let it out. "Because it was one of the parts of me I kept away from you. I was an idiot, Lena. Do you trust me now?"

Trust him? Trust him when he seemed to be trying to convince her he was the prince she had always believed him to be—after convincing her that he wasn't? Hell. "What if I hate it?" she asked.

He smiled. "You're going to love it. I promise."

"But what if I hate it?"

He crooked a brow. "Fine. If you hate it, we'll strip it back down to the drywall and start over."

"Promise?"

"Yes. Now go take care of your mother before she hurts herself."

So she did.

10

Aside from a big blank spot in her memory and a persistent headache, her mother seemed fine. Still, Lena spent the entire day sticking close to her side. She finished her stenciling project in the kitchen and decided to declare the rest of the afternoon a baking day. It was something she and her mom did every so often, especially on really cold days, so the oven would do double duty by heating up the house. Today wasn't particularly cold, but it was damp and miserable.

Her mom fell right into the rhythm. They spent hours mixing and kneading and rolling and measuring. And laughing. Lots of laughing. They had music blasting from the iPod, nestled in an impossibly small speaker dock that had concert sound quality. They sang along at the top of their lungs, puffed flour into each other's faces and tasted their efforts way too often, and they laughed until their sides ached.

They enjoyed each other. Always had.

It was a good way to distract herself from giving in to her curiosity about the nursery. Ryan had been upstairs all afternoon, and he'd made several trips out through the rain to the truck and back, carrying stuff upstairs each time. Big stuff. Lena smelled paint. She'd seen the cans he'd carried up the stairs, but it had been impossible to tell the colors. She'd already had paint picked out, and she hoped he wasn't replacing her colors entirely. She was just about dying to peek by dinnertime.

He came downstairs, not even a speck of paint to be seen anywhere on his person, the cheat. He'd showered, changed clothes. He took one look at the kitchen counter and his eyes went round. "Is *this* what I've been smelling every time I poked my head out of the nursery?"

"Uh-huh," Selma said, waving a hand like a TV spokesmodel. "Apple pie, carrot cake, chocolate chip cookies, cinnamon-swirl bread, whole wheat rolls and, since we had extra pie-crust, homemade chicken and veggie pot pies for dinner."

"This, after the night you had?" he asked.

"Pssh. Lena did most of the work."

But Lena saw the color rushing into her mom's cheeks. She was eating up the flattery.

And *he* was eating up the chocolate chip cookies.

"Dinner is only five minutes out," Lena told him. "Save some room."

"Oh, trust me, I'll manage to stuff it in." He popped another cookie into his mouth. "If I stay here very long I'll have to take up jogging again."

"Yeah, well, if you stay here very long," Lena said, "you can tag along behind me. 'Cause I'm gonna need to jog off a ton of baby weight pretty soon."

He stopped with a cookie halfway to his lips, and

his eyes took her in, head to toe and up again, slowly. "You've never looked more beautiful, Lena. And that's the truth."

Not only did the blood rush into her face, but hot moisture flooded her eyes, as well. She had to turn away to hide it from him, because it was so inexplicably sappy of her. Her excuse was to reach up into a nearby cabinet for dinner plates.

But he was behind her, pressing up against her back and reaching around to get the plates himself. "Let me do that. You should be sitting with your feet up. It was a long, hard night, and you've obviously been knocking yourself out all day."

She frowned and looked up at him.

Don't do it. Don't fall head over heels again, not until you know for sure he's not up to something.

But he *wasn't* up to anything. He couldn't be. She would know. Wouldn't she?

Both Bahru and the ghost tried to warn you. Maybe you should check the chalice again later. Maybe you can scry for the truth. It's the most powerful tool you've ever had. Use it.

Or maybe she could just check his cell phone. See who he'd been calling. If he'd been talking to a custody lawyer just before coming here, it would probably still show up in his call log.

Absolutely not. I'm not that woman.

"Lena?" Ryan was looking at her funny, probably because she'd stopped moving to have her internal argument. "Okay. I'll sit. Come on, Mom. You too."

"I think I could get used to this royal treatment, Lena. Maybe we ought to keep him around."

She was pretending to be teasing, but Lena knew she wasn't really.

Dinner was over and the dishes waiting for morning, because she was beat. But she and Ryan kept their date. Doc Cartwright had come by to quickly check on Selma, who had gone to bed afterwards, still seeming fine. Now Lena and Ryan were sitting together on the little sofa in front of a roaring fire.

Lena and the Prince in the Oasis was open on his lap, and he was smiling indulgently as he flipped the pages.

"I hope you're right and our baby is a girl, and I hope she's just like her mother," he said.

"That's a lovely sentiment, but it's not why I showed you these."

He met her eyes, and she swallowed hard. Nothing ventured, nothing gained. He thought he wanted her and the baby in his life, well, he might as well know it all. "I didn't just make up these stories, Ryan. I...I *saw* them."

"I don't...follow."

She pursed her lips. "I saw them in a magic mirror when I was first learning how to scry."

"Scry?"

"You know, when someone sees images in a crystal ball? That's scrying. We can do it in rippling water, in dancing flames, in black mirrors. The very first time Mom let me try it, I saw this entire story unfolding before my eyes."

He didn't laugh, didn't look at her as if she was nuts. That was gratifying.

"It's not supposed to happen that way. Usually you see bits and pieces, or symbols that you have to try to interpret. This was different. Powerful and full-blown. As a little girl, I thought they were dreams. Fantasies, you know? And so did Mom."

"Sounds like you don't think that anymore," he said, flipping another page, looking from the crayon drawings and painstakingly printed words on construction paper back to her.

"No, I don't. In hindsight, it's very clear to me that these stories were coming to me from a past lifetime."

"*Your* past lifetime?"

She held his gaze steadily as she nodded. And then she forced herself to say, "And yours."

He blinked. "Mine."

"You were the prince. I recognized you the very first time I saw you. You're identical."

"Well, yeah, clearly I have purple hair and everything." He was smiling, trying to lighten the mood a little.

Lena smiled back. "Obviously you're not identical to the drawings. I was barely eight. I couldn't draw what I was seeing. But what I *saw* in that mirror, and in my dreams so many times from then on, was you. Everything, your eyes, your smile, your mannerisms. I was seeing *you* in those visions. And I know it probably sounds crazy to you, Ryan, but I believe those dreams and visions are true. I believe we were together in another lifetime. Long ago, in some desert kingdom. I think...I think it was Babylon. And...I don't think it ended well. I think I was murdered. And you were trying to save me, but you couldn't get there in time."

"Holy shit. You're serious about this."

"I know, this probably makes you— Maybe I shouldn't have said anything, but…"

"Hey." He covered her hand with his. "It's okay, Lena. I'm starting to think there's more to all this stuff you believe in than I knew."

"Thanks for not laughing at me," she said.

"Maybe that's why you're having these weird dreams now, because you're…seeing me again. You think?"

"I think it's connected, but I just don't know how."

He nodded very slowly, his eyes thoughtful. As if he was seriously turning everything over in his mind, not just humoring her. "So that's it, that's what you wanted to tell me tonight."

"Yeah." She sighed, relieved that it was out and he hadn't reacted with disbelief or ridicule. "That, and that I think we found each other again for a reason. To make it right this time around somehow. Finish something we didn't get to finish back then. But yeah, that was it." She studied his eyes. "What did *you* want to tell *me?*"

He was staring into her eyes, seemed to have gotten lost in them, and then he shook his head a little and blinked. "Oh, right. Um… There were some guys in the hardware store today. They were talking about a couple of animal murders right here in Milbury."

"Animal murders? What…?"

"Someone apparently slit the throat of a calf last night and caught all the blood. They must have taken it somewhere for…something."

She grimaced at him. "That's terrible."

"They said it was the second time in a month. And when I kind of insinuated myself into the discussion, they asked who I was. I said I was out here visiting you, and the hardware store guy said he'd heard you and Selma were witches, and that these animal murders hadn't started until after you'd moved to town."

"Oh, *hell,* Ryan. This is awful. People out here won't understand, especially if they think we're out sacrificing baby animals by moonlight." A shiver whispered up her spine as she recalled sidelong glances and murmurs behind hands the last few times she'd been in town. She'd written them off as the result of old-fashioned attitudes about unwed mothers, but now she understood.

"It's more than awful," he said. "It's dangerous. And I couldn't help but wonder if someone else got the same idea and maybe did something to your mom the other night in the woods."

"Or not." She frowned, processing the thoughts swirling through her head into logical order. "She saw something out in the woods, right? Something that made her get out of her car and go out there for a closer look. She came across what looked like a ritual circle, and she must have thought it was important, because she took pictures of it."

"Did you ask her about those pictures today?"

"Yeah. She doesn't remember taking them. But she does remember her circle with her friends, and she says she definitely didn't take any pictures there. Which I pretty much already figured. It's very bad form to take photos in a Wiccan circle, especially when there are broom-closeted practitioners taking part."

"So she took the photos in those woods," Ryan said. "And *then* something happened to her. Maybe it wasn't someone blaming her for calf murders. Maybe it was someone trying to keep her quiet about them instead."

"But how? I mean, what the hell could they have done to make her lose her memory like that?"

"A roofie would do it," he said softly. "And they could have poured some liquor into her so everyone would assume she'd been drinking."

"Dammit, Ryan, I don't like where this is going. I don't like it at all."

He put a strong, reassuring hand on her shoulder. "I don't think you need to be too concerned. I mean, think about it. You've got some kids messing with the occult, they kill a couple of animals and maybe roofie your mom to keep her quiet when she stumbles onto them. That might be the extent of it. I'm betting they got a good enough scare by almost being caught to make them give it up, or at least take it somewhere else."

She shook her head slowly. "What if they're not just a bunch of kids who don't know what they're doing, messing around with the occult?"

He blinked, clearly not having considered that.

"Magic is real, Ryan. Dark magic as well as light. And the people who know how to wield it have real power. If they don't have a moral code along with that power—then they could be truly dangerous."

He nodded. "I'm not even doubting you on that. Listen, that's double the reason you and your mother need to be very careful from here on. Not just so you don't get blamed for what's going on, but so no one targets you for any reason." He sighed. "I'll watch your backs. You've got nothing to worry about as long as I'm here. I promise."

Lena looked up at him, and she went all soft inside. "I believe you."

He slid his arms around her, pulled her close, and slowly bent nearer, then nearer still. She felt his breath, featherlight on her lips, and let her eyes fall closed. "Ryan," she whispered.

And he kissed her. Just like that, he kissed her, and all her warnings about taking it slow, about making sure, about not falling for him again, melted away like snow in the springtime sunlight. She opened her mouth to him, and he tasted her with his tongue. She was on fire, her fingers splaying in his hair, her mouth feeding from his, reveling in his hands on her back and tickling up and down her nape beneath her hair.

The quiet chirping of his cell phone shattered the spell, and their lips parted, clinging, reluctant to let go. Ryan rested his forehead against hers. "Sorry. I'll shut it off." He pulled the phone from his pocket, and she lowered her eyes, since he was holding it practically under her nose.

Even though the caller's name was upside down, it was clear enough.

P. Reynolds Atty.

Atty? Attorney!

Something hammered in her chest, and she jerked backward, breaking contact. "Go ahead and take it. I… this was a mistake." She fled upstairs, heading straight into the temple room. He called her name, but she just kept on going. She didn't owe him any explanations. Bahru was right. He *had* been consulting a lawyer.

He just inherited several billion bucks, and a butt-

load of businesses, dummy. There are a thousand reasons why he might be talking to a lawyer.

Right, and Bahru's warning—not to mention the one from her own house ghost—were what? Coincidence?

"There's no such thing as coincidence," she whispered.

She took a deep breath, knowing by her frantic squirming that she was upsetting the baby. Okay, time to calm down. This wasn't good for either of them. She lit a few candles, enough to let her shut off the lights and still see what she was doing. And then she opened the big old cabinet that lined one wall and inhaled the scents that spilled from it. The familiar aromas she associated with witchcraft soothed her mind instantly. Sandalwood, sage, mint, roses, vanilla, her personal favorite, dragon's blood, and more all mingled together in an almost visible cloud. They were a trigger for the ultra-calm state of mind known as alpha. The state in which magic could occur.

She reached up unerringly, plucking out a tiny bundle of white sage and sweet grasses, dried and twisted together with a few of their own strands. When she touched the ends to a candle's flame, the dried herbs flared to life, snapping and sizzling. Flames leapt high and hot. She gave it a beat or two, then blew out the fire. Now the herbs wafted fragrant smoke in spirals and swirls.

Her mind grew calm and her body relaxed, nerves uncoiling. She carried the smoking herbs to the little table near the window, picking up the vulture feather that rested there. Illegal to possess, she knew, but the huge turkey vulture had dropped it for her, so she considered it a gift, one she could not refuse. Picking it up, she used the feather to wave the smoke around her body, bending to waft it over her feet and up her legs, moving the smoking bundle behind her and then in front again, lifting it higher, until she reached the top of her head.

When she felt perfectly cleansed of every negative vibe, she moved around the room, still wafting the smoke with the vulture feather, sending it into every corner, nook and cranny, and ending where she had begun. Then she tapped the bundle almost out in a little dish and let it lie there, a few ribbons of smoke still winding up from it.

With her hand held palm out, she projected energy. It wasn't imaginary. It wasn't visualization. It was genuine energy. She could almost see it beaming out of her palm, painting a path of white light as she cast a circle in the room.

Here, in this room, she never took the circle down, just reinforced it every time she needed to work magic. This room was sacred space, and nothing evil could get inside. Only goodness. Only love.

By the time she finished her preliminary steps, she was feeling very calm, very peaceful. She went to the cabinet again and took out the chalice Bahru had given to her. Since her first experiment with it had been almost frightening, she decided to cleanse it and bless it, which she did quickly and easily, as any seasoned witch could. It didn't require a big elaborate rite. She wafted a little smoke from the still-smoldering sage bundle over the cup. Then she moved the cup through the candle's flame. She drizzled it with holy water and sprinkled it with sea salt, and then she held her hand over it and beamed that same white light energy into it. And it was done.

"You serve the gods now, little cup, and likewise you serve me. Nothing evil, only love. Now show me what I need to see."

After pouring a bit more holy water into the chalice, she sat down on the floor, her legs crossed, the cup in the crook of them, and gazed down into the water. Her breathing slowed and softened, until it was nearly impossible to tell where inhale ended and exhale began. It was all one flow, like the waves of the ocean. She felt the air swirling around her nostrils, rushing along her windpipe, filling her lungs, dancing out into the room again. Focusing on that allowed all other thoughts to cease. When they tried to return, she gently tugged her attention back to the breaths moving in and out, in and out. Her eyes relaxed, her vision going blurry.

Soon she felt herself sinking into that beautiful, blissful state of oneness with the All. Her body was no longer an individual being but rather a vantage point for spirit. A vehicle for spirit to ride in during its journey through the physical realm.

Clouds formed in the cup, swirled and parted.

"Show me what I need to see," she whispered.

And then she was no longer in her temple room but in her bedroom, floating on the ceiling, looking down at her own body in the bed. She was sweat-damp and straining, and her knees were pointed ceilingward and parted, toes curling and digging into the mattress as she pushed.

Doc Cartwright was there. Nurse Eloise, too. And

Mom, but she was in a chair in the corner, slumped to one side. Sleeping?

Dead?

Panic clutched at Lena's heart, but she ignored it and fought to stay focused.

Ryan was there, Bahru right beside him. Thank God. She would be all right. And the house ghost—he was there, too, hovering in the corner like a thick, vaguely human-shaped pillar of black smoke. He was far denser than he'd ever appeared before, and much more *real* looking. Less like a shadow. More like a being.

Then she was both hovering by the ceiling and in her body in the bed, and she was in pain. The baby was coming. She felt her little girl's head pressing through her into the world, felt as if she was being torn in two. And the ghost in the corner opened his eyes, like darkness parting to reveal fiery red orbs.

Suddenly she was afraid. She looked up, saw Ryan pulling that golden blade from its sheath and raising it above her, point down. His eyes were red, and he was wearing a crystal on a silver chain around his neck.

Three firm knocks on the door yanked her out of the vision. She dropped back into her body so abruptly that she felt the impact as if she had physically fallen to the floor.

She gave her head a shake and tried to catch a final glimpse of the vision in the cup, but there was only water. She'd lost it.

Sighing and fighting not to allow anger into her sacred space, she parted the energy curtain with a sweep of one arm before opening the door.

Ryan met her eyes. "Did I do something to make you angry?"

"I'm busy right now."

His gaze darted past her, taking in the dancing candles, the smoke hanging in the air, then the chalice on the floor. "Wow, that's…that's something. That cup. Where did you…?"

"Your father left it to me."

His brows went up. "He did?"

She nodded.

"Does it…*do* anything…you know…unusual?"

Lena blinked. How could he know that? "What an odd question. Why do you ask?"

"Humor me. I'm opening my mind about all this, and I have a good reason for asking. Trust me."

Unfortunately, she *didn't* trust him. Not enough. Yet she didn't see any harm in being honest about the chalice. "It's pretty amazing, actually. I use it for scrying."

"But that's nothing you haven't done with other cups and mirrors and stuff, right?"

"True. I've done it all my life."

"But with this cup, it's different?"

"Yes, it is." Lena frowned. "It's more powerful. Even a little scary at times."

"Yes. Scary," he said softly, nodding. "So what do you do about that? When it's scary, I mean."

"Just keep working with it, same as I would with any new tool. The more you use it, the more it becomes like an extension of you. Like driving a car, you know?" Her irritation with his interruption was quickly being pushed aside by her love of talking about her favorite subject and her genuine pleasure at his interest, which still seemed sincere. She leaned against the door frame. "Remember being sixteen and behind the wheel for the first time? How you felt completely out of control behind the wheel? Maybe you were even all over the road. But now you drive almost without thinking. It's automatic. You've sort of melded with the car, like it's an extension of your body. Magical tools are like that."

"I'd never thought of it that way."

"Of course, I cleansed it first."

"Cleansed it?"

"Yeah. I mean, I do it with any new tool, but especially one that feels at all…scary. It's a simple rite to get rid of any negative energy that might be clinging to… Why are you so interested in my chalice all of a sudden, Ryan?" She suddenly wondered if he was wearing a hidden recorder, trying to gather evidence of her nontraditional beliefs to use against her in a custody battle.

Stupid thought. He would never.

Oh, yes, he would. The guy he was back in New York would, anyway. The prince he'd been in a former life? Not in a million years. The guy he was trying to convince her he was now? Well, that remained to be seen.

He shrugged. "You're the mother of my child. I think it's important that I understand your…belief system."

"The same belief system you once called 'cute'?"

He nodded. "I've apologized for that. More than once, I think."

She just stood there, waiting.

He finally sighed. "Look, I don't know what happened downstairs, but…I don't have a single regret except that we were interrupted. And I want—"

"I'm not ready, Ryan." She shook her head, sighed,

looked at her feet, then met his eyes again. "Okay, I suppose it's obvious that I still have feelings for you. And the fire between us…that hasn't gotten any smaller, either."

"Bigger, I think."

She wanted to bask in that reply. But she clenched her jaw and resisted. "Ryan, you know how I am about honesty, so I need to be honest with you now. The truth is, I don't trust you. I don't know what the hell you're really doing here, or what you really want from me, and I'm just not ready to put my heart or my child into your hands. Not yet. I need to take this slow. Okay?"

He studied her eyes for a long time. "Okay. I guess I deserve that. But…Lena, is it that you think I'm only pretending to still have feelings for you, because of the baby? Because that's not true. Even Bahru will tell you that's not true. I've been miserable since you left. I wish my father was still here. He'd tell you." He looked at the chalice. "Maybe you could ask him yourself."

"Maybe I will."

He nodded. "Okay, I… You take your time. I'm not going anywhere. And, um…I'm sorry I interrupted your…ritual."

"It's okay."

"Okay. Well. Good night, I guess."

"Good night, Ryan." She closed the door, swept the energy curtain together again. "I want to believe him so, so freaking bad," she whispered.

Ryan took her rejection on the chin and told himself he just had to work his way past it. Hell, he'd only been there a couple of days. He couldn't expect her to believe in the new and improved Ryan two-point-oh he was trying to sell her in so short a time. He'd spent way too much time selling her the old version. Ryan one-point-oh. Or one-point-a-hole, which he figured was probably more accurate.

It was going to take some time.

Meanwhile, he thought she'd given him some massive insights into what to do about that crazy-ass magic knife his father had left him. He needed to practice with it, to master it. But first he needed to cleanse it.

She'd started getting suspicious about all his questions, so he'd had to let that part go. But he knew where he could find the answers.

In the attic, in those boxes upon boxes of books he'd carried up there only a couple of days ago. So that was where he headed. Part of him wanted to get back to work on the nursery, but he couldn't really paint until the primer was dry enough, which meant tomorrow morning, so he had nothing but time on his hands tonight.

He found a handy spot on the attic floor and then began pulling the volumes out of the boxes, one after another, flipping through them in search of an explanation on how to "cleanse" a magical tool.

An hour later he'd found what he needed, a list of numerous methods of cleansing objects.

1. Tie the object up tight in a netted bag, like the kind onions come in, and drop it into a running stream. Weigh it down with rocks or tie it to something so it won't float away, and leave it there for three nights.

Well, that was simple enough, but it would take too much time.

2. Bury the object in salt, or in the earth itself, and leave it overnight.

That might work.

3. Bathe the object in an infusion of mugwort and—

No, that wasn't any good. He wouldn't know a mugwort from a toad's wart.

4. Lay the object out in direct sunlight for three full days.

Too likely it would be seen. And too much time again.

5. Cleanse and consecrate with holy water, sage smoke, candle flame and sea salt inside a ritual circle.

He didn't know enough to do that.

It looked like number two was the one. He just needed a small shovel, and he prayed he could find a patch of ground that wasn't too frozen—though that shouldn't be a problem, given the mildness of the winter. He already knew where he was going to start looking for the right spot. That little patch of trees out back, at the edge of the lawn, where he'd first experimented with the blade. That was it.

Lena frowned at the computer screen where she had uploaded the photos from her mom's cell phone and clicked the "enhance" button. There was clearly a fire, and there were several figures standing around it, but they were all covered from head to toe in dark, hooded robes. Like monks' robes.

She glanced at the stairs, then at the front door. The computer desk was nestled in the little bank of bay windows in the deepest part of the living room. Ryan had gone out. He hadn't taken the truck, so he was either out walking or he'd gone over to see Bahru. Not very likely.

He wasn't around, though, so she minimized the photo-editing software, opened a private browsing tab, so there would be no trail in the history, and then typed *P. Reynolds Attorney* into the search bar. Her finger hovered over the enter key. Should she do this? It was an invasion of privacy. And yet, if he was laying the groundwork to fight for custody of their daughter, she needed to know, right?

Lena hated dishonesty, along with lying and sneaking and covert actions of any kind.

But for her baby, she figured she could put her values just very slightly aside. Decision made, she tapped Enter. In seconds the search results came up. The very first one was Paul Reynolds, Family Law Attorney, specializing in Marital and Custody Law in New York, N.Y.

"Son of a—"

The door opened, and she closed the screen so fast anyone would have thought she'd been caught watching porn. Then she looked up at Ryan, her heart breaking. Because it was true. He was talking with a custody lawyer. Damn him for getting her hopes up. She tried not to look guilty, even though she'd obviously had good reason for her snooping.

Then she realized he was looking guilty, too. Avoiding her eyes and wiping his hands on his jeans for some reason.

"What have you been up to?" she asked him.

"Just walking around, looking at the stars, thinking."

"Oh." Lies, all lies.

"You?"

"Oh, um, I've been playing with those photos on Mom's phone. Want to see?"

"Dying to." He pried off his shoes. Mud was caked on the bottom. Then he headed into the kitchen and washed his hands. "Can I bring you something?" he asked. "Personally, I'd like a hot cocoa. All this tea we drink around here is fine, but sometimes you just need decadence."

She smiled, growing warm. Loving him. Then she squashed it all down. "Cocoa sounds great. If you use two packets in a big mug and add whipped cream, it's even better."

"I'm all over that." He rattled around in the kitchen. She took the time to make sure that her recent web search had indeed vanished from the history and then shut the browser down.

A few minutes later he brought in the cocoa, whipped cream piled on top like soft-serve ice cream on a cone. He handed her a cup, and she made a heartfelt "mmm" sound and took a sip.

When she lowered the cup, he looked at her, and there was something beaming from his eyes that looked like adoration. Yeah, he was that good. "How did I ever think…no, never mind." He reached out to touch the tip of her nose and said, "Whipped cream. Just a little."

"Oh." She lowered her eyes. It would be too easy to believe what she was seeing in his.

"What did you find out?" he asked.

Her head came up fast. "F-find out about what?"

"The photos?" He was looking at her oddly, as if he'd totally noticed her defensiveness. She might as well have blurted *"I wasn't snooping on you!"*

Oh, right. She nodded at the screen, where the first image was enlarged but blurry.

He frowned at it and said, "I'm really sorry if this offends you, but that photo gives me the creeps."

"Why would that offend me?"

"Well, they're witches. Aren't they? The fire, the robes, they're standing in a circle, in the woods, at night...."

"I don't think they're witches." She put her finger on the screen. "No cords. Witches who wear the same ritual robes would more than likely be part of a coven. In most covens there are cords to signify the various degrees. A novice wouldn't have any cords, but after a year and a day of study, should he or she pass muster, he or she would become an initiate, a first-degree priest or priestess, and would normally receive a cord. A second-degree, or adept, would get a second cord, and a third-degree, or master, would have three cords. Sometimes an elder receives a fourth."

"Do you have cords?" he asked.

He seemed genuinely interested. He was awfully convincing, if it was all an act. She wasn't usually easily fooled. "No. Mom and I are—well, not exactly solitary. More a fam-trad. Family tradition."

"Like Hank Williams Junior?"

She grinned, growing warm again, then forced it away. "We don't do cords or degrees. We just...*be*."

"You're a rebel, even among witches. I should have known. So you don't think the people in the photo are a...fam-trad?"

"No. Those robes are dark. Formal. But no cords. I don't think they're witches at all. I don't see any of the traditional tools of the Craft nearby. Do you see a chalice or candles, a sword…anything?"

He leaned closer, scanning the screen, and she felt his breath right on that sensitive area where her neck met her shoulder. She wished he would put his lips there instead. No, she told herself, she didn't.

"Not a pentacle in sight. Just them."

"We witches like our stuff. We take rattles and drums into circle with us. We wear our pentacles outside our robes, we don't hide them within, not in circle. And the hoods. The hoods are weird."

"I can't see a single face," he said. "Just those damn hoods."

"It's like they planned it that way."

He nodded. "I'm going to walk back out there tomorrow. *With* the sheriff or *without* him. In between working on our little guy's room." He gave her a grin.

"Girl. She's a girl. I hope you're trusting me on that as you work on her room." *And why is he doing all that anyway, if he's planning to take the baby and leave?*

"I'm making it unisex. We don't want her growing up thinking she has to love pink just because she's female, do we?"

"You know me too well." She blinked slowly and pushed her chair away from the desk, then got to her feet. "It's late. And I get tired really easily these days."

"I'm not surprised. You've been carrying a lot of extra weight around—not just physically, either."

He straightened, clasped her shoulders, looked into her eyes. "Good night, Lena."

She could tell that he wanted to kiss her, but he was waiting for her to make the first move, to lean closer or close her eyes, or even just lick her lips. A signal. She sighed, wishing she could trust that his concern for her was real, and forcibly lowered her head.

He let his arms fall to his sides, and she felt his disappointment wash over her.

Just as if it was real.

Turning, she headed up the stairs, checked quickly on her mother—who was sound asleep—and went into her room. As she closed the bedroom door behind her, she glimpsed that shadowy form, now so familiar, lurking near her window. She waved dismissively at it. "Go away. I've got no patience for you tonight."

Do not trust him.

She had accompanied her command with a flick of her hand, as casually as she would tell a dog to "go lie down," and she had fully expected the house ghost to comply.

But he hadn't. He'd pressed his message into her mind instead. And that made her stop in her tracks. Since when could a ghost refuse to obey the command of the home owner—particularly if that home owner was a witch?

She blinked at the shadowy form, wondering for the first time if it was really a ghost at all...or something else. Because a ghost should have vanished almost before she had finished telling it to. Oh, it might have come back later, but...

This dude was breaking the rules. "What are you?" she asked.

You must send him away. Send him away now.

"I asked you a question," Lena said, her voice soft

but firm. "You're not a ghost at all, are you? What *are* you, then? And why are you here?"

No reply.

"I command you to answer me. What are you, and why are you here?"

It refused to respond. She felt its resistance, like a solid brick wall, and then she felt more. Anger. Rage. Menace.

The child in her belly kicked her so hard she gasped in pain and pressed her hands to her belly. And then there was a rush of silence, of emptiness, and she knew the being had gone.

11

The shadow dissipated, vanished. Just like that. Lena rubbed her arms and decided a major house cleansing was in order. She was no longer comfortable with that dark presence hanging around.

Moreover, she was sick to death of beating around the bush with Ryan.

He had gone to bed. She'd heard him come up while she'd been arguing with the ghost, or whatever it was, in her room. So she flung her door open and marched across the hall, opened his without knocking and walked right in as if she owned the place—because she did.

He looked up fast, his expression guilty again. He'd been reading in bed, and she was stunned to see the titles, not only of the book in his hands but the other three lying open, facedown, on the bed beside him. Every single one was about the practice of witchcraft.

He set the books down as she frowned at him. "You okay? Is your mom—"

"Fine, I just— What's up with the books, Ryan?"

He shrugged. "Like I told you, I want to know about…you know, what you believe in. And you got so suspicious when I asked you that I figured I should just find out for myself. Seemed like everything I could ever want to know was probably in those books up in the attic, so I picked a few that looked interesting and brought them down for some bedtime reading."

She drew a deep breath, sighed and reaffirmed that honesty was the best policy here. Because what if he was being sincere? What if he really meant it when he said he wasn't the man he'd been pretending to be?

Moving closer, anger dissipating, she sank onto his bed. "When we were kissing before, and your phone rang…"

"Yeah?"

"It was a lawyer."

He blinked. "Yes, it was. How did you…?"

"The phone was practically under my nose and I saw the caller ID. "

"Oh."

She swallowed hard, lifted her chin and went on. "I looked the name up online tonight. I know it was really awful of me, snooping like that, but I had my reasons. He practices family law, Ryan." She watched him closely, probing his eyes, waiting for the guilty reaction, but there wasn't one. "Are you planning to fight me for custody of Eleanora?"

He blinked three times, slowly, and then he smiled. "Eleanora? That's what you want to call her?"

She lowered her eyes, trying not to sigh in frustration. "That's her name. She sort of…told me." Glancing up at him nervously, she added, "But if you don't like it…"

"I think it's beautiful."

"You do?"

"Maybe I can pick the middle name?"

Shrugging, she chose not to answer. "What about the lawyer, Ryan?"

"Paul is my best friend. My only real friend, I guess. He happens to be a lawyer, but he's not working for me. Not in any way, Lena."

"Then…then you weren't discussing a father's rights with him?"

"No. I wasn't."

Lena frowned. That meant Bahru had lied to her. But why?

"Paul has a side project going with a small group of engineers and inventors, and I'm funding it."

She set aside her concerns about Bahru, for the moment. "I didn't know that."

"No one knows that. I've kept it very quiet."

"But why?"

"Frankly, because I was still trying to keep my façade intact. You know, unattainable, irresponsible, self-centered playboy. It would have blown my image. And besides, I didn't want my father or his boards of directors swooping in trying to take it over."

She was even more interested now. "You think they would have done that?"

"If they thought they could make a profit off it? Sure they would. And it's not that kind of a project. It's not about profits. Not yet, anyway. Maybe someday, but the important thing is to get it up and running."

Sinking onto the edge of his bed, she let herself indulge her curiosity. Everything about him was fascinating to her, especially now that she was—maybe—seeing the real Ryan. "What kind of project is it?"

He closed the book with a snap and set it aside, then yanked his laptop from the nightstand and opened it, excitement glittering in his eyes. A few keystrokes later she was looking at a full-color drawing of a sprawling field filled with solar panels.

"Solar farms, but with a twist. Paul's group is buying up land with excellent sun exposure all over the country and installing these solar panels that follow the sun's motion across the sky."

Lena frowned in thought. Not because of what she was seeing on the computer but because of what she was seeing in his eyes. Something she had never seen before.

He spun the laptop toward him again, clicked a few more keys and spun it back. Now she was looking at schematics or blueprints or something, and it was completely Greek to her.

"This is the home conversion kit, the key to the whole thing. The batteries that store the excess energy will be small and affordable, unlike the bulky, pricey ones available up to now. Plus they've come up with these conversion kits that they're going to provide free of charge to every household within range of the solar farms. The goal is to make everyone in the immediate vicinity of our farms one hundred percent solar by the end of the first five years. The people would pay only for the energy, not for the equipment. And we'd guarantee to keep even that cost capped at whatever the big power companies are charging. But that means the initial funding really has to come from investors. The start-up costs, the equipment costs, the research and development, and then buying the property, all that is expensive."

"Millions."

"Billions," he said. "But if we passed that cost on to consumers, no one would be willing to convert. Most couldn't afford it even if they wanted to. This way the investors take it on the chin, absorb the loss and accept that it might be up to twenty years before we can expect to see any of this even begin to turn a profit."

"Then why do it?" she asked, watching his face, awaiting his answer.

"Somebody's got to." He shrugged. "I don't want my father's money. I'd give it all to Paul if I could."

She was completely stunned. "How long have you and...Paul been working together on this?"

"Five years. But I only handed over the big bucks last year."

"I wish you'd told me."

Sighing, he closed the computer. "You worked for Dad. You were his PR wizard. Him getting involved in something like that would have made for excellent press. I just...didn't want that."

"You didn't trust me."

He lowered his gaze, so she knew she'd nailed it.

"But it was more than that. I told you, I pretty much haven't told anyone. This was *mine*. My own thing. I wanted to keep it that way. And Dad had taken enough from me." He rolled his eyes. "I mean, not *from me, but—*"

"That's exactly what you meant."

He frowned.

"I get it, Ryan. I don't think *you* do just yet, but you're getting closer." She put her hand over his. "I'm sorry I jumped to the wrong conclusion. So then, you're not planning to fight me for custody?"

He met her eyes, held them steadily. "Losing my mother was the worst thing that ever happened to me, Lena. I would never deliberately put my own child through that."

She believed him and nodded to tell him so. "Okay." And then she smiled a little. "Okay."

He seemed relieved. She got up from the bed, ridiculously glad she'd decided to just be direct and ask him for the truth instead of keeping tight-lipped and making flawed assumptions. "Thanks for telling me about it, Ryan. And you can trust me to keep your secret until you're ready to go public." She smiled again. "But when you do, man, is New York society in for a shocker. 'Cause you're right about one thing—this is going to set your irresponsible, lazy, entitled image on its head."

"I don't care what New York society thinks about me. I really don't."

"Good for you." She nodded slowly. "Good for you, Ryan." Then she indicated the books. "If you want a little more info on magic and ritual, let me know. Okay?"

"Thanks."

She backed out of the room, pulling his door closed behind her, and then stood there for a long moment, just feeling.

A huge weight had been lifted from her shoulders, that was the first and clearest sensation making its way into her awareness. She believed him. She knew, though, that there was more. Lots more. His issues and feelings about his mother, his father, even Bahru, were all tangled up with this new zeal for her and the baby. And though that interest might be real, it wasn't…gut-deep. It was all mental. He wanted them on a practical, logical level. But she still didn't feel it was coming from his heart.

And though she would far rather err on the side of believing in him completely, she still sensed he was holding something back, maybe keeping a secret.

But it was progress, that was for sure. It was progress.

The crack of dawn found Ryan kneeling on the damp ground, digging in the soft soil and tugging out the magic blade. He had the box open beside him, because he didn't want to handle the thing too much this close to the house. Lena had said the key was practice. So practice he would.

He tugged the knife out of the cold, wet earth still encased in the sock he'd used as a temporary sheath. Then, holding the toe of the sock, he more or less poured the blade out into the box, managing not to handle it much in the process. Even just nudging it with his fingertips to get it into place for transport made him jumpy.

But no flames shot from the thing, and he sighed in relief.

It was only seven, and barely light outside. He'd noticed that the women tended to get up and around by nine, and today had been no exception. No one else had been awake yet. He had time to work with his dagger. Besides, he'd been wanting to get back to those woods where Selma had been wandering to see what he could see in the light of day.

It had grown colder overnight, so the rain had turned

to snow. But now the sun had returned, and the temps were already above freezing. The dusting of snow that had fallen overnight wouldn't cover much—assuming anything was left—and it would probably be gone within a couple of hours.

Clutching the box under one arm, he walked around the house and down the driveway to the dirt road that flanked the field and then the woods on the left, opposite Bahru's cottage. He had to walk right past the place but didn't sense any movement from within. Maybe the guru was still asleep, too. He hoped so. He wanted privacy for this.

The field was mostly weeds and dead grasses, stiff and brittle now. It had been a vineyard once, and he could easily visualize it being one again. Grapevines abundant in neat rows, lush and deep, dark green leaves, heavy bunches of purple fruit dangling, glistening with morning dew.

It was a nice vision, one he would like to see realized.

If he wound up staying.

Hell, he'd pretty much given up the idea that he would be living anywhere else. If Lena and his child were here, *he* would be here. If Lena wanted them to be together as a family—well, he could get into that. It made sense. They got along, they had great chemistry. He honestly loved being around her.

Yet, when he thought that way, there was a part of him that wrapped itself up in emotional Kevlar. As if just thinking along those lines made him vulnerable to the same old patterns his life had shown him so far. People didn't stay. He had to keep that in mind right from the get-go, so it wouldn't hurt as much when they checked out.

He never wanted to feel again what he'd felt at the death of his mother. He never wanted to feel the way he'd felt when his dad just up and left him.

But mostly he never ever wanted the death of one person to have the same life-altering impact on him that the death of his mother had had on his father. It had destroyed him.

He would never let that happen to him. Never.

The field gave way to trees, white birch and pine, looking like a Christmas card. He kept walking until the dirt road ended in a T junction at the pavement. Then he turned left, walking along the front edge of the woodlot until he reached the spot where Selma's car had been parked. The tire tracks were deep enough to still be visible on the soft shoulder. He left the road, hopped the shallow drainage ditch and entered the woods right where she must have.

Only a few steps in, he had to stop for a minute just to indulge in the sensory feast of this place. There were so many birds singing that it was hard to believe it was real. It felt like an overly ambitious Disney soundtrack, but it was real. There were squawks and caws, but also tiny little flute solos and full symphonies being played just for the sheer joy of it. And the smells! God, he'd never breathed such delicious air. The pines and their tang, and the rich, earthy scent of damp soil and decomposing twigs, leaves, conifer needles and cones, all mingled with every breath. He wished he could bottle that smell, but he knew he couldn't, because it was all tied up with the coldness of the air and the touch of the morning sunshine. And you couldn't capture that.

This place was amazing. No wonder his father had wanted his grandchild to grow up here.

After basking in his surroundings for a couple of minutes, he shook off the pleasure and continued on. He had a two-pronged mission this morning, and he hoped to get back to the house before anyone knew he'd been gone, so it was time to get moving.

He followed the occasional print where Selma's small foot had sunk deep enough into the soft, wet earth that an impression still remained, and when he couldn't find any more prints he chose a landmark: a pine tree that stood taller than those around it and had a large bird's nest way up near its crooked top. From there he walked in increasingly larger circles, keeping the tree as his center, in hopes of finding anything that might qualify as a clue.

On his third circle, he did: a charred log that stood in sharp contrast to the dusting of white snow clinging to one side of it and to the ground nearby. Moving closer, he bent and brushed the snow away. No question, the log had been burned. And as he explored the area around it, he found other partially charred branches and several blackened coal-sized chunks on the ground.

Someone had made a fire out here, then scattered its remnants. To make it harder to spot?

He straightened, looking around the area. If those bits of wood were from the fire Selma had photographed, it must have been nearby. He doubted the robed figures in her pictures would have carried charred logs far—especially if they'd still been hot, even smoldering. Hell, most likely they would simply have kicked the smoking coals around and called it good.

So everything must have happened here. Right here.

Looking around, he asked himself where he would make a fire if he were looking to start one in this vicinity and noticed that the trees here seemed to form a natural circle. The middle, about five yards to his right, would make a good spot.

He walked over and looked at the ground in search of any sign of a fire, certain he was in the right place but not seeing anything to prove it. And then he stopped and shivered. Damn, the temperature seemed to be dropping all of a sudden. He'd expected it to get warmer as the morning progressed.

He flipped up the collar of his denim coat, looking up as he did, and found himself staring at the trunk of a white birch tree dead ahead of him. It had been smeared or splashed with red paint. In fact, so had the one beside it.

Frowning, he turned in a slow circle and realized that all of the trees surrounding him had been daubed with red. A near-perfect circle of red-stained birch trunks.

And the red, he knew with sudden perfect clarity, was not from paint at all.

Lena headed downstairs to put on the coffee and found her mom in the kitchen making her famous blueberry waffles. Well, famous to the two of them, anyway. And to Ryan. Lena had spoiled him with her mother's recipe before they'd split up.

"Ahh, perfect timing," Selma said, smiling at her

daughter. "Admit it, you smelled them all the way upstairs."

"I did. Ryan better get his butt out of bed soon or he'll miss out."

"Oh, he's up. I just saw him outside, sticking something in his shiny new truck. Did you notice he bought the one with the backseat?"

"Why would I notice something like that?"

Her mother gave her that "we both know better" look, and Lena didn't argue. Of course she had noticed. He was thinking about the baby.

It also occurred to her that she was dying of curiosity to know what he had just been putting in that truck. And yet snooping on him had only led to a horrible misconception earlier. She wasn't going to go against her own values and repeat the mistake. If she kept looking for trouble, she would surely find it. Right?

He came in through the front door with an armload of firewood, stomped the mud and snow off his boots, and deposited the logs in the rack near the fireplace. A good thing, too, as the fire had burned down to embers overnight.

"It would have taken me four trips to bring in that much," Lena called.

"Would've taken me five," her mother said. "You're getting extra blueberries in your waffles this morning, Ryan." She reached into the bowl for a handful and sprinkled them into the already blue-stained batter, moving her hand in a clockwise circle and saying, "You fit right in our little nest. I hope you'll stay. I think it's best."

"Mother!"

Selma sent Lena an innocent look and shrugged. Poor Ryan was just frowning at them, clueless that Selma had just tossed a little magic his way.

Ryan went back out for more firewood, and Lena joined her mother at the counter, wiggled her fingers over the waffle iron. "Free will to all and harm to none—"

"And as I will, it shall be done," Selma put in quickly. Then she slanted Lena a look. "Don't try to out-witch your mother, dear."

Lena grinned at her. "Things between us are nowhere near where you think they are yet."

"I love that you said 'yet.'" Her mother shrugged. "They'll get there. It's meant to be. He's your prince, after all."

"I hope so. But he's still very…what's the word? Practical. Just…too logical, you know?"

"Hmm. Maybe protecting himself?"

"I think so. And speaking of protecting, we need to do a little house cleansing while he's working on the nursery today."

Selma frowned as if perplexed. "A cleansing? Why?"

"I don't think our ghost is a ghost. I'm starting to feel…very uneasy about it. It spoke to me—twice now. Both times to tell me that Ryan is not to be trusted."

Selma's frown became a look of surprise. "Why would it tell you that?"

"I don't know."

"Do you think it might be right?"

Lena shook her head, surprising herself by her own certainty. "I don't think so. I mean, what does *your* gut tell you about Ryan, Mom?"

"I like him. I've always liked him. I think he'll make a great father. And I think he's wounded, way down deep, and doesn't want to address it. I get the feeling it's festered and healed over, and it needs to be lanced to let the poison out."

"Me too. That's exactly the sense I'm getting. That's why he's so…careful."

Selma took the first two perfect waffles and dropped them onto a waiting plate. "So if we're right about him, then it's our ghost who's lying." She tipped her head to one side. "Maybe he's jealous. I mean, we pick him up as a masculine entity, right? He's had us all to himself up to now. Maybe it's just a guy thing. Territorial or something."

"Well, even if that's what it is, it's negative, and if it escalates it could be dangerous. I think it's time to send him packing to wherever he belongs. Agreed?"

Her mother nodded. "I've got some asafetida tucked away for just such an occasion."

"And some air-freshener for afterward, I hope."

"Ryan's back with more wood. Get the door for him, hon."

Lena headed to the doorway but caught her mother muttering something as she dusted Ryan's waffles in powdered sugar. *"Mom,"* she warned.

Selma glanced at Lena over her shoulder and winked.

Ryan had learned a lot last night while perusing those books. More, in fact, than he'd ever needed to know about the lesser known uses of daggers. Or athames, as the witchy types called them. He had already known that they were phallic symbols. But he'd discovered that they were associated with the fertilizing force of the masculine aspect of the divine. A God-Rod, so to speak. In magic, they were used to control and direct energy, and one was never supposed to cut anything physical with one's ritual blade.

None of which told him how to wield his. But practice, he thought, would make perfect.

He spent the day painting the nursery and by mid-afternoon had finished. The ceiling and every bit of wood trim were all done in a soft eggshell color. White would have been too harsh. The walls were two-tone, a pastel sea-foam green from floor to waist height, and a slightly lighter-than-sunshine yellow from there up. The paint needed to dry before he could move on to the small hand-stenciled border and the giant animals. He had it all planned out in his mind.

It was kind of surprising to him how much pleasure he was taking in this project. Probably because it was for his own child.

His own child. Imagine that.

Someone knocked on the nursery door. Frowning, he went to it and, standing close, picked up a rancid scent. "Who is it?"

"It's me," Lena said. "I need to come in."

"You can't. It'll ruin the surprise. God, what is that smell?"

"Just open the door a crack. I promise I won't peek. Okay?"

"All right." He looked behind him and could have sworn he saw a shadow move in the corner, but then it was gone. So he cracked the door, peeked through and saw smoke, then drew back in disgust. "God, that's rank!"

"That's the idea." She thrust an oblong shell, filled with smoldering weeds, through the door at him. "Take it."

He took it, and she handed him a feather, too.

"What the hell *is* this?"

"Asafetida."

"Smells like the ass of something-dead-it-a."

"That's the idea. It's also known as Devil's Dung. I want you to walk around the baby's room wafting the smoke with the feather and visualizing anything negative being driven out. Understand?"

"As fast as humanly possible. Got it." He turned.

"The other way."

"What?"

She pointed. "Widdershins. Counterclockwise."

"Naturally." He pushed the door shut with his foot and, grimacing, waved the smoke with the feather. "Ghosty, ghosty, go away, don't come back another day. Get your ass away before she finds some stuff that stinks much more!"

He heard her giggle from outside the door, completed his lap around the room and shoved the shell out at her.

She poked a small, pretty bottle through next. "Now draw an equal-armed cross—like a plus sign—on every window, and on every electrical outlet and register."

"What is this, and what's it do?" he asked.

"Holy water. Keeps what we just booted out from coming back in."

"Ah. Gotcha." He closed the door and dampened his finger in the water from the bottle, drawing the cross everywhere she'd told him to. "Why do I feel like I should be speaking Latin?" he called.

She laughed again. He felt warm at the sound and then wondered why that warmth was suddenly chased away by an icy chill. As if someone had just opened the door of a giant walk-in meat locker right behind him.

He stopped what he was doing and frowned, turning in a slow circle, but of course nothing was there. Still...

He went back to the door, opened it just enough to squeeze out, bottle and all, then pulled it closed behind him. The stench wasn't left behind, though. It permeated the entire house.

"God, what have you two crazy women *done* to this place?"

Lena shrugged. "I thought it was time we got rid of our ghost. He was starting to make us feel uncomfortable." She rubbed her arms and looked nervously around. "Frankly, I was expecting a little resistance from him, but I guess he wasn't all that strong."

"Well, the smell certainly is. How soon can we air the place out?"

"After a few hours." She walked with him down the stairs. Selma was going around "sealing" the windows and doors just as Ryan had done in the nursery. Lena set the bottle of water on the coffee table, then tamped out the foul-smelling weed before sinking onto the sofa.

For a second, Ryan just stayed where he was, standing in the doorway, staring at her. All that wild red hair fell around her shoulders in curls he'd always loved. He remembered them falling onto his chest at night, tickling his face during sex. They'd always been so silky-soft beneath his palms. And they'd always smelled of incense and exotic smokiness. Magic. Her hair smelled like magic.

Well, most of the time. He figured right now it probably smelled like Devil's Dung.

She looked up, caught him staring, smiled. "What?"

"Let's go out for dinner," he said, finally shaking himself free of the spell just looking at her could cast. "Let's get out of this house for the rest of the night so the stinky smoke can do its work, and when we get back we can open all the windows for a while and air it out. Okay?"

He saw her delight at the idea right there in her face, but only briefly. She chewed her lip a second later. "I don't know if I want to leave Mom when there's so much going on."

"Don't be silly," Selma said. She was capping her bottle, apparently finished. "Go on, have fun. I can probably have the place smelling like home again by the time you return."

"Come with us, Selma," Ryan told her. "I have a brand-new truck neither of you has even ridden in yet. And you know what? On the way back from town I noticed this restaurant right on the lakeshore. It looked like the kind of place you'd love."

"I know the one you mean." Lena looked at her mother. "The Southern Cross. Remember?"

"Mmm, nice place."

Lena frowned. "It's a bit of a drive, though."

"You have a pressing appointment?" Ryan asked.

She smiled down at her bulging belly. "Not for a few more weeks." Then she nodded. "What do you say, Mom?"

"I say I'm perfectly fine staying home by myself. My goodness, I don't need a babysitter."

"Yeah, but Mom—"

"I want you two to go. Have a beautiful dinner and take your time. I'm going to take a long, hot bath full of scented bath oils, and by the time I'm finished, it'll be time to open the windows."

Lena looked at Ryan, and he frowned. He didn't like leaving Selma, either, especially given her recent health scare.

"Look, Bahru is just a few steps away if I need him," Selma said. Then she blinked as if puzzled by her own words, shook herself and went on. "But I *won't* need him. Plus the sheriff's two miles away and Doc Cartwright's even closer. If you don't go, it'll hurt my feelings."

"We really need to get a phone or something hooked up out in Bahru's cottage," Lena said, eyeing her mother and looking hesitant.

"I can flash the outdoor light to get his attention if anything goes wrong. But it won't. Lena, I swear, I have been fine on my own for years now. I had one bad night. A very *oddly* bad night, but still, I promise you, I'm fine."

Lena nodded slowly. "All right. I guess you're on. Let me just change into something less…fragrant."

"Fantastic, I'll warm up the truck," Ryan said.

He was going to call Sheriff Larry while he was alone, tell him what he'd found in those woods and ask him to check in on Selma tonight. He didn't think telling Lena he'd found blood—probably all that missing calf blood—on her property would be a very good idea.

Stress was bad for the baby, and her knowing wouldn't do her any good, anyway. She needed less to worry about, not more.

Damn, but he was going to wine and dine that woman tonight, he decided. Okay, not literally—she couldn't have wine. But still, he needed to remind her how good it had been between them once. It made sense for them to be together as a couple, to raise their baby together as parents, so she—or *he,* he reminded himself—could have the childhood she deserved.

He was going to talk to her about that tonight. And she would hear him. He knew she would. It was all going to be okay.

If he could just get that smell out of his nostrils.

When he stepped out the front door it slammed behind him—*hard.* So hard he damn near jumped out of his skin, then spun to look back at it.

He looked through the glass pane. But Lena and her mother were right where he'd left them, though they were both staring at the front door as if they were as startled as he was.

He shrugged at them in a "damned if I know" way and headed out to start the truck. Must have been a draft.

12

Lena was excited about her night out with Ryan. He was her golden prince, after all, and she'd waited a long time for him to start acting like he was acting now. Attentive, kind, interested in her spirituality and, apparently, in being a parent.

There was still something lacking, though. The passionate *I'll-wither-and-die-without-your-love*-ness of her desert prince. He was still very practical, caring, polite, but…ah, hell, she didn't know. She told herself that maybe that part of it had been only her own fantasy all along, not a true memory. More like wishful thinking. But then again, it felt real and always had. And she wanted it. Whether it had been true in the past or not, she wanted it now. Fire. Passion. Someone who would kill for her, would die for her, would give his all to make her his own. Instead of waiting around for her to chase him.

Still, tonight was progress, and Lena was glad. So they climbed into the giant truck, and he pointed out its many high-tech features. "There's a backup camera," he said, pointing at the screen. He even demonstrated when he put the truck into Reverse and it showed a wide-angle—almost fish-eye—view of what was behind them.

"Nice," she said.

"Navigation system." He punched in the information and hit Search, and within seconds their fully mapped route popped onto the screen.

"That's fantastic. Mom would love to have one." She nodded at the dash. "Sound system?"

"With satellite radio."

"You thought of everything." And had shown her everything, too, she thought. Except for whatever he'd hidden away in the big truck.

"They hated to part with it. It was their floor model, the one they use to show off every imaginable extra. But I wanted the best, all the safety features. They even threw in a top-of-the-line baby seat, but they had to have it shipped from the manufacturer."

She couldn't stop her adoring gaze from roaming his face, and hoped it didn't show too much, how this touched her. "You're really excited about being a father, aren't you, Ryan?"

He slanted her a smiling look but let it die, his eyes turning serious. "More than I ever imagined possible." He had to look back to the road, but he wasn't finished. "If you decide you don't want me at Havenwood, I'm going to buy a place as close as humanly possible."

"I guess that would be the log cabin perched on the hill above us. You can just see it from the second floor of the big barn. I'll have to show you sometime."

"Is it within walking distance?" he asked.

"Yes, if you're up for a hike. There's a path through the woods—not the woods Mom was in but the patch off the other side of the drive, between the house and the lake."

"Uh-huh."

"You head out to the cliff about halfway up the mountain and then twist back the other way up a pretty steep slope. There's a log cabin up there. Really nice. I think it's owned by a priest."

"Really?" He shrugged. "Well, priest or not, I'll bet I could make him an offer he wouldn't refuse. Though I really hope I won't have to."

He was asking. Or was he?

It was so hard for her not to scream *Yes, yes, yes!* and say to hell with everything else. But she wasn't yet sure of him. He wasn't giving her all he had to offer. And there was still the dream of him getting ready to drive a blade of gold into her heart. The silence was becoming awkward as she tried to figure out her reply, and then she was saved by the navigation system.

"Turn right ahead," it said, in an inflection-free female monotone. "Then take the highway."

"Huh," she said. "Your GPS sounds just like Nurse Ironbottom."

"It does, doesn't it?" He laughed.

Great. Tension broken.

As they drove onto the more well-traveled highway and headed south, the evening skies changed.

Lena looked through the windshield and pointed at the oddness unfolding in the sky. "What the hell, Ryan?"

He frowned, too, easing off the accelerator. Earlier they had been treated to a clear blue sky that had darkened as nighttime gathered, dotted with twinkling stars that had blinked on one by one at first, then two by two.

But now a thick black wall was literally crossing the sky in front of them. On their right the sky was still clear and star-spattered. On their left a towering smoke-black cloud looked like a dark curtain being pulled across the universe, dragging an ice storm and tree-bending wind behind it.

"That came out of nowhere," Ryan said, slowing still further, cranking on the wipers as the sleety mixture began to pound the windshield. He strained to see. The sleet was horizontal, dense as a deluge. The wind blew so hard it actually forced the huge black truck to shudder. "I can't see crap. We need to pull over."

There was a flash, and she jumped. "My God, was that lightning? In January?" She knew it was by the crack of thunder that followed. It resonated in her chest as she hugged her belly in the instinctive need to protect her child.

Ryan continued driving, or trying to, with visibility down to a few feet, at best. He inched the truck forward in search of a safe place to stop, so they wouldn't get rear-ended by another vehicle coming from behind—although at that point the road seemed deserted. Still, he couldn't stop in the middle of the lane. That would be suicidal.

And then suddenly something *huge* came crashing down as if from the sky, landing crossways in front of the truck, hitting so heavily that it felt as if the vehicle bounced up into the air with the force of its impact.

Ryan hit the brakes, and Lena braced her hands on the dash and thanked her stars she was buckled up as the truck came to an abrupt stop.

It was a tree, a giant tree, with a trunk three feet in diameter and limbs reaching up as high as a house, dark against the night, wet with the freezing rain that was rapidly becoming a coat of ice.

"Are you okay?" Ryan asked.

She nodded, then realized he wasn't even looking at her and said, "Yeah, I think so." They sat there, the windshield wipers snapping back and forth at full speed, staring through the storm at the enormous tree. Lena was shaking, vibrating with an awareness that was only just beginning to make its way into her brain.

"Turn around," she said.

Ryan nodded, the motion jerky, and he managed to back up and turn the large truck until they were facing the other way. He started toward home.

Within seconds the storm stopped.

The skies ahead were clear. The clouds skittered away, leaving a pristine starlit night ahead. Lena looked back. The tree was still there, but the sky was clear in that direction, too. Even weirder, it was also clear to either side—including in the direction the storm had been moving.

"Ryan, pull over and look back."

He did, coming to an easy stop on the shoulder and turning in his seat to stare behind them. "It's gone. Where the hell did it go?"

"I don't know, but that was just…weird."

"More than weird." He pulled back onto the road.

"You're right, more than weird." She swallowed hard. "It didn't feel natural to me, Ryan. It felt…it felt *super*-natural."

He smiled over at her, not like he was happy or playful, but with more of a comforting smile, like he was trying to be reassuring. He put his hand over hers. "Well, maybe you're in a bit of a supernatural state of mind right now. I mean, you and Selma *did* just perform a full-fledged, foul-smelling, ghost-be-gone ritual, after all."

"Mom!" Lena's heart thudded hard against her rib cage. "We need to go home right now. This was related."

"I really don't think—"

"Please, Ryan?"

He met her eyes, nodded. "Okay. Okay, we'll go home.'"

"Just…drive fast, Ryan. I've got a bad feeling."

Lena burst through the front door, Ryan at her side.

Selma was standing in the middle of the living room, looking around with round eyes.

"Mom, I—"

"Shh!" Selma held up a hand. "Listen."

They went still. In the silence they heard a distant rattling sound, like a vibration. At first Lena thought the heating system was responsible. Maybe the furnace was shuddering or there was air in the pipes, or… But then it grew louder.

The windows were all open. She knew, because she felt the cold draft wafting through the house. They must have been open for a while, because the smell of the Devil's Dung had dissipated, and the scents of lemon balm and mint had replaced it.

The vibration got louder. The cool breeze lifted her hair and sent icy chills down her neck.

"There are storms in the area," Ryan whispered. "We should close the windows."

"I did—twenty minutes ago," Selma replied, speaking very softly, her wide eyes meeting his.

Suddenly the rattling and the wind died at the same time.

Selma stayed where she was, standing in the middle of the room looking ready to flee. "That wasn't... earthly."

"Neither was the freak storm that came out of nowhere, knocked a giant tree across the road in front of us and then vanished without a trace," Lena said.

"Freak storm?"

"Thunder and lightning, Mom. In January. In upstate New York."

"But you're okay," her mother said, looking her up and down as she came closer. "You're okay, right?"

"I'm fine."

"Me too. I'm fine, too," Ryan said.

Selma looked at him and smiled. "I'm glad. And how did the new truck fare?"

"Not a scratch."

"Well, thank goodness for that." She drew a deep breath, looking around the house. "Something's going on here," she said. "Though whatever it is, it seems to have calmed down for the moment."

Lena did not like the feeling that her haven had become unsafe. "Do you think our house cleansing today—"

"Pissed off our supernatural houseguest?" Selma interrupted. "Yeah, I'd say so. Big-time."

"I don't think he's a ghost, Mom."

"No. Neither do I."

Lena hugged her mother. "What are we going to do?"

Ryan was looking at them oddly. "You two really think you have a ghost who's not a ghost, and that he got mad because you tried to bust him today?"

"Yes," Lena said.

"And that this...this thing, whatever it is..."

"I'm leaning toward demon," Selma said.

"Maybe a really pissed-off Elemental," Lena suggested.

"And you think this *thing,*" Ryan went on, "managed to throw a storm and a stray tree at us out of anger?"

"Yes," Selma said. "Yes, that about nutshells it, wouldn't you say, Lena?"

"Uh-huh. And if he can do that, it worries me what else he can do."

"Come on, now. I mean, I'm trying to keep an open mind, but you guys are over-the-top here."

Lena rolled her eyes at him. "Don't you *feel* it, Ryan? Just stop thinking with your damned logical mind for two minutes and *feel,* will you? Something is wrong here. It couldn't be more obvious to me if there were a fire-breathing dragon in the middle of the living room."

"We'll figure it out," Selma said. "Maybe you should try scrying in that chalice again, Lena. I know it's been frightening for you so far, but there must be a reason you received this powerful tool just before all this began to unfold. You know there's no such thing as coincidence."

"You're right. I'll try, Mom."

"And as for you, Ryan, you keep an open mind. Okay?"

Ryan sighed, then nodded. "Okay, consider my mind

wide open. Now, in the meantime, does anyone care if I order pizza? I'm starving here."

Lena nodded. "Go ahead, Ryan." She watched as he went to the kitchen and picked up the phone, then shook her head at her mother. "He just doesn't get it."

"He said he'd keep an open mind." Selma sighed. "I'm beginning to think we ought to take a little vacation from here—at least until the baby is born. Just in case. What do you think?"

"I think that's a really good idea, Mom. Maybe we can go back to Brooklyn? Or maybe Ryan would let us stay at his dad's place until…"

"I'm sure he wouldn't mind. We can decide everything else later." Selma looked at Ryan. "I wish he believed. You know, *really* believed."

"So do I," Lena whispered. "But you can't believe in magic without being in touch with your own emotions. And he's keeping his all walled up inside him." She sighed as she gazed into the kitchen at him, willing him to remember the prince he had been—the man she had loved. No. The man she *still* loved. The man who had loved her back. That was the man she was missing. Aching for. Dreaming about.

"Tomorrow, honey," Selma said. "We'll get out of here tomorrow."

Selma and Lena saw reasons for everything, Ryan thought, as he stood in that tiny copse of trees in the backyard after the women had gone to bed. To them, everything that happened was some kind of sign, all of it fitting together like the pieces of a big paranormal jigsaw puzzle.

Well, hell, there was definitely something going on, and it was definitely something weird. And they were the experts on weirdness. So if they thought it was all part of something bigger, then maybe he should be thinking the way they were.

What if he was here for a reason? What if his coming here when all this was going down was part of some bigger plan? If that were the case, what could that plan be? What was the reason for his presence?

Well, the obvious answer was that he was here to protect them. Lena, the baby, even Selma. Things were happening around them, dangerous things. Selma in the woods the other night. Locals murdering calves and doing God only knew what kinds of rituals in the woods, either trying to frame the two innocent witches or for some other nefarious purpose. The house ghost who wasn't a ghost and could conjure storms, hurl trees, rattle pipes and blow cold wind through a house with all the windows closed.

There has to be a logical explanation for everything.

Right. And what about the knife? Was there a logical explanation for the knife?

There has to be a reason why you received this powerful tool just before all this began to unfold. Selma's voice rang clear in his mind as he stared down at the engraved, antique box. *You know there's no such thing as coincidence.*

Ryan picked up the knife from its red velvet nest, bracing himself for it to come to life. If there really was no such thing as coincidence, then he'd received the blade for a reason. And since that reason could not possibly be to thrust it into Lena's heart, despite what she'd dreamed, it must be to do something else.

But whatever it was, he had to master the thing first.

He held it upright, its blade aimed toward the night sky, and felt torn between *God, I must look ridiculous* and *God, I feel like some storybook hero.*

And then he thought, *Storybook. Lena's storybooks. She thinks I really am some kind of storybook hero.*

Can I ever live up to that?

He looked at the blade. "Work for me, dammit."

It spat a few sparks into the night. He drew it back down and, very intently, pointed it at a tree and tried to mentally force it to release a blast of energy. He actually *pushed,* but the knife only glowed.

He lowered it, shook his arm to loosen the muscles, raised the knife again and this time took aim at a rock. *Blast it to pieces,* he thought.

Nothing.

He took a deep breath, lowering the blade again, then closed his eyes and tried to gather his focus. Finally he raised the knife again and aimed it at a clump of weeds that were swaying in the breeze.

Still nothing.

"I knew it wouldn't work. It's not possible for a knife to shoot fire, and if I think I've seen proof otherwise, I must have been hallucinating. Because knives do not have supernatural powers. Even ancient golden ones."

In frustration, he stomped back toward where he'd left the box. "Freaking thing. The question is, how am I supposed to use it to protect my—my *family*—if I can't even get it to--" A blast shot from the tip, nearly hitting him in the foot.

He dropped the blade and jumped away from it. *Dammit!* What the hell was he missing?

Carefully he moved the open box next to the knife and managed to get the blade in using the toe of his boot. He slammed the box shut and carried it back around the house, then returned it to its spot under the front seat of the truck. He locked the doors, dropped his keys in his coat pocket and went inside, prepared to spend another long night reading and researching.

Lena couldn't sleep. Something was very wrong. She had an entity in her home that was furious about being forced to leave and kept trying to tell her not to trust Ryan. She had a man in her house who refused to believe, even though he said he was keeping an open mind and pretended to be trying to learn about the ways of magic. He might be trying, but he simply *couldn't* believe. He was out of touch with his own feelings, and magic and emotion were so tightly entwined that one could not exist without the other. And beyond that, she had a very strong intuition that Ryan was still keeping something from her, starting with what he was hiding in the truck. And that bothered her, given her recent dream.

So when she saw that truck light come on outside, saw him tucking something under the seat and then locking the vehicle up tight with the remote, she made up her mind. She had to know what he was hiding out there. *Had to know.*

He dropped the keys into his coat pocket. She went to the top of the stairs and hid in the darkness, then watched from there as he came back into the house, shrugged off his coat and hung it on a hook near the door. And her decision was made.

She waited until he'd returned to his bedroom. Even after that, she gave it another hour, pacing her bedroom floor in her socks, trying to be quiet so he would drift off to sleep and she could go snooping.

Snooping. God, she hated the idea! She was racked with guilt before she'd even done anything. And yet she had to know. She'd been hurled back and forth with the shifting currents of her belief in him. Not her love for him, never that. But dammit, she had to find out about his feelings for her, had to know whether they were genuine, even if shallow and cool. She got up, crept to his door, which was slightly ajar, and peered inside.

He'd fallen asleep reading. His head was crooked over onto one shoulder, his dark hair falling across his forehead in a way that made her ache to tiptoe closer and smooth it out of his eyes. But she resisted that urge and backed away.

Softly, so softly that her steps made no sound, she went down the stairs and to the door. As she slipped her hand into his coat pocket she caught his scent in the fabric, and her heart twisted into a knot. God, she loved him. And she hated spying on him this way.

She cupped the keys in her hand, so they wouldn't jingle, slid her feet into a pair of boots and didn't bother with a coat. She would only be a minute.

Twisting the doorknob as gently as if it might break, she opened it, almost holding her breath, willing it not to creak or groan, then breathed a silent thank-you when it didn't.

She stepped out, closed it behind her ever so carefully, and then she turned and faced the big black truck. Everything in her rebelled against doing this. Sneaking, spying, snooping, deception, they were the last things she had ever thought she would do.

And yet she found herself walking down the porch steps and across the crispy frosting of ice on the ground to that truck. She turned to look up at Ryan's bedroom window. Empty. Taking the key ring from her pocket, she clicked the unlock button and the truck obeyed with a snapping sound.

Her hand trembled as she touched the driver's door, and the night wind drove goose bumps across her skin as she pulled it open. Swallowing hard, she reached beneath the seat and felt a box there. She pulled it out, admiring the elaborately engraved wood. It looked like an antique.

Don't do this, Lena, her mind told her. *Just slide it back under the seat. You don't have to look. It's not too late. Stop now, before it is.*

"I have to know," she whispered.

Bracing herself, she opened the box.

And there was the knife. The golden athame she had seen in her dreams—her nightmares. The one she dreamed Ryan used to kill her. She flashed on the recurrent vision again. Saw him standing over her bed with the others all around, wearing those stupid crystal pendants, their eyes gleaming red as they reached for her baby and Ryan, her child's father, lifted the knife and prepared to drive it straight into Lena's heart.

It wasn't a dream. It was a premonition. A warning. The ghost was right. So was Bahru. She *couldn't* trust

Ryan. He wasn't seeing a lawyer to steal her baby girl from her. He didn't need to. He was just going to murder her instead.

The next morning, she managed to keep her horror from showing, or hoped so, anyway. She hadn't told her mother yet, because she would want to murder Ryan if she thought he was a threat to Lena and the baby. And not Bahru, because she hadn't seen him yet. But she was remedying that now.

Right after breakfast she had piled a basket full of fresh fruit, a couple of blueberry muffins and some of her mother's specially blended teas, and tucked a towel around the lot of it, and now she was on her way to see Bahru. A shiver ran up her spine as she passed by the big black pickup truck with that golden blade hidden inside.

She kept telling herself that there could be a dozen reasons why Ryan would hide the blade away, keep it a secret from her. But that dream kept returning, fluttering through her mind like a giant hairy moth, confronting her with the vision in which he plunged that blade straight into her heart in the seconds after their baby was born.

Her dreams were never without meaning. Even if they sometimes seemed random and nonsensical, they always made sense eventually. And yes, sometimes in hindsight the meaning turned out to be something far different from what she had at first believed. But it didn't seem there were too many ways to interpret this one.

Were there?

Bahru opened the door to her knock and greeted her

with a genuine smile. "I am so glad to see you, Lena. Come in, come in. How are you feeling?"

"Tired, stressed. A little bit paranoid, maybe. But I think the baby's fine. How about you?"

"Good," he said. "I am very content here." He closed the door behind her as she entered his cottage. She handed him the basket, and he moved the towel aside to see what it held as she shrugged off her coat and stepped out of her boots. "Oh, this is wonderful. Thank you, Lena."

"Don't thank me. It's a bribe. You mind if I sit?"

"Of course not." He quickly set the basket on the small wooden table and pulled out a chair for her. "You're troubled, you have been since we arrived here. I can see it in your eyes. What's happened, Lena?"

She sighed, wondering where to begin. "Well, a lot, actually. There's a ghost in our house…or something. It's never been a problem before, but now I'm feeling impatience, even anger, from it. And it feels…I know this will sound odd, but it feels possessive of me."

He nodded slowly, his eyes hooded, as if he were looking inward. "Yes, I, too, have sensed the presence in your home," he said, stroking his beard. "But the energy I picked up was more protective than possessive."

"Protective? Really?"

He nodded again. "Yes, definitely protective."

"I guess it makes sense, then, that it would be acting out more now that Ryan is around. It doesn't seem to like him. Even warned me not to trust him."

He watched her, listened intently, but didn't say more.

"Bahru, do you think Ryan is capable of harming me?"

His eyes widened. "Why would you ask such a question?"

Lena got up from the table, paced slowly away. Bahru sat down, the picture of patience. "I keep having this dream about having the baby. You're there, and Doc Cartwright, and that nurse he keeps pushing on us, Eloise Sheldrake. And Ryan's there, too. You're all standing around my bed, and he's right beside me. Mom is in a chair in the corner, but she's either asleep or unconscious or...or I don't want to think what."

"Bizarre."

"Oh, I'm just getting started on the bizarre part. Everyone's eyes are glowing red," she said. "And they're all wearing quartz pendants, like yours." She frowned as Bahru lifted his necklace and examined it.

"Where did that come from, Bahru?"

He smiled. "I was meditating in a cave not far from here the last time Ernst and I came to town. We were just getting things ready to put Havenwood on the market. I'd discovered the cave before and been drawn to it. Always...so drawn." He had a faraway look in his eyes, and his voice had softened, deepened.

"And...?"

"I found a very large deposit of quartz, and I just couldn't resist helping myself to the few pieces that were loose. It felt...it felt like they were meant for me. Like a gift. I kept one for myself and gave the rest as gifts to people who admired them. They're harmless, Lena. I promise you."

She sighed, nodding slowly. "I don't know why they would seem so important in my dream," she said softly.

"Nor do I. But go on. Tell me the rest. You are in

your room. We are all there around you. And you're about to give birth."

She nodded. "The ghost, or whatever he is, he's there in another corner, watching, waiting, bigger and... denser than ever before."

She paused in her pacing to look at Bahru. He was listening intently.

"I feel the baby emerge from my body. And I feel consumed with fear. And then I look up to see Ryan raising this blade up over me, like he's going to plunge it straight into my heart."

Bahru jumped to his feet. "*Ryan* is holding the blade?"

She nodded, pacing away again. "I wake just as he starts to bring it down, but I feel the horrible pain in my chest even though the dream is over. Bahru, what can it mean?"

He was standing in front of his chair, his palms pressed to the table. He opened his mouth, closed it again, then closed his eyes and took a deep breath, as if he had to steady himself. Softly he said, "In the dream, what does the blade look like?"

"It's very unusual," she told him. "Gold, not silver or stainless. The hilt and the blade are both covered in odd etchings, symbols, like some kind of ancient writing. Double-edged. Like an athame."

She shook her head slowly as the guru listened. He rubbed his hands together as if they were cold, and his eyes were so intent on her that she knew this all meant something. "There's more. I can see there's more," he said softly.

She nodded, swallowing down her fear and heartache and nerves. "Bahru, I told Ryan about the dream. He swore he would never hurt me. But I saw him hiding something under the seat of that new truck of his, and I couldn't bear not to know what it was. So last night I sneaked out there after he'd gone to sleep to take a look." She closed her eyes, shaking her head as she lowered it in shame. "I know it was wrong."

His hands on her shoulders startled her, and she looked up fast, surprised he'd crossed the room so quickly.

"What did you find?" he asked.

"The blade from my dream. The same one."

"Ryan has the blade?"

A red flash in his eyes made her suck in a sharp breath and jerk backward, so that his hands fell to his sides. "What the hell was *that*?"

13

Bahru frowned. "What was *what,* child?"

"Your eyes. Your eyes, they just… They were…"

His expression turned to one of extreme sympathy and concern, and he studied her with care. "Dear, sweet Lena. You asked for my advice, and I will give it to you now. I believe you are suffering from an extreme amount of stress. It makes sense, with your body in flux, your hormones raging in your bloodstream, your mother having just suffered a health scare. You've lost a friend in Ernst—more than a friend, the grandfather of your child. And you've been reunited, for good or bad, with your baby's father. I believe the things you've been observing of late are more medical than magical. The nightmares, the fear, the hallucinations—symptoms, Lena, not events."

"I did *not* hallucinate that blade."

"Are you sure, Lena? Are you *very* sure?"

"Positive." She'd backed up all the way to the door and was reaching behind her for the knob, fumbling to grasp it.

"It makes no sense for you to be afraid of Ryan, nor

of me, Lena. Think about this. Neither of us would harm you, not ever. I distrust Ryan, but I know he wouldn't physically hurt you. And I've lived my entire lifetime as a pacifist, you know that."

"Yeah. I know. It's fine. I have to go." She got hold of the knob, twisted the door open and all but stumbled outside.

"Talk to Doctor Cartwright, Lena. At least consider that there might be more at work here than you realize."

"Sure, I'll do that." She turned and ran down the three short steps to the driveway, then kept on running until her side cramped up so bad it almost put her on her knees. As she stumbled to a stop, bending over and clutching her belly, that black cat darted across the drive in front of her and vanished into the woodlot that overlooked the lake. *Black cat crossing my path. Again. This can't be good.*

Panting to catch her breath, she turned and looked behind her.

Bahru was nowhere in sight.

Then she straightened, rolled her eyes at her own panic and realized how ridiculous that thought was. As if Bahru would be chasing her through the snow in his flowing robes and sandals. What the hell was wrong with her? She started walking again, limping due to the hitch in her side.

His eyes flashed, dammit. And not for the first time.

Come on, Lena, her logical side argued. *You know magic isn't about special effects and flashing eyes. It's about focus and will.*

That chalice sure is a special-effects machine, though. I mean, it's not like any sort of actual scrying

*I've ever experienced before, not mental images but
real ones, real visuals and an almost time-travel sort of
effect, the way it sucked me in. What about that, huh?*

Well, what if you hallucinated that, too?

She reached the house, breathless, mounted the steps
and stumbled inside to find her mom and Ryan in the
living room, holding mugs of cocoa, smiling and apparently in the middle of a conversation—until they
looked her way. Selma pressed her fingers to her lips
and her eyes widened. Ryan slammed his mug on the
coffee table and crossed the room in two long strides, his
arms going around her shoulders fast, as if he thought
she was on the verge of collapse.

"What happened? Are you okay?" He helped her to
the sofa and lowered her onto it.

"Where were you?" Selma asked, bending over her.
"Hell's bells, your face is as red as a beet!"

"I'm fine." Lena tried to straighten, but her mother
pressed her down onto her back, while Ryan moved to
her feet to pull off her boots.

"Guys, really, I'm fine. I just...I spooked myself and
ran a little, which is really not a great idea when you're
carrying a watermelon in your belly."

"I'll get you some water," Selma said. "Or tea. Yes,
tea."

"Some of that cocoa you guys are drinking sounds
better." She tried to inject some lightness into her tone,
but Selma still looked worried as she hurried to the
kitchen.

Ryan helped her sit up, his arm wrapping around
her, and it was so much like an embrace that her heart

tripped over itself in response. Stupid, if he was just going to stab her later. And yet she couldn't help herself.

It would be wonderful, really, if all this really were due to some kind of hormone-induced mental lapse. Women went crazy from hormones sometimes, right? Postpartum psychosis was real enough. Women heard voices, believed them, did terrible things. Not that she would ever—*could* ever—harm her daughter. But still, it happened. So what about *prepartum* delusion? Was that even a thing?

She let Ryan peel off her coat, and then he lowered her back down and took the boots and jacket away. He set the boots by the door, hung the jacket on one of the hooks there. Selma was rattling things in the kitchen.

"So what spooked you?" he asked.

Lying, sneaking, they just didn't suit her, despite her actions last night. "I was talking to Bahru, and I swore I saw his eyes glow red. Just for a second. But it seemed so real. And in that dream I had, that nightmare vision thing, everyone's eyes were glowing red, and it scared the hell out of me."

He frowned hard. "That dream where I'm going to stab you?"

She nodded. "Yeah. That was what I went out there to talk to him about. I thought he might have some… insight."

"And did he?"

She pressed her lips together and swallowed hard. "He thinks I've gone mental due to stress and hormones."

Ryan lowered his chin, sighed soft and deep.

"You agree with him?"

He met her eyes, and his seemed…angry? No, that wasn't it. Intense. No, not that, either. Something she hadn't seen in them before. And then he said a single word that shocked her right to her toes. He said, "No."

"No?"

"No, Lena, I don't think you're *mental*. I think there's something going on here, and I'm damn well going to find out what." And then his face softened. *Way* softened. His eyes were swimming, and he stroked her hair up off her face and back behind her ear. "Are you sure you're okay?"

Okay? She was baffled. If he was planning to kill her, why wouldn't he agree with Bahru and try to convince her that she was having a preggo-induced nervous breakdown? And why was he looking at her now just the way she'd been dreaming he would look at her since the day they'd first met—in this lifetime, at least?

"Yeah, I'm okay."

He put his hand on her belly. "How about you, Peanut? You okay, too?"

The baby kicked, right on cue. And Ryan's face lit up like a kid's on Christmas morning. His smile was full and genuine, and his eyes gleamed. Not in a demonic way, like Bahru's had, but in a beautiful way. "It's like she's answering me."

"Maybe she is. She's a witchling, after all."

He met her eyes, his smile fading slowly. "Thank you, Lena. I haven't said it, but…thank you."

Lena blinked. "For what?"

"For this." He ran his hand over her belly. "You didn't have to keep her. It's just now hitting me how hard this must have been on you physically, to say nothing about—"

"It's not hard, Ryan. It's…magical. And blissful. And beautiful. I'm in love with her already, and she's not even here yet."

"I am, too."

Oh my Goddess, she thought. *I believe him.* He loved their baby. She no longer had any doubt about that. *But what about me?* her heart cried. *How do you feel about me?*

Her mother came in with the cocoa, looked at them briefly, and then the worry in her eyes evaporated. "Here you go, honey."

"Thanks, Mom." Lena blew on the top of the mug, then took a tentative sip.

"Ryan was just saying he was ready to show us the nursery," her mother said. "Weren't you, Ryan?"

"I just have to pick up a few drop cloths. There's no furniture yet, no curtains, but I can't wait for you to see it."

Lena stared at him with what felt like puppy-dog eyes as he backed away and darted up the stairs like an excited kid. God, she loved him.

Please don't let him be planning my murder!

As soon as he was gone, she turned to her mother. "I want you to do something for me as soon as Ryan and I go upstairs."

She frowned. "What, honey?"

"His truck keys are in that coat pocket." Lena pointed at Ryan's big fleece-lined denim coat, hanging on the hook beside her own. "Take them. Go out there and look under the front seat, driver's side. Tell me what you find there."

Her mother's frown deepened. "What do you *think* I'm going to find there, Lena?"

"An ancient ritual dagger tucked inside an ornate wooden box. The box looks a lot like the one my chalice came in." That was the first time she'd put those bits of information together in her mind, she realized. And since the two tools were intimately connected, there must be something there, something more for her to mull on. But first she had to be sure the knife was really there.

"Either it's real and he's hiding it from me for some reason, or I imagined or dreamed it was there. I need to know which it is. Please?"

Selma's concerned eyes searched Lena's face. "Are you sure you're okay, hon?"

"I honestly don't know, Mom."

Ryan came back downstairs and held out his hand toward her. "Ready?"

Lena nodded and started to get up, but before she made it to her feet he jumped over the coffee table and grabbed her hands to help. Something had changed in him. She was sure of it. He led her to the stairs, and they started up. She spared her mom a parting look full of meaning, and Selma gave a firm nod. She would do what Lena had asked her to do.

Then Lena turned her focus to the nursery door, which was standing slightly ajar. They reached it, and Ryan pushed it wide and opened one arm with a flourish. "Ta-da!"

Her jaw dropped, and she clapped her hand to her

mouth in surprise. The walls were green on the bottom, yellow on the top, with a row of turtles stenciled along the middle where the two colors met, each and every one of them unique. Some were smiling, some looking up, some down, some had tufts of hair or whimsical ponytails, one wore glasses. One wall also sported larger animals. A happy elephant and a tall giraffe. The elephant had painted its toenails red, and the giraffe wore a necktie. He'd added a playful monkey wearing tennis shoes, and a prancing zebra with a laughing little cartoon girl on its back. She had wild red curls and big green eyes.

Her own eyes filled. "Oh, Ryan…"

"Do you like it?" he asked, almost nervously.

"It's wonderful." She moved closer to the wall, soaking up the details. A palm tree in the corner, fronds extending to either side, bananas and pineapples and coconuts all growing from it, and a brightly colored toucan on one limb. Tall grasses extended from the floor to waist height, and as she looked more closely, she saw a pair of lion cubs at play there. "You did all this by hand, in just two days' time?"

"Yeah, I've been on fire."

As she turned to stare at him in wonder, he moved around the room. "I figured the crib could go here, by the window. Sunshine is supposed to be good for babies, right? And see, I already set a hook in the ceiling. One of your books says that every child's room should have a crystal prism in the window, so I thought we'd find a really amazing one and hang it right there, over the crib. But on the foot end, not over her head, so it can't fall and bop her on the noggin," he added quickly.

He moved to another spot. "My mother's antique rocking chair can go here, if you want. It's still in Dad's house. It's the one she rocked me in." He turned to the third wall. "We'll put a dresser over there, maybe a changing table. There's still space left, but I don't know what else we might need, or—" He'd turned to face her again as he went on and stopped suddenly, tilting his head to stare at her. "You're crying!"

Her stupid face just crumpled, and she nodded as jerky sobs tore through her heaving chest.

"Why? Is it the color? 'Cause we can change—"

She hurled herself against him, wrapping her arms around him, mashing her tear-wet face to his chest and her bulging body to his solid one. His arms came around her, strong and soothing, as she proceeded to soak his shirt with her tears. She couldn't talk. She heard her mother come in, heard her delighted gasp and almost breathless, "Oh, my!"

"You like it?" Ryan asked.

"Oh, Ryan, I had no idea," Selma said. "This is amazing!"

Lena nodded, so he would know that she agreed, then sniffled and tried to look up at him. "It's even better than I could have imagined."

He seemed relieved and hugged her closer, one hand in her hair. "You had me worried."

"She was probably knocked speechless with surprise and sheer joy," Selma said. "Ryan, if you hang around us a while, I'll help you learn how to tell happy tears from sad ones from furious ones, okay?"

"That would be extremely helpful." There was laughter in his voice.

"And by the way, Lena dear," her mother went on. "You know that bracelet you lost, the one you asked me to look for?"

Sniffling, Lena lifted her face from Ryan's chest and looked her mother's way, wiping her cheeks with the back of one hand. She was terrified her happiness was about to take a nosedive.

"I looked right where you told me you thought it might be, and there wasn't anything there."

"Nothing?" Lena blinked in surprise.

"Not a thing, honey."

Bahru was right. She *had* been stressed out. And it had been awfully late when she'd gone out to look under the seat. Very late. Maybe she had dreamed the entire thing, or even sleep-walked out to the truck and imagined seeing the knife of her nightmares there.

Worse things had happened to stressed-out, hormone-flooded women.

And that meant…that meant that she could believe… this. She could relish this. She looked up at Ryan's face, vaguely aware of her mother backing out of the room.

"I'm going to the grocery store now," Selma said, pausing in the doorway. "I'll be…a while." She pulled the door closed.

Ryan looked right back at Lena, and then he bent and met her lips with his. Everything inside her was shouting *I love you, I love you, I love you!* It was hard to imagine he couldn't hear her on some level.

Then he scooped her up into his arms and carried her, somehow making her feel tiny and light, into his room and laid her down on the bed. He closed the door softly, turned the lock and lay down beside her, kissing her again. The kiss grew hotter, their tongues entwining, mouths open, as if he'd been as starved for her as she had been for him. Her blood heated, and rushed faster and faster through her veins as her heart galloped. Eagerly, she unbuttoned his shirt and pushed it down off his shoulders. And her hands ran over his skin, his hard shoulders and delicious corded neck, and she moved her face over it, too, tasting him, inhaling him. It had been so long. She wanted to drink him into her.

He lifted her blouse over her head, but she caught the bottom edge and pulled it back down. He covered her hand with his own. "I want to look at you."

"Like this? Ryan, I'm—"

"You're like a rare fruit, all ripened and ready to fall from the tree. You've never been more beautiful, I've told you that. I want to see you. I want to see you all full of my baby."

Blinking, still self-conscious, she nodded and let go of the blouse. Ryan tugged it up over her head. Then he peeled off her bra and tossed it to the floor as his eyes roamed her breasts and darkened with appreciation. "Wow."

"Yeah. I know. Two cup sizes, and they tell me once she gets here, I'll go up another one."

He smiled. "And you didn't want to show me this?" He caressed her heavy breasts, kissed them, gentle, easy. He pushed her pants down and she kicked them off, and then he was running his hands over her belly, kissing it all over. Eventually he shifted and lay on his side next to her, head propped on one elbow, his free hand tracing her body up and down. "I wish I were an artist," he said. "I'd paint you just like this. You're amazing."

Then he kissed her again, and again, and again. And it was beautiful and amazing, and she wanted him inside her. She wanted to make love. But he didn't. He just kissed her and caressed her, and continued to rub her all over. "It's so close to your due date," he said. "I don't want to do anything to hurt the baby. Would it? If we...?"

"I don't know. I haven't had any reason to ask." His hands, rubbing circles on her lower back, were absolute heaven. His touch, the tone of his voice, the look in his eyes, everything was light-years beyond what they had been before she'd left him.

It was happening, she thought. He was falling in love with her. Right there, right then, she was watching this man fall in love with her.

"I can wait for the sex," he whispered. "But I want you to know it's killing me."

"I think that's for the best—and it's killing *me*, too."

"But I can hold you, kiss you. I can touch you."

"Yes," she whispered. "And maybe we can stay right here for the next two weeks, until the baby comes."

"That's okay by me."

It was good. Lena's entire being told her that it was good. Everything was good. It was all going to be fine. Not only was Ryan *not* hiding a ritual dagger or planning to kill her with it, he was starting to embrace his emotions, to let them escape through the widening cracks in his armor. He was becoming that prince she'd loved lifetimes ago. And it was only a matter of time before he loved her as much as she loved him. Only a matter of time.

* * *

They spent the day putting together the crib Ryan had brought home. Yellow and green, with a matching dresser. They took the musical mobile Selma had found ages ago and attached it to the head of the crib, then wound it up to let it play its tinkling version of Brahms's Lullaby, watching as a herd of colorful stuffed animals—elephants, giraffes, hippos…all with wings— swirled and spun. Lena brought out the boxes full of baby clothes she and Selma had been collecting for the past six months, and started putting them away in the little dresser. It was truly a beautiful set, she thought. They even put a sheet on the crib mattress and laid a receiving blanket on top, ready and waiting for someone to swaddle.

Lena looked around, her throat tight, her eyes moist, as they had been for most of the day. "This makes it all so…so real."

"I know what you mean," Ryan said.

"We still need curtains. And an electrician to install the light fixture."

"And a crystal prism to hang in the window. And my mother's rocking chair."

"And diapers and bottles and—"

"We need to shop." He grinned at her, apparently in love with the prospect.

She pressed her hand to the small of her back. "Tomorrow, okay? I'm about all-in tonight."

He nodded, then slid his arms around her and ran his big, warm hand up and down her back. All her breath whispered out of her, and she leaned in, resting her head against his chest. "That feels so good."

"Then I'll keep doing it."

And he did, for a little while, until she lifted her head and said, "I smell something fabulous."

"Thank you. I haven't showered since this morning, but it's good to know my natural musk—"

She batted him playfully. "I mean from the kitchen, but we've been messing around up here all day."

And they had been. They'd lain around in bed, making out like a couple of high school kids. He'd given her a full-body massage. And then they'd played in the baby's room for hours, talking and laughing and planning.

What kind of swing set should they get? They would design and build one themselves.

Were they for or against backyard trampolines? For.

How old should Eleanora be before she got her first puppy? Old enough to ask for one.

And what would her middle name be? Sarah, after Ryan's mother.

Selma had made her grocery run and returned, put it all away, then busied herself downstairs for the rest of the day. She'd never set foot on the stairs. Because, Lena thought, she was the best mother in the world. And now…

"Smells like Mom's cooking dinner," Lena said.

"Oh. I suppose the polite thing to do would be to go down there, then." Ryan pouted, then lifted his brows. "On the other hand, it smells *really* good."

He kept an arm around her, as if it was the natural, normal thing to do, and they walked into the hallway. She stopped, turning to look up at him. "Are we…are we *together* again, Ryan?"

He frowned at her. "Well, we're having a baby together."

"I know, but...then what?"

He blinked and lowered his eyes. "I'm being totally honest with you here right now, Lena. I haven't even had a chance to think that far. This is all... It's happening fast. A few days ago I didn't even know about Eleanora, so I'm just struggling to keep up."

"I know. I know, I didn't mean to push or..."

"Can we let it unfold for a little bit and see where it's going?"

No.

"Sure," she said. "Sure we can." And then she trotted down the stairs ahead of him and hurried into the kitchen, where her mother was opening and closing cabinets, and looking flustered. "What's up, Madre?"

"Oh, hell's bells, I'm just so absentminded." She looked at Lena, made a sheepish face and pushed her hands through her curls. "I spent all afternoon making my special pasta sauce and meatballs—"

"We smelled it upstairs," Ryan said as he came into the kitchen. "It lured us in like a siren's song."

"Well, there's no pasta. Nowhere in this house is there a single strand of spaghetti." She sighed, then brightened. "Ryan, I don't suppose you would run down to the little store in town for me and pick up a box? The Grapevine is only fifteen minutes away, and they're open for a half hour yet."

"Only if I get the biggest meatball." He headed straight for the door and grabbed his jacket, put it on and dipped into his right-hand pocket for his keys. Then he frowned, patting himself down. The keys jangled when he hit the left-hand pocket, and he pulled them out, still frowning. "Huh. That's odd."

Lena cringed, realizing her mom had put them back on the wrong side. Selma met her eyes and shrugged apologetically. "Just a box of spaghetti. We've got everything else."

"All right. I'll be back ASAP." Key snafu forgotten, Lena thought. He headed out to the truck, but Lena found herself looking out the window, watching until the truck was out of sight.

"Things took a turn for the better today, hmm?" her mother asked.

Lena glanced her way, her face heating, and couldn't stop herself from smiling.

"Oh, gosh, look at you. I haven't seen you this happy since...well, since we left New York," Selma said.

"I think it's happening, Mom. I think he's starting to fall in love with me. I really do."

"Oh, baby. How could he not?" Selma smiled and turned back to the fridge, taking items from it one by one. Lettuce, salad dressing, a cucumber.

Lena turned for one last glance out the window and saw that this time someone was looking back at her. That black cat, sleek and gleaming, with huge green eyes. It was sitting halfway down the driveway with its tail curled around its body, watching her. *Staring.*

"Mom, there's that cat I told you about again."

Her mother came quickly, wiping her hands on a dish towel and leaning in to peek out the window beside her. "I've seen her twice over the past week," Selma said. "She's *such* a witch cat. I wonder if she's lost and waiting for us to help her out, or if she's trying to adopt us?"

"Give me a meatball. I'm going to see if I can lure her inside. Or at least leave it out there somewhere. I think she's been bunking in the small barn."

Selma rushed to the pot on the stove, while Lena headed to the front door to put on her parka and boots. Her mother brought her half a meatball, mashed into small pieces in a plastic bowl.

"Don't be long, okay?" her mother said. "And be careful."

"I need some fresh air, Mom. A walk will do me good. I've got a lot of thinking to do."

"All right." Selma returned to making the salad, and Lena went outside into the dusk, where she could see her breath. The cat just sat there, still watching her— waiting for her, she thought. Odd, when it usually ran away the minute she made eye contact.

She was glad her mother had seen it, too. At least she didn't have to worry that she might be imagining it.

She walked down the driveway toward the cat, which waited until she was almost close enough to touch it, then turned and trotted away, straight into the copse of trees behind Bahru's cabin. Unlike the woods where Selma had wandered the other night, these led all the way to the lakeshore. The cat entered near the start of a narrow trail, one Lena had never explored very far before.

She was intrigued, because the cat paused at the trail-head and looked back at her, then moved on again, almost as if it wanted her to follow.

So Lena left the bowl on a rock and followed, calling, "Here, kitty kitty" in a silly falsetto that she had to admit would never have worked on her, had she been a cat.

Every little while the sleek black feline would stop and wait for her to catch up, then stalk forward again.

She found herself following the meandering path through the tiny woodlot and out the other side, then uphill for a little way, until she emerged at the prettiest spot she had ever seen. She'd known it was here. The log cabin that had once been owned—maybe still was, for all she knew—by a priest, was farther along the path, which took a steep upward jog from here. This spot was plus or minus the halfway point in between, and while she'd glimpsed it from below, she'd never come up here to check it out, though she'd wanted to.

A waterfall tumbling from an even higher spot splashed into a small pond. The pond hadn't frozen over—probably couldn't, with that waterfall pounding down into it.

The cat was sitting near the water's edge, waiting for her. She moved closer, and saw that just to the right of the pond the ground dropped off sharply—and it was a long way to the lake below. On the far side, behind the waterfall, there was an opening.

A cave?

And voices. Definitely voices.

The cat bounced from its spot to the top of a boulder on Lena's left, then jumped off the back. Lena ducked behind the boulder, too, wondering why she felt as if she had some reason to keep from being seen.

And she guessed she did have. A gut feeling. No more than that. But she always trusted her gut. Her mother had taught her that, and yeah, maybe she'd been hallucinating some stuff lately, but still…better safe than sorry. So she crouched there, peeking around one side and waiting to see what happened.

To her utter shock, she spotted Bahru. He seemed to be coming out of the cave, but he stopped just on the other side of the waterfall. He was a liquid blur of red and white. But he was speaking loud and clear, and despite the cascade's splashing, she heard every word.

"If I had known they would banish you from the house, I'd have convinced them not to, Master. I swear I would. But it does not matter."

Did he just say "Master"?

"It won't matter. Once the baby comes, it will be done. Her power will die. And you will live again."

Lena gasped, then clapped a hand over her own mouth to shut herself up. What the hell was going on here?

"It has to be soon. She is catching on."

She leaned out a little further, trying like hell to see who he was talking to. There was definitely someone else there. But she couldn't make him out. Just a dark shadow beyond the waterfall.

Wait a minute, a dark shadow?

If I had known they would banish you from the house…

Was it their house ghost? Was their house ghost—or whatever he was—conspiring with Bahru? And what the hell did all this have to do with her baby?

The cat bumped Lena's hand with its head, and she looked down as she complied with its demand to be stroked. And that was when she noticed that it wore a collar with a phone number woven into the fabric. No dangling metal tags to disrupt kitty's hunting fun. It must have particularly insightful people. Lena made a mental note of the number, crouching lower as Bahru emerged fully from the cave, walking right through the waterfall, though he held a dark cloak of some sort over his head to keep him from getting soaked, and—

A dark cloak. Just like the ones those people in the woods were wearing in Mom's photos.

She flashed back to when her mother first regained consciousness and had been muttering Bahru's name. Maybe she hadn't been asking for him at all. Maybe she had been remembering who she'd seen in the woods that night.

Lena huddled lower as he came forward, whipping the cloak off his head and giving it a brisk shake before bundling it under one arm, all without breaking stride.

He walked right past her. She prayed the cat wouldn't move and give them away, but when she glanced at the animal, it was crouching low, tail twitching in agitation and emitting a deep growl.

Holy shit.

Lena couldn't trust her favorite guru anymore, that much was clear. But how the hell was she going to find out what he was up to, much less prevent it?

She had to see what was inside that cave, she decided. Stroking the cat, she whispered, "All right, cat. You've delivered your message. You wait here, okay? I'm going inside." She got to her feet, drew a fortifying breath and headed for the waterfall.

14

Lena pulled up her hood, braced herself and darted through the waterfall as fast as she possibly could, then quickly shrugged off her coat and shook it hard. It was wet but not soaked through. Good enough.

She pulled it back on again as she looked around the interior of the cave, and shivered. Whatever entity Bahru had been conversing with was not in sight. It wouldn't be hard to miss a being that resembled a shadow, though. There were shadows everywhere. Still, she didn't feel its presence. She'd always known when the house ghost was near, long before she'd started catching glimpses of it. And she didn't feel that nearness now.

Wishing for a flashlight, she moved deeper into the cave, her steps slow and careful, her eyes gradually adjusting to the darkness. The cave seemed to penetrate deep into the hillside, and it seemed to curve away as it receded into the distance.

Something moved in the darkness, and she froze, sucking in a breath so fast it hurt her chest.

"Mrrow."

Squinting, she leaned forward. "Cat?"

"Mrrrrrow."

The cat trotted toward her a few steps, then stopped and waited.

"How did you get in here? Did you run through that waterfall?" But it couldn't have. Even in the near-darkness she could tell it wasn't as drenched as it would be if it had come through that cascade. There must be another way in. And now the cat seemed to be asking her to follow. Again.

"All right, but I can't stay in here much longer." Bahru might come back.

And yet, even if he did, she didn't think he would venture this deeply into the cave. Something told her he never had. This place had an empty feel to it. The air was stale, and it felt devoid of any hint of human energy.

She started toward the cat, which turned and pranced a few feet farther along, then stopped and sat down. It sat tall and regal, and groomed a paw while it waited for her. She stopped. "Now what?" she asked.

The cat looked at her, then gave a slow, arrogant blink as only a cat could.

Sighing, Lena looked around, seeing nothing but the stone floor, the stone wall, the little pile of stones that—oh, wait. That pile of stones. That wasn't natural. That had been put there.

She went closer, kneeling awkwardly for a better look. "There's something under here," she said, and began moving the stones aside one by one until she uncovered it. A miniature treasure chest with black metal bands around it. It looked old. Hands trembling, she lifted the lid, surprised that though it appeared to be locked, it opened easily.

Inside lay a cylindrical bundle tied up with a thong. Her hands trembling, she untied it, unrolled it and saw that there were parchment pages inside. As she flattened them out, an envelope fluttered to the cave floor and lay there looking up at her.

It was too dark to read the pages, but the printing on the front of the envelope was big and easy to see, even inside the cave. It was a modern envelope, not old, like the rest. And it had a single word handwritten across the front.

Magdalena

"That's just not possible," she whispered. But there it was. She explored her own mind, to try to determine whether or not she might be hallucinating this entire event. Or dreaming it. But the stone walls felt real when she pressed her palms to them. Hard and cool. The air tasted the way it should. The water had been icy cold and wet. The cat rubbed itself over her legs, and even it felt the way a cat should feel.

It was real. Someone had left this chest and a note for her to find in this cave. And the cat had led her to them.

She set the pages and envelope aside, and closed the box, then carefully buried it again, covering it with loose rocks to hide it from view. It was too awkward to carry back to the house, too big for her to sneak it in unnoticed, and she had a feeling she needed to keep this to herself until she figured out what was going on. The box was beautiful, possibly even valuable, but it wasn't important right now. The pages and the note *were*. She folded the envelope and stuffed it deep into a coat pocket. The scroll she tucked inside the jacket, under her arm. Then she scooped up the cat, who allowed it but didn't seem amused. Stuffing the cat, too, inside her coat, she pulled up the hood and ducked through the waterfall again. Then she took the poor feline out from under her jacket but continued carrying it as she hurried back to the house. The cat, which Lena decided was female, didn't seem inclined to escape. By the time she got back she was tired from the long walk, but also fired up. Ryan had been right. She hadn't hallucinated any of this. Something was happening. She'd been right about that all along. It was real, it was supernatural, and it was important. And it involved her *and* her baby. But she had help. Of that she was sure. She had the cat, and she had the ancient pages and note, and she was going to figure this out.

She reached the house and saw that Ryan's truck was back in the driveway. Eager to see him and show him her finds, she went inside, then froze as she saw Dahru sitting in front of the fire, sipping tea, while her mother and Ryan set the table.

Ryan sent her a smile as she walked in. "I was just about to go looking for you," he said, walking over to her and raising his brows at the cat. "Who's this?"

"I found her wandering. Thought I'd keep her safe until I can locate her owner." Her eyes shifted to Bahru, and she plastered on a smile that felt stiff and phony, hoping he couldn't tell. "Hi, Bahru."

"Hello, Lena. How are you feeling?"

The cat hissed and dove out of her arms, then tore through the room and up the stairs like a black streak. Ryan frowned at the cat and then at Lena. He saw through her fake smile, she knew that much.

"Bahru's joining us for dinner," her mother called

from the kitchen, and even *her* voice sounded strained, the cheerfulness hollow. "Isn't that nice?"

"Awesome." Lena kept that false smile in place. "I'm going to need some supplies if we're going to keep the cat around. The Grapevine's closed until tomorrow, though. Maybe after dinner we should take a drive into Ithaca."

"Sleet and freezing rain are predicted for the evening," Bahru said. "It might be best to wait until morning, see how the road conditions are."

"It's funny you'd know that, Bahru," Lena said, trying to sound conversational rather than challenging. "You don't even have a television out there in the cottage."

"I do not watch television. I do have a radio, however."

"Oh." She shrugged. "And of course you're right. No point in taking unnecessary risks just for kitty litter."

"There's a pile of sawdust in one of the outbuildings," her mother called from the kitchen. "We can use that for tonight." She smiled at Lena. "Did she eat the meatball?"

"No, she wouldn't touch it. I forgot the bowl, though. I'll get it later."

"No problem. We'll find her a can of tuna. She won't turn her nose up at that."

Lena considered her options, upset that Bahru had just effectively stolen her excuse to get out of the house tonight. She'd been thinking of taking her mother and Ryan along with her and maybe not coming back. Probably a big overreaction, but still…

Selma set a steaming pot of sauce and meatballs in

the middle of the table, then went back for a bowl of freshly cooked spaghetti and still-warm garlic bread. The salad was already there. "Dig in," she called.

But Lena was still standing in front of the door with her coat on, to hide the bundled pages hidden under her arm. She heeled off her boots and then, without explaining herself, headed up the stairs.

"Lena?" her mother called after her.

"I, um—I don't want the cat up here. I'll just grab her and bring her back down. Won't be a minute."

She had no idea if anyone believed her, but she gave them no time to argue. She made a beeline for the temple room, and closed and locked the door behind her.

Peeling off her wet coat, she let it fall to the floor and took the scroll to the cabinet, tucking it far in the back, out of sight and nearly out of reach. Then she arranged jars and bottles artfully in front of it. She pulled the letter from her coat pocket and eyed it, wondering if there was time to read it.

"Lena?" her mother called. "Are you okay up there?"

"Yeah, Mom. I'm coming." She put the letter in the cabinet as well, then closed it and left the temple room to head down the stairs, stopping to hang up her coat on the way.

Somehow they got through the meal. Lena caught Bahru looking at her oddly once or twice, especially when he asked how the baby was doing, and she felt the blood drain from her face as she answered him. "My baby is strong and healthy, and she's going to stay that way."

He smiled. "I'm certain the child is male."

"Then you're wrong. She's a girl."

His expression turned to one of confusion for a moment, but at least she'd distracted him from her almost angry reaction to what seemed, on the surface, a casual, even thoughtful, question. She knew he was up to something. She *knew* it.

And with every minute that passed, she felt more and more certain that she had to get herself and her baby the hell away from Bahru and the shadowy presence that had inhabited the house, away from the cave, and even away from Havenwood. And Mom and Ryan needed to get away, too. They should all leave together. Tonight. As a family.

Finally Bahru left. Lena followed him to the door, eager to be rid of him but smiling all the way. She opened it, saying goodbye, good-night, sleep well, all the usual crap. But she didn't feel relief when she closed it again. She didn't feel relief until he'd walked halfway back to his cottage, and she was still peering out the window, watching him, as he disappeared into the darkness.

"Lena, what is going on with you?" Ryan asked. "You're as antsy as hell tonight."

"Nothing." Not until Bahru was back in his cottage and the lights were on, she thought, still staring out into the night. Then she would tell him.

"Are you sure?"

"Yes. No. I mean, there *is* something, but… We'll talk later." Her mother was in the kitchen, clearing up all by herself. "I should help Mom." She gave one more glance out the window. Bahru had to be almost back to the cottage now.

"Well, give me just a minute first, will you?" Ryan

asked. "I have something I want to ask you, but...in private."

She raised her eyebrows, and a whole new sort of nervousness flooded into her brain and body, completely tugging her attention away from Bahru and the cave, the letter and the parchment pages. Everything tingled. Her stomach knotted. He had something to *ask her?* In *private?*

"Um...sure. Okay." She glanced toward the kitchen, where her mother was humming as she ran hot water into the sink. "Where do you want to...talk?"

"Here is fine." He led her back to the sofa, and she sat down. "And don't worry about the dishes. I'll go relieve your mother momentarily. You should just rest. Okay?"

"Okay." She wondered if he would get down on one knee. She wondered if she should tell him about Bahru first—but that would really ruin the moment, wouldn't it?

He took a breath. She could tell he was nervous. But he didn't get down on one knee. He just sat beside her on the sofa. "All right, here it is. I wanted to tell you sooner, but after you told me about that dream, I didn't dare."

She blinked, completely confused. What did her dream have to do with his proposal?

"My father left me something—something...weird."

Her eyebrows pushed against each other. "Something weird," she repeated, beginning to suspect this wasn't going to be a marriage proposal after all.

"The note he left with it warned me not to tell anyone about it. But I need to tell you, because the thing is...it's enchanted or something."

"Your father left you an enchanted...*something?*"

"A knife," he said.

He could have gut-punched her and not driven the wind out of her lungs any faster.

"Gold, all engraved with symbols. It came in a carved wooden box that looked antique. Possibly ancient."

She had to remind herself to breathe, and when she did it was in short, openmouthed little gasps, which didn't provide enough air at all. She thought she was going to pass out. "Why didn't you tell me before?"

"I was going to," he said. "But then you had that dream, where you thought I was going to…"

"Kill me."

"And the description of the knife—it matched."

"So you hid it from me."

"I put it under the seat of the truck," he said. "I didn't want it in the house. I thought it was dangerous to have it around you and the baby."

The baby. Always the baby. She got to her feet, looked toward the kitchen, wondering if her mother had lied to her, too, when she'd said there was nothing under the seat of his truck.

"Lena, don't look like that."

"Like what?" She was standing between the sofa and coffee table. He was still sitting, blocking her escape in that direction, but she could back up, and she did, one trembling step at a time.

"Like you're afraid of me. I would never hurt you, I swear it. It's just that…the knife disappeared. It's not where I left it, and I was wondering if you maybe found it or moved it, or…?"

"Yes. I found it. I saw you hiding something from me, so I went out there and looked to see what it was. I found the very same blade that you used to murder me in my vision."

"Dream. *Nightmare*. Not vision."

"Vision. I saw the same thing in the chalice. The one your father left to me."

He frowned. "That's right. And the chalice has powers, too. You said—"

"The power is in the witch. Tools are just tools." But even as she said it, she knew it wasn't true. And she also knew that the chalice and the blade were intricately bound to one another. Mated.

"Yeah, well, this knife is considerably more than just a tool, believe me." He looked at her inching away from him and pushed his hands through his hair in frustration. "Every time I pick it up, it…it shoots sparks. Fire. It blasts things, Lena."

She stopped inching.

"I set the curtains in Dad's study on fire the first time I touched it. Then, the other night, I set the weeds on fire out back."

Lena's heart was pounding with something she'd never felt in his presence until now. Fear.

"I was reading one of those books my dad left you, and I found a chapter about how to cleanse and consecrate magical tools, so I thought that might help. I tried burying it outside overnight. You know, in case it had… bad mojo or something."

"And how did that work out for you?" Her voice was trembling. She clamped her jaw and cleared her throat.

"I don't know. I still can't seem to control the thing." He lifted his eyes to meet hers. "Or I couldn't, last time I tried. But now it's gone and I don't know who has it, and between what I've seen it do and what you've dreamed of it doing—"

"Of *you* doing."

"I think the thing is dangerous. I think we need to find it." He swallowed hard, rising to his feet. "God, I hate seeing that fear in your eyes. Lena, how can I make you believe I would never hurt you? I swear, I wouldn't."

"I know." But she didn't. She didn't know at all. She didn't even know how he felt about her. Just today she had thought things were beginning to change, but up to then it had just been practical for him to be here, to be close by, two parents, one child. There had been no love. Not the wild, all-consuming, die-without-you kind of love she needed from him. Passion from time to time, yes, but not that fiery, unbridled, soul-fire kind of love. Not the kind she remembered from the prince of her past.

"You said you found the knife," he told her softly. "Why didn't you say anything?"

She shrugged. "I had Mom check, and she said there was nothing there. I thought I had…hallucinated it."

"Well, you didn't. And that should tell you that you can trust me, Lena, because if I meant to hurt you, it would have been better for me to let you go on believing you had imagined it. Wouldn't it?"

"That makes sense."

"Did you tell anyone?"

She held his eyes, searching them, wishing she could read his soul. "I told Bahru. I thought he might know something about it." *But then his eyes flashed red, and later I saw him talking to a demon in a cave behind a waterfall, and the cat thinks he's evil.*

She didn't say any of that last part out loud, though. How could she? For all she knew he and Bahru were in this thing together.

Doesn't make any sense. Ryan hates Bahru, always has.

You willing to risk your baby on that?

"No," she whispered.

"No what?" Ryan asked.

She stopped inching, just turned and walked away. "I don't want to talk about this anymore."

He lunged after her, grabbing hold of her arm and turning her to face him again. "Lena, you can't honestly believe—"

"Let go of me." The words fell like chips of ice, emotionless, deep, commanding.

He looked down at his hand on her arm, then let go. "I wouldn't hurt you or the baby, you have to know that."

"Right now all I *know* is that I don't want to be anywhere near you or Bahru or the damn house ghost or—"

"The house ghost? I thought he was gone."

"Not far enough." She moved past him to the kitchen, and this time he let her go.

The dishes were finished, the house in order, and Ryan was in the attic, poring over books on mysticism as if his life depended on it. Lena tugged her mother into the temple room with her, then closed the door and turned the lock.

Interior doorknob locks were pathetic at best. Easily picked, she knew, but she hoped that wouldn't matter. She hurried to the window to take a look outside. The sky was clear and dark blue, sparkling with stars that seemed to blink into existence out of nothing with every few seconds that passed. "Sleet-storm warning, my ass," she muttered.

"Honey, what in the world is going on with you?"

She let the curtain fall back into place and turned to face her mother, noticing the cat for the first time. She was curled up on the altar, blinking as if they had disturbed her from a very important nap. "I should have known this is where you'd be," Lena said. "I think you're smarter than all of us. This is the safest room in the house."

Her mother blinked and looked at the cat, then back at Lena. "Tell me what's wrong. You acted like you wanted to throw Bahru out the door at dinner."

"Yeah, well, you weren't exactly gushingly friendly to him, either. Why is that, Mom?"

Selma averted her eyes. "I don't know. I feel…nervous and unsettled around him. But only since—"

"Since that night you can't remember?"

Selma met her daughter's eyes again, frowning. "Yes. Since that night. How did you know?"

Lena lowered her head, pacing away, circling naturally in a clockwise direction. "You know those pictures on your cell phone? The ones you don't remember taking?"

"Yes. People in monks' robes standing around a fire in the woods."

Lena nodded. "Today I saw Bahru with a robe just like that."

"When? Where, for goodness' sake?"

"When I went out after the cat." She paused by the altar and ran her hand over the animal's silky soft head, down her back. "She was leading me, Mom. I swear she was leading me."

Selma's eyes shifted from the cat, then back to Lena, over and over. "Leading you where, honey?"

"That spot with the pond and the waterfall that overlooks the lake. There's a cave behind the waterfall that I didn't know was there."

Selma frowned. "A cave? I've never seen a cave."

"Well, it's there," Lena said harshly, and saw her mother's eyes widen at her tone. "Bahru was just inside, talking to someone. A large, dark, shadowy shape."

"A dark, shadowy shape…like the house ghost?"

Lena nodded. "Bahru told it that if he had known we were going to banish it from the house, he would have stopped us."

Selma's eyes widened even further.

"He called it 'Master' and, worse, he said once the baby comes my power would die and then 'it' would live again."

"My God. Are you sure?"

Lena nodded hard, deciding not to mention the letter or the pages. Not until she knew what they contained. Goddess, she was half afraid that when she went to look at them again, they would be gone. Vanished. Afraid she'd been imagining them this whole time.

"We can't trust Bahru, Mom. And I don't think we can trust Ryan, either." Then she finally told her mother about her visions of him stabbing her with a golden knife immediately after the birth of their child. The same knife she'd had her mother look for in his truck.

"But it wasn't there," Selma said.

"I know. He said someone took it. He told me about

it earlier. He has it, Mom. Or *had* it. That exact blade, only now it's missing. And the only person I told about it was Bahru."

Selma listened, and her face grew harder with each word Lena said. In the end she put her hands on her daughter's shoulders. "We're going to leave here—just the two of us. Tonight. We'll leave everything behind."

"Mrrrow," said the cat.

"Everything but the cat," Selma amended. "We'll go where no one can find us, and that's where we'll stay until the baby comes. All right?"

Lena nodded. "That's exactly what I was going to say. But we have to be sneaky. We have to get out of here without Ryan or Bahru knowing about it."

"If Ryan is somehow involved in…in whatever is going on here," her mother said softly, "if he's got some kind of mystical connection to you and the baby, then how can we get away without him knowing, honey?"

"I don't know."

Drawing a deep breath, then releasing it all out at once, Selma moved across the room to open the wooden cabinet, then reached to the back and brought out a small burlap pouch with a drawstring closure. She unknotted it and drew out a tiny ornate bottle of smoky dark glass with a pewter vulture for a stopper.

"What's that, Mom?"

"Belladonna," she said. "A few drops in his tea—or, better yet, cocoa, because the sweetness will cover the taste—and he'll sleep for hours."

Lena stared at the vial. "A few drops too much could kill him."

"I know. I'll err on the side of caution. In case we're wrong and he's innocent."

Lena bit her lip, her heart bleeding, her mind swirling. Images of the prince who would have done anything to save her warred inside her troubled mind with the Ryan whose attitude until recently had seemed so indifferent, so dispassionate. And both men battled in her mind against the image of the man standing over her bed, raising a dagger over his head to drive it into her heart.

Which one was real?

Lowering her head, she shook it slowly. "I can't let you do it, Mom. I can't risk hurting him. I love him so much. I want to think I'm wrong. I want to believe there's some explanation for the dream, the vision."

"You're risking your child's life, Lena."

"No, I'm only risking my own. He won't hurt Eleanora. I know that much for sure."

"Would you risk the life of your child if you *weren't* sure?" Selma asked.

Lena shook her head. "Of course not, Mom."

"So how can you ask me to risk the life of mine?"

"I'm an adult. It's my life to risk. I love him. I'd die for him. It's worth it. I *do* want to sneak away, I *do* want to have the baby somewhere safe and figure out the rest of this afterward. I want to stay alive to raise my child. But I can't risk Ryan's life to do that. What if I'm wrong?" She closed her eyes and prayed that there was a rational explanation for everything she'd seen in the chalice. "We'll get out of here, Mom, but we'll find some way to do it that doesn't involve poisoning Ryan. All right?"

Selma looked down, blinking tears from her eyes. "All right, hon. If that's what you want."

"That's what I want."

15

"Ryan?"

Ryan looked up from the book he was perusing, all about hauntings and ghosts and banishing them, to see Selma poking her head up through the trapdoor into the attic. He'd had one brief, idiotic moment when he'd hoped it was Lena. But no, he'd scared the hell out of her, destroyed any trust she'd had in him, and it was going to take something huge to win it back.

If he could. It was beginning to feel to him as if she stopped trusting him every time he hiccupped lately. And he wondered why that was.

"I'm not interrupting, am I?" Selma asked.

He shook off his brooding and smiled a welcome. It felt weak, but she would understand. She came the rest of the way up, a steaming, chocolate-scented cup of cocoa in her hand, the smell tickling his taste buds to life.

"I was having cocoa before bed, and I thought you might want some, too." She crossed the dim attic carefully and set the mug on an upturned wooden crate near his side. The light was on, a dusty bulb dangling from the ceiling with a long pull-chain attached. It was great for reading but awful for people. Even sweet Selma had an almost evil hue to her under that harsh over-head glow.

"Thanks for that," he said with a nod at the mug. "How is Lena doing?"

"Oh, I think she'll be fine. Hormones and pregnancy really do a number on a woman's nerves. We tend to worry about everything this close to delivering. I think she'll come around. Just give her a little time."

"She doesn't trust me," he said. And then he thought, why not just throw it right out there, put his cards on the table? "I know I did a number on her before, when we were dating. Worked so hard to convince her I was a player that she bought it a little too much. But I keep getting the feeling there's more to it than that."

Selma sighed and sank down onto an old black metal trunk. She seemed deep in thought for a moment. "You know, you might be right."

"You think?"

"I hadn't given it much thought, but…yeah. When a woman brings a child into the world, she starts thinking big-time about her own childhood. The good things she wants to pass on…the not-so-good things she doesn't want to repeat."

He shook his head. "I've never heard Lena say anything bad about her childhood. She loved growing up with you, Selma. Don't try to take the blame for—"

"I know she loved growing up with me. But she also grew up without her father." Her brows drew together. "She was only three when he left us. She cried for him for days, but she was so little…I honestly thought she'd forgotten all about it."

"She's never mentioned it since?"

"Not once. But I should have known it was in there, maybe deeply buried…but still there. Kids don't forget that kind of thing. And you know, it might very well be why she's so quick to mistrust you. She might not even be aware of it."

He reached for the mug and brought it to his lips.

"Ryan, wait!"

The cocoa burned, and he jerked it away again with a hiss. "Ouch. You're right, that needs to cool for a minute." He set the mug down.

She sighed in apparent relief, looked from the mug to him, and wrung her hands a little.

"You okay, Selma?"

She nodded, forcing a smile that was as weak as his own had been earlier. "So what are you reading about?" She nodded at the book.

"Bound spirits. You know, bound to a house the way that ghost of yours seemed to be."

"What made you want to read about that?"

"Just something Lena said about it seeming to be angry about your ghostbusting. She said it seemed almost…irrational. Desperate."

"And what have you learned?"

He frowned. "Well, for one thing, they're not always ghosts. Any number of things can pass from their plane—into ours through a…a doorway, but that wasn't the word they used."

"A portal," she said.

"Yeah, a portal. If it's left open, you can get a lot of

traffic. I mean, I never believed in any of this stuff, and frankly, I'm a little stunned to find myself researching it as if it's real. But I've seen so much since I've been here…." He gave his head a shake. "If there *is* one of these portals nearby, then theoretically at least, all sorts of beasties could have come through. Demons, spirits, divinities, lesser gods even." Then he shrugged, feeling a little sheepish. "Listen to *me* telling *you*. You already know all about this stuff." He reached for the cocoa.

She covered his hand with hers. "Still too hot. Please, keep talking, Ryan. There's no way I know everything in every one of these volumes. A wise woman never stops learning."

"Okay," he said nodding. "Okay. So if there *is* a portal nearby, and if your house ghost or whatever he is did come through it, then he might be stuck here. The book says entities that enter our world that way can sometimes be bound to the area in the immediate vicinity of the portal until and unless they manage to…what was the term?" He opened the book, flipped pages, then said, "'Manifest in the physical.'"

She blinked. "And does the book say how, precisely, such an entity would go about doing that?"

"Not that I've found so far."

"Mom?"

They both turned to see Lena coming up the ladder to join them. "I just checked outside. It's a full-blown sleet storm, just like Bahru predicted."

"Were you planning to go somewhere?" Ryan asked.

She shrugged. "Not really, I was just nervous. I could have the baby anytime, after all. I want Doc Cartwright to be able to get to me. Right now the news says no unnecessary travel. A lot of secondary roads are already closed."

She met his eyes. "Ryan, I'm sorry about earlier. I was—" She broke off as she looked around, taking in the books piled around him, the cocoa cooling on the nearby crate. Then, out of the blue, she sent her mother a furious look. "I said *no!*"

"I made an executive decision," Selma said. "But I'm already having second—"

Ryan reached for his cocoa as he wondered what the hell they were talking about. It had to be drinkable by now.

"Ryan!" Lena lurched toward him, tripping over nothing at all and flailing wildly. He sprang to his feet to catch her, and she hit the mug and sent it flying across the attic. It smashed into a wall and shattered just as he caught her and drew her against his chest to keep her from falling. Though the contact felt good, she'd damn near scared him gray. "What the *hell,* Lena?"

"I...saw a mouse."

He frowned until his eyebrows met, searching her face, completely certain he was in the middle of a conversation that was flying right over his head. "Are you okay?"

She nodded and gazed up at him in a way that made him think she was over whatever had upset her earlier and was back to adoring him again. God, her mother had been right about pregnancy hormones. One minute she was terrified of him, the next she was looking like she wanted to kiss his face off.

He knew for sure that *he* wanted to kiss *her* face off. He felt himself being pulled closer but stopped when he heard her mother gently clear her throat. His hands on Lena's shoulders, he waited as she steadied herself.

"Ryan was just reading about spirits sometimes being bound to areas near the portals through which they entered our world," Selma said. "The text says that in such cases they can break that bond only if they can manifest in the physical."

"Yeah," Ryan said. "But how do they do that, exactly? 'Manifest in the physical'?"

Lena blinked and looked from him to her mother and back again. "It means it needs a body. It can't leave the area until it gets one."

"So it can't let the body it wants leave the area, either," her mother said.

Lena's expression had changed again—to a look of pure, undiluted terror. Her eyes were huge, and darting back and forth. "That's what happened with that freak storm the other night and the tree falling across the road right in front of us, and with the sleet storm tonight. We can't leave," she whispered. "It won't *let us* leave."

"Lena, what do you mean?" Ryan asked.

"It wants our baby!"

She turned and scrambled down the ladder so fast he was afraid she would fall. He heard her feet pounding through the hallway below, heard a door slam, and looked at Selma as if for answers.

She had tears running down her cheeks.

Lena ran to the temple room, and slammed and locked the door. She got it now. Their house ghost was no ordinary ghost. Somewhere near here—*the cave, it has to be in the cave*—there must be an open portal to the Otherworlds.

She grabbed the sea salt from the cabinet, waved her hand over it to empower it, then scattered it in a sloppy clockwise circle around the room.

This thing, whatever it was, had come through the Portal, and now it was looking for a body. Her baby's body! Did it make any sense? No. She had no idea why this being thought becoming a newborn infant would serve its purpose, whatever that might be. But did she believe it anyway? You bet she did. And Bahru, a man she had once thought was her friend, was helping it!

She threw the plastic container of sea salt aside and grabbed a bundle of herbs. Not sage alone, not this time. She wanted, needed, more power. She grabbed angelica, patchouli, sandalwood, orrisroot, snatching pinches of each dried herb from its jar and dropping them onto a concave abalone shell. Crunching and charging them all at once by rubbing them between her flat palms, letting them fall into the shell, scooping them up again and repeating. She visualized a ring of smoke that hardened into one of pure, impenetrable power, and muttered words to her unseen enemy as they came to her, without thinking first.

"I command you by heaven, by earth, by the river, by the power of mountains and lakes... The house I enter, you shall not enter, the door I close, you shall not open."

And then she bit her lip, because while her mind had heard those words, had understood them, her lips had been speaking them in some other tongue. Some long-ago language. *Akkadian,* someone whispered inside her mind. And she began again, without even knowing how.

"Uta am i-i-ki, ana am, ersetam, nara-am..."

She grabbed her lighter and flicked it to life, touching the flame to the herbs and whispering the chant over and over.

The entity that had come through the portal wouldn't let her leave this place, she knew it for sure. Whatever it was, it didn't want her to escape its reach until her baby was born.

But that didn't mean she was going to stop trying. And she would succeed, dammit. She *would*. Because she was a witch.

She carried the smoking herbs around the room, strengthening the circle she had made, and then setting them on the altar and letting them continue to smolder.

She had to get out of here, out of Havenwood, out of Milbury. But it would be easier and safer by day. Getting herself and her baby killed in an escape attempt would do no good at all. She just had to get through tonight. One more night. Just one. And then she would get out of town tomorrow. She would walk if she had to.

She got some holy water, the good stuff she'd been saving, collected from a midnight thunderstorm on the Summer Solstice and charged again beneath a lunar eclipse. A tiny pebble taken from the grounds of Stonehenge, a gift from a friend years ago, rested in the bottom of the bottle. She shook out the water, sprinkling a small, tight circle all around her. Then she sat in the center, her knees drawn to her chest, her wand in her hand.

The cat came and rubbed against her legs. Reminding her of the parchment pages, the letter. She quickly got up and retrieved them, sat back down, then sprinkled the water around herself again for good measure.

"It can't get in. It can't get in. It can't get in," she whispered.

Someone knocked on the door, and she damn near jumped a foot off the floor. But it was only her mother and Ryan. They took turns reasoning with her, pleading with her to come out.

"I'm not coming out until morning," she told them. "It won't hurt you as long as you're not trying to stop it. You'll be fine if you just leave it alone. I'm safe in here. The baby, too. We're not coming out. So just leave us alone."

She heard Ryan sigh. "Lena, please, hon. I'm not going to let anything hurt you. You know that. Please, babe, just come out. Things were going so well—can't we get back to that? Please? You can't stay in there all night, there's not even a bed. Lena, come on, be reasonable."

She went to the stereo, an old-school all-in-one that had dual tape decks in the front, a five-disk CD changer and a radio tuner. She pushed play, not caring what was in there.

"The Goddess Chant" began to play. She cranked it loud enough to drown out her mother and Ryan outside the door, and eventually they went away. But she kept the music playing. Its harmonies unfolded, built, entwined, empowered the energy of protection around her. Her arms around her belly, she sank to the floor in the center of the room, invoking her protectors to surround her on this night. To protect her child, and her, from whatever evil had set its sights on them. To empower her to take her daughter to safety at the first light of dawn.

Feeling stronger by the minute, she opened the envelope with her name on it, and began to read.

"It's not good," Ryan said. "She just doesn't trust me." He hung his head and walked away from the closed, locked door, knowing he wasn't going to get through to Lena. Not tonight, anyway. Not now that she knew about the knife.

"But *I* do." Selma put a hand on his shoulder. "I didn't, when I first learned about the athame—the knife—but I do now, Ryan. Listen, she's scared. I told you what she said happened out there tonight, and I believe her. Thinking back, it seems that cat has been trying to get us to follow her since she first showed up here. And Bahru—I've got to tell you, Ryan, I've been feeling *very* uncomfortable around him since that night I blacked out. It all makes sense."

"That there's some kind of demonic force looking to take over our baby's body? That *makes sense* to you?"

She shrugged. "I admit it sounds far-fetched, yes. Even to a witch. But look at her point of view, Ryan. She either chooses to believe it and do whatever she can to protect her baby, or she chooses not to believe it and risks the baby's life. Not to mention her own. Which one is she supposed to choose? Which would *you* choose?"

He sighed. "I just wish she'd let me join her in that choice. It's my baby, too. I want to protect her just as much as Lena does, but she's shutting me out."

"Well, on that I disagree with her. Now, I mean. Hell's bells, I don't know. But she must have a reason."

"It's that damn knife," he said.

Selma lifted her brows. "Then you really were hiding it under the seat of your truck?"

He shot her a look. "Yes."

"She asked me to take a look, tell her what I'd seen. I think she thought she might have imagined it or dreamed it or something. I looked, and there was nothing there."

He sighed. "My father left it to me. Every time I touch it, it shoots sparks, sets things on fire. I've been trying to master it, but I thought it was too dangerous to keep in the house."

She blinked at him. "And you didn't tell her about this magical blade?"

"I intended to. But then she dreamed of me stabbing her in the heart with it as she gave birth. She described it to a T. I couldn't very well tell her I had it after she told me that, could I?"

Selma looked at him as if he was stupid. "She found out anyway, Ryan. Wouldn't it have been better coming from you?"

"I suppose." He looked back at the closed door. "Hindsight's twenty-twenty."

"Well, at least the solution is simple."

He shot her a stunned look. "It is?"

"Of course it is. Give her the knife. Let her get rid of it or lock it away or mail it to Tibet."

Rolling his eyes, he muttered, "Why the hell didn't I think of that?"

She shrugged. "Because you're male. You really have no idea where it is now?"

"That's just it. I don't. Someone took it from the

truck, and it clearly wasn't her, and it wasn't you, either, so that only leaves—"

"Bahru," Selma said. She turned and looked toward the closed temple room door. "You know, I'm not altogether sure she's wrong to stay where she is until morning. Tell you what, I'm going to put up wards of protection around this house tonight. And *you* need to figure out how to get that blade back from Bahru. And *then* you need to shift the focus of your research just a little. Because your father didn't just leave you a blade with some kind of mystical power. He left Lena something, too. A chalice. And those two tools are very closely entwined in the mystic traditions of the world. *Very* closely. There's more to this than the two of you are seeing."

He nodded, again looking at the door to the temple room. "What about Lena?"

"She couldn't be anywhere safer tonight. It doesn't look very likely that we can get her out of here before morning without risking all our lives. But unless you can get that blade back from Bahru, she's not truly safe anywhere, Ryan."

"You believe her dream, then? You think I—"

"Not you. But perhaps the blade. You *must* get it back, Ryan. And even then, we need to get Lena and the baby far away from here at first light." She pressed her lips together. "If we can."

Dear Magdalena,
My name is Indira, and I am your sister. I would say I was once your sister, in a previous lifetime, but the thing is, that lifetime never really ended. Because we left things undone, you and Lilia and I.

"Lilia," Lena whispered. "Oh, my Goddess, is this for real?"

Long ago, we were harem slaves in Babylon. The king found out that we were also witches—and also that Lilia was in love with his most trusted soldier, Demetrius. We were arrested, tortured and executed…

"Yes, pushed from a cliff. As the prince raced toward us…but he couldn't save us in time."

Her eyes returned to the page, racing over the lines.

But for Demetrius, a far worse fate awaited. The high priest, an evil bastard named Sindar, stripped him of his soul and sentenced what was left of him to eternity imprisoned in a dark Underworld realm.

But we had a plan, we three. We did not cross over when we died. Our spirits snatched Demetrius's soul from Sindar's evil grasp. We split it into pieces and bound it to us, hiding it in magical tools that we then secreted away. Only we could find them. Or they would find us. And we each vowed to help Demetrius and set in motion the wheels that would make all this right again.

I found my magical tool, an amulet, and when I used it, it restored one small part of Demetrius's soul and released him from his prison.

Now you must find your tool. I do not know what it is. I only know that when you use it correctly, it will restore another part of his soul to him. And then it will be Lilia's turn.

But you must be careful, because Demetrius has been imprisoned so long that he no longer remembers his humanity. He's a dark and raging beast who cares for no one. He's dangerous. But we made a vow, and we cannot be free until we fulfill it. In fulfilling my own small part in this, I found the love I had lost in that long-ago lifetime, and I hope the same will happen for you.

I don't know where you are, or where you will be when your turn comes to pass, so I've hidden this letter along with the details of our history in a cave near the portal, knowing you will find it there somehow. But the writings will not tell you what to do with your magical tool. That's something you have to figure out on your own. I can tell you this much, however: Love is the key. Love is the whole of it. Love is all there is, really. Look to love for the answers and all will be well.

I hope we meet soon. I feel it's destined that we will. Take care, my sister, until we are reunited again. And blessed be.
Indira

Lena refolded the letter and returned it to the envelope. Then she unrolled the parchment pages, but they were written in a language she didn't recognize. Still, it didn't matter. This Demetrius...maybe he had been innocent, even heroic, once, and maybe he had been tormented beyond her wildest imaginings, wrongly, horribly.

But she knew what he wanted from her. And she didn't care how many lifetimes ago she had vowed to help him. He was *not* getting her baby. Period.

Ryan hunched against the freezing rain and slashing wind as he made his way toward Bahru's cottage, his flashlight virtually useless in the storm. He wasn't convinced of any of the crazy theories Lena and her mother had come up with to explain the weirdness going on around this place—yes, there was definitely something supernatural going on, but a rogue spirit that wanted to take their baby's body? He didn't think so. Still, he didn't have any better theories to offer. So he figured if he could get the knife away from Bahru, take it back to the house and make Lena watch him break it in two with a sledgehammer, maybe she would trust him again.

Lena afraid of him was a sight he disliked more than just about anything he'd ever seen. It ranked right up there with the sight of his mother in her casket at the wake. It was just that unnatural, just that surreal. Dead people who looked as if they were only sleeping and Lena Dunkirk looking terrified. Those things didn't match up, didn't make sense. Didn't jibe in his brain.

As the image of her fear kept bubbling up in his mind, he flashed on something that brought him to a halt in the middle of the sleet storm.

Lena again, only…not. Or not exactly, anyway. Dark hair, not red. Tanned skin, not pale. Clothes from some other time, and not many of them. Hands bound behind her back. Two women by her side. Standing on the top of a cliff. Just a flash, there and then gone. But in that instant he felt a scorching sun pounding down on him, and the heat and pungent sweat of a horse beneath him. He felt the pounding motion of the stallion galloping over burning sand that blew into his eyes and nose, and coated his tongue. He heard the flapping and snapping of his own robes and wrappings in the wind. He felt the paralyzing, desperate, horrifying realization that he couldn't get to her in time.

There and gone. Full-blown. A second long. No more.

He shook himself free of the lingering aftershock that image had left and felt a brief sense of dislocation as he came back to the here and now. He was standing in a sleet storm, with freezing wet wind buffeting his face, not sand and searing sun.

"What the hell was that?" he whispered.

But there was no one there to answer him. He tried to get hold of his senses, but it was harder than it should have been. He felt as if he'd checked out for a minute there. Stepped into another existence, another realm.

It hit him that if Lena's visions were that real, and more than a second or two in duration, then it was no wonder she believed in them so strongly.

Okay, okay. He was overtired, stressed, and his brain had obviously had a bit more to deal with than it could handle lately. The death of his father, Lena's pregnancy, a knife that shot fire. Who wouldn't be on the verge of a breakdown?

Sighing, he pushed on to the cottage where Bahru had to be hiding that blade. The cottage was dark and even from outside, it felt empty. Where the hell could Bahru have gone in this weather? He opened the door, walked inside to make sure, checking the little bedroom, even the tiny bath. No sign of Bahru, and though he opened drawers, closets, even looked behind the firewood bin and under the furniture and mattress, he didn't find his knife.

Frustrated and angry, he went back outside, debating his next move. The wind hit him in the face, and he turned away from it, then stopped himself and faced it full on, sniffing the air. Was that…was that *fire* he smelled?

Smoke, from the fireplace in the house. That's all.

But no, the wind was blowing *toward* the house. This smoke had to be coming from somewhere else.

"That way," he whispered, facing the woods on the other side of the dirt road. The same woods where Selma had photographed hooded figures around a central fire. "Maybe they're at it again."

Remembering what had happened to Selma, he took his time, moving slowly, silently, using the trees as cover. He walked through the woods, his senses overwhelmed by the scent of pine and earth, rotting wood, and that distant woodsmoke. Keeping his flashlight turned off, he moved only when the wind blew and stood still in between gusts. The sound of the sleet on the skeletal trees was like bacon sizzling in a pan, only dark, menacing.

He stepped softly, ice-coated leaves crunching under his boots, and he crouched low, using those bare crystalline trunks for cover. It was like tiptoeing through a forest of glass, where everything he touched shattered and tinkled noisily to the ground.

Finally he spotted the fire, a soft glow broken up by shadows as the participants in some arcane ritual passed in front of it. A little closer and their voices reached him, too, dull murmurs at first, blending in with the freezing rain, the ice, the wind, but then becoming clear enough for him to distinguish what they were saying.

He was close enough to count the hooded figures around the fire when one of them lifted a box. *His* box.

"I have the Master's Blade! There is no longer any obstacle to our mission."

"Praise be the Master," the others intoned.

"Who will be the one to wield it?" someone said. It was a male voice, and one he kept thinking he should recognize.

"I will, of course," said another vaguely familiar voice. "The mother must die *before* the child takes its first breath."

"Is it truly necessary?" a woman asked.

Why was it so hard to identify them? It was almost as if there was a layer of insulation around that fire, something that muffled and altered their voices. And he couldn't see their faces, which were deeply hidden within the cowl-like hoods of the robes they wore.

"Yes, I'm afraid it is. She's a powerful witch, more powerful than even she knows. Her magic would prevent the Master from entering the body of the child. The blade must be driven into her heart, so that the Master enters with the newborn's first breath."

"And what of the child's soul?" another man asked.

"The Master will banish it to the other realms, with no harm to it at all. It will simply await another opportunity to be born."

The man with the box turned, and Ryan got a look at his hands. Long, gnarled fingers, caramel skin. Those hands were familiar to him. They were Bahru's hands.

His pendant was dangling on the outside of his monk's robe, and now that he noticed that, Ryan realized they all wore them. Crystal prisms on longish chains.

Bahru lifted the lid of the box and gazed down into it. Then he grasped the knife and picked it up.

Immediately there was an electrical crackle, a flash of light, and the knife fell to the ground, while Bahru yelped in pain. He gripped his own wrist and examined his palm. "I do not understand."

"Let me try," said someone else.

Holy shit, was that Dr. Cartwright?

"No! *I* am the chosen one, I am the one called by the Master to gather you all. It must be me." Bahru bent low and grabbed the knife again, but the same thing happened, and this time he jumped backward, falling on his ass on the ground. He pressed his palm to an ice-coated rock nearby.

"I will try," said a woman—that nurse, Ryan realized. The one Lena had hated on sight. What the hell was her name? Sheldrake. Yes, that was it. Eloise Sheldrake. She reached for the knife. "Maybe it has to be a woman."

But she couldn't pick it up, either. In fact, none of them could. One by one they tried. And one by one they failed.

Ryan saw his opportunity and stepped out from behind the tree where he'd been hiding. "There's only one person who can wield that knife," he said. "And you're looking at him."

A couple of men he hadn't seen emerged from the trees outside the circle and grabbed him by both arms. The rest were more careful than ever to keep their faces averted, their voices low, but he didn't think he would recognize them even if they hadn't. Wait, was one of them the guy from the hardware store?

They held him steady, but he didn't fight. He was concocting a plan on the spot, hoping to hell it would work. "Let me show you," he told them. "Just let me show you." He nodded at the blade.

Bahru stepped up to him, apparently not caring that Ryan could see his face clearly. "Go ahead, show us. Pick it up."

The hands holding him let him go. He had a plan. He was going to pick up the blade, and this time he was going to master it. He was going to spin around and shoot fire at these freaking hooded maniacs, blowing them to pieces if that was what it took. Because yeah, they were insane. There was no way they were going to be able to evict his baby from its body so some demon could take up residence there. And he would be damned if he was going to stand by and let them try.

And no one was going to hurt Lena. *No one.*

He straightened his jacket, looked at the blade, clenched his jaw. *Okay, ready. Make it work this time. Lena's life depends on it.* He walked to the knife, bent down, closed his hand around the handle. "See?" he said, still crouched. "I told you I could—" He rose and spun and thrust the dagger toward them all in one smooth motion.

Fire spat from the thing, setting someone's robes alight. And then something stung his neck—a dart, he thought—and his vision went cloudy. He told himself to hold on to the blade as the world around him swam and he dropped to his knees.

Bahru looked down at him, smiling. "It's all right,

Ryan," he said. "You were right. You *are* the one who has to wield the blade. But first you have to *see* as we have all come to see. And I'm going to help you do that."

He held up a chain with a dangling quartz prism at the end of it that was glowing like fire. Like hellfire, Ryan thought. He ducked his head to avoid it, but Bahru only smiled. "There's no point in trying to fight. You won't remember this tomorrow. But you will awake seeing the truth. You must. Because we need you."

He lowered the chain around Ryan's neck, and Ryan felt its power licking at his brain like a hungry fire at dry kindling.

"You will be a hero, Ryan. You will right a wrong that has persisted for more than three thousand years. You will free an innocent soul, restore that which was taken from him, and you will be richly rewarded."

"You're nuts. You're all freaking insane."

"Drop the knife into the box, Ryan." Bahru was holding the box open, waiting for him to give up the knife.

"No fucking way," he whispered, but his hand let go of the blade and it fell into the box. How the hell had that happened? *He* hadn't opened his hand. It was as if someone else had taken control of his body. Oh, this was bad. This was really bad.

Bahru closed the lid. "Relax. It will all make sense to you soon. The Master's stone will clear your mind. Relax, Ryan. Father of the Chosen One who shall be the Master's host. It makes sense, somehow, that you should be the wielder of the blade."

16

Lena had begun her night in the temple room all but cowering in fear. But by the time morning approached, just as the sky began to pale from the dark gray of a stormy night to the pink and deep blue of predawn, she felt a little bit foolish for being so terrified. She was a witch. She was not powerless. Whoever this being was, one-time hero or otherwise, she had banished him from her home and apparently kept him from coming back inside. She was *strong*.

The house was silent. Everyone was asleep. So she took out the enchanted chalice, filled it with holy water and sat on the floor, gazing into its depths. As her vision lost focus and the mists swirled into shapes and forms around her, she saw herself as she had been before, a condemned captive in that other lifetime. She stood on a precipice, her hands bound behind her stinging, bleeding back. Her sisters stood beside her, the wind whipping their hair. Beautiful, proud, powerful women.

A bed of jagged rocks awaited them far below, and yet they were not afraid. She was filled again with the knowledge that death was not an ending. That in fact one was far more alive on the other side than one could manage to be while condensed into a tiny physical body.

In the distance she saw a lone rider racing across the desert, sending up a plume of sand in his wake. Her prince, determined to save her.

She hadn't told him the secret she kept. It was that secret that made her so afraid to die. It wasn't the loss of her own mortal life she feared, but the loss of the child she carried.

I was pregnant then, too. That's what made it so horrifying.

She felt again the hands on her back and her toes trying to cling to the stone beneath them, and then…nothing. She was airborne, plummeting, falling, knowing she was about to die.

And that even if her prince had reached her in time, he would have died, too. The high priest was in a rage. The king—her prince's father—was dead, killed by her sister Lilia's lover, Demetrius, in his rage to set his woman free. And the three sisters knew that Demetrius would pay with more than his life. He would pay with his soul.

But they had a plan, the three of them. They had a plan to make it all right. A plan that was even now playing out as intended. A plan she had to see through to the end.

No. Not if it means giving him my baby…

In the magic chalice, she saw an image. The chalice—this *very* chalice—held in hands that might have been her own. And the blade, the golden blade she so feared, poised above the cup in hands that were unmistakably Ryan's. She knew those hands so well. She knew their touch, their strength, their warmth. Then she heard a voice, a powerful voice that was vaguely female but more than human. It whispered from the echoing, cavernous, bottomless cup in which the vision swam: *As the rod is to the God, so the chalice is to the Goddess, and together they are one.*

You can trust your love. But you must save my *love. You gave your word.*

"Not at the cost of my child."

Only love can save your child. The kind of love you know so well. You know the love I mean. What are the passwords, Magdalena? How do you enter the sacred circle of the wise?

"In perfect love and perfect trust." She whispered the words uttered by students of the Craft down through the generations, the passwords that allowed them entry into the circle of the witch.

Perfect love and perfect trust, the voice from the chalice repeated. *They are your only hope. Keep the chalice within reach at all times. Keep it near.*

The vision faded. The cup sat in silence, and Lena stared into it in disbelief.

She didn't know who or what to believe. But that voice felt true. It felt genuine. It felt personal, close to her. She was pretty sure it was the voice of her childhood imaginary friend Lilia, who she had since come to believe had been one of the women standing beside her on that cliff. One of those two who'd died with her. One of her sisters in that lifetime. And it was telling her the same things as the note claiming to be from her other sister, Indira.

She trusted those two women—or spirits or memories or whatever they were—intuitively.

And yet she had trusted Bahru, as well. And now it seemed he was evil. She had believed the house ghost to be good. Now it seemed that it wanted to take her child from her.

How strange to trust a voice coming to her in a vision in a cup. A cup given to her by Bahru himself.

She didn't tell you to trust her. She told you to trust Ryan.

Lena closed her eyes. "With my life? With my baby?"

His baby, too.

She got to her feet, her knees shaking. She didn't know what she was going to do next, but she was still certain that leaving this place like her feet were on fire was near the top of the list. She opened the circle, grounded the energy, and then carefully, slowly, she unlocked the temple room door and opened it.

Ryan was sitting on the floor in the hallway, his back against the wall, his breath coming slow and steady, his eyes closed.

He'd slept outside the door. To keep her safe?

Her heart contracted a little, and she bent far enough to touch his face. "Ryan?"

He opened his eyes, looked up at her, and then blinked the confusion away as he looked around. For a moment he looked as if he didn't know where he was or how he'd gotten there, but then he seemed to shake it off and got—a little unsteadily—to his feet.

His eyes were puffy and red-rimmed. "Are you all right?" she asked, searching his face.

"Yeah. I— Damn, what a headache. And the dreams. The dreams…"

She lifted her hand to his head, smoothed his tousled hair. "Let's get you some coffee. Some breakfast. You'll feel better."

"Wait." He gripped her wrist, and when she stared into his eyes, he stared right back, searching. "I don't remember going to sleep out here last night."

She blinked. "No?"

"No. But I remember the dream I was just having. It was you, but it wasn't. And me, only not really. I was trying to get to you. You were going to die, and I was supposed to save you, but I couldn't get there in time."

He was blinking back moisture, agitated, almost… anguished.

"You were on horseback in the desert," she told him. "And I was on a cliff with my sisters. Only my hair was dark then, and my skin was bronzed by the sun."

His eyes widened. "Yes! Did you…did you dream it, too?"

"I saw it in my chalice just now. A vision. You were so close that you must have…tapped in somehow."

"It was so real."

"It was. I think it was another lifetime, Ryan. I think it's part of what all this is about. But I still don't know how. Or why. Or what we're supposed to do, besides reenact the Great Rite with my cup and your blade."

He blinked and actually took a step back, away from her. "My blade…?"

She nodded. "You're a mess."

He blinked at her, shaking his head slowly. "I don't know what I'm supposed to do."

"I only know one thing I'm supposed to do."

"And what's that?"

"Trust you," she said. She slid a hand around his neck, cupped his nape beneath his hair. "Come on. We need food. We'll think better on full stomachs."

He nodded, but didn't look convinced.

They headed down the stairs to the kitchen, where Selma was already up and cooking. Lena could smell coffee, and she was damn well going to have a cup this morning. Just one. And there was bacon, too, sizzling and filling the kitchen with its delicious aroma.

She went to the coffeepot, filled two mugs, set them down and turned to her mother, who was facing the stove as she turned the bacon. "I'm sorry about last night, Mom. I...I kind of freaked."

"That's understandable, honey." Selma turned to face her daughter, smiling as warmly as ever. Putting her hands on Lena's shoulders, she said, "But everything looks better this morning, doesn't it? We're all going to be just fine. You, me, the baby, Ryan. All of us. I promise."

Lena frowned, wondering at her mother's serene assurance, and then she saw it.

Selma was wearing a crystal prism on a chain around her neck. It winked at her in the morning sun that slanted in through the window beside them. Lena took a backward step, staring at it. "What the *hell* is that?"

"What?" Selma looked down, and Ryan, curious, looked over to see what had happened to change the tone in Lena's voice so completely.

Selma was wearing a crystal pendant of some sort.

As he stared at it, something burned against his skin, beneath his shirt.

"Oh, this?" Selma asked, picking up the quartz crystal and turning it in the slanting morning sunlight. Rainbows painted the ceiling. "Bahru gave it to me. Isn't it pretty?"

"When?" Lena croaked. It was more a demand than a question.

"The day he arrived, after I complimented him on his. I just hadn't gotten around to wearing it until now. I'm starting to wonder if we might have misjudged him, hon. I really think all this has been one big misunderstanding. I mean, it just doesn't seem logical that he would go from spiritual pacifist to servant of some dark, body-snatching entity overnight. He might actually be able to advise us on this. Maybe if we just sit down and talk to him, it will all make— Lena, what's wrong with you?"

Lena was backing away from her mother. "I want you to take it off, Mom."

Yes, Ryan thought. *Take it off. Take it off, it's evil.*

"But why? It's so pretty."

"They were all wearing them." Lena's voice was hoarse, low, quivering. "Everyone in my dream, the dream where I have the baby and Ryan…Ryan has that knife. The crystals were all glowing, and they all had red eyes, and I just have this horrible feeling. Mom, *please*. Take it off."

"Of course." Frowning, Selma lifted the necklace over her head and held it out to her daughter.

Lena jumped away from the thing as if it were a poisonous snake. "I don't want it. Just…just get rid of it."

The burning against Ryan's chest was getting worse. He had to get away from the two of them, so he could look underneath his shirt. But he had a really bad feeling he knew what he was going to find when he did. And it was sure to break Lena's trust in him once and for all, if it turned out he was right.

"Here, give it to me," he said, holding out a hand, putting himself between Lena and the thing that so frightened her.

Selma smiled and dropped the necklace into his palm. "Either bury it or toss it into the stream."

He looked at Lena. "Is that okay with you? I can smash it with a hammer first, if you want."

She nodded.

"Okay. And then I'll bury it. I know just the spot." He closed his hand around the crystal, but it didn't burn his palm. It didn't heat or glow or vibrate. He turned toward the door.

"How did it go last night, by the way?" Selma asked.

He blinked. "How did...what go?"

"Last I saw of you, you were going out to see Bahru, to demand the return of that blasted knife." At Lena's sharp gasp, Selma rushed on. "He was going to give it to you, honey. To show you that you could trust him."

Lena turned to Ryan and asked, "You were?"

"That was the plan."

"So how did it go?" she asked. "Did you find it?"

He racked his brain, but last night was a blur. Vaguely, he recalled leaving the house, walking through the snow, thinking Bahru's place looked empty. He was going to go inside and look for it. Had he?

Yeah, he was pretty sure he had. God, what had happened to his memory?

"Ryan?"

"Uh, no. No, Bahru wasn't there. I searched the cottage, but…" He shook his head. "Nothing."

She nodded. "I appreciate that you tried," she said. "But I still think getting out of here is the best bet."

"Yeah. I think so, too," he said.

But even as he spoke, a cacophony of discordant whispers filled his head, each voice twisting around the next, and yet their words were clear enough.

But she won't be able to leave.

The Master will see to that.

She has to stay within his reach…

…until the child is born.

Yes, until the child…

…until the child is born.

What the hell was happening to him? Why was his memory of last night so spotty? So foggy? He looked at the crystal in his hand. It was just an ordinary piece of quartz on a silver chain.

Closing his hand around the thing, he shoved his feet into his boots, pulled on a coat and headed out back, pausing near the woodpile, where he picked up the old rusty axe that looked as if it hadn't been used in a dozen years.

The minute he was out of sight of the house, heading over the back lawn to the little copse of trees where he'd been practicing with his knife, he pulled his shirt open and looked down at his chest.

A quartz pendant rested there. It was suspended on a long silver chain, and it was glowing. He moved to take it off, but when his hand got close to the thing, it froze. It was as if he couldn't move it any further, as if he'd somehow lost communication between his brain and his arm.

It was controlling him. The damn thing was taking over his mind. He strained, baring his teeth in the effort, but his hand refused to move, and finally he let it drop to his side with a rush of breath.

Opening his palm, he looked again at the necklace Selma had given him. She'd removed it easily. Not even a hint of effort.

"It's not the same," he said softly. He didn't know why Bahru had given it to her. Maybe to make it seem like the stones meant nothing? Maybe to make Lena feel she couldn't even trust her own mother? Maybe just because Selma had asked about the piece and he wanted to shift her focus away from it. But he was certain the stone was not the same as the one that had somehow magically appeared around his own neck overnight.

What was he going to do? How the hell was he going to get this thing off? How much power could it possibly have over him? And for how long would it last?

He looked at the shovel, which was leaning against the tree where he'd left it. Only…not quite where he'd left it. Turning, he looked at the spot where he intended to bury Selma's necklace, even though he didn't think the thing posed any threat.

He knew immediately that something was wrong. After cleansing his knife overnight by burying it in the earth, he'd dug it up and filled in the hole. He'd patted the dirt down nice and flat with the back of the shovel when he'd finished. But now it was all loose and mounded up on top.

"What the hell...?"

Grabbing the shovel, Ryan plunged the blade into the dirt, easily turning it. It didn't take long to feel that there was something there. He knelt to pull it out. It was hard, square, wrapped in plastic. He knew, not just by its familiar shape and weight, but by the feeling that hit him as he brushed the dirt off it, what it was. But he unwrapped it anyway.

The intricately carved wooden box was too heavy to be empty. He opened the lid to look all the same.

And there was his knife. The one he was supposed to use to kill Lena.

Pick it up.

Go on, take it...

...it's yours, it's...

...your destiny. Do it!

Pick it up!

His hand moved toward the box, and once again he wasn't the one telling it what to do. How easy would it be to commit some horrible crime if he couldn't control his own body, his own mind?

Think of Lena, he screamed inwardly. *Think of the baby.*

He'd lost her once before.

You survived it then.

You'll survive it now, said the loudest of those mental whisperers. *As long as you don't let yourself care too much.*

Not too much, Ryan...

Not to the point of madness, like some men do. Not

*to the point where losing her means giving up your life,
your son, your family, and spending the rest of it traveling the world in search of a reason why.*

...like your father did, Ryan...

*Nothing is worth that. You must never, ever let your-
self care that much for anyone.*

...not ever, Ryan...

It's certain doom.

The voices weren't telling him anything he didn't already know, he realized, and then he was aware of his
hand closing on the handle of his knife, lifting it from
the box, feeling its power buzzing against his palm.

*Fulfill your destiny and you can have anything you
want.*

...anything you want, Ryan...

"I can *already* have anything I want," he said softly.
And yet something in his mind said that what he *really* wanted was to obey the whispers that would not
let him go.

Lena wondered what was taking Ryan so long and
started getting nervous. She headed out after him,
around back where he'd said he had buried his knife to
cleanse it before. She was nearly there when she heard
him talking softly, as if someone else was there. She
went still and silent, creeping slowly closer, peering
through the limbs to see him standing there wearing
a gleaming piece of quartz around his neck on a silver
chain and holding the knife he'd claimed not to have
found last night. Holding it right in his own two hands.

She backed away, her heart breaking into sharp, glittering fragments that first cut her and made her bleed,

and then froze into shards of fear. She had to get out of here, and she had to do it now. Without him. Without her mother. Without anyone. She was on her own. She could trust no one.

The voice said to trust him. Perfect love and perfect trust, remember?

But he's got the knife. He lied to me. I have to put the baby first.

It wasn't hard to get back to the house without him seeing her. Nor to slide in the front way while Selma was putting a delicious breakfast on the table. She called out, "I've got a really bad backache, Mom. I'm going to soak in the tub for a while, okay?"

"Of course, hon. Are you all right?" Her mother peeked around the corner at her, so she took off her boots. "It's not labor, is it? It can start with lower back pain, you know."

"No, it's not like that. I'm sure it was just…um… from sleeping on the floor last night."

"Oh, yeah, that's most likely it." Selma looked relieved. "But don't you want breakfast?"

Lena shrugged off her jacket, hung it on a hook and started upstairs. "I couldn't eat right now if I wanted to. You guys go ahead, and I'll be down when I feel better. Save me a plate, will you? I'll come down after my bath—and maybe a nap, since I didn't sleep much last night—and I'll warm it up and eat it then."

"Okay, honey."

Lena padded the rest of the way up the stairs, went into her room, turned on the water and closed the bathroom door, then shoved her purse and a change of clothes into a backpack. She took an old coat from her closet, and put on a pair of hiking shoes, as well. She turned off the water, and when she left her bedroom she locked the door from the inside before pulling it shut behind her.

She realized she hadn't heard Ryan come back in yet.

She slipped into the temple room and grabbed the chalice, remembering the warning to keep it close to her. Then she buried it deep in the backpack.

Good. All she had to do was get downstairs and outside undetected. Easy.

The cat wound around her legs and looked up at her.

Nodding, she scooped the animal into her arms and slipped quietly down the stairs, making almost no sound at all. She turned the doorknob as if it were made of nitroglycerine, opened the door slowly, then slipped outside and pulled it closed very softly behind her. And then she ran across the driveway into the open field, and cut at an angle across it, heading for the woods. This was the crucial part of her escape, she knew, because she was in plain sight, no cover. Bahru would see her if he so much as looked out the front window of his cottage. Her mother would see her if she looked out the door. Ryan would see her if he came around the corner of the house.

She ran full out, which wasn't easy with the cat in her arms, the backpack bouncing up and down, the chalice bruising her spine and the weight of her baby straining her abdominal muscles. She kept one arm around her belly to support it and ran despite the pain. Icy needles of fear, the kind you felt when you *just knew* someone was after you, prickled up and down her spine and along her nape, until finally she was in the woods, lost in the sheltering embrace of the pines.

If they hadn't seen her yet, they wouldn't see her now. She paused just long enough to turn around and look back, peering through the fragrant needled boughs. But the house was still and quiet. As she watched, Ryan came around the corner, and she ducked back quickly. But he only walked slowly to the front door and went inside.

He hadn't seen her. Good. And since he didn't pop right back out again, her mother must not have seen her, either. She looked toward Bahru's cottage. It was still and silent. Maybe, just maybe, she was going to pull this off. But she was going to have to hurry.

She probably wouldn't be able to leave town, so she needed help. She needed to find someone she could trust. Turning, she headed through the woods again. Help was within walking distance, and she knew she could get there safely if she was fast.

However, the sprint from the house to the woods had taken its toll, and the backache she'd only been making up earlier had become a reality now. Lies. Nothing good ever came from them.

17

Ryan returned to the house feeling as if his head was floating somewhere in the stratosphere and only connected to the rest of his body by an ever-thinning, ever-weakening thread. Everything he did felt as if it was being controlled by someone else, as if he were on autopilot. *Walk. Go inside. Enter the kitchen. Sit down. Eat.* At the same time, from somewhere far, far away, he could hear, very faintly, his own voice calling to him. *Over here, Ryan. Pay attention! You've got to fight this possession. You've got to save Lena and the baby. You've got to resist!*

Possession? Really, was that what this was? The thought was dispassionate, as if it was coming from a part of his brain where no emotion resided. And for a second it hit him, in that faraway place to which his brain had emigrated, that he used to be just that emotionless most of the time. Perhaps not quite as robotic, but emotionless. Living his life from a safe distance, never caring too much about anything or anyone.

And the most shocking part of that bit of self-realization was that it wasn't true anymore. He'd stepped out of that safe place. He cared. He cared more than he had ever imagined he was capable of caring.

He loved Lena.

Selma is speaking to you. Answer her.

His head moved as if someone was controlling him via remote. He looked at Selma, but he felt as if he was seeing her through a camera lens. His own body, his own eyes, were machines now. Just tools.

"Ryan, you look really off this morning," she said. "Are you sure you're all right?"

His head nodded for him. His lips formed words. He honest to God didn't know what they would be until his ears heard them and his brain interpreted. "I'm fine. I was up all night, and it's catching up with me."

"Worrying about Lena, I'll bet."

"And the baby."

She nodded, her face softening. She patted his hand. He looked at the contact in some surprise, because he didn't feel as if it was his hand at all.

"Well, she's going to be fine, I promise."

Where is she?

"Where is she?" Ryan asked, still as if someone else was wielding a master control. A master control? Or just a *master?*

"It was a long night for her, too," Selma said. "She's soaking in a hot bath. Said she was going to take a nap when she gets out."

Ryan's head turned toward the stairs as Selma set a plate of food in front of him. His stomach grumbled in hunger. He told his hand to pick up the fork and was surprised when it did so.

Hunger. A basic human need that enabled him to

take control, however feebly. Good thing to remember. He shoveled some food into his mouth, eager to fill his stomach while he was still able.

Go check. Make sure she's upstairs. The master's voice. *The Master.*

He decided to try to ignore the command, to try to eat a little more, just to test himself. He had a shaky grip on the reins, but they were slick and pulling against him. He ate another bite, the biggest one he could fit into his mouth, sensing he couldn't keep control much longer. Then he eyed his coffee and managed to bring it to his lips, despite a burning pain in his arm, as if he were trying to lift a thousand pounds instead of a cup of coffee. He managed to take a sip before he lost his tenuous grip.

The cup slammed to the table so hard the contents sloshed over the side. *Dammit!*

But he was already rising, turning, through no will of his own, walking out of the kitchen, through the living room to the staircase.

"Ryan? You can't possibly be full."

"I have to check on Lena," the Master said through Ryan's lips.

"Well, be quiet about it, okay? Try not to wake her. She really needs to— Ryan?"

But he was already halfway up the stairs.

He went to Lena's door, paused outside to listen.

Open it.

He didn't want to be anywhere near Lena right now. Not with the blade tucked into the back of his jeans and the pendant burning his skin. Not when he wasn't in control of his own body.

His hand began to rise. He forced it down again, tried to hold it at his side, but it was shaking, trembling as a force like a two-ton winch began to lift it again. He fought as long as he could, but the hand snapped up, twisted the doorknob, breaking the lock. He shoved the door open wide.

Lena wasn't inside. Thank God.

The bathroom. Check the bathroom.

His feet moved, obeying even as his true self—his soul, maybe?—resisted. It was no use. When he tried to stop it felt like the muscles were being torn from his bones. Pain, burning, ripping pain. He tried, but he was physically unable to hold against it. Within a few seconds he was opening the bathroom door.

She wasn't there, either.

Run, Lena, he thought. *Run as far as you can. You were right not to trust me.*

Go after her, the Master commanded.

I won't.

You don't have a choice. Or have you not realized that yet?

Lena hugged her coat around her as she picked her way through the woods, moving as quickly and silently as she could manage. Neither one was easy, given the size of her belly and the ice that coated everything around her. Every footstep crunched and crackled. Her back screamed and pulsed in pain.

The sun was beaming down, though, and the woods looked like an enchanted forest, every limb, every twig, completely encased in a layer of clear ice that sparkled in the sun. It was as if they'd been painted in liquid diamonds that had hardened on contact. It was breathtakingly beautiful, and the scent of the pines on the cold, cold air was heady.

It was Imbolc, she realized. February 2nd, one of the High Holy Days of her faith. The mundane world had co-opted only one of the day's traditions—using nature's signs to predict the arrival of spring—and called it Groundhog Day. The rest had been mostly forgotten. It was in fact a holiday that honored Brigit, goddess of the forge, and of the creative fire of the artist. The day was sacred to poets and musicians and writers. It was the halfway point between the winter solstice, the shortest day of the year, and the vernal equinox, when day and night were equal. It was a time of magic. A day of power.

And she could use all the power she could get today.

She kept on moving and whispered a prayer to Brigit. "Lady of the fiery forge, I call on you now to protect my child from evil and from harm." She wished she could take out her chalice and ask it which way to turn, but she couldn't stop long enough to do that.

Not yet.

Eventually she emerged from the woods and onto the closest main road. She'd kept to the woods until they ended and estimated she was a solid mile from her house at this point. Doc Cartwright's place was just a few hundred yards back the other way. She could see the roof of his house, a ribbon of soft smoke wafting from the chimney.

But Doc Cartwright had been wearing one of those pendants. As had everyone in the dream. Even her own mother had worn one this morning, and then Ryan…

Oh, Ryan...

She didn't know what the pendant meant, but she didn't dare risk finding out. Enchanted crystals were not unheard of. Using them to turn a good person into an evil one would take magic far beyond any she'd ever heard of. But to use the crystal as an entryway into a person's mind? That was a well-known type of manipulative magic. Dark magic. It was a form of possession, and it was strictly forbidden in the Craft of the Wise.

Could it be what was happening here? She didn't know, but she couldn't take the chance that it might be.

So Doc's place was out of the question.

Sheriff Dunbar, on the other hand, lived just another mile or so down the road. If she could make it that far with this screaming pain in her back—which felt like a steel band was wrapped around her and tightening— she would be fine, she thought. She just had to get there before anyone came looking for her.

The roads were glare ice, probably still closed. No wonder there was no traffic.

And yet, no sooner had that thought crossed her mind, than she heard a deep-throated motor in the distance behind her. She didn't dare wait to see who it was. It sounded too much like that massive black truck Ryan had bought. She scrambled into the ditch along the roadside and lay down on her side, hiding herself as well as she could, given her condition. Too late, she discovered that there was an inch or so of icy water in the bottom of the ditch. But she couldn't move now or the driver would see her for certain.

She huddled there, terrified, as the vehicle drew closer and thought of the irony if this *was* Ryan. In her hazy memories of that past life, her prince had been trying to come to her rescue, racing across the desert on a mighty white stallion.

In this lifetime his "steed" was black, and he was coming to kill her. To do her in so some demonic force could take her baby.

God, I don't want to believe that.

Their destinies were entwined, just as she had always known, but not in the way she'd expected. It made her heart ache to admit it. Damn him for refusing to love her, to be the man he'd been before and to complete this horrible cycle by saving her now as he'd been unable to save her then.

The truck rumbled past. She only saw it from behind, but it was him. Damn. He was out looking for her already. She had very little time.

As soon as the truck was out of sight she climbed out of the ditch, hugging her belly against another really bad cramp and forcing herself to keep moving despite the agony. She could handle the pain. She had to.

She hurried down the road, figured she'd covered a third of the distance to the sheriff's place, when she heard the truck coming back.

Again she lay down in the ditch, her clothes soaking up still more frigid water. And again he drove by without seeing her.

This time when she got out and stumbled onward she was shivering, despite the warm sun and climbing temperatures. This was February, and "unseasonably warm" meant hitting a high of forty, at most. At the moment it was maybe thirty-five, only a few degrees above freezing.

She kept on moving, and thankfully she didn't hear the truck again. Finally the sheriff's house came into view around a bend in the road. The stitch in her belly and pain in her lower back were worse, and she wanted to sit down and rest so much that she could barely stand it. But she was *so close*. So freaking close.

She heard an engine again, far behind her, and she began to run as best she could. If she just could get all the way around the bend, she thought, she would be out of sight for a few seconds longer and might even make it to the front door before anyone could spot her. So she poured on every ounce of power she had as the motor grew louder.

She dropped the cat, who had been remarkably compliant through everything, and pushed around the curve, her feet sending gravel flying behind her. Crisp winter air filled her lungs as she panted, air so cold it hurt. She was still shivering, but now she was damp with sweat, too, and her abdominal muscles were screaming in painful protest.

She wrapped one arm under her belly to support it, pumping the other as she ran. Her legs were trembling in exhaustion, and she wanted to sink to the ground, but she willed herself on. To the house, to the woodpile near the front door, around it and then hunching down, fast, as that big black truck came around the bend.

Safe. She was safe.

She crouched behind the woodpile, smelling the tangy essence of maple and sawdust. Peeked out between the stacked firewood and saw the truck passing by. It was moving slowly now, so slowly that she could see Ryan craning his neck to look into the ditches as he passed.

That was the only reason she'd been able to make it this far, she thought—because he'd slowed way down to search the ditches. Thank the Goddess he hadn't thought of that before.

A creaking hinge made her turn her head sharply. Molly Dunbar, the sheriff's wife, was standing in the doorway, holding it open and frowning at her.

Lena brought one finger to her lips and felt hot tears burning on her cold face. If Molly gave her away it was over. *Please,* she thought at her. *Please!*

Molly shifted her focus to the truck that was creeping along the road. So did Lena. She could see Ryan looking at the woman oddly.

She looked back to see what Molly would do. She was a cop's wife—small-town, but still—it ought to be obvious that Lena was in trouble.

As Lena held her breath and spoke with her eyes, Molly Dunbar pasted a great big smile on her face, waved hello to Ryan and walked over to the woodpile. She took a log off the top, as if that had been her intent the whole time, and went back into the house without even hinting there was anything unusual going on, like a freezing, wet, pregnant neighbor hiding behind her neatly stacked firewood.

Ryan had slowed to a near stop. As the door banged behind Molly, he *did* stop, then looked around the place, giving Lena a chance to really see his face. She knew there was something terribly wrong with him. His face was blank. Just...empty.

And that damned pendant was dangling down his chest, gleaming in the winter sun.

Or was it the sun at all? It looked almost as if it was glowing from within.

After what seemed like forever he stepped on the gas and moved on. Lena sighed in relief and waited until she was sure he was out of sight before she got up and went to the door.

Molly was standing on the other side, waiting. She quickly pulled the door open and helped her inside. The sheriff's wife had short dark hair and narrow blue eyes that nearly disappeared when she smiled, and she was, Lena thought, the most beautiful thing she had ever seen.

"My goodness, child, what in the world is going on? You're soaked. And freezing."

The pain hit Lena again, and she realized at last that this wasn't just a muscle cramp from exertion. "I think I'm in labor," she said. "Oh, God, not now, not yet."

"Oh, honey, these things happen in their own time. You know that. Shall I call your mother for you?"

Lena wanted nothing more than her mother right then. But the memory of that pendant hit her and she shook her head. She would call her mom later. "Molly, you have to get me out of here. You need to call your husband and have him take me to a hospital. Please, Molly. People are after me. After my baby. Please, please, you have to help me."

Molly's expression went from friendly worry to downright astonishment, and her comforting smile vanished. "*Of course* I'll help you! All right, all right now, it's all gonna be fine. I'm gonna call Larry right now. And Doc—"

"No." Lena bit her lip. "No. Just the sheriff. No one else. Please, Molly."

"All right. Okay. If that's what you want." She was clearly confused, but at least she didn't argue. "Let's get you into some dry clothes before you catch your death. How far apart are the pains, honey?"

A half hour later Lena was dressed in a warm flannel nightgown, pink with yellow flowers. It had buttons up the front, big, round, plastic ones, and it was fuzzy and soft and comforting. Over it she wore an equally snuggly plush robe, cream-colored, and on her feet, cushy pink slipper-socks infused with aloe, according to the package. Everything was brand-new. Molly had brought them to her one by one, all wrapped in pink-and-blue giftwrap with tiny rattles and baby booties all over it, and the most beautiful ribbons and bows on top.

Lena had been a little perplexed until Molly explained that they'd already been intended for her. There was to have been a surprise baby shower for her that night. But given the situation, Molly had decided that the "little mommy" should have the things now.

There were more gifts, too, from other people. Baby things, wrapped in far smaller packages, but Molly said Lena would have to wait until later for those, as she led her to the biggest, most comfy-looking chair in the living room and eased her into it. "I called Larry, while you were changing," she said. "He's on his way. With the roads as bad as they are, there've been accidents and such, but he's not far out. And as soon as he gets here, we're gonna bundle you into the Explorer and we'll be off to the hospital."

"I don't know if there's time," Lena whispered between bouts of pain and pressure. "Maybe we should go now. He can meet us there." She refused to consider how the ghost or demon or whatever it was might try to stop her from getting beyond its reach. She couldn't think about that. Not now. This had to work. She had to get away.

Molly smiled down at her. "It's still a good ten minutes between contractions, sweets. First babies tend to take a while, but even without that, ten minutes apart means you've got lots of time. Besides, he'll be here in fifteen. That's only one more pain, maybe two. Does everything fit all right?"

Lena lowered her eyes in sheer gratitude. "Everything's perfect. I can't remember ever feeling more warm and cozy. Thank you, Molly. Thank you so much."

"Oh, it's nothing. I'm just glad you came to me." Molly smiled. "How lucky am I to be right by your side during this blessed event, hmm? Why, I never expected such an honor. *I* should be the one thanking *you*." She headed to the kitchen, summoned by the whistle of a teakettle. "Be right back. By the time we finish our tea, Larry will be here and ready to rush us to the hospital— which is, I'll remind you, only a half hour away. Twenty minutes with lights and sirens. And I think the ice is melting enough to let us go pretty fast." Lena heard the water pouring, the clattering of spoons against china cups. Then Molly was back and handing her prettiest china teacup and saucer, delicate white porcelain with gold trim and a pink rose on its face.

"These are gorgeous."

"Aren't they? They were my grandmother's. Sip, now. It's hot." She took her own cup and saucer, and sat in a chair opposite Lena.

Lena sipped the tea. It was sweet and strong, and just what she needed to warm up her insides to match her outside. She watched the clock, though, jumpy and knowing she would be nervous until she was safely ensconced in the maternity ward. Another contraction started to tighten around her middle. She felt it in time to take one more drink of the soothing tea, then put the cup down on the end table before it gripped her fully.

Molly came to her, bending down to hold her hand. "Five more minutes, honey. Larry will be here in five more minutes. You'll be fine. I promise."

She smoothed the hair away from Lena's forehead, and Lena squeezed her eyes tight and let the pain move through her like a wave, stronger, stronger, peaking, then easing back. As she relaxed again, her eyes still closed, she felt the teacup being held to her lips and took a long, grateful drink. So good.

As Molly took the cup away, Lena opened her eyes and sent the woman a grateful smile. "Five more minutes?" she asked.

Molly nodded. "Mmm-hmm. Now, finish your tea. It's my own blend."

"It's so good I might want another. You have to give my mom the recipe. It's very soothing," Lena said as Molly handed her the cup again.

"I'm just going to clear the kitchen while you drink, all right, hon?" Molly said.

Lena nodded and drained the cup as Molly headed toward the kitchen.

Water ran, dishes clattered. Aching, tired, even dizzy now, Lena suddenly realized she desperately needed to use the bathroom. The downstairs bathroom was right across the hall. Molly was busy in the kitchen, but surely she could manage such a short distance on her own. She'd made it *here,* after all.

She got out of the chair without difficulty and into the bathroom, peed—as she had to do at least once per hour at this stage of her pregnancy—and was washing her hands when she glanced up into the mirror over the sink and noticed the odd dark streaks on the inside of the closed shower curtain behind her.

A shiver went up her spine. One of those shivers she just knew better than to ignore. Something was wrong. She reached to turn off the faucet and missed. Her vision doubled, tripled, then righted itself again. And that dizziness was back in a rush, making her sway a little. She had to grab the edge of the sink to keep from falling. She held herself up, cranked off the water and turned slowly around.

The shower curtain was streaked with what looked like a handprint that had smeared something dark in its wake. And there was a smell, a smell that part of her mind recognized and the rest refused to acknowledge.

She grabbed hold of the shower curtain and, clenching her jaw, yanked it open.

Sheriff Larry Dunbar lay in the bathtub, the entire front of his uniform soaked in blood. His eyes were wide open. But they were never going to see anything again. He was dead. Shot in the chest, she thought.

She had to get out of here. She had to pretend she hadn't seen, pretend she knew nothing, distract Molly somehow and then sneak out the door. She was on her own. Again.

Trembling now, she gripped the knob and pulled the door open.

Molly stood there waiting for her, a quartz crystal dangling from a chain around her neck. It must have been tucked under her blouse before.

"Oh, honey, I wish you hadn't seen that."

Lena tried to slam the door shut again, but a big hand loomed into view to keep it open. Molly stepped out of the way. "Did I mention your ride is here?"

Ryan. His face was expressionless, his eyes glassy and empty.

Lena's head was swimming, and she realized much too late that Molly must have put something into that tea. No wonder it had been so soothing. Her knees buckled, and Ryan reacted quickly, grabbing her shoulders to keep her from hitting the floor.

"My...my bag," she whispered. "The baby's things..."

He scooped her up into his arms, carrying her through Molly's house, past the chair where she'd been sitting, grabbing her backpack on the way. "Meet us at the house," he told Molly in a monotone that didn't sound anything like him. And then he kicked open the front door and carried Lena out to that awful black truck.

Her vision blurred, she saw the black cat crouching near the woodpile and hissing as they passed. Then it spun and ran flat out away from them.

18

Lena was groggy but not unconscious. Whatever they'd used to drug her hadn't been strong enough to knock her out. She figured they needed her conscious so she could give birth.

They were going to take her baby. And then they were going to kill her.

She fought for coherence, clutched at the console to pull herself up from her boneless slump in the passenger seat. "Ryan, please don't take me back there."

"I have to."

"Ryan, listen to me. This isn't you. You're under some kind of—some kind of mind control. Possession or something."

He stared straight ahead and kept on driving.

"Ryan, they're going to take our baby!"

Awareness flickered in his eyes. It was brief, but she saw it.

"You're still in there, aren't you? I have to reach you, have to get to you. Ryan, dammit, I know you can hear me. Listen to me. Fight this thing, Ryan. Fight with everything you have! Don't let them take our daughter."

He turned the truck into the driveway, drove right up to the front door, shut it off, got out. Lena wrenched her door open, trying to get out, intending to run even though she knew she wouldn't get far. But Ryan was there before she even got both feet on the ground, picking her up in his strong arms.

"Ryan, you loved me before. In that other lifetime. You remember, I know you do. You dreamed it, just like I did. You were racing across the desert to get to me, to *save* me."

"You died," he said.

"I know I did. I know. And I'm sorry, Ryan. I died and left you behind, even though you loved me so much. I died and left you just like your mother did. Just like your father did. And I'm sorry, Ryan, I'm so sorry I did that to you. I didn't want to."

"I couldn't get to you in time."

"I know. But this time you can, Ryan."

He blinked. She saw it and pressed on. He would hear her, he would come back to her, she knew he would. He had to, and she had to believe in him. Perfect love, perfect trust. What else could that message have meant?

"Don't you see, Ryan? That's why we've been given another chance. This time you *can* save me. This time it can all come out right for us. Don't you see?"

His eyes were brimming. Yes, she was reaching him. She knew she was. He kicked open the front door, carried her through and up the stairs. The house was silent. That sent yet another frisson of fear up Lena's spine. "Mom?" She looked around as best she could, her head heavy, her vision distorted and out of focus. "Mom, where are you?"

No answer. They were at the top of the stairs now, heading down the hall, and she balled up her fist and swung it at Ryan's head with all the strength she had left. Her knuckles connected with his skull. "Snap out of it, damn you! What the hell have you done to my mother?"

He blinked at her.

"Please, Ryan, tell me you didn't kill her like Sheriff Dunbar, did you?"

He blinked. "Dunbar?"

"Larry Dunbar. The sheriff. You said you liked him. You trusted him. He was in the bathtub at Molly's. Someone put a bullet in his chest. He's dead, Ryan."

"Dead."

"Murdered. By the same people who want to take our baby. Who want to murder *me*. The people you're helping right now. Where is my mother, Ryan?"

He frowned as he carried her through her own bedroom door to the bed, then dropped her down onto the mattress. She scrambled to get up, lunging after him as he dropped her backpack on the floor, walked out and closed the door in her face. Seconds later she heard power tools at work on the other side.

He was putting a lock on the outside of her door. She knew it, knew there was no stopping him, but she pounded on the wood anyway. "Dammit, Ryan, where is my mother?"

No response. She collapsed against the door, giving in to the rush of despair. Tears flowing, she turned around. She needed her bed, just for a minute. Another contraction was coming on. That was when she spotted her mom. Selma was slumped in a chair by the bedroom window, her mouth slightly open, her eyes closed.

"Mom?"

The contraction came on strong, and Lena gripped the bedpost, hugged herself with her other arm, panted and prayed for the pain to pass. It seemed to last longer than the one before. When it eased, breathless, she shuffled over to her mother, fell to her knees in front of her and touched her face. "Mom?"

She was warm. Lena searched for a pulse and gasped in relief when she felt one, then saw the rise and fall of her mother's chest as she breathed. She was alive, thank the Goddess. They'd probably drugged *her,* too.

Again. There was no longer any doubt in Lena's mind that her mother had been drugged that first night with something that had localized amnesia as one of the side effects. Rohypnol, the famous date-rape drug known as a roofie, or something like it. Ryan had been right about that.

Ryan. Her eyes burned with tears. She needed him to come back to himself. Back to her. "Back to us," she said, hands on her belly.

Damn, what was she going to do? She turned, scanning the room for an answer. The phone sat there on the nightstand, and she went to it, even knowing it was probably hopeless.

No dial tone. The phone was dead.

Her cell!

She snatched her backpack off the floor and dug for her phone, but instead she encountered the familiar shape of her enchanted chalice.

Keep the chalice with you at all times. It's your only hope.

Blinking as she recalled the words of her sister, she took out the chalice and, moving as quickly as she could, given what was happening to her, she tucked it under the pillows on her bed, edging it underneath, plumping them over it.

Then she went back for her cell phone.

The door opened, and Ryan caught her red-handed, on her knees and digging through the bag. Without a word he bent and grabbed it by one strap, then left the room again, taking it with him. Lena curled up on the floor and cried.

The door opened again and Nurse Eloise Sheldrake came in, old-fashioned uniform, hat and all. She smiled as she bent over Lena, who was still lying on the floor sobbing. The nurse's eyes were dead. Like the eyes of a shark. Emotionless marbles. Just like Ryan's. "There now, you shouldn't be down there. Let's get you into bed." Her hands closed on Lena's shoulders.

"Don't touch me!" Lena jerked away from the nurse's grasp.

The woman stood up, hands going to her hips. "Then get into bed yourself. We're not going to have you giving birth to the Master's new body on a dirty floor."

"Get out of my room. You can't—"

"Dr. Cartwright? Molly? A little help in here," Nurse Sheldrake called.

Molly and Doc Cartwright appeared in the doorway, their eyes just as dead, just as lifeless. They wore smiles that were sick, frightening, like the plastic grin of a mannequin, and came at Lena, reaching.

She screamed, pleaded, scooted awkwardly away

from them, but they closed in around her, and their ice-cold hands clasped and clawed. It was like being mauled by corpses. They picked her up and wrestled her into the bed. A contraction wrapped its iron band around her. Lena twisted onto her side, turning her back to them, hugging the pillows and her chalice beneath them, and burying her face to hide her pain.

When the contraction passed and she dared to sit up a little and look around the room again, Bahru was there, too, smiling down at her. But his eyes were not his own. Not just dead, like the others. Someone else was looking out at her through his eyes. She felt the presence of the house ghost but didn't see him, and then she knew—he was inside Bahru. He was perhaps, somehow, inside *all* of them.

She gathered her power, reminding herself that she was a witch and he a disobedient spirit. "I banished you from this house! Get out. Get out now."

"I'm afraid that won't work. We made your mother take down the wards and open the protective circle," said "Bahru" softly. "We told her we would kill you if she didn't."

"Did you tell her you were going to kill me either way?"

She saw her mother's body twitch, knew she must have heard, must be coming around. Luckily she was behind the others, who were all surrounding the bed and looking down at Lena. All but Ryan, who was Goddess only knew where.

"Get out of my room," Lena said, sitting up slowly, calling up the magic from deep inside her. "By the power of Brigit, Goddess of the Forge, whose sacred day this is, I command you! I banish you! Get. Out. Of. My. Room!"

She waved a hand as she spoke, and her bedroom door flung itself open. They all started moving toward it, walking slowly, as if against their will.

Keep pushing, it's working, Lena thought.

"By the power of three times three, by witch's rage, I banish thee!" She repeated the charm as they moved closer and then closer to the door, and then she repeated it again. Another contraction was coming, but she held strong. They shuffled into the hallway. "Be gone!" she said, giving a final push, and the door slammed in their expressionless faces. She pointed her finger, engaging the lock.

"G-good," her mother whispered. "That was…really good."

Lena's gaze shot toward her mother. Her head was up, but she was clearly weak. Puffy-eyed. "Mom!"

"Cast…" Selma panted for breath. "Circle."

Lena's entire body was tightening with another contraction, but she lifted a hand, projecting power through it. "I conjure thee, oh circle of protection. *Unh.*" She bent double. "Goddess, I need help."

"I conjure thee," Selma said softly, and when Lena could lift her head, she saw her mother's hand outstretched, her arm quivering, finger pointing. She lifted her own hand to match.

"We conjure thee, oh mighty circle…" Together they managed to cast a circle, and Lena kept adding layers to make it stronger.

"I'll try to hold it. Call for help, honey." Selma was

rising from the chair, clinging to it with one hand, holding her arm out with the other.

"The phones are dead. They took my cell—"

"Use the chalice, then. Tap into its power. Quick, now, before they come back."

Nodding, the contraction easing, Lena yanked the cup from beneath her pillows, stared into it, tried to relax her vision, her tension, but it wasn't easy with a murderous horde outside. "Lilia, I need you. Lilia, please…"

The chalice emitted a swirl of light, and Lena was instantly sucked inside.

She was in the past again, standing on the cliff, high above the desert. The scorching winds whipped her raven hair and the sheer white fabric that was knotted at her hips. Around her breasts, another scrap of white. Her feet were bare. She had been stripped of jewelry. Her back burned, and she knew she had been whipped. Scourged.

She gazed out across the desert, and she saw him, her prince. He was galloping toward her on a mighty white horse, sending a tail of sand in his wake, and yet still so far away.

"He won't make it in time, my sister," said Lilia.

Lena turned and looked into her sister's eyes. Jet eyes, hair like her own, features more delicate, the smallest of noses and a cupid's bow mouth. "He has to," she whispered. Looking down at her flat, bare abdomen, she went on. "I carry his child."

"I know. But take heart. All is not lost."

"How can it not be, if we're about to die?" Lena

started sobbing. Lilia rocked into her with her shoulder, almost tipping her over the edge.

Soldiers laughed as she gaped at her sister.

"Look behind us. While your love races to your rescue, mine prepares to meet a fate worse than death."

Twisting her head around, Lena saw him: Demetrius, once the king's most beloved soldier, bound and being forced to watch them die. He lifted his gaze, looked right into her eyes, and she saw his heart there. His tortured, tormented, anguished heart. He was a good man. And she knew, somehow, that he had fought to save the three of them. Sisters. Witches. In his rage over their death sentence, he had murdered the very king he served, a man who had been his friend. "It's cruel," Lena whispered. "He acted out of love."

"The fat high priest plans to strip my love of his soul," Lilia said, her voice breaking on the final words.

"And imprison him in an underworld realm for all eternity," another woman said. Lena's other sister. Indira. "But we have a plan."

"Yes, you must not forget the plan," Lilia said. "You will live again. Over and over, for as long as it takes, the two of you will return, always witches, always powerful—"

"Always with the same names, so we can more easily find each other," Indira said.

"And you, Lilia? What about you?" Lena asked.

"I will remain between the worlds, awaiting the right time to call you into action. To save my beloved. To right the wrongs done here this day. To restore you to your own true loves, robbed from you…and your child, the child you carry, Magdalena. She, too, will return to you. But only if we keep our vow and break the curse."

Lena swallowed hard. "I remember now. When we die and our souls leave our bodies...we will not—cannot— cross over."

Lilia nodded as Indira picked up the tale. "We must linger here, find the pieces of Demetrius's soul and steal them from the high priest. In magical tools we will embed them, bind them to us, and then hide them away on the astral plane, waiting to be restored to him one day."

"I understand," Lena said. And she frowned, because she was...remembering...the future. As she stood on that cliff, things that had not happened yet filtered into her mind like memories. "Indira's tool was the amulet."

"Yes," said Indira. "I've returned that to him. And in doing so, I freed him from the Underworld. He entered through the portal."

"My turn is next, then. And I'm to—" Lena felt her eyes widen, and the child within her kicked, though it was far too young. "I'm to return the second piece of his soul and restore Demetrius to human form. I'm to give him...a body?"

"Yes," Lilia said. "You see? You *do* remember."

"But he wants my baby for his body! He wants my baby! He wants—"

"He knows nothing of magic, Magdalena. He knows only darkness, hatred, anger and rage. For more than three thousand years he's been imprisoned without a body, without a soul, and only hate for company. He knows nothing, Lena. Especially of love."

"So then...it's *not* my baby he wants?"

"It's not your baby he *needs*. Oh, he'll try. And kill the child in the trying, unless he's stopped. But it will do him no good."

"How can I stop him?"

"Only by saving him. Use the magical tools, the tools entrusted to you, the tools imbued with Demetrius's soul and bound to your own by our magic. Only you can restore his body, Lena. Only you. Use the tools. And the most powerful force of all."

"But I don't know what they are. I don't know how to—"

And then it flashed into her mind. *The Great Rite. The blade and the chalice were to be used together, when it came to the moment of truth. Force and Form. Male and Female. Combined, they create life. Combined in love, they are unstoppable. The chalice had found its way to her, and so had the blade, but through her one true love, her soulmate. It had brought them together again, and together, it would save them all—and save the one who would destroy them, as well. Through perfect love and perfect trust.*

"Save him, Lena. It is your destiny."

Ryan felt as if he were standing a long, long way from his own body, and at an even greater distance from Lena. He could hear her, could see her, but it was as if he was looking at her from far away. Someone had taken him over.

And he was afraid that same someone was going to use *his* hands to plunge the golden knife into Lena's heart.

No. He couldn't let it happen.

Ryan.

That voice! That voice that wasn't Lena or the one he'd come to think of as the Master or—

Ryan, dammit, pay attention.

Dad? he asked inside his head.

All your life, you've been avoiding the one thing that can help you now, you stubborn spoiled brat. All because you didn't want to be like me.

Ryan frowned in confusion, because his brain was beginning to clear and he could see…something. Somewhere. He wasn't in Lena's house anymore. He was in what looked like a desert.

And, he realized in shock, he was apparently on a horse. His father was standing on a sand dune a few yards ahead of him, dressed like some kind of ancient desert dweller. What the hell?

Tell me why? Why are you so afraid of it?

Somehow he knew what "it" was, in a disconnected, no-idea-how-he-knew sort of way. And he found himself answering even before he planned to say anything at all.

It drove you crazy.

When she left me, you mean?

When she died. *You abandoned everything. You abandoned me.*

His father lowered his head, closed his eyes. *I'm sorry. I'm not proud of that. I was weak. I didn't realize how quickly the time would pass. I didn't understand how, once we were together again, it would seem like only seconds had gone by.*

Ryan watched as a beautiful young woman walked into sight from somewhere beyond a swirl of wind-whipped sand. It was only as she drew closer that he realized who she was. *Mom?*

Hi, baby.

Mom, is it really...?

All that pain. His father was speaking again. *All that mourning and weeping and aching for her. Such a waste. When my time came, it was instant. Closed my eyes, opened them again. Like a blink. There she was, holding me. And it felt as if no more than a minute had passed since the last time I saw her.*

It was the same for me, my love. Ryan's mother stroked his father's face, love beaming from her eyes.

Ernst nodded. *It was only then that I realized I'd wasted my time on earth, aching for something I'd never really lost. I should have spent that time with you, son. Maybe you wouldn't be so messed up if I had.*

He's not messed up, Ernie, he's just scared.

I don't know what you're trying to tell me, Dad.

I'm dead now. And I'm in paradise. That's what love will get you, son. That grieving I did? That wasn't because of love. That was because I didn't understand. But now I do.

What is it, Dad? What do you understand now?

That loving your mother with every part of me, heart and soul, body and spirit, was the best thing I ever did. The best *thing. My salvation. And loving Lena, that will be yours, Ryan. You've got to open your heart, lay it bare, risk it all—because there's really no risk at all. Just ignorance.*

Love, Ryan, his mother whispered into his mind. *Love is the answer.*

The answer to what, Mom? I don't know the question.

It doesn't matter, honey. It's the answer to every question there is.

His father swept his mother into his arms, and out of nowhere a dust devil rose around them. When it was gone, so were they. Ryan was alone again, his horse pawing the sand with its massive hooves. He looked up, and in the distance he saw three women standing on a cliff. He knew Lena was one of them, and he felt his heart swelling in his chest as if it would burst. He had to get to her.

This time he had to save her.

With a whoosh, Lena was back in her body, back on the bed, back in the grip of a powerful contraction that refused to let up. She had no idea how much time had passed. Her mother's arm was trembling, her body shaking as she fought to maintain their magic circle. The hordes in the hallway were pounding her door, which was rattling and shaking.

"Let it go, Mother," she grunted in anguish. "Let it go and pretend to be asleep."

Selma's arm dropped to her side, and she sank back into her chair. "I'm sorry, Lena."

"It's all…right." She could barely speak for the pain. "I think I know…what to…do."

The circle dissolved and the bedroom door burst open, her captors all but hurtling in. They surrounded the bed only seconds after Lena managed to shove the chalice beneath the blankets as her daughter fought to emerge from her body.

Not yet, little one. Not just yet.

"Ryan!" she cried.

He stood beside the bed. His eyes were not his own, but she knew he was in there, distant, powerless perhaps, but there all the same. "Ryan, please," she whispered. "Please, before I die, I want to kiss you one last time. *Please.*"

He looked at Bahru, almost as if seeking permission.

Lena looked at the guru, too. "You know, don't you, Bahru? All of this is tied together somehow. You know how long I have loved this man. How long he has loved me. How long we have waited to find each other again, only to be torn apart, just like before. Please, I beg of you, for the sake of whatever humanity remains in you, grant me my dying wish."

Bahru frowned. Lena could see his internal struggle.

"Demetrius," Lena said softly. "My destiny is to save you. I know that now. Grant me this boon in return."

Bahru nodded, and then Ryan sat down on the bed beside her, stiff, uncertain. He slid his arms around her shoulders, lifted her from the pillows. She stared deep into his eyes, and with everything in her, she channeled the woman she had been all those thousands of years ago and spoke to the devoted prince he had been then. "I love you. I have loved you for all time, it seems. Do you hear me, my prince?" She pressed a hand to his chest, projecting her emotions into him with all she had. "I love you. I love you. I love you. And I trust you completely."

He blinked rapidly, and his eyes seemed to spark to life again. His gaze shifted almost imperceptibly left.

"The baby is coming, Ryan. Take out your blade."

His back was to the others, but she saw the horror in his eyes.

"Trust me as I trust you, my love. I know what must be done."

There were tears in his eyes—and questions, endless questions—but he did it. The blade was in his hand.

"Remember the first time we made love? Remember how I explained the symbolism? Male and female. The Great Rite of the Craft. The Blade and Chalice?"

She shifted her gaze, saw his follow, and she could tell by his expression when he glimpsed the chalice, visible for his eyes only where she'd lifted the covers.

"I thought it was a kiss you wanted," his voice said. "Take it, then, so we can proceed."

But his eyes said more. So much more.

Lena nodded. "Kiss me, then, my love."

He bent and pressed his lips to hers. Softly, gently, slowly. He gathered her close and, with her body for cover, lifted the knife to the chain around his neck. Then he gritted his teeth and seemed to squeeze the tiniest flame from the blade. He'd learned to control it, she realized. Like a laser, it sliced clean through the silver chain.

Lena felt his body tense, heard him grunt with pain as the flame licked his skin, and then the chain and its deadly crystal fell onto her chest. She quickly swept them under the blankets, shoving them away so they didn't touch her.

Another contraction, and she hugged his neck. With her face buried there, she whispered, "The Great Rite, Ryan. It will work. I know it will."

He nodded, the barest motion, but she felt it.

She prayed he truly understood what he had just agreed to.

Then she grunted in pain, and he stepped away.

Nurse Eloise stepped forward decisively and pushed the covers up past Lena's bent knees, followed by her nightgown. "It's coming," she said. "Dr. Cartwright, the child is coming. It's time."

The doctor had vanished into Lena's bathroom, but he returned now with his hands dripping. He hadn't forgotten basic medical sanity, then. He went to the foot of the bed, nodded at what he saw. "Bear down on the next contraction, Lena. Are you ready?"

"Lena?" her mother said. She got up, wandering slowly toward the bed.

"Doctor?" asked the nurse. "Should I...?"

"It's fine. What can she do at this point? Selma, sit down or we'll be forced to drug you again. Go on, Lena, there it is. Push now. *Push*."

Lena pushed. Her mother defied the doctor and moved around to the left side of the bed to hold her hand. Ryan stood close on the right, one hand on her shoulder, his eyes downcast. His lashes were wet.

"Again, Lena," the doctor said. "Push."

She pushed, and then she pushed some more. Everyone was too busy staring at the child emerging from her body to notice the tears running from Ryan's eyes.

And then suddenly the baby slid out. Lena felt a rush of relief, and her head fell back against the pillows.

"*Now,* Ryan," Bahru said. "Do it *now,* before it breathes." Doc Cartwright was reaching for the baby, cutting the cord, then standing ready with a bubble syringe to suction her nose and mouth.

"Hurry, Ryan," Bahru insisted. "The child must breathe. Do it now."

Ryan lifted the blade and met Lena's eyes. "As the rod is to the God," he said.

"So the chalice is to the Goddess," she replied, and as the others all blinked and frowned, just beginning to wonder what was going on, Lena pulled the chalice from beneath the covers.

Bahru saw it and lunged toward her. "No! No, what is this?"

Ryan turned, pointed the blade at him and fired. A blast of energy shot out, knocking Bahru into the far wall. Molly and Doc Cartwright charged Ryan next, even as Lena scrambled to gather her baby into her arms so she could clear Eleanora's mouth with her fingers. Ryan stood between her and the others, and he blasted with the dagger again, once, twice, and then Dr. Cartwright and Molly were shuddering on the floor, smoke spiraling from the burned clothing at their chests.

The nurse sank slowly to the floor, weeping. "Oh, Master, Master, all is lost...."

Facing Lena again, Ryan met her eyes. She was still working on the baby, frantic, smacking her little bottom as a last resort.

And then Eleanora cried. She *cried!* A snotty, snuffly, lost lamb sound, and Lena cried with her.

Ryan's smile was shuddery, and he bent over them, hugging the baby and Lena as one.

"Behind you, Ryan!" Selma shouted.

He spun, wielding the blade, and Bahru went flying again.

"Ryan," Lena whispered, wiping her eyes and gazing at the miracle in her arms in absolute awe. "Ryan, we have to finish it." She looked up at her mother, who took the baby from her, wrapping her in a warm receiving blanket that had been waiting nearby.

Lena set the chalice on her belly and looked up at Ryan again. The love radiating from her for this man was beyond anything she could have imagined.

He lifted the knife.

She closed her eyes and felt him lower the blade into the chalice.

"And together they are one," they whispered in unison.

The tip of the blade touched the bottom of the chalice, and a soundless flash of white light filled the room, then faded as if it had never been.

Ryan had been bent over to protect her. Now he straightened and looked slowly around the room. "What *was* that?"

Lena didn't know, but she was pretty sure another piece of his soul had just been returned to the unfortunate and misguided Demetrius. Her chalice and Ryan's blade had vanished. And she no longer felt the so-called house ghost's presence. In fact, the entire place felt as if a pall had been lifted.

Selma gathered little Eleanora closer. "I'm going to get her all cleaned up and warm. We'll be right back." She took the baby into the next room, stepping over the people still lying on the floor.

Doc Cartwright had ended up near the chair where Selma had been sitting. He blinked up at the ceiling. "What in the world is going on?"

Nurse Eloise was at the foot of the bed, rubbing her forehead and sitting up slowly, frowning as if she didn't know what had hit her. "How did I get here?" she muttered.

Bahru was out cold—perhaps dead—lying near the wall. Molly Dunbar lay still, eyes open, unseeing, skin already turning blue.

She was dead. Lena knew it and thought it was for the best. How could she have lived with knowing she had murdered her own husband while under the power of some mad spirit?

Nurse Eloise crawled on hands and knees toward her. "Doc, we have to start CPR."

"We can't. She signed a DNR in my office not a month ago," he said softly. "It's almost like she knew." He rose from the floor, then helped the nurse up, and the two of them moved to where Bahru lay and began checking his vitals.

Selma returned, placing little Eleanora into Lena's arms. The baby was all cleaned up, diapered, dressed in a pretty T-shirt with a matching little cap that had moons and stars in yellow and blue. She was bundled in a fresh, clean blanket, and her face was scrunching up comically.

Ryan, who was sitting on the edge of the bed with one arm around Lena, smiled down at their daughter, then looked back up at Lena. "I can't…believe it. Look at her."

"Eleanora," Lena whispered.

"Eleanora Sarah," he said.

Lena smiled. "After your mother. Eleanora Sarah… Dunkirk? Or McNally?"

He met her eyes, and his were moist. "It would be

kind of silly to call her Dunkirk, wouldn't it? She'd have a different name than her dad—and her mom."

Lena blinked.

"I remember," he whispered. "I more than remember, Lena. I loved you so much it damn near killed me to lose you back then." His voice went tight, his throat choked with tears. "And I love you just as much now. I've loved you the whole damn time, I was just in denial, walling it up inside me. I love you, wildly, passionately, madly, insanely. I love you, I love you, I love you."

Epilogue

Lena was rocking week-old Ellie in front of the fire. Her mother and Bahru were in the kitchen, arguing over how much mint to put into the latest batch of her newest tea blend. Ryan was reading one of her *Lena and the Prince* stories to Ellie as she nursed. It was yet another construction-paper creation, but they would soon have hardcover versions. He was having them all printed, so Ellie could keep them forever and hand them down to her own children one day. They were working together on the illustrations.

The cat was lying on the hearth, purring to her heart's content.

Molly had died. Her husband's body had been found, and the medical examiner—Dr. Patrick Cartwright—had determined that she had suffered a mental breakdown due to a brain aneurism, shot him, then died a few hours later. And most of that was even true. She *had* died of a brain aneurism. The stress of what had happened in Lena's bedroom had probably been what caused it to rupture, but that part didn't go into the report. No one would have believed the truth anyway.

Doc Cartwright didn't know what had really happened, either. Neither he nor Nurse Eloise, who—once she was released from Demetrius's control—turned out to be a wonderful woman with a wicked sense of humor, had any memory of the past few weeks. As for Bahru…well, Lena thought he *did*. And she thought he was ashamed that he hadn't been strong enough to resist Demetrius's power.

None of them had any idea what had become of the house ghost, which they now knew had been the long-tormented Demetrius. Lena hoped he had found peace. A body, maybe, or release of some kind. It didn't matter which.

Her part in his story was done, Lena thought. Her bond to that past life was broken. Her life was her own now, hers to live in the present, with no more ancient spells or curses allowed to interfere.

All she had now was peace, serenity and absolute bliss. Her dreams had come true.

"'And then,'" Ryan read, "'the royal prince rode his mighty stallion through the desert sands and saved the beautiful harem girl. And the tiny princess inside her, as well. But what surprised him the most was that those beautiful witches saved him right back.'"

"'And then they lived happily ever after,'" Lena said.

He met her eyes, leaned in and kissed her slowly. "And ever after, and even ever after that." A knock at the door interrupted them, and he whispered, "I'll get it."

He went to open the door, and Lena watched from his mother's rocking chair, which had been delivered the day before, as two people stepped inside. A gorgeous, stylish blonde with the most killer boots Lena had ever seen, and a darkly handsome man who looked to be Hispanic.

"We had a message on our machine," said the woman. "It said you'd found our cat?"

"Oh, the cat!" Lena nodded at the feline in question, who hadn't even bothered to lift her head, though she was blinking her green eyes slowly at her mistress.

The blonde smiled. "That's her all right."

Lena got to her feet, laying the baby in her nearby bassinet, and scooped up the cat. Stroking the animal, she said, "We're going to miss you around here."

"We only live a little further around the lake, or up the trail through the woods if you don't mind a hike," the blonde said as Lena carried the cat over to her.

"The cabin?" Lena asked. "The one that belonged to a priest?"

The other woman nodded with a wry glance at her husband. "We've been away, and Pyewacket here ran away from her sitters."

She met Lena's eyes, and it felt to Lena as if the blonde was looking deep inside her. "I'm surprised we haven't met before," Lena said.

"Like I said, we've been away. Out of the country, in fact. Honeymoon." She smiled up at the man beside her, then returned to her steady perusal of Lena and offered a hand.

"We're the Petrosas. This is Tomas, and I'm Indira. Indy for short." She clasped Lena's hand as she spoke, and Lena felt as if an electric buzz passed between their palms.

"Indira?" Lena asked, disbelieving.

The other woman blinked, nodded.

"I'm Magdalena. Um, Lena for short."

The blonde's eyes widened. "Oh, my Goddess," she

whispered. "Oh, my Goddess, it's *you*." She threw her arms around Lena, then turned to her husband. "It's her, Tomas. It's Magdalena!" When she stood back and looked at Lena, there were tears in her eyes. "Man, do we ever need to talk," she said.

"I guess we do." Lena looked back at her sleeping baby, her beloved Ryan, the comfy fire crackling in the hearth. She'd thought this was over, but maybe she'd been wrong.

Indira put a hand on her shoulder. "Not now, though," she said as Lena faced her again. "We haven't even un-packed, and you—"

"I need some time. We've...we've been through a lot in the past week."

"I can only imagine."

Lena nodded. "Tomorrow, then?"

"Tomorrow," Indira agreed with a nod. "I have so much to tell you." She hugged Lena, and Lena hugged her back, feeling a rush of affection for the woman she'd only just met and knowing they were not strangers. They were sisters.

Sisters. Imagine that.

The couple left with their cat, and Lena watched them all the way to their ancient-looking off-white Volvo, then down the drive and out of sight. Ryan came up behind her, reached past her to close the door, then turned her to face him and wrapped his arms around her.

"I thought this was over," she whispered against his shirt. "Oh, Ryan, I'm not ready for any more. I don't know if I ever can be."

"It's gonna be okay," he told her. "We've already proven that we can get through anything as long as we're together. We've got the most powerful force in the world on our side, Lena. Perfect trust and—"

"Perfect love," she said with him. "It *is* perfect, isn't it?"

He nodded, turning her in his arms and walking her to the bassinet, where they gazed adoringly at their sleeping daughter. "It's beyond perfect," he whispered. "It's a miracle."

And then he kissed her, and she knew they could face anything as long as they were together.

* * * * *

Look for
BLOOD OF THE SORCERESS,
the final volume of
"THE PORTAL,"
by New York Times bestselling author
Maggie Shayne,
coming in February 2013
from Harlequin MIRA

Author's Note

The Great Rite mentioned throughout this book is actually better called the Symbolic Great Rite or The Great Rite in Token. It's symbolic of ritual sex. The "Actual" Great Rite, ritualized intercourse for magical purposes, has been practiced throughout history. In many ancient cultures the High Priestess would offer her body to be used by the Goddess and engage in ritual sex with the chosen king, who was the earthly representative of the Gods. This act served as the king's anointment and ensured that his reign would be blessed by the Gods, and his lands and people would be fertile, fruitful and productive. The entire idea is based on the understanding that form and force equal life. Form is female energy, the womb. Force is male energy, the seed. The two combined create all life. And this is why Witches today honor that knowledge by recreating the Great Rite symbolically at the beginning of most of their magical workings, through the use of the chalice and the blade.

Also, you may notice that I did not capitalize the word *Witch* in this book. Normally I would, but in fiction there would have too many instances where the copy editor would have had to figure out whether the word was being used to identify a follower of a given path or with a more general meaning, which would change whether it should be capped. We opted to simplify by using lowercase throughout. Likewise, my use of the word *magic,* as it pertains to Witchcraft, would normally (among practitioners, at least) be spelled *magick* to differentiate the kind practiced in the Craft from the kind performed by stage magicians. However, *magick* is not a word many people know, and it was going to drive the copy editors mad, so we used the mundane spelling.

For more information on Witchcraft and magick, visit: www.ThePortalBooks.com/online-book-shadows.

REQUEST YOUR FREE BOOKS!

2 FREE NOVELS FROM THE PARANORMAL ROMANCE COLLECTION PLUS 2 FREE GIFTS!

YES! Please send me 2 FREE novels from the Paranormal Romance Collection and my 2 FREE gifts (gifts are worth about $10). After receiving them, if I don't wish to receive any more books, I can return the shipping statement marked "cancel." If I don't cancel, I will receive 4 brand-new novels every month and be billed just $21.42 in the U.S. or $23.46 in Canada. That's a saving of at least 21% off the cover price of all 4 books. It's quite a bargain! Shipping and handling is just 50¢ per book in the U.S. and 75¢ per book in Canada.* I understand that accepting the 2 free books and gifts places me under no obligation to buy anything. I can always return a shipment and cancel at any time. Even if I never buy another book, the two free books and gifts are mine to keep forever.

237/337 HDN FEL2

Name _____ (PLEASE PRINT)

Address _____ Apt. #

City _____ State/Prov. _____ Zip/Postal Code

Signature (if under 18, a parent or guardian must sign)

Mail to the **Reader Service:**
IN U.S.A.: P.O. Box 1867, Buffalo, NY 14240-1867
IN CANADA: P.O. Box 609, Fort Erie, Ontario L2A 5X3

Not valid for current subscribers to the Paranormal Romance Collection or Harlequin® Nocturne™ books.

**Want to try two free books from another line?
Call 1-800-873-8635 or visit www.ReaderService.com.**

* Terms and prices subject to change without notice. Prices do not include applicable taxes. Sales tax applicable in N.Y. Canadian residents will be charged applicable taxes. Offer not valid in Quebec. This offer is limited to one order per household. All orders subject to credit approval. Credit or debit balances in a customer's account(s) may be offset by any other outstanding balance owed by or to the customer. Please allow 4 to 6 weeks for delivery. Offer available while quantities last.

Your Privacy—The Reader Service is committed to protecting your privacy. Our Privacy Policy is available online at www.ReaderService.com or upon request from the Reader Service.

We make a portion of our mailing list available to reputable third parties that offer products we believe may interest you. If you prefer that we not exchange your name with third parties, or if you wish to clarify or modify your communication preferences, please visit us at www.ReaderService.com/consumerschoice or write to us at Reader Service Preference Service, P.O. Box 9062, Buffalo, NY 14269. Include your complete name and address.

MAGGIE SHAYNE

32980	TWILIGHT PROPHECY	___ $7.99 U.S.	___ $9.99 CAN.
32875	BLUE TWILIGHT	___ $7.99 U.S.	___ $9.99 CAN.
32871	TWILIGHT HUNGER	___ $7.99 U.S.	___ $9.99 CAN.
32808	KISS ME, KILL ME	___ $7.99 U.S.	___ $9.99 CAN.
32804	KILL ME AGAIN	___ $7.99 U.S.	___ $9.99 CAN.
32793	KILLING ME SOFTLY	___ $7.99 U.S.	___ $9.99 CAN.
32618	BLOODLINE	___ $7.99 U.S.	___ $8.99 CAN.
32498	ANGEL'S PAIN	___ $7.99 U.S.	___ $7.99 CAN.
32497	DEMON'S KISS	___ $7.99 U.S.	___ $9.50 CAN.
32244	COLDER THAN ICE	___ $5.99 U.S.	___ $6.99 CAN.
32243	THICKER THAN WATER	___ $5.99 U.S.	___ $6.99 CAN.
31333	MARK OF THE WITCH	___ $7.99 U.S.	___ $9.99 CAN.

(limited quantities available)

TOTAL AMOUNT	$ _____
POSTAGE & HANDLING	$ _____
($1.00 for 1 book, 50¢ for each additional)	
APPLICABLE TAXES*	$ _____
TOTAL PAYABLE	$ _____

(check or money order—please do not send cash)

To order, complete this form and send it, along with a check or money order for the total above, payable to Harlequin MIRA, to: **In the U.S.:** 3010 Walden Avenue, P.O. Box 9077, Buffalo, NY 14269-9077; **In Canada:** P.O. Box 636, Fort Erie, Ontario, L2A 5X3.

Name: _____

Address: _____ City: _____

State/Prov.: _____ Zip/Postal Code: _____

Account Number (if applicable): _____

075 CSAS

*New York residents remit applicable sales taxes.
*Canadian residents remit applicable GST and provincial taxes.

HARLEQUIN® MIRA®
www.Harlequin.com

MMS1212BL